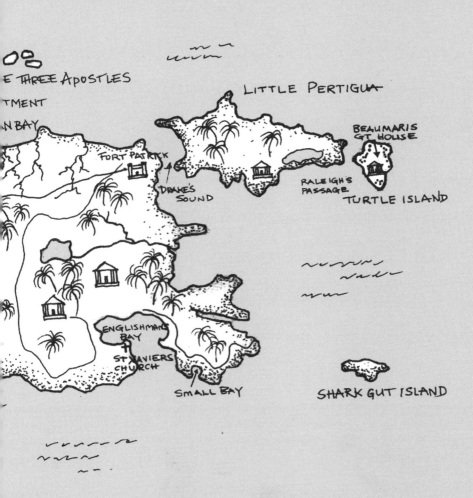

E THREE APOSTLES

TMENT

N BAY

LITTLE PERTIGUA

BEAUMARIS
GT HOUSE

FORT PATRICK

DRAKE'S
SOUND

RALEIGH'S
PASSAGE

TURTLE ISLAND

ENGLISHMANS
BAY

St XAVIERS
CHURCH

SMALL BAY

SHARK GUT ISLAND

illa

ESCAPE ROUTE : ‑ ‑ ‑ ‑

Reap the Forgotten Harvest

REMI KAPO

Milestones in the author's life include: seagoing experience with the Merchant Navy, rising from cadet officer to watch officer on vessels trading along the West African coast; contributing journalist for the *New Statesman* and *New Society*; researcher for documentaries with Yorkshire Television and Thames Television's TV Eye programme; co-director of the visual arts gallery, Peoples Gallery, incorporating Gallery One and Nelson Mandela studio; author of *A Savage Culture* published by Quartet Books; director of The Roundhouse Arts Centre; produced *Moon on a Rainbow Shawl* at the Almeida Theatre, Islington, directed by Maya Angelou and opened by Oprah Winfrey. Lately completed the *Reap the Forgotten Harvest* trilogy.

Reap the
Forgotten
Harvest

REMI KAPO

QUARTET

First published in 2009 by
Quartet Books Limited
A member of the Namara Group
27 Goodge Street, London W1T 2LD

A catalogue record for this book
is available from the British Library

ISBN   978 0 7043 7152 1

Typeset by Antony Gray
Printed and bound in Great Britain by
T J International Ltd, Padstow, Cornwall

For Tunde and Segun

It's late at night, all's well and my watch is over. I write these words for you, my sons, so that you and your generation may comprehend some of the difficulties faced by mine. And in doing so, may find a shared understanding that encourages you to journey on with faith for a more united future.

Remi Kapo
Oxford
29 December 2008

Acknowledgements

The sun is climbing above the eastern hills and I turn to my acknowledgements.

At the conclusion of this trilogy, which has claimed so many of my years, it gives me great pleasure to be able to sing the praises of those who have helped me.

Many thanks to Naim Attallah who called me on a bright autumnal day in a Gloucestershire country churchyard. During that exciting exchange, he expressed his interest and gave me his assurance. This book is a testament to his word. And many thanks to David Elliott, for his untiring professionalism, warmth and camaraderie throughout the production process. My thanks also to the friendly, energetic and conscientious production team at Quartet Books.

Huge thanks to friends who watched over me for such a long time. To them I extend my heartfelt gratitude for they not only kept faith with me but also spurred me on: Olatunji Akeredolu, for that unforgettable journey on tramp steamers along the West African coast, Grace Amadiume, for her insight into old Nigeria, Gavin Douglas, Armet Francis, Susannah Gault, Annie Hayward-Hughes, Mohammed B. Hassan, the late Vincent Joseph, Christopher J. O'Dell, Dr Jill Sudbury, for her apposite counsel and repetitive rereads, Sasha Waddell, for her advice on seventeenth and eighteenth century costumery, G. Levi Wilson and Beth Wooldridge, for her genuine love of Africa.

Sincere respect for my editor Honor Borwick, who believed in this book at the outset, and whose astonishing expertise, attention to detail and humour lent a sparkle to the editing process; and to Bob Solly for his skills restyling the map of Pertigua.

There were others who helped me along the way, with gestures great and small, I give you all my thanks.

And many many thanks to the curators of Cape Coast Castle,

Ghana, and the miniscule museums and archives along the West African coast and the islands of the Caribbean, to the staff of the Humanities and Map Room of The British Library and The National Maritime Museum, Greenwich.

A special tribute to my dear sweet mother, who never ceased to love me and who furnished me with all the tools I would need in that land across the Ocean, and to my father who never lived to see his dreams realised, for both his children and his country.

Reap the Forgotten Harvest

. . . a delicate sorrow wafts
in human hearts, a whisper
of torment called conscience.
Whither it goest is truly within
the grasp of every lifetime. That
weight named fate is merely the
delicious torture of the blind.
Sight is a visual fantasy –
sound – an echo. In decisive moments
today and tomorrow repair,
to reap the forgotten harvest
for time cuts thru' air . . .

Prologue

The former monastery of Saint Francis of Assisi,
Stillingfleet, Yorkshire: December 1616

He heard a muffled sound. An icy chill scurried down his spine. He raised his head. Aye, there it was again. Pocketing his rosary beads, Father Thomas shut his prayer book without a sound. Rising painfully from his knees, he pulled open the door and peered into the dark passageway. A cloaked figure was silhouetted in the faint dawn. Then a hoarse whisper shot out of the shadows.

'For the sake of our faith,' the cloaked figure hissed, 'protect this with your life.'

'Who are you?' he asked. 'Who sends you?'

There came no reply. A vellum scroll was thrust into his hand and the figure faded into the freezing shadows of the long stone passage. Closing the door to his cell, he secreted the scroll in his habit and set about his ablutions. It was past the hour of prime when he finished his salt-water rites. Still shaking from the encounter he sank to his knees, bowed his head and called to the Virgin Mary for her help and protection in a testing age.

Soon after, he made his way along the dark passage, past the doors of his fellow monks, until he reached the last one. Knocking sharply, he pushed it open and walked into the austere, glacial cell of the Father Superior. Like the others, his tallow-lit cell was damp and musty, with a miniscule window set high up in the wall. In keeping with the authority of *patria potestas*, the cell had a small oak trestle table and two chairs. Ending his prayers, the Abbot, Father Matthew, rose slowly to his feet. Thomas considered the slightly built man. During these harrowing times of Catholic persecution, he could not fathom why the chapter of the monastery had elected a man of such limited moral fibre. He was convinced that the Abbot would let something slip inadvertently into the ears of the Puritans.

'Good morrow, Abbot.'

'Good morrow, Father Thomas.'

'I trust you have concluded your observances?'

'For now, Father Thomas. Why so?'

'I bring tidings that cannot wait.'

'Then indeed you have my ear.'

Sitting down, Thomas lowered his voice.

'I have word of the emissaries from Rome.'

'Good,' said the Abbot, 'I have been concerned that they have not yet appeared.'

'It is not good,' Thomas whispered, sharply. 'Two days ago, carrying correspondence from the Holy Father, they entered the city of York disguised as journeymen and tarried the night at the Boar's Head.'

'As journeymen?'

'They could hardly appear dressed as Catholic monks,' Thomas replied, curtly. 'Lamentably, while downing tankards of ale, a Puritan overheard the intoxicated blabbermouths employing the Latin tongue.'

'Latin,' the Abbot groaned. 'They may as well have assembled their own scaffolds.'

'After sending word to the Deputy Lieutenant,' said Thomas, 'the Puritan landlord locked them in their chamber while they slumbered.'

The Abbot farted with shock.

'Have mercy on us!' he cried. 'By now the letters from the Holy Father will be in the hands of the Deputy Lieutenant. We must be gone from here post haste. And you say they were drinking ale?'

'Journeymen are generally awash with ale,' replied Thomas, scathingly. 'The emissaries could scarcely behave any differently. On the word of the Landlord, a man who has close dealings with the Deputy Lieutenant, they were tried within the hour in Clifford's Tower and summarily burned at the stake. You are undoubtedly right Abbot, the Deputy Lieutenant will most certainly have those letters in his possession by now.'

'What would you advise?'

'To proceed with extreme vigilance,' replied Thomas, 'for even the slightest display of curiosity in their fate is certain to draw attention. We cannot do anything. We must not do anything. 'Twill not be long before the Deputy Lieutenant draws up on our threshold. Then we must brazen it out.'

'Lest there be interrogations,' said the Abbot, 'we must make certain that no inkling of this episode passes to any other.'

Leaving the Abbot's cell, Thomas was vexed. Back in his own cell, he sought comfort in the habitual tasks of an anchorite. His life was one of almost continual solitude, with the monks gathering only for morning mass, afternoon vespers and the night office. Opening the monastery's copy of *An Epistle of Comfort*, written surreptitiously during the Protestant persecution of 1587 by his favoured author, Robert Southwell, he began to read. Finding little cheer in the author's letters of consolation to persecuted Roman Catholics, he shut the volume. Slipping to his knees and clasping his hands together, he began to pray.

Approach road to Stillingfleet.

In the early hours of that icy morning, Sir Frederick Cuthbert, Deputy Lieutenant of the county, wheeled his mount off the toll road onto a snow-covered, rutted lane. Morion-helmeted musketeers, hastily mustered overnight in York, plodded behind him on foot. In the bleak dawn, the company of thirty recruits rattled grudgingly through the snow, icicles hanging from the hinged cheek-pieces of their burgonets and freezing breath ascending in clouds. Just visible in the smoky distance was the slumbering village of Stillingfleet. Pressing his spurs into his mare, Cuthbert brought her abreast of his companion the High Sheriff, Nycholas Norris.

'Dissolution didn't sever the nerve of the papists then, Nycholas?' he asked, staring ahead.

'Are you certain of that, Sir Cuthbert?' asked the Sheriff.

'Squire Fleming of Augustfields is up to no good, Nycholas. I know it. If we're not on our guard, England will be crawling with his like again. Papists like Fleming will never prevail in this county while I breathe.'

'Fleming?' asked the Sheriff, stopping his mare and for once turned to look directly at him. 'How that name rises to the surface.'

The musketeers clattered to a disorderly standstill behind them. Irritably, Cuthbert swivelled around and shouted at the Captain of the Guard.

'Move on.'

His men resumed their march. Cuthbert cantered ahead on his chestnut mare. She's spirited today, he thought, perhaps affected by my own eagerness. The smell of burnt wood made him lift his gaze. Up ahead, wisps of smoke were rising from behind a cluster of oak trees. He could hear the faint strains of a Gregorian chant. He was about to signal the

Sheriff when a fox scurried across the track. His horse shied taking him by surprise. Casting an angry look at the animal disappearing into the frozen white undergrowth, he waved at tall chimneys now visible through the trees. The Sheriff nodded. Leading his men off the track, past the acrid stench emanating from the reredorter latrine and into the bleak courtyard, Cuthbert crunched to a halt before the great oak door of the monastery.

'Fetch out the traitor, Father Thomas!'

'Aye, Sir Cuthbert,' replied the Captain of the Guard, who stepped forward and struck the door with his gauntleted fist. 'Open up in the name of the Lord Bishop of York!'

The Gregorian chanting continued without interruption. Annoyed now, the Captain drew his sword and hammered on the door with the pommel.

'Open up or we'll batter down the door!'

Cuthbert's mount whinnied and pawed at the cobblestones in the bitter cold. The Sheriff sat in lumpen silence. A hatch jerked open and a crusty voice sprang from behind the iron lattice.

'Who is there and what do you want?'

'Open up!' yelled the Captain of the Guard. 'It is Sir Frederick Cuthbert, the Deputy Lieutenant, on the Lord Bishop's business.'

'Wait there!' snapped the face, slamming the hatch shut.

The Gregorian chanting stopped at once. For a few minutes nothing stirred from inside. A gust of wind ruffled the ivy-covered façade, dumping a layer of powdery snow onto the shoulders of the waiting officers. Aggravated at being kept waiting, Cuthbert scowled at the Sheriff, hunched impassively on his black mare. Scraping bolts being drawn back turned his head. The massive door creaked as it inched slowly open.

In hooded brown habit and crude sandals, a lone monk stood with his hands cuffed in his sleeves. Cuthbert's nostrils twitched with disdain, as he watched the monk hesitate, step over the threshold and out into the snow. Drawing back his hood to expose his tonsured scalp, the monk raised his eyes.

'Good morrow, Sir Cuthbert,' he said respectfully. 'What business does the Lord Bishop want with us?'

Contemptuously, he scrutinised the monk's deadpan features.

'Mind your tongue, monk,' he said sternly. 'You will answer questions not ask them. Who are you?'

'Father Matthew, Sir Cuthbert. Here we care for the needs of this inconsequential commune. I meant to ask what service the Lord Bishop seeks from us, for you come to a refuge where we tend only to the wants of the poor.'

'I have here a warrant for the arrest of the traitor, Thomas. Stand aside and let us be about our business.'

'May I humbly see this warrant, Sir Cuthbert?'

Cuthbert leapt off his mare. It was his signal to the Captain of the Guard, followed by six men, to shove the cleric aside and march directly into the monastery. The Sheriff dismounted heavily onto a box.

Heeding the commotion at the great door, Father Thomas's heart faltered. Recognising the voice in the courtyard as that of Sir Frederick Cuthbert, he knew that his presence almost certainly meant that the Vatican letters had been deciphered. Crossing himself, he continued his contemplations. His door flew open. Hell burst into his cell. Two musketeers marched in, seized his arms and dragged him into the passage.

'Thomas the monk,' said Cuthbert, 'I have here a warrant for your arrest.'

'Arrest? For what?' he asked. His whole body felt clammy with sweat.

'The Lord Bishop of York who signed this warrant knows you to be a papist. His Lordship seized letters off two emissaries from that purple-caped, pot-bellied braggart in Rome. I myself also have proof that you have officiated at a Catholic Mass in this parish, and all that, Father Thomas, is treason.'

Father Thomas trembled.

'I beg you, Sir Cuthbert, I have done no wrong and have not anything to hide. 'Pon my oath, I know not anything of Catholics in this county or any other.'

'You hide your faith and their names, monk. Denying it will do you no good. I have the evidence and a sworn witness.'

His throat dried and his chest tightened. Slumping against the wall of the passage, he envisioned his own mangled bloodied body dangling in the torture chamber.

'Search him and rummage around in his cell, Captain,' said Cuthbert. 'Convey everything in it to the Merchant Adventurers' Hall. Escort this traitor to the dungeons of Clifford's Tower. There I shall extract the names from him.'

'It'll do you no good withholding the intelligence we seek,' the Sheriff said, attempting to assert himself. 'Is that not so, Sir Cuthbert?'

With an irritated look at the Sheriff, the Deputy Lieutenant muttered an oath and rolled his eyes.

'I am innocent, Sir Cuthbert,' Father Thomas pleaded. 'I swear I am innocent. I know nothing of the Catholics.'

Smiling scornfully, Cuthbert replied.

'I shall determine if that is so on the rack.'

Yanking him to his feet, two musketeers marched him out of the monastery, past the cowed Father Matthew and into the courtyard where the intimidated inhabitants stood shivering.

'For your sake, monk Matthew,' shouted Cuthbert, 'I trust you harbour no more enemies of the Lord Bishop.'

Trussed inside the gaol-cart and sodden with freezing sweat, Thomas watched the Deputy Lieutenant remount and wheel out of the courtyard, followed by the Sheriff and the militia, drawing the cart behind them.

Augustfields – an estate six miles from Stillingfleet.

Later that overcast afternoon, returning from a visit to York and unaware of Cuthbert's chilling transactions, William Ampleforth Fleming smiled with contentment as his carriage jolted through the portals of his extensive estate.

'Stop, coachman,' he yelled, throwing open the carriage door. 'I shall walk from here.'

'Aye, Squire,' said his coachman, jerking the carriage to a halt.

The carriage trundled around the bend. Thankful for a moment alone, he sank into reflection and began to walk. Halting briefly beneath a mature oak, he scanned the snow-sprinkled avenue of poplar trees sweeping gracefully towards the stately entrance of his home – August-fields. Beneath a mantle of snow, with smoke from her hearths billowing out of her tall chimneys and spiralling into a leaden sky, his mansion house sat like a waiting parent – steadfast, silent and safe. Stepping back onto the carriage-drive, he carried on walking. Despite the evident threat of religious persecution hanging over the county, he had found it exceedingly pleasant to have luncheon with friends. But in York, he also learned that the two emissaries from Rome with whom he had hoped to meet had been arrested and burned at the stake the day before. Nearing his home, foreboding seized his spirits. Marching through the front door and down the passage, he stomped into the library. Unbuckling his sword, he flung it onto the oak settle. A man who had been warming himself by the hearth leapt to his feet and removed his hat.

'Who the devil are you?'

'Ned Atwell, Squire, messenger from York,' said the man. 'Father Thomas has been arrested by Sir Frederick Cuthbert and taken to Clifford's Tower.'

William swallowed deeply.

'Good God man! Who told you this?'

'Squire Wheatcrofte sent me to put you on alert,' replied the messenger. 'Sir Cuthbert's men are searching for the whereabouts of a mass held in a secret chapel around these parts.'

'How long have you been in Squire Wheatcrofte's service?'

Ned Atwell began to fiddle with the brim of his hat.

'I've been in his service all me life, Squire,' he said. 'My kin have served as his ostlers for four generations.'

'Stop fidgeting man. When and why did Squire Wheatcrofte impart this sensitive intelligence to you?'

'At the Merchant Adventurers' Hall this morn, when he saw the militia dragging in the monk's possessions. He sent me at once to forewarn you.'

'Tell me, Ned, what is your persuasion?'

'Begging your pardon, Squire, I know not what you mean.'

'What faith are you, man?'

'Catholic, Squire. As is Squire Wheatcrofte and I believe yourself.'

Scrutinising the scrawny, ale-soaked man before him, William's heart beat hard. The idea of a servant being in possession of information capable of sending a man to the scaffold was disturbing. Furnishing Ned with a watery smile, he pulled a cord to summon his manservant.

'You will mention this to no one,' he said.

''Pon me soul, Squire,' said Ned. 'May I burn in hell if a word of this ever passes my lips.'

'I shall myself set light to the faggots and you'll burn on earth first if you do.'

A knock on the door silenced them both.

'Enter!' he said.

Phipps, his manservant, shuffled wearily into the room.

'You rang, Squire?'

'Take good care of this man and have Squire Wheatcrofte's horses fed and watered. Ask Mistress Charlotte to join me in here.'

Heaving a sigh, William laid a few logs in the hearth and sat mesmerised by the crackling flames. For weeks, ever since that last visit from the indefatigable Deputy Lieutenant, he had felt that something abominable was about to happen. There had been that note of suspicion in Cuthbert's voice when he was enquiring about the attitude of the local gentry to the Puritans. William had always found the Deputy Lieutenant to be a deeply unpleasant man with his sunken black sockets and bulbous pocked nose. He could still feel those icy eyes probing his own as Cuthbert questioned him.

'My agents keep me well acquainted with the practices in this part of the county,' Cuthbert had said. 'You wouldn't know anything about these secret masses would you, Squire Fleming?'

'Nay, Sir Cuthbert, I know not.'

'Make no mistake, my Honourable Squire,' Cuthbert had retorted. 'We shall wheedle out those sinners who attempt to pervert the word of Our Lord and our King.'

Shortly after the Deputy Lieutenant's visit, William began hearing stories about gangs of Puritans stopping people and demanding to know their religion. Anyone suspected of being Catholic was forced to admit their faith in public examinations, often with the aid of Skevington's Daughter. When the iron contraption had been used on one of his farm workers accused of heresy, he had been obliged to be present in Clifford's Tower. He had watched the man's head being forcibly pressed to his knees until blood appeared from his ears and nose. Nightmarish visions of the sufferer, whom he had known all his life, had flooded his thoughts for weeks afterwards. Choosing not to alarm his wife, he told her nothing, particularly his feeling that the Deputy Lieutenant suspected he was privy to the names of religious dissenters in the area. It seemed only a matter of time before he was openly accused.

Arriving in the library, Mistress Charlotte found her husband slouched on the oak settle, staring into the flames. Putting her arm around his shoulders, she sat down beside him.

'What did the messenger want, William?'

'Father Thomas has been arrested by Cuthbert.'

'Good God, William, are you certain?'

Taking her hand, he spoke sincerely.

'We're no longer safe here, Charlotte. Francis Wheatcrofte was in attendance at the Merchant Adventurers' Hall when they carried in Father Thomas's possessions and papers. Cuthbert is set to put him to the rack.'

Her hand flew up to her mouth.

'Father Thomas – is – to be racked?' she stuttered.

'It is inevitable.'

'The instant he is threatened with a tad of pain, let alone the rack, that ill-fated monk will confess.'

'A foregone conclusion. And on the rack, he will howl out a tale with our names writ large.'

'Holy Mary, Mother of God, we must do something, William.'

'We must be gone,' he said, 'before Cuthbert returns. Let us repair to the chapel. There it will be safe to talk.'

Lighting a candle and vacating the library, he led her across the hall and along the oak-panelled gallery. He stopped beside the grandfather clock, which possessed two unique features. The first was a dial that showed the four phases of the moon, and the second a mechanism which, when he pulled it, opened a rectangular panel, about two feet wide, in the wall. Stepping into the narrow vestibule and closing the panel behind them, he led her down a narrow stairway to a second door. This he also unfastened. Taking her hand, he led her into the chapel, the object of the Deputy Lieutenant's search. In the light of the candle, their shadows flickered eerily about the walls of the small musty refuge. The chapel could accommodate twelve worshippers on four oak pews. William turned to his wife.

'Let us pray for deliverance,' he said softly.

She knelt down beside him.

'*Tantum ergo Sacramentum,*' he murmured. '*Veneremur; Et antiquum documentum. Novo cedat ritui; Praestet fides suupplementum. Sensuum defectui.*'

Rising from his knees, he took her hand. Facing a night of great uncertainty, he had to ensure that she understood the gravity of their situation and what action they must take.

'In these testing times, Charlotte, we must accept that we might have to pay a political price for our religious beliefs.'

'You see politics in everything, William.'

'Religion and politics are currently inextricably linked, Charlotte. So much so it is now a question about loyalty.'

'Loyalty?' she asked.

'We need more light hereabouts,' he said.

He examined her countenance in the additional candle glow. As heir to the Augustfields fortune, he had acquired her like everything else, effortlessly. She was seven years younger than he, with dark eyes and fine raven hair. At their first meeting, he realised that she was more instinctive than he, more outspoken and more opinionated. But for him an aspect of her desirability lay in her feisty disposition. It made him believe that his marriage would be a lively and good match. Before the nuptials, while looking intently at his bride-to-be, he had declared:

'I shall want a wife who shall please me and who shall be pleased to do so.'

'Likewise I wish to be pleased,' she had replied. 'But, sir,' she added, with a flirtatious glimmer in her eye, 'I cannot be truly pleased if you are not.'

They were married on a bright October day in 1595, in Saint Mary's Church, Ampleforth. He cherished the memory of his wedding night. In the subsequent years, they were blessed early on with two children, Harry and Mary, but since then she had been unable to carry any baby to full term. Despite this setback, after twenty-one years of matrimony, she still possessed a spark – different from all that time ago, but a spark all the same.

He smiled at her hesitantly. She stared back at him.

'Charlotte, since Pope Pius excommunicated Queen Elizabeth, our beloved land has been divided between those who pledge allegiance to the throne and those who are bound to Rome. The Puritans have concocted what they call the Bloody Question.'

'The Bloody Question?' she said, putting her hand over her heart. 'What manner of question is that?'

'It is this,' he quoted grimly. '*If the Pope or any other by his appointment do invade this realm, which part would you take, and which part ought a good subject to take?*

''Tis a fraudulent question,' she said dismissively.

'Undoubtedly. But it sits at the heart of the issue. It is also to our misfortune and now a well-established fact that any Catholic will be declared a heretic. Therefore, he, she, you, I and the children are certain to be hung, drawn and quartered, roasted or both.'

'Blessed Mary! 'Tis a grisly report. William, we must act speedily.'

'Indeed we must.'

The air in the chapel had grown stale.

'Charlotte,' he said gravely, 'I feel certain that Cuthbert suspects us. Sooner or later, I am convinced he will turn up here.'

Clutching his arm, she gasped.

'Good God, William – we are lost!'

Disquieted by her apprehension, he turned to the altar, crossed himself and knelt down. His thoughts streamed over the pastures of his beloved Yorkshire in happier times. He envisioned a family in a carriage trotting happily across the dales to a garden party. Surrounded by meadows, woods and waterfalls, he floated high above the twelfth century nave of Bolton Abbey beside the River Wharfe. In the distance, out of York, the old Gothic Minster rose majestically into the heavens. It was springtime and crocuses speckled over the rolling grasslands. At his very core, he knew they would have to bid farewell to Augustfields, for there was no longer any avoiding the threat to their existence.

The far-off sound of hammering jolted him back from his reverie. Looking aghast at Charlotte, who had turned ashen, he unbolted the lower door of the chapel. Closely followed by her, he hurried up the steps and emerged beside the clock, where he collided with Phipps his manservant. It was dusk and the candlelight cast ghostly shadows across the main hall. The persistent pounding on the front door had thrown the house into a state of confusion. Servants frantically darted about, while others stood rooted along the wall flanking the main door, anxiously awaiting instructions.

'Who pummels our door, Phipps?'

'The Deputy Lieutenant's men-at-arms, Squire,' the panting manservant replied.

'How many?'

'About ten, Squire. And well armed.'

Charlotte tugged at his sleeve.

'Go to meet them, William, lest they rummage through our house.'

Pushing the manservant in the direction of the front entrance, he was firm.

'Unbolt the door, Phipps.'

Apprehensively, the manservant slid back the bolts and pulled the great oak door slowly open. An officer stepped over the threshold. The tramp of unsolicited boots echoed across the candlelit hall and a grim-faced Captain came to a standstill before him. Alarm coursed through his frame. He blurted out his challenge.

'You come to make an arrest, Captain?'

'Nay, Squire. Sir Frederick Cuthbert seeks your assistance and ordered me to escort you to York.'

'In such inclement weather?'

'Aye, Squire.'

'Where in York are we bound, Captain?'

'Clifford's Tower, Squire.'

Turning to Charlotte, her eyes shrieked the threat he felt. Knowing at once that he must certainly attend, he bit his lip and swallowed deeply to moisten his throat. Not to abide by the directive of the Deputy Lieutenant would be as good as confessing that he had something to hide.

'Very well, Captain. Following a private word with my wife, I shall indeed accompany you to York. For it would not do to deny the request of the Deputy Lieutenant in the performance of his important duties of State.'

'Nay it would not, Squire,' said the Captain. 'Be not too long.'

Enveloped in a cloak, William boarded the black-lacquered four-in-hand. With Wheatcrofte's man at the reins, they clattered out of Augustfields' lofty gates into the night, behind the Captain of the guard and closely followed by his mounted troop.

'Shall I wait for thee, Squire?' asked Ned, anxiously, when they arrived on the outskirts of the snowbound city.

'Aye. Dally in the courtyard of the Tower.'

It was apparent that the Deputy Lieutenant had dispatched the armed escort to guarantee his attendance at the cross-examination. But had Father Thomas already succumbed and divulged his connection with the Holy See? He focused on the impending ordeal, for his own liberty hinged on the resolve of the monk, especially if, when he reached the

Tower, the monk was still *compos mentis* – enough to recognise and identify him. Dropping down the Tower's spiral stone steps, he shuddered at the thought of the unfortunate who made it to the rack. On the bottom-most step, the Captain heaved open the door. A searing blast of hot air rasped his face. Adjusting to the oil-soaked light, his eyes discerned diabolical forms gliding about the rugged stonework of the large vault. Making out the implements of torture hanging on the walls, his whole being revolted. Then his eyes fell on the rack.

'Good God Almighty!' he gasped.

In the company of his masked inquisitors, the Deputy Lieutenant was standing, hands on hips, in the stifling chamber. Kneeling before him was a whimpering monk, whose teeth had been forcibly extracted and arranged in a neat row on an anvil. Behind the Deputy Lieutenant was the scrivener, sweating copiously, quill in hand. Backing away from the men stoking the white-hot coals of a brazier, Fleming caught the pain screaming from the eyes of the monk.

'This monk is bull-headed, Squire Fleming,' said the Sheriff, keeping tight hold of his nose with a podgy hand while dabbing the blood spatters on his silk doublet with a shred torn from the monk's habit.

The Deputy Lieutenant swung around with a triumphant look.

'Fret not, Squire Fleming, you have not been summoned here for questioning.'

'Why then have you had me escorted here?'

'I seek merely your assistance.'

'My assistance with what?'

'I believe that this monk may be known to you, Squire.'

'I know him not.'

'The elderly are believed to be repositories of wisdom, Squire Fleming. But the monk you see before you is a seasoned obstruction to change. Nevertheless, I urge you to impress upon him to use his good judgment by telling me all he knows. It would go easier on him.'

The Deputy Lieutenant had him backed into a corner. All he could now hope was that the toothless monk would not howl out his name in the expectation of easing his agonies. To put his antagonist's conjecture to the test, he stepped confidently before the monk, whose head was then forced up with an iron bar, to look directly at him. Not an iota of recognition flickered in the grey eyes that were either so deadened by pain, or else past caring, or indeed, the monk was a very brave man. The lifeless eyes drifted away and the tonsured head slumped down. From somewhere in the mists of his consciousness, Father Thomas heard the words: 'Rack him.'

Forcefully stripped by the masked men and shackled to the rack, the handle was cranked. His limbs lifted from their sockets. An anguished groan issued from the monk.

'Look, he speaks,' said the Sheriff, excitedly.

'Aye, but what does he say?' asked Cuthbert.

Again, the handle was cranked. Obedient to the agony, the monk turned his head. Putting an ear to the bloodied mumbling lips, the scrivener started to write. Each name was uttered slightly out of William's hearing. He could feel the Deputy Lieutenant's eyeballs scrupulously probing his face. Maintaining his composure, he fervently prayed that his name would not emerge from among them. Following what felt a lifetime, the monk passed out and though still breathing, could not be revived. The Deputy Lieutenant snorted.

'This monk has not disappointed you, Squire Fleming. He has kept his own counsel.'

Odium welled from deep within him. He hovered on the edge of drawing his sword and running through the Deputy Lieutenant. But a greater desire for survival prevailed.

'I know not what you imply, Sir Frederick. This monk has never kept counsel with myself.'

'I shall persist with my cross-examination after noon on the morrow, Squire, when once again I shall require your presence.'

'As you wish, Sir Cuthbert,' he said, lurching past the Sheriff without giving him as much as a glance.

It was late by the time he re-emerged. Outside, the air was icy. His face and hands began to freeze. From somewhere in the distance, church bells chimed ten o'clock. He walked unsteadily to his carriage, and with Ned once again at the reins, they passed beyond the precincts of Clifford's Tower and out onto the open snow white road.

'To Augustfields, Ned, and then you must return to Squire Wheat-crofte and acquaint him with what has transpired.'

'As you wish, Squire.'

Tightening his grip on the handrail, his knuckles turned white. Time was his enemy and he knew that he must take his wife and children and flee. He had to get them out of the reach of the Deputy Lieutenant before the monk was questioned at noon on the morrow. The tormented monk was ultimately bound to break.

10 December 1616

She had completed the arrangements for their departure from August-fields. Through frosty windows and misty eyes, Charlotte Fleming watched the wagonette, bearing her servants, housekeeper and governess, trundling down the carriage-drive and out onto the road bound for Whitby. Settling her children snugly in the heavily laden six-horse carriage, she slumped onto the padded seat next to them. Her husband sat opposite with a glassy-eyed look, swathed up to his neck in a thick cloak. Tucking the ends of her lapmantle under her legs, she pulled her cloak around her.

'We take a substantial load, William,' she said.

'Apart from ourselves, our food, apparel and the coachmen,' he replied, 'we carry a chest bearing muskets, sacks of flint and gunpowder, all of which have been stowed in the box.'

'My point precisely,' she said. 'Will that not be too much weight? Might we not get caught up in the snowdrifts?'

'Do not vex yourself, Charlotte,' he said. 'We are obliged to take muskets for we travel a dangerous road. For our greater comfort and protection, I have had this carriage especially strengthened with oxen-leather thoroughbraces. Believe me when I say that it is more than up to the task. These coachmen are the finest and are on an extra stipend. Beloved, we have no more time for these questions.'

Knowing he could turn disagreeable when he was challenged, she fell silent. Though he appeared confident, she also knew his propensity for riding out a storm with a certain smile. She was not fooled by his bravado nor impressed by the mechanical virtues of his horse-drawn carriage.

'We should be gone, William.'

Poking his head out of the window, he shouted.

'Coachman! Away with you.'

The shawled coachmen clambered up onto the box. Flicking his whip, the driver urged the horses off into the freezing darkness. Making slow progress along the potholed roads, Charlotte's unease deepened. Rumbling through the village of Thorganby and a short way past Black Dog Farm, a snowstorm sprang up and made the going even slower. Her spirits fluctuated between panic and a belief in her husband's ability to protect them. Putting a hand to her breast to calm her faltering heartbeat, she cast a mother's eye over her sleeping children.

'In this night of Hades,' she whispered, 'this mother will do her utmost to protect the lives of you innocents.'

'As will their father, Amen,' William said, leaning forwards to kiss her fully on her lips.

The carriage lurched over a rut and threw them apart. Giving him an affectionate smile, she leaned back. Placing an arm around each child, she sighed and sank into imagining.

Inevitably, her thoughts returned to Augustfields. Having become a Fleming through marriage, like her husband and the generations before him, the house dwelt in her bones. She loved it passionately and already felt a sense of loss. In her heart, she knew that there was every chance that she would never again set foot in any part of it. Wandering through her cherished garden in her mind's eye, she pictured the hollyhocks against the south wall. Every year was marked by the vibrant display they presented. During the day, her only moments alone were when, in the early hours, she took a stroll around the exquisite flower gardens to bask in the familiar, comforting scent. Though he had said nothing, she had caught the distress in her husband's eyes and heeded the sorrow in his voice when the moment had come to depart. Only such a current threat to his family would ever have prised him from Augustfields.

The carriage lurched and terminated her reflections. On the outskirts of York at Monk Gate crossroads, they turned sharply towards the market town of Malton. Ten more snow-covered miles beyond Malton brought them to the outer edge of the moonlit town of Pickering, where the carriage threaded its way through deserted snowbound streets. She noticed her husband once in a while looking anxiously behind them.

'No one pursues us, William,' she said.

'I fear I hear horses and am certain they are Cuthbert's,' he said anxiously. 'My neck has quite developed a crick.'

'Could it not be the wind in your ears, William? Cuthbert will surely not set after us this night?'

Burrowing deeper into his cloak and closing his eyes, he muttered.

'I hope not.'

Notwithstanding the freezing conditions and her own exhaustion, she stayed doggedly awake. Snow continued falling heavily as the carriage jerked and jolted through the town until they arrived at the heel of Pickering Castle, where they shuddered to a halt. William remained sound asleep, as did the children. Thrusting her head out of the window, she snapped.

'Why have you stopped coachman?'

'We must tarry awhile to make repairs here, milady,' yelled the head coachman. 'And as well we must make ready for the passage through Dalby Forest.'

'Make haste, make haste, coachman.'

'Aye, milady.'

For over an hour, she watched the coachmen repairing the carriage. By the time they set off, the wind had risen alarmingly. Hard by the village of Thornton-le-dale, the carriage entered the forest. A stiff north-westerly gust thrashed the snow into a blizzard, reducing visibility. Her heart pounded as her finger found the trigger of the blunderbuss pistol beneath her cloak, an item she had concealed from her husband. Drawing back the portière in the howling wind, she peered into the swirling snow. Fearing the appearance of the highwayman, Henry Pitt, who was known to haunt stretches of the Whitby Road, she had secretly slipped into William's armoury before leaving Augustfields and taken the pistol. Only a few weeks had passed since two highwaymen had held up a Whitby-bound stage. Terrorising the female occupants of the stagecoach into giving up their possessions, they had shot the husbands dead.

William stirred and opened his eyes.

'You are troubled?' he asked, softly.

'Until we reach Falling Foss on the far side of the forest, we are prey to highwaymen, William. For now, there is nothing you can do. We shall need your strength when we reach Whitby. Why don't you sleep? I shall keep watch.'

Needing no encouragement, his snores soon filled the carriage as it rocked on its reinforced suspension. About seven in the morning, the coachman's face appeared at the frosted window.

'We be long past Falling Foss, milady. We be outside the village of Sneaton.'

Momentarily relieved, she knew the nearer they got to their destination, the less likely it would be that her family would fall into the clutches of the Deputy Lieutenant.

'When we reach Whitby, coachman,' she said, 'make for the harbour wall and draw up at the sign of the Bo'suns Locker.'

Tapping the brim of his hat with his whip, the coachman reassured her. 'We be there 'fore long, milady.'

Her eyes wandered over her slumbering family. Whitby, renowned for fishing, whaling and smuggling, lay ahead – and beyond that, the sea and exile. In such close proximity to the seaport, her confidence rose, her eyelids grew heavy and she fell asleep.

Snow was still falling when the carriage rattled along the harbour wall and stopped outside the Bo'suns Locker. Roused by the coachman's whip tapping against the frozen pane, she woke the children. Her husband yawned and stretched. The carriage door was suddenly jerked open by a tubby figure who she scrutinised with some unease. Bull-headed, scarlet-faced and swathed in a grimy leather apron, he stood there hastily sprucing up his scruffy brown hair. She readied the pistol beneath her cloak.

'Good morrow, Squire Fleming,' said the man, breezily, his face partially masked by clouds of breath.

Given the stranger's warm-hearted greeting, she heaved a silent sigh and removed her finger from the trigger. Alighting onto the cobble-stones, her husband turned to help her down from the carriage.

'Good morrow to you too, Innkeeper,' he replied.

'Your Good Wife?' asked the innkeeper, with a gap-toothed smile.

'Aye, Innkeeper. May I present Mistress Charlotte.'

'Noake,' he said, touching his forelock, 'Thomas Noake, innkeeper of the Bo'suns Locker at your service Good Mistress.'

Acknowledging his hospitable greeting with a smile, she kept her distance.

'Has the carriage with my servants arrived, Innkeeper?' she asked.

'Surely, Mistress Charlotte, everything is in hand. You be right frozen after your passage through this bitter climate,' said the innkeeper, waving a grubby arm at the whitewashed tavern. 'A grand fire blazes in the hearth for thee.'

'We had little time to snatch but a morsel before we left,' she said, shivering, 'so we are ravenous.'

'A feast awaits thee in the parlour, Good Mistress. My good wife will take right good care of thee and thine.'

A plump, freckled-face woman stood near the doorway of the tavern. Her hair was drawn back beneath a plain scarf and a full-length beige petticoat shrouded her huge backside. Warmly ushering them into the oak-beamed inn, she chirped:

'Just call me Alyce.'

The innkeeper's wife led the children to the parlour. Following her husband and the innkeeper, Charlotte walked down the worn stone steps to the taproom.

'Are you certain you can do this, Innkeeper?' she heard her husband ask.

Closing the door quietly, the innkeeper thrust pewter goblets into their hands. Dispensing brandy into their goblets and pouring a tankard of ale for himself, he lowered his voice.

'Only the day last past I were talking with Captain Prendergast of the barque *Eventide*. He alerted me to an execution that happened right nearby. A husband and wife it was, Catholic they were, roasted at the stake before each other. A friend had betrayed them. Nay, Squire, I have no taste for these common-kissing apple-johns. I am more than happy to serve thee. I have everything well prepared, just as ordered by thee.'

She was heartened by the relief in her husband's visage.

'From the depths of my soul, Innkeeper, I thank you for your diligence,' he said. 'You take a great risk to help us and you will be well rewarded.'

'I thank thee, Squire. You sail this night, Good Mistress. The owner and captain of the *Lady Margaret* of Whitby will come shortly to agree terms with the Squire. Captain Becket is a Lancastrian Catholic from Morecambe. His missus is of the faith and she lost her son to the pox a while back. What with the persecutions of those of the faith, she thirsts to leave the old country. The captain and his crew of nervous Catholics are right anxious to sail.'

'Your intelligence gladdens me, Innkeeper,' she said.

'If we are to sail on the tide, William, had we not better transport our chests speedily to the vessel?'

'Nay, Mistress, my men are loading them as we speak,' said the innkeeper.

'Good man,' said her husband, proffering a small leather pouch. 'Two hundred gold crowns for your services and your silence, Innkeeper?'

'Right gladly, Squire, and I thank thee. Thou hast the silence of me and my men. With such a grand sum we can as well care for the carriages and horses till thee returns. And . . . '

Doggedly shaking her head, she cut him short.

'Keep them all man.'

'Aye keep them all,' her husband reiterated.

'The carriage, the wagonette and twelve horses as well?'

'We shall have no need of them at sea,' she replied. 'And as for our homecoming, God only knows when that might be.'

'I thank thee kindly, Mistress. And may God look just as charitably upon thee.'

Caring not for the way he sat waggling his finger in his ear or picking his nose, she was nonetheless captivated by the tall, thickset, lantern-jawed seafarer who appeared in the taproom at noon. Captain Edmonde Becket of the *Lady Margaret* had the sea in his eyes and the smell of adventure about his avuncular person. And the curly black hair that tumbled from beneath his black tricorne united with his tousled beard. A pillar of rock, she thought, gladly shaking the man's huge hand, the back of which was lined with thick cord-like veins. Fortunately he's a Catholic rock.

Captain Becket noisily downed a tankard of Whitby brown ale and wiped his mouth on his sleeve. In a deep Lancastrian voice, the master mariner then accepted from William the sum of one thousand gold sovereigns for their passage to the New World.

'She is square-rigged and well found,' said the captain, stroking his beard. 'Leaks a bit. Nothing to fret about. Passage will take two maybe three months.'

Alarmed by the image of a leaking vessel, Charlotte threw a startled look at her husband and then glared at the captain, who rose from his seat for another tankard of Whitby brown.

'We have little time to lose, for the prick-ears are right close,' said the captain. 'This night they will lodge at a village inn about ten miles from here. Cuthbert leads them and is heading this way.'

She gasped.

'That evil man I know well,' she said, 'but who are the prick-ears?'

Waggling a finger inside his ear, the captain belched. She glowered at him.

'The current epithet for Puritans, Mistress,' said the captain, grinning. 'Prick-eared, 'cos they cut their hair short, cover their heads with a black skull-cap, which is drawn tight leaving the ears exposed.'

'Reminiscent of a giant rabbit,' she scoffed.

The three men chuckled.

'How long before they get here?' she asked.

'Not till first light I reckon, thus we have little time, Mistress. We sail at sunset with the ebbing tide.'

Clasping her hands together in prayer, she cried out.

'Thanks be to God. In your greater wisdom you have heeded the intercession of the Blessed and Glorious Mary, ever Virgin, Mother of God, to guide us on our journey.'

'Amen,' said the three men.

From the quayside, she watched her children follow the governess, Emma Chapman, along the length of the harbour wall. They walked down a path snaking beside the wharf and stepped onto the waiting *Lady Margaret*, a scruffy barque of one hundred and ten feet. She herself led the servants. Following a final poignant look around the harbour, her husband followed her, bringing up the rear.

From the captain she had learned that the *Lady Margaret's* complement totalled forty-three Catholic souls, including the crew, his wife and a priest called Father Clement. Boasting provisions that he had assured her would last about two years, the vessel carried tubs of biscuits, oatmeal, flour, butter, cheese, salt pork, salted beef, barrels of oil, casks of Pease, port, Madeira, beer and tuns of iron-hooped casks filled with freshwater. For fresh meat and milk in the New World, pigs, goats, hens and cockerels had been loaded on board; and for building purposes and their wellbeing, a large quantity of tools, as well as a chest of medicinal supplies.

About to set sail, Charlotte stayed on deck to watch, in awe, the aerial tricks of the men aloft in the yards. Misgivings about their course of action washed over her. In an attempt to reassure herself, she squeezed her husband's hand as the crew wound up the hawsers. But the finality of the moment overwhelmed her. She blinked back her tears. Momentarily breaking through the grey cloud cover, the sun dipped below the western horizon. Sails flapping wildly in the biting wind, the *Lady Margaret* was under way. Daylight waned, her mainsail billowed and she crossed the bar. She gave her husband a hesitant smile. Breathing in deeply with a fixity of purpose and lovingly taking her arm, he waved at the dock head. Tight-lipped, she gazed after the receding silhouettes of the innkeeper and his wife providing a meagre send-off.

'Fare-thee-well,' yelled the innkeeper.

'God speed,' cried the innkeeper's wife.

Hours later, they were specks in the distance and England lay astern.

Adversaria

The Journal of Emma Chapman

Occasional reckoning of the voyage proposed by God's help in the ship *Lady Margaret* of Whitby. Captain Edmonde Becket commanding, from Whitby in England we flee for the Ocean Sea and anonymous, began the 11 December 1616, who God preserve and send us an auspicious voyage and scatheless landfall. Amen.

God be compassionate and bless us and shew us the light of his countenance and give us his peace.

Emma Chapman

Governess

17 December

Gales, blizzards and freezing rain.

It pleased Our Lord that at midnight I set down these words as we venture into the unknown. I look to my Missal for consolation. May the Blessed Virgin watch over us. The threat in me knows no bounds in these freezing tumultuous conditions. Seasickness, lassitude, famine and fright plagues Augustfield's sodden servants. Flooded are the decks and lubricious with vomit. Headfirst did a seaman butt with the mast. Yielding much blood the insensible fellow bled to death – may God rest his soul. Akin to crossing the North York Moors the cold doth exact a toll – above all to my charges and the servants. Exempt the seamen are not. I pray for the intercession of the Virgin Mary ever blessed. Who will confess me? Should I perish – will I receive the last rites? My charges appear not to be infected by like spirit. Alas arithmetic and Latin edify not any soul in these frightful conditions. Beset by seasickness soon after we sailed I took to my cot. Mistress Charlotte likewise indisposed dispatched Nicholas Savage one bedraggled boatswain to determine my wellbeing. Confirming I was exceedingly sick, the poor man counselled a flagon of seawater. I sent him away. Are we damned? Shall we lay eyes on the morrow?

Christmas Day: 25 December

Fresh gales and a Great Sea.

Mountainous seas this blessed day. We are hurled to and fro. Thick black clouds sully the skies. Rising from the cot I perdured a titanic effort to assemble with the ship's company. Sighted ships struggling in seas of a monstrous size. A maudlin miscellaneous assemblage imbibed the seasonal goblet of port. Salt beef salt pork and biscuits were the fare and greatly tainted they were by salt water. Much of the flesh was inedible with well nigh all suffering from want and sodden apparel. Dizziness assails me constantly. Squire Fleming's forced attempts to kindle mirth came to naught. The man is a citadel of self-belief tho' his good mistress appeared ashen. We are off The Needles. I sighted not any. In the late afternoon the ballast shifted. Awhile the ship leaned dreadfully to its right. Amid awful shouts and curses upper yardsmen scurried aloft in freezing rain to trim sail and steady our little vessel as others put the ballast aright. A man was flung into the sea from the yardarm – may God rest his soul. The other wretched devils were soaked entirely. O Lord will we mislay any more? Nicholas pronounced a hulking vessel to be a warship of His Majesty's Navy. She was a redoubtable and stirring sight. He asserted we are off Land's End – on the frontier of the Ocean Sea. Forthwith we set for alien shores. I pray the Virgin Mary and the Saints watch over us. Reverted queasily to the cot. Expended eventide in the matchless company of Mistress Charlotte. These perilous times have fashioned a novel familiarity with my Mistress and have quite drawn us together. Shall we lay eyes on the morrow?

1617: 6 January

Thick weather and freezing rain.

A sodden-coated Nicholas visited at daybreak. This boatswain is exceedingly attentive. He is well liked – indeed I find him fetching. Scarcely edible portions issued – cheese biscuits and untainted scraps of salt beef. Rife is hunger and harsh is the regime. A callow sailor reaped twelve lashes for stealing cheese witnessed by all. Galled by the bloody sight Charlotte swooned. What with Cuthbert's execution of her friends she doth grieve yet again. All afternoon wan and showing the trembles Charlotte lay next on my cot thickly wrapped in old Jackcoat. Shall we lay eyes on the morrow?

15 January

Thick weather and freezing rain

Mountainous seas soaked our little ship. Sailor washed over the side with scarce a sound – may God rest his soul. Attended by my good Mistress who shewed much diligence in her consideration. I have seen not the slightest of my Master tho' ofttimes I heed his bellow. Being of consummate ill health this day I stayed in the cot. Nicholas is solicitous for my care with paltry victuals. I could bear not to so much as look at any fare. Shall we lay eyes on the morrow?

31 January

Gales and Great Seas

The gales fume with such ferocity. Saints preserve us. Shall we meet another day? Mightily sick with cramps and ague. Though gaunt from hunger Charlotte cheers me so with her company.

10 February

Mighty winds and Great Seas

A satanic wind angered for three days and nights. O Lord we know not where we are. Charlotte kept constant watch over me. We have little food and tainted water. During our discourse she confided the Master on occasion meets with doubt – as does Captain Beckett. What will befall us? Nicholas shews not these past days. Father Clement is beset with ague. Who will confess me? Shall we lay eyes on the morrow?

15 February

Fair weather and smooth water

Charlotte confided her courting by the Master. Indeed she did further impart her trysts before her marriage. I apprised her of Nicholas and that met with her delight. Amid much clamour frigate birds alighted on the mast – an omen of land it is said. Though we are lost on the Ocean Sea laughter again stirs our spirits. In the cordial climate lies the cause.

19 February

Blue is the unclouded sky and sultry is the atmosphere.

Land tho' three specks each larger than the other. Praise be to God. Everywhere the environment is itself hot. Salvation is upon us. Through the intercession of the Blessed Virgin Mary we are saved.

Landfall

Latitude 18° 46′N Longitude 67° 40′W
19 February 1617

'Land ho. Land ho.'

'Where away?'

'Fine on the larboard bow.'

William's heart leapt. Two months of torrential rains, gale-force winds and the icy line squalls of the Atlantic had gone by. Clambering exhausted to the forepeak, he set eyes on the longed-for landfall. The leaking *Lady Margaret* limped along with the alien coastline abeam. An easterly breeze stirred her shredded sails and rigging. Within the hour the boatswain took soundings with the lead. Clearing the decks, the crew anchored the square-rigger off a palm-fringed sandy nugget of land. Soon the barque was virtually motionless.

The early morning heat shimmered above an azure sea. Laughing gulls, ship-borne voices and a rippling breeze were all that ruffled the tranquillity of the anchorage. From the seas of frightening height, now it was as if they had stumbled into paradise. The enveloping peace spoke to him of clement currents, a respite from persecution and favourable prospects. Unaccustomed to the humidity he was sweating torrents. Happily, he stripped down to his cotton jerkin and breeches.

'Sweet is this air, Captain Becket,' he said, 'and this heat gladdens my blood.'

The captain gave him a broad smile.

'Did you ever believe you would encounter an inferno like this in February, Squire?'

'Nay I did not. To think some ten weeks ago we were easy pickings for the Puritans and highwaymen like Henry Pitt. Here we stand this day in this heavenly province. I give thanks to God we're a long way from Cuthbert and his prick-eared villains.'

'Verily, I am of the same mind,' said the captain, chuckling. 'And you can be sure Cuthbert is livid you have slipped through his fingers.'

'Aye, that beef-witted thug will be incensed,' said William, grinning. 'But I have worried on the fate of the innkeeper and his wife. I pray they are safe. We could not have made it to this unimaginable haven without them. Never before have I beheld a spectacle like this. Look, look at it.'

To larboard was a low-lying island dotted with coconut palms. Mangroves formed a barrier either side of a wide stretch of sand – so white and so immaculate that it seemed to him that no human had ever set foot upon it. Scores of blue crabs scurried about probing the waterline for food. Black-headed gulls feasted on the unsuspecting crustaceans. Half a league to starboard lay two larger islands swathed in dense forested vegetation and expansive tracts of grassland.

'A Garden of Eden, Captain,' he said.

'I trust it is as idyllic as it appears, Squire.'

''Tis more tranquil than the North Yorkshire moors, Captain. As if a teardrop had tumbled from the blessed eye of the Virgin Mary.'

'An enchanting thought, Squire.'

Gazing down the length of the main deck, fatigue and malnourishment met William's eyes. But the deck was also in celebratory upheaval. His children were playing on the forepeak. His wife was chattering excitedly with the governess. Seamen were giving the maidservants tipples of brandy. Shrieking at the vibrantly coloured birds, the slightly fuddled young women giggled at the exotic features of the isle. At the poop rail, under a black biretta and on bended knees, was the solitary figure of Father Clement. The priest could be heard thanking the Virgin Mary for guiding them onto terra firma and beseeching her for her continued protection.

Though apprehensive of the unfamiliar, William was encouraged by the open nature of the smallest island. Ambling along the main deck with the captain to the gateleg table on which lay the charts, he posed the question.

'Is this the New World then, Captain?'

'I think this is not the New World, Squire, but it be hereabouts.' Wiping his brow, the master mariner opened his worn copy of the *Lord High Admiral's Directions for Mariners*. 'Nay, I have us near an island that was sighted and named, *Insula Perdita*, by the Spaniard, Admiral Cristóbal Colón. It is in the Indies as it says here on the chart.'

From the outset in the Bo'suns Locker, William had liked what he saw in the tough, shrewd captain – a man with an optimistic tendency and agreeable manner. He also favoured the candour of the tousle-bearded mariner, though he was somewhat disturbed by the information he had just imparted.

'Is it claimed by Spain then, Captain?'

'Nay, Squire, it does not appear to be,' said the captain. 'According to the *Directions*, Colón was driven back by a hurricane and never actually effected a landing.'

'*Insula Perdita* is an intriguing designation, Captain.'

'Why, Squire?'

''Tis Latin for Lost Island. I conclude it was so named because the Spaniard never found it again.'

Smoothing his beard thoughtfully, the captain grinned at him.

'There are in fact three islands,' said William.

'Aye, Squire, that be so.'

'To which one does the designation *Insula Perdita* belong?'

Smiling broadly at the expediency of his logic, the captain said:

'Admiral Colón should not have been so ambiguous, Squire.'

'I have been considering another matter, Captain.'

'And what might that be, Squire?'

'That it would be to our advantage to secure these islands, then by all means, if they are not suitable, let us persevere in our quest for the New World. What say you?'

Scribbling in the Ship's Log, the captain straightened up, narrowed his eyes and scanned the archipelago.

'I find your proposition appealing, Squire. My crew is fatigued after such a turbulent voyage and with all the gales, my ship is in need of repairs. Look at the undergrowth and forest on the two largest islands. 'Tis nigh impossible to see through them at what is on the ground. Then again, this, the smallest island appears uninhabited, so if you have no objection, Squire, on the morrow I shall lead a well-armed party ashore to explore it.'

Stepping forward, William lodged the primacy of his position.

'I have financed this expedition, Captain Becket,' he said. 'So I shall also go ashore with your party.'

Picking up his black tricorne, the captain set it on his head, drew back and announced:

'As Master of the *Lady Margaret*, I am responsible for your safety, Squire. I think it best that me and my men have a close look at this here island before you and your family set foot ashore.'

'As Master, you are indeed responsible for your vessel,' William replied. 'But then again, let us not forget that I am the means by which you find yourself here. To be more precise, my family and I have not fled the shores of England to replace one regime with another. Therefore I shall go ashore with the party, Captain Becket.'

An awkward silence ensued. Then guffawing with camaraderie, the captain slapped him on the back.

'As you wish, Squire, I concede your prerogative.'

The landing party set out at noon of the next day. William sat between Father Clement and the captain. No sooner had the craft grazed the lip of the sandy shore, William leapt into the foaming wavelets in his leather brogues. Dropping to his knees on the crest of the shoreline, he kissed the land and clasped his hands in prayer. Rising to his feet and taking a step forward, he stumbled over an animal about a foot long, encased in a horny green shell and paddle-like flippers, pulling laboriously for the sea.

'Mother of God, what manner of abomination is this?' William asked.

Picking one up and waggling its leathery underside in his face, the captain chuckled.

'Turtle, Squire.'

Grimacing and taking a step back, William was uncomfortably aware of the pleasure the captain was getting at his expense.

'Seamen who frequent the tropics eat them,' said the captain.

A queasy sensation seized his belly.

'Have you ever partaken of its flesh, Captain?' he asked.

'Aye, and a right morsel they are too. Besides the livestock we shipped from England, the turtles, shark, barracuda and flying fish in these waters should provide us with ample meat.'

'I do not relish much of the fare on your list of options, Captain.'

The captain and his crew laughed loudly. With a taut smile, William turned inland.

'Shall we explore our new colony, Captain?' he asked.

Palm trees, woodland, mangroves and slow-moving turtles occupied the island's interior. Knowing a little geology and after an examination of the rocks, the captain proclaimed the island to be of coral limestone with red topsoil. Crystal fresh waters gushed from a bedrock of boulders in the northeast, which then plunged into a deep pool and streamed away to the southwest. Along the eastern shore, mangroves claimed a broad strip. A plateau formed the heartland and positioned around the edge of the raised ground, in a crescent of sorts, were tubers, coconut palms, clumps of palmetto and fruiting trees. From this elevated central setting, they could see all parts of the island, which looked to be about three miles by two.

'We'll call her Turtle Island, Captain,' said William. ''Tis an apt title for an isle inhabited by these strange gentle beasts.'

'A fitting soubriquet for our tropical islet, Squire,' said the captain. 'I second it. A man could have a right fine life for himself in these climes. We must construct an encampment before twilight and use the leaves of the palmetto for shelter. My men will put up a holding-pen for our farm animals. Then again, Squire, on such a small island, it will be child's play to fetch them as we need. We should let them run wild.'

At the word 'wild,' William's ears pricked up. For as long as he could remember, the theft of a handkerchief, a hatpin, an apple or a leg of mutton, branded a person as 'wild' in the eyes of England's authorities. It was routinely rewarded with a lengthy prison term, in atrocious conditions, inside rotting hulks on various rivers and places of confinement. Standing on the uncertain periphery of the New World, where the limits were circumscribed entirely by the physical confines of the island, to run wild signified the freedom to do so.

'Aye, Captain, we should let them run wild.'

Musket fire startled him and sent nesting birds fluttering. The boatswain showed up moments later flourishing two brilliantly feathered birds and cradling his fowling piece.

'A brace for your table, Squire Fleming,' he said.

'Why, thank you, Master Boatswain.'

'Turtle Island is undoubtedly uninhabited,' said the captain. 'Come, Squire, let us return to the *Lady Margaret*.'

Raising a crucifix above his head, the priest said:

'Should we not first give thanks for our deliverance, Squire Fleming?

Though his words were softly spoken, they sounded like a command. The seamen looked uncertainly at one another. William scrutinised the gaunt withdrawn figure. Throughout the voyage, the cleric had stayed below decks and kept to himself, save for the occasions he had observed him furnishing the governess with religious instruction. He now appreciated the captain's enlistment of this remote man of religion – the rationale being that the priest would be the spiritual instrument for conducting the religious ceremonies during births, deaths and marriages aboard the *Lady Margaret*, and in the New World.

'We did not save ourselves, Squire,' the priest insisted. 'A greater hand had reason for our salvation.'

'Of that there can be no doubt, Father Clement,' agreed William.

It dawned on him that apart from the priest, the captain and himself, few members of the landing party had had any experience of the communal act of worship. Taking the captain aside, William spoke quietly.

'These rogues and rascals have fled English society,' he said. 'They have crossed a tempestuous ocean to land on an anonymous island where, if all goes well, they will in due course become landowners, an occupation which they are also unfamiliar. Until now, superstition of the sea has been the mainstay of their faith. Look at every man jack of them. They have only ever bent a knee to scrub the decks or to beg.'

'Spiritual matters are indeed unfamiliar to them Squire,' the captain agreed.

Still holding the crucifix above his head, the priest addressed the seamen directly.

'Men, we did not save ourselves,' he said. 'A greater hand had reason for our salvation. Do you wish to incur the wrath of Our Lord from the outset?'

Without even a murmur the seamen acquiesced and dropped to their knees. Thrusting the crucifix at them, the priest intoned.

'O Salutaris Hostia. Quae coeli pandis ostium. Bella premunt hostilia, Da robur, fer auxilium.'

'Amen,' muttered the company.

Beneath cerulean skies, William strolled back to the tender along a shore swept by temperate breezes. Heartened by the sun-drenched environment, he was finding a degree of optimism for his new and extremely uncertain existence. The overladen tender, by and by, ferried supplies and much of the ship's company to the shore. William pondered over their presence on the island. He had no way of knowing who had been there before them – or whether unfriendly eyes were watching them – even now?

Late into the afternoon he toiled with the seamen building shelters. The women prepared supper of salted pork, boiled potatoes and stewed fruit. A fresh breeze wafted in and the shadows grew longer. The sun slipped below the horizon and the day drew to a close. Laughing at his children and Augustfield's servants ducking for apples in the glow of the firelight, his spirits improved. A few seamen gambled with cards, while others jigged to the hornpipe. The festivities ended with yarns, sea shanties and hymn singing around a heartening fire. Beside his wife and children inside their makeshift home, he soon fell into a deep sleep – the first since their flight from England.

A tug at his sleeve awakened William.

'Squire, Squire,' whispered the captain. 'We have company.'

It was in the early hours with a dark and star-studded sky. Sitting up, he rubbed open his eyes in the direction of the captain's outstretched arm. Making out two flames moving slowly in a straight line high up on the mountainside of the closest island, the hairs on the nape of his neck bristled. For over an hour he monitored the progress of the torches until at last, they disappeared from sight.

'We may have to make a fight of it, Squire,' the captain whispered.

'I think not, Captain,' he replied. 'I have a notion that if they were hostile, we would have seen their canoes soon after we anchored. 'Tis clear from the lack of any clues of human habitation that this island is of little use to them. It would be wise though, to send a party to parley with them in a day or two.'

'A commendable strategy, Squire, but we'd best go careful.'

Two days went by before a scouting party set out from the *Lady Margaret* to explore the source of the flaming torches. In addition to William, the party included the captain, the priest and eight seamen, armed with parrying-daggers, cutlasses and muskets. Once ashore, William took the lead and marched them into the forest. Walking along a narrow path for some distance high up on the slopes of the wooded mountain, above a river, they arrived at the outskirts of an outwardly deserted village. William was struck by the uncanny silence. Comprising fifteen small sphere-shaped houses of woven straw walls and palm-thatched roofs, the settlement was sited around a central open space, abutting cultivated vegetable grounds.

'It would be wise to fully cock your muskets, Captain.'

Cocking his flintlock pistol, the captain gave orders.

'Fully cock your muskets men and keep your wits about you,' he said. 'What do you intend, Squire?'

Drawing out his double-edged rapier and wiping both sides deliberately on his sleeve, William replied.

'To enter the village quietly, Captain Becket, and give a good account of ourselves if we run into any difficulties.'

Birdsong and chattering monkeys were all that was evident in the patently empty village. In front of a dwelling, William's nostrils smarted at the spicy alien aroma issuing from a stoneware cauldron containing leafy parcels simmering in a crimson broth over a fire.

'Smells good,' said the boatswain.

'Don't touch it,' said another. 'It might be right poisonous.'

'Why would they want to poison themselves?' William asked, irritably.

Striding past nets strung out between poles, he grew aware of the pious presence by his side.

'It would seem that our natives are fishermen, Squire,' the priest said.

'It would also seem that our fishermen are not here,' William replied. 'Perchance they witnessed our landing and promptly departed in some haste. But do they lurk in the shadows, Father, or were they truly frightened off?'

It was evident that the inhabitants of the village had left in a hurry. A hollowed log had been overturned, spilling dry corn and a wooden pestle in the dirt. Reaching the uppermost boundary of the village near the summit of the mountain, he gained sight of the entire archipelago and the *Lady Margaret*. Of the inhabitants though, there was neither sight nor sound. It made him anxious.

At a distance of about fifty yards, a figure slipped out from behind one of the houses. William halted abruptly. Ambling towards him was a sinewy brown-skinned man, who stopped at about ten paces. Young and stern-faced, with thick black hair, his semi-naked body was adorned with paint and shells and a cloth covering his loins.

'What manner of being is this?' William asked himself.

Not anything in his experience had prepared him for such an encounter. He grew aware that not one man in his party had moved. He turned to the captain, who glanced at his men, who in turn gazed nervously askance at one another. William looked back at the stranger, whose dark and serious countenance had not changed. He forced himself to approach the stranger. Drawing closer, he was satisfied that the man, though presenting a fierce-some appearance, was unarmed.

'Lower your muskets, Captain.'

'Aye, Squire. Easy men,' the captain said. 'Half cock and lower your muskets. Keep your eyes peeled on the outskirts of the village.'

'*Niorouba. Niorouba* – Sit down. Sit down,' said the stranger, pointing to the ground.

William frowned. Sinking gracefully without taking his eyes off them, the stranger sat cross-legged on the footpath. Maladroitly settling himself down in like manner, William scrutinised the stranger. Noting a small scar on the cheek of the broad face, he examined the thick lips, wide nose and clear dark eyes. For what felt like time without end, he gazed at the brown face that gaped back at him. William turned to the priest.

'We are people from different times, Father, separated by an epoch of ideas. But are we from irreconcilable civilisations because we are so ignorant of each other?'

'You have a point, Squire Fleming. But are we not also here to reconcile our differences by doing the Lord's work? Have we not a duty to do that, Squire?'

Before he could answer, the stranger snapped what sounded like a question.

'*Alouti ouekelli balanagle?* – White man come by sea?' he asked.

William assessed the intentions behind the fierce dark eyes. His greatest fear was that they were being surrounded as they spoke. Were they about to be overwhelmed and perhaps even eaten? Slapping his chest in earnest and conjuring up a smile, he raised his voice.

'Friend,' he said. 'Friend. Friend.'

He waited for a reply. Nothing about the stranger's demeanour conveyed he understood. Suddenly the brown man broke into a smile and gestured towards his mouth with budded fingertips and said:

'*Kouraba biaka. Kouraba biaka* – You eat? You eat?'

William smiled back at him. Employing a few simple words coupled with sign language, a laborious exchange was gradually cobbled together. He ascertained that the stranger's name was Taya, his island was called Patigaa and his people were the Arawak, who inhabited the island of Xaymaca, which lay to the west. With his wife very much in his thoughts, William ordered the boatswain to light a signal-beacon notifying the watch on the *Lady Margaret* that all was well with the scouting party. Then he insisted that they stay for a few days exploring the islands.

On the evening of the third day following their encounter with the stranger, William addressed the landing party.

'Our friend Taya has cooked for us,' he said. 'We should accept, above all, by eating what he has so generously offered.'

'Aye, Squire,' said the captain, 'and it smells right good.'

Being as hungry as William now cared to admit, he had little difficulty swallowing the peculiar repast of green turtle, followed by mangoes, papaya and pineapple. Producing a short reed with a tiny cup at one end, Taya crumbled dried green leaves into the cup and set fire to it. William's mouth fell open. He was further alarmed when Taya put the other end of the reed between his lips. Smoke unexpectedly billowed from Taya's nostrils – a blissful expression suffused his features, and then he cackled loudly.

In the spirit of the alien but cordial occasion, William filled twelve noggins with brandy and merrily passed one to the smoke-haloed man.

'Gentlemen, a toast to our friend Taya.'

'Aye, Squire,' said the captain, raising his noggin.

Recovering from the fiery effects of the brandy, Taya again put the reed between his lips. More smoke billowed from his nostrils.

'*Youli* – tobacco,' said Taya, offering him the pipe.

Hesitantly, William accepted the proffered reed pipe.

'*Youli*,' he repeated.

Putting the end of the reed pipe between his lips, he sucked in smoke. Much to the amusement of them all, he burst into a coughing fit with tears streaming down his cheeks.

'By the Virgin Mary, do they do this for pleasure?' he squeaked.

Following his turn with the pipe, the priest coughed himself a vibrant red.

'This night doth veer into such wondrous colours,' he said. 'I must nod off to pray.'

Rocking with laughter at the cleric's stupefied condition, William accepted the reed pipe for another turn.

'I daresay that this *youli* would fetch a handsome price in the taverns of London,' he said.

Given the influence of the *youli* and the balmy evening, he felt relieved of all cares and was soon laughing nonsensically. It was for him a remarkable yet harmonious spectacle – a Squire, an Arawak, a Master Mariner and a Catholic priest, carousing and smoking under the stars of the tropics with scoundrels from Whitby's taverns.

Addressing the gathering of the ship's company on Turtle Island in the morning, William fleshed out their prospects in the archipelago.

'We should bring order to these islands,' he said.

'Take possession of them, Squire,' said the captain, waggling a finger inside his ear. 'Though it would be unwise to make our intentions known to the little brown scallywag.'

'Captain, I am of the opinion,' he said, 'that we should construct our fortifications before the Spaniards return.'

'A first-rate strategy, Squire,' said the priest, 'and our Church will be the richer for it.'

Leaping to her feet with annoyance, his wife interrupted the male-only discourse.

'Apart from the church and almost everyone else present, William, what is also needed here is a woman's judgment,' she said. 'Why should we not stay where we are? We have meat and fish and although out of the ordinary, the land is stocked with identifiable fruit and vegetables. The men can build and hunt, and we women can sew, cook and care for the children and the sick. And we are a free people. What say you, Emma?'

Having never heard his wife invite the opinion of the governess on any subject, William gazed at her. He began to reappraise the woman who stood before him. At first he thought that their seafaring tribulations had taken a toll. Having lost a great deal of weight, she was now endowed with a gaunt look. And there was a new challenge in her expression as her eyes engaged with his. Certainly they had both been transformed by their forced exile. She had borne witness to many brutal incidents normally never imagined by women from such a genteel family. It was *now* he grasped that their shared experience had granted them an equality of sorts; for the look that met his no longer reflected a compliant wife.

Her invitation to the governess to proffer her opinion was so uncharacteristic that it rendered him speechless. He recalled how kindly his wife had nursed this servant, when a week out of Whitby the governess had taken to her cot. His wife had spent several hours every day tending to her needs. There now existed a seasoned bond between these two women that he had singularly failed to register before this moment.

'You are indisputably right, Mistress Charlotte,' replied the governess. 'Rest here awhile until we are robust enough to continue, or stay and assemble our own state.'

He narrowed his eyes suspiciously. How readily this woman concurs with my wife, he thought. This servant who had hitherto barely been a presence had acquired a new confidence. Perhaps all the servants felt that their common experience aboard the *Lady Margaret* had levelled their status. This notion bothered him greatly. It was true that they all lived in a never before conceived proximity and dependency, but he had thought that that was the extent of it. Now his innate sense of order had been critically undermined. There was no denying it – they had strayed into uncharted territory and due to their exiled circumstance, they were all changed beings. He wondered, more intensely than usual, what fate awaits our morrows?

'Your thoughts on a name for our island habitat, Squire?' the captain asked.

'I propose we name the principal island Pertigua,' he replied, un-equivocally, 'and the smaller one, Little Pertigua. Happily, this accords with the Arawak name, Patigaa, which apparently, if I understood it correctly, means the land of the green mountain.'

Given that he was the financier of the expedition, his opinion carried weight and thus his proposal was unanimously endorsed. On the seventh day, the boatswain reported to him the presence of a large party of Arawak seen landing on the two larger islands.

At sunset of the following day, much to his surprise, an Arawak messenger appeared with an invitation to eat with his people on Little Pertigua. Following an exchange with the captain, William announced that twelve men including the priest would attend. The remainder of the men were to stay behind to guard the women and children on the *Lady Margaret*. With William seated on the stern thwart, the tender set off across the channel. Despite the sociability of the approaching event, he was aware of his own fears during the crossing. Drawing up at the eastern end of the island, the tender slid alongside cedar wood canoes made fast to the spit.

Beneath a sparkling moon exposing the length of a wide sandy shore, a bizarre display unravelled before his eyes. Walking to the village along a trail marked out by two rows of flaming torches, he passed the smiling diminutive Arawak assembled either side. At the entrance of the settle-ment stood the elders, clad in scarlet robes of woven cloth, trimmed with gold thread and decorated with wedges of solid gold. He caught his breath at the gold he saw everywhere – gold bracelets, gold bangles, gold rings and even ornate gold headpieces. In a white cloak, the Cacique, the elderly leader, was even more richly decorated, and resting on his head was a gold diadem in the shape of a birdman. A poignant harmony greeted him as he followed the headman down a further avenue of torches. The symphonic cadence of song delighted his ears.

'I have never come across such an affable people,' William said. 'I hope they will be just as happy to have us as neighbours, as they are to have us as guests.'

'There is land here enough for all of us, Squire,' said the captain, 'if only they will share it.' On a more sinister note, he added. 'And if they will not, we will have no option but to take it.'

Making no reply, William ambled down the torch-lit avenue that brought him to the centre of the village and a large elegant rectangular house with a small porch – the habitat of the Cacique. An area decked with straw had been cleared before the woven-straw dwelling. A small bowl containing a dark liquid, distilled from the potato into a brew called *mobi*, was thrust into his hands. Invited to sit before a strip of matting on which had been laid the mouth-watering carcass of a roasted hog, his belly rumbled vociferously. Though he was somewhat disturbed by the dishes of goat, barracuda, corn, cassava and yams, he was horrified at the sight of two roasted iguana huddled in a dish beside a rat-like rodent lying on a wooden platter, as if in the depths of sleep.

'Holy Mary,' said the priest, 'do they really want us to eat these creatures?'

''Tis curious I must admit, Father,' said the captain. 'But they might well be affronted if we reject their fare. Would you not agree, Squire?'

William nodded.

'Aye, they well might,' he said. 'Come, Father, let us eat. The church should demonstrate to our new friends how we appreciate their charitable hospitality. If they are happy to share their food, they might be just as happy to share their land and also the source of all this gold.'

At the mention of gold, the priest began eating with relish. Arawak musicians played bronze and copper bells, nose flutes made from cane and drums of hollowed logs. With the repast ended, William gave the Cacique a gilt mirror, a sword, and a gold-topped cane bearing his own family crest. The captain donated a newly invented refracting telescope. Following his observation of the moon through the eyepiece, the chief chattered excitedly. The priest furnished the old man with a silver crucifix and a leather-bound copy of the Holy Bible.

'A Bible?' William asked. 'Why Father Clement, the man cannot read English.'

'I shall tutor him, Squire,' replied the priest. 'I shall also instruct him on the veneration of the Virgin Mary, after which I shall baptise the fellow. Thereafter he shall be called John.'

Winking at the captain, William raised his eyes in pretended despair. Breaking away from the gathering, he accompanied the Cacique to his house to parley. At least an hour went by before he re-emerged with a broad smile.

'The old goat has agreed to let us to remain on these islands,' said William.

'And right glad am I to hear it, Squire Fleming,' said the captain.

Rising to his feet and removing his biretta, the priest met him with a cold reception.

'For how long can we remain on this island, Squire Fleming?' he asked.

'As long as we want, Father Clement.'

There was more than a trace of suspicion in the priest's manner.

'That extent of time, Squire, might prove to be exceedingly short,' he said.

Scowling directly at the preacher, William responded.

'I am heartened by their munificence, Father Clement. On a planet where division is commonplace, in a corner of the New World our peoples have met to share a new experience. Two peoples, Sir priest, who cannot comprehend each other's language or fathom each other's ways, have come closer through the language of friendship. Notwithstanding your reservations, Father Clement, on the morrow we shall explore this little archipelago.'

Donning his biretta and pursing his lips, the priest dropped his eyes.

At first light, accompanied by the captain and six seamen, William embarked on a mission of discovery. Sailing west from Turtle Island, half a league across a channel he named Raleigh's Passage, they landed on Little Pertigua, an island that the captain estimated at some thirty-six miles by fifteen. A range of hills extended nearly one-third of its length, culminating in a sizeable mountain. To the east of the island, he came upon a fresh water lagoon. To the west, across a stretch of water he christened Drake's Sound, they waded onto the main island of Pertigua, which by the captain's reckoning was about one hundred miles long and forty-five miles wide.

At some five thousand feet on the summit of Pertigua's highest peak, which he named Mount James, William marvelled at the sight and sound of birdlife – parakeets, parrots, macaws and pigeons flitting about the trees. He revelled in the splendour of the landscape, swathed in mist, out of which shimmered the rainforest, tree ferns and intensely coloured foliage. Beyond the coastline were the distant rolling breakers of the Atlantic battering the windward side of the island. His spirits soared when he saw the magnitude of a subterranean reservoir, which the captain said would in all probability supply a sizeable population with fresh water. He was however not prepared for what he saw when he strode out onto a plateau.

'Good God,' he exclaimed.

Stretching for miles before him along the north-western coast of the island lay thousands of acres of lush grassland. The spectacle filled him with optimism and a renewed conviction that their fortunes were changing. Being a landowner, he knew the profitable yields such fertile soil could generate. Buoyed by what he saw, he grinned at the captain. He would persuade the exiles to build the first houses in the sweeping horseshoe-shaped bay with its deepwater harbour, on the side of the island facing the Caribbean Sea. Deeming their agreement to be a foregone conclusion, he christened the settlement Jamestown.

One sparkling afternoon, several months after arriving in the archipelago, William invited his wife and the captain to take a walk with him along the shores of Jamestown.

'Look. Look at it,' he said breathlessly, sweeping his arm across the full extent of the horseshoe-shaped bay. 'There is land here enough for all.'

In the golden light, a patchwork landscape of foliage greeted them – jade, emerald, olive, lime, bottle green and sea green. Puncturing the lush landscape were huge swathes of flowers, bristling with hummingbirds, in colours of tangerine, yellow, white, orange, ruby red and lilac, toppling down to the water's edge.

'I share your judgment, William,' Charlotte said, smiling. 'I have greater hope for our morrows here, where being of the Catholic faith is not an offence, than I did on England's problematic shores.'

The captain smiled benignly.

'Our prospects have greatly improved, Squire,' he said. 'I have it in mind to engage in husbandry and plotting a course athwart fields of corn.'

William laughed.

'And so you shall, Captain,' he said. 'In due course, others will come to assist us in our quest to establish the state of Pertigua. Jamestown shall be our capital. To bring this about, we will have to exert ourselves greatly to cultivate the land, or perhaps pursue a notion I chanced on in Whitby.'

'What notion might that be, William?' she asked, softly, with a searching tone of voice.

With his back to his wife, William addressed the captain.

'Am I right in thinking, Captain, that English merchantmen have been transporting slaves from Guinea, to cultivate sugar on Spanish plantations in the New World?'

'Aye, that is so, Squire,' replied the captain. 'My old shipmate, Captain Rogers, of the barque *Elizabeth Jane*, amassed a princely sum, after shipping slaves from the coast of Guinea to plantations in the Indies and importing sugar into England. In fact, from one voyage he obtained sufficient profit to commission a new barque.'

'A considerable sum indeed and I say we do likewise. We shall not be commissioning a barque, Captain Becket, instead, we shall be colonising these islands.'

Giving him a horrified look, his wife was emphatic.

'You propose to establish our morrows on slave labour, William?' she asked.

Closing his eyes, he shook his head with irritation.

'And what is wrong with such a noble scheme?' he asked.

'We could do it, Squire Fleming,' said the captain, excitedly.

'Ship in slave labour and fashion our fortunes, Captain, by sowing this island's fertile acres with cane sugar.'

'And not before time, Squire. Spaniards, Portuguese, French and Dutch grow rich from this trade. Why not we?'

'Slave labour!' his wife reiterated, with an increasingly agitated manner.

'It contravenes no English laws,' William replied.

''Tis against the laws of God!' she snapped.

'Who told you that? Show me which of the Ten Commandments state, Thou shalt have no slave.'

'By everything that's holy, what abomination is this?' she asked, indignantly. 'You have so concealed the genuine article all these years, William. Why, I cannot recognise the man I married.'

Embarrassed by the captain's gaping mouth, the atmosphere between himself and his wife intensified as their difference of opinion grew.

'I suppose you would have us sail back to Cuthbert's Inquisition?' he enquired. 'Mountains have been known to move, Charlotte, but I am certain that that always requires the violence of an earthquake. I do not believe such a fundamental change of heart in the Deputy Lieutenant is possible, do you?'

Provoked by his wife's openly aired hostility, he turned to scan the bay and let the wonderfully pleasant breeze cool his face and neck. Red-billed laughing gulls plunged into the sea, before soaring into the blue, blue firmament.

'Will they not ache for their families, Captain Becket?' he suddenly heard her enquire.

Gazing at her with incredulity, William took hold of her arm.

'Piffle,' he said, frowning with displeasure.

Clearly ill at ease, the captain looked in the direction of the *Lady Margaret*.

'That is just what we might expect from a woman, aye, Captain?' he asked, scowling at his wife.

'You're hurting my arm, William,' she said. 'Will the slaves not be fettered?'

Dropping his wife's arm, he was brusque.

'Do you want us to regain Augustfields or not? We shall not maltreat the slaves. A windfall awaits us if we get a foothold and take advantage of this trade.'

'A king's ransom could be put together, Squire' agreed the captain. 'It may take a bit of persuasion but with the right men as overseers, slaves will not suffer overmuch . . . '

'What of the Arawak?' she said, with a sudden, forthright and un-explored line of attack. 'And what kind of persuasion do you propose to employ?'

'Within a few years,' he replied, 'we shall outnumber the Arawak.'

Her lips curled with an expression of unqualified distaste.

'We shall grow a colony,' he said. 'We can offer England sovereignty over these islands, in exchange for the return of my Yorkshire estate and your dwelling in Morecambe, Captain. We have until then the required skills among the men here to build houses, a governess to instruct the children, and under the priest's auspices we shall all receive the Catholic scriptures. Good wife, we should thank God and Captain

Becket this day that we can be certain of the morrow.'

Glancing uneasily in Charlotte's direction, the captain was concise.

'I am in full accord with your reasoning, Squire. I think now would be a judicious moment for me to return to my vessel.'

'I daresay it would, Captain,' said Charlotte, acidly.

'As you wish, Captain Becket, my wife and I shall walk awhile.'

A flight of yellow parrots squawked across the clear blue sky, as the foaming tide rippled gently along the sands.

'Come my beloved, you know I am right.'

'Are you certain Our Saviour will look kindly on your decision, William? For such a grim deed once implemented can never be rescinded.'

He turned and gazed at her. Tears were standing in her eyes, she had a grimace on her lips and she exuded an angry silence. Taking hold of his proffered arm, he heard her sigh of resignation. Without another word, he started walking along the silken shore. Like a founding father gripped by imperial thoughts, he murmured.

'It can be a somewhat painful assignment, bringing home the morrow.'

Guinea

A long long time ago in the Gulf of Guinea, a Yoruba village came to life on the eastern bank of the River Ogun. Bounded by dense rainforest, people settled in this fertile area with long days of tropical sunshine and seasonal rains. Maturing into a large village, it boasted laterite-red, clay-brick houses topped by leaves from the forest and the long grasses of the savannah. Traders journeyed from all over the region to its weekly market.

On any day the heady aroma of cooking drifted through the prospering village – the banana-like *dodo* frying in palm oil, *egusi* stews with scorching hot peppers, roasted yam and concoctions of bitter-smelling herbs. Acquiring a burgeoning mercantile reputation, the villagers named their village Ake and appointed a *Bale* – Mayor. It grew to become the head village of the fifty-three surrounding villages. Ake's houses were set around a large rectangular area of baked, fiery-coloured earth, on which stood statues and shrines to the various cults of the Yoruba pantheon, especially to the god Sango, who played a pivotal role in the life of the villagers.

Sango had not always been a god. He was the fourth king of the Yoruba, the son of Oranyan and the grandson of Oduduwa, the legendary ancestor of the Yoruba people and founder of the city of Oyo. Tutored by a divine being, Sango was given a potion that granted him the ability to draw lightning on command. Doubting the properties of the concoction, Sango tested it out on his own home. In the subsequent storm, lightning struck the palace, killing his wives and children. Mortified by his actions, Sango abdicated and hanged himself from a tree at Koso. Following his death, it was announced that Sango 'disappeared' at Koso. On hearing of her husband's death, Oya, his only surviving wife, committed suicide and 'disappeared' at Ira. With Sango's disappearance, only the Bariba, a distant clan in the far north of Yorubaland, possessed the formula. Henceforth, the pious devotees of Sango, the Mogbas, were empowered to preserve the name of the god, uphold his decrees and interpret his laws. From that day forward, whenever thunder and lightning struck together, it was said that Sango had returned to punish wrongdoers by inserting beneath the house a thunderbolt in the shape of a smooth, black, oval-shaped stone. In September of 1749, Ake's villagers were unaware of converging atmospheric currents . . .

And so it begins . . .

Lightning streaked over the dark forest between voluminous black clouds, followed by a strong gust of wind that swept across the savannah, arching the palm trees and flattening the long grasses. Like a stirring giant, thunder rolled ominously across the night sky as the storm drew near the village. Thunder and lightning struck simultaneously. Voices began to shout their homage to the god Sango.

'*Ka boo ka biye si.* Welcome Majesty, long live the king.'

Skulking in the shadows of a house was a hooded figure, shielding the fiery embers he carried in a clay pot. Using a machete, his hooded accomplice effected an entry through the outer mud wall of the house. Inside the compound, they traversed the outdoor area and made it to the wall of the interior building where the Sodeke family slept. Standing on a stool under the eaves, one began spreading the glowing cinders into the cavities and corners of the dry thatched roof. The other hurriedly burrowed beneath the wall of the house, where he buried a smooth, black, oval-shaped stone. Refilling the hole, he flattened the ground with his feet. As the cinders ignited and flames spread inside the roof, rain began to fall. Melting into the shadows beneath the eaves of the outer wall, the villains lingered briefly to make certain the fire took hold.

Unaware of the conflagration happening over his head, Kayode, the striking, sinewy scion of the household, lay inside in the depths of sleep.

From the distance the cry came again.

'*Ka boo ka biye si.*'

A bolt of lightning lit up the sky and an ear-splitting thunderclap shook the village as flames rose from the roof of the house. Kayode heard the cry in his dreams.

'*Ina! Ina!*' – Fire! Fire!'

'Fire', he dreamed, 'cooks my delicious *egusi*.'

'*Ina! Ina!*'

Dreaming that he was wandering through a freshly cut maize field, he saw farm workers firing the leftover *koriko* grass. They were shouting and frantically beckoning to him from the far side of the field. He ran towards them until the flames cut off his escape, and he veered away. His foot plunged into a hole and he awoke with a jolt in a smoke-filled room. Violently coughing, he leapt to his feet.

'Fire!' he screamed.

'*Ka boo ka biye si*,' a voice shouted.

'Fire! Fire!' another voice yelled.

The cry came again.

'*Ka boo ka biye si.*'

Flames were crackling in the roof. Dense smoke was clogging his nostrils and filling the room with a bitter stench. Through the wall he heard the coughing and gasping of his parents and his elder brother's wife as they stumbled from the house. He must wake his house-visitor, Habib, the storyteller. Sinking beneath the thick black smoke and pulling himself along the floor to the next room, he grasped the storyteller's arm.

'Fire, Habib!' he shouted. 'Get out! Get out!'

Shaken awake and speedily on his feet, the drowsy storyteller fled from the house. Looking back from the front door, chaos met Kayode's eyes. Rain was entering the house and turning the dirt floor to mud. The roof was a blazing canopy, hissing when raindrops hit the flames. As the dundun drum began to 'talk' the news of Sango's visitation, he joined his family beneath the eaves of the outer wall. There is something strange about this blaze, he thought. How can a roof burst into flames with so much water falling on it? An instinct made him turn his head, in time to see two figures sprinting away from the outer wall and disappearing into the dark forest. The protection of his kinfolk was his first concern. Later he would hunt down the men responsible for the fire. Torrential rains descended, covering up the tracks and sounds of the intruders. It was sky-river. Wafting on a warm breeze came the soft sorrowful rattle of a *sekere*. The mournful tones of a flute injected dark tense notes into the unfolding events.

Kayode turned to Habib.

'When the sun rises,' he said, 'this catastrophe will be reported to the

Alafin of Oyo – the King of the Yoruba. This night we must sleep in the blacksmith's forge. Come, Habib, help me get my family there.'

He led his family down the waterlogged track that ran alongside the forest. Arriving at the forge, he waited until his inconsolable mother had crossed the threshold, before drawing his father aside to speak out of her hearing.

'I will return to our house with a palm wreath, Baba' he said.

'Take Habib with you.' said his father, with a cracking voice.

Trailed by the storyteller, Kayode hurried down the dark track.

'A wreath?' asked the storyteller.

'The wreath is nailed to the front door,' he said. 'It forbids anyone from going inside the house until the kings and chiefs appear to pay their respects to Sango.'

'At least your goods will be safe then,' said the storyteller.

Fastening the wreath to the door, he frowned at the storyteller.

'What use are possessions without a house?' he asked.

Dropping his eyes, the storyteller fell silent.

By the time they returned to the darkened forge, a light warm rain was falling. They were welcomed by the blacksmith's toothy smile.

'*E'kabo* – welcome, Kayode,' said the blacksmith, 'and you too Habib, you must be weary, my friends. I have prepared sleeping mats for both of you.'

'*E'kabo*, Babarimisa.'

Pointing to a tidied corner of the forge, the blacksmith lowered his voice.

'Things look bad now, Kayode, but your friends will help,' he said. 'Get some sleep. *O'daro* – goodnight, my friends.'

'*O'daro*, Babarimisa.'

Lying on his back, his thoughts drifted to the blacksmith, a man the village turned to in times of trouble. He recalled a severe thunderstorm that had flooded the Ogun River a few years previously. While people scurried about panicking, the thirty-year-old blacksmith had led a rescue team and erected a dam to divert the oncoming torrent away from the village. Buttresses had snapped from time to time under the pressure of the floodwaters. Single-handedly, the blacksmith went without sleep for nights on end, shoring up the dam with new props.

Listening to the patter of raindrops, his mother's anguished voice, the blacksmith's whispered tones and the sweet notes of a finger-piano, the touching words of a song drifted into his hearing. A tear crept into his eye.

The cockerel woke him. He dressed while the sun was hovering above the horizon veiled in a light mist. This is going to be a long, hot day, he thought, as he walked back through the village with the storyteller. Goaded by white-robed Mogbas, an angry crowd were circling the charred house.

Kayode scowled.

'Scavengers,' he snarled.

'Sango has cursed them,' shouted a Mogba.

'Sango has spoken,' a man shouted.

'They must have done something really wicked,' said a woman.

He shook his head at the malicious mutterings of the crowd.

'To think that some of these rats were our friends,' he said.

'Your father insulted the Mogbas,' a voice shouted.

'It smells strange to me,' said another voice. 'I think somebody is after their land.'

'How dare you question this sacred event,' a Mogba cried.

The mood of the crowd turned ugly. Stones and clumps of mud rained after the fleeing sceptic.

'Is Sango angry, Kayode?' the storyteller asked.

Grasping the storyteller by the arm, he pulled him away from the crowd.

'The Mogbas are making mischief, Habib,' he said quietly. 'It all began a few days ago. My father arrived at the bridge over the Ogun River. A Mogba suddenly appeared at the opposite end. By tradition, my father should have stepped aside and let the Mogba cross before him. He did not, which angered the narrow-minded Mogba, whose friends are now out to wreak vengeance. I am angry because their actions will make them rich.'

'Make them rich?' the storyteller exclaimed.

Habib was clearly perplexed. Hailing from the Fongbe, a people with an entirely different language and culture, he was an itinerant teller of tales who knew nothing of the ways of the Mogbas.

'You ask me how the Mogbas would enrich themselves, Habib?'

'I ask only to understand,' replied the storyteller.

'Our ruin and dishonour begins when the Alafin sends kings and chiefs to our house to pay homage to Sango,' he said. 'According to our laws, my father must give to each of them eleven heads of cowries, a goat and a slave, in three payments.'

The storyteller gasped.

'Are there not forty cowries to one string?' he asked.

Kayode nodded.

'Fifty strings make one head,' he said, 'and ten heads make one bag.'

The storyteller gasped again.

'Every king and chief will be given more than one bag of cowries?' he asked.

'Besides the cowries,' Kayode continued. 'My parents must give their youngest son to the Mogbas, who will then be ransomed, and the kings and chiefs will receive even more cowries for themselves.'

'Kayode you are the youngest,' the storyteller exclaimed. 'That means . . . '

Cutting the storyteller short, he said:

'That is not all, Habib. When my father has amassed enough cowries for the ransom, only then can he ask the authorities to perform the ceremony to appease Sango. Then they will remove the thunderbolt from under his house. After that he must then pay more cowries to allow him to seek permission to rebuild his house.'

The storyteller was incredulous.

'Your father must pay to ask permission to rebuild his own house?' he asked.

'From that grasping Alafin,' he replied. 'And it is to him that my father must pay the cowries, which he himself will share with the town council. My parents will then have to give their eldest son to the Mogbas, to be become a Mogba, a disciple of Sango.'

'That is your brother, Taiwo,' cried the storyteller. 'They seek to destroy your family, Kayode.'

'That is also Sango's decree, Habib,' he replied. 'The Mogbas say that Sango's ruling was confirmed by our ancestors. But I think they have created these customs to suit their thieving. From this day, Sango's followers can take anything they want from any hut or house in our village – goats, chickens, clothes, furnishings – in truth anything from any house. The whole village will suffer terribly.'

'In the name of Sango?' asked the storyteller.

'We have to wait and see what the Mogbas demand when they come to the house,' he said. 'I am certain that the Mogbas have eyes on my father's land . . . '

Catching sight of two men striding towards them, he stopped abruptly. One wore a richly embroidered *agbada*; the other was dressed in the white robes of a priest.

'Here comes the Ologbo accompanied by a Mogba,' he whispered to Habib.'

'Who is the Ologbo?' the storyteller asked.

'The official witness and the King's historian who must listen, remember what is said here and commit to memory any agreement that is made this day. Believe it or not, Habib, at the King's command, the Ologbo can chant all the dealings about land ownership and the history of the Yoruba in the area.'

The two men halted before Kayode – a surly, pockmarked priest of about forty, and the elderly, jowly, affable Ologbo.

'Where is your Baba?' snarled the Mogba. 'When is he going to clear this big, big debt?'

Bowing respectfully to the Ologbo, Kayode turned to the priest – a cold, resentful-looking man with darting eyes and a hideous blemish on his neck in the shape of a distorted crescent moon.

'My father is the only one who can properly give you an answer. I cannot speak for him. *Bale ni oloran awa* – the master of the house must be privy to all secrets.'

'Tell him that I wish to speak with him when the sun is at its highest. Talk to your *Iya* – mother – and get her to advise her husband not to cheat us. Sango must now be appeased.'

Stifling the impulse to punch the contempt back into the Mogba's face, he retorted.

'Would you not agree that I cannot tell my Iya how to instruct my Baba? *Obe ti Bale ile kinije Iyale ile kifise e* – the sauce that the master of the house finds unpalatable, the mistress of the house must not cook. I cannot act against the will of my father. I will go now to give him your words.'

Entering the forge, Kayode was instantly aware of the despair within. He beckoned his elder brother outside.

'*Egbon*, your wife is about to give birth,' he said, 'and Baba is too old to submit himself to the disrespect from this Mogba.'

'What do you want, Kayode?'

'I want to take Baba's place at this parley with the Mogba.'

More than content to be left behind, his brother heaved a sigh and nodded.

'So be it,' he said.

It was noon and sweltering when Kayode left to go to the agreed meeting. Outside the Bale's house, he found his antagonist sitting between the two sapele wood house pillars of the mayoral residence – one pillar depicted a kneeling Sango priestess offering a fowl in thanks, and the other a kneeling priestess holding her breasts in respect. In the steamy heat of that sombre afternoon, Kayode sat impassively on a stool and faced the Mogba. Pressing a cup of fermenting palm wine into his hands, the Ologbo greeted him, while the Mogba buried his face in a carved wooden goblet, raising his head only to acknowledge passers-by. The Mogba eventually turned to him.

'*E'kasan* – good afternoon, Kayode.'

'*E'kasan*,' he replied, quietly.

'I have been sent by the Town Council,' said the Mogba, 'to inform you that four kings and five chiefs will call on your house to pay homage to Sango. They are each to receive a gift of one *egbawa* of cowries. That is one hundred and ninety-eight thousand cowries in all. Does your father have such a sum?'

Kayode gasped with incredulity.

'I have never seen such a sum in my entire life,' he exclaimed. 'My father is a poor farmer. My family will starve if we lose our land.'

Tactlessly, the Mogba began picking his teeth.

'What land does your family hold?' he asked.

It was a question shrouded in subterfuge and Kayode knew it. He had to be truthful, for he was certain that the Ologbo had spoken to the Town Council beforehand, and would have informed them of the extent of his family's landholding.

'My father owns an *oko etile* – home farm – behind his house,' he replied. 'He also possesses an *oko egan* – forest farm. He can look down and look up, for he owns the land as well as all the trees, and he grows sweet potato, koko, cola-nut, yam, bean and calabash.'

Clearing his throat, the Mogba expectorated. His discharge kicked up a layer of dust near Kayode's bare feet. It was an act that was tinged with ill will. Raising his eyes slowly from the phlegmy green mass, he stared at his tormentor.

'That does not sound paltry to me,' sneered the Mogba. 'You and your neighbours will have to sell all of your *oko egans*. And if that is not enough, as the youngest son, you will be ransomed.'

With his thoughts racing, Kayode maintained a deadpan expression.

'Your village will also bear the cost of entertaining Sango's worshippers who pay homage at your house,' said the Mogba. 'And finally your elder brother will be delivered unto us to become an initiate and be taught Sango's mysteries.'

He fought the impulse to reach out and crush the hideous birthmark on the Mogba's windpipe with his thumbs.

'Your words for the Town Council, Kayode?' the Mogba asked.

Taking a deep breath and raising his head, he gave the Mogba an unwavering look.

'It is said that we must follow the old ways and we cannot refuse Sango's judgment,' he replied. 'Following such a convenient visitation it is better I keep my mouth shut.'

'What do you mean?' snarled the Mogba. 'What have you not said?'

'What is said is not said, until I say it,' he retorted, angrily. '*Bi owo eni ko te eku ida a ki ibere iku ti o pa Baba eni* – If one has not grasped the handle of his sword he should not attempt to avenge the death of his father.'

Leaping up from his stool, the Mogba snapped:

'Insolent agitator!'

Rounding on the King's historian, the Mogba was vehement.

'You hear that Baba?' he said. 'You hear that?'

Kayode looked closely at the Ologbo. Opening his eyes even wider, the historian's jowls shook when he coughed. And with his eyeballs rolling from one man to the other, he maintained the mandatory silence.

'Sango has descended and you are not in awe, Kayode?' the Mogba asked. 'What is wrong with you? I make no decrees. A long long time ago, our forefathers set down what must happen when Sango has descended. Yet you who are worthless question their wisdom?'

By staring stolidly into the distance, Kayode further infuriated the priest who resumed his seat.

'What cheek,' the Mogba scoffed. 'You who are nothing dare to pour scorn on our sacred traditions?'

'Your tongue runs away with you,' Kayode replied, raising his voice. 'I have said my family will accept Sango's judgment. But our ancestors did not say we must like it.'

Clearing his throat, the Mogba again expectorated thick green phlegm that landed even nearer Kayode's feet. There it lay between them – silent, inert and nocuous. With that, he knew the examination was at an end. Rising to his feet and keeping his eyes fixed on his inquisitor, he spoke with a firm voice.

'I will go and speak with my father,' he said. '*Ohungbogbo ti a se l'aiye, li a o de idena Orun ka* – whatever we do on earth we shall give an account at the gates of heaven.'

Shrugging his shoulders, the Mogba stood up with the King's historian.

'I feel your pain, Kayode,' said the Ologbo, with watery eyes.

Scowling at the Ologbo for offering words of sympathy, the Mogba stepped aside to let him pass. Bowing to the historian, Kayode turned and strode away. From the edge of the compound his friends shouted words of encouragement, and so with horns, flutes and fiddles, rattles and bata drums, they fell into a heartening beat. Despite the tension and dread in him, he still waved appreciatively at them.

The light was fading by the time he arrived back at the forge. The long tailed white okin birds were landing on the roof, and parakeets were settling harmoniously in the trees with the monkeys. Alone, he imparted the details of the Mogbas cowrie demands to his father. Surrounded by his family and the storyteller, Kayode tucked into his favourite dish, a bowl of the melon-seeded *egusi* soup. At the end of the meal he downed some palm wine to steady his nerves and spoke.

'The Mogbas started the fire.'

'How do you know?' his brother asked.

'Intruders were inside our house that night,' he replied.

'Are you sure about this, Kayode?'

'There were two of them,' he replied, quietly but firmly. 'Before I left I saw their muddy footprints inside the house. With the thunder masking their entry, they cut a hole through the wall of the compound.'

His brother gasped.

'Are you saying that Mogbas set fire to our house?'

Leaning closer to his brother, Kayode asked:

'Has anyone heard any villager say they saw lightning strike our house?'

'I have not.'

Looking around the forge, he saw everyone shaking their heads.

'If a man witnessed Sango arrive,' he asked, 'would he be able to keep his big mouth shut?'

'He would not,' agreed his brother.

'The Mogbas say our house was destroyed by Sango's visitation,' he said. 'I say the Mogbas lit that fire.'

Their father raised his hand for silence.

'I think what Kayode says is true,' he said.

With this paternal concurrence, Kayode launched into a furious monologue against the ancient rites of the Yoruba – absurd customs, outdated traditions, covetous Mogbas and the acquisitive Alafin of Oyo. So, he helped his family totter across the consecrated divide between blind faith and logic. From her sleeping mat, their tearful mother prayed.

'*Oluwa* – God, you must stop this nightmare,' she cried, 'you must stop it.'

His brother's wife began to sing softly. He could not quite make out the words of her song, but it struck a mournful note.

His father, who had been silently mulling over their predicament, suddenly interjected in a quiet urgent voice.

'I think there is only one way to defeat those wicked Mogbas.'

'You know a way, Baba?' asked Kayode.

Throwing guarded looks about, his father leaned towards them. He spoke out of the hearing of the women.

'Have any of you ever heard about a people called the Bariba?'

'I have told tales about them,' said the storyteller. 'But are they not a myth?'

'They are no myth, Habib,' said their father. 'They are a clan of the Yoruba who live beyond Gbere, a town in the far far north of Yorubaland. Solely they possess the *sese* bean – the only known remedy against Sango's ruinous visitations.'

'I too have heard about the *sese* bean legend, Baba,' said Kayode.

'It's more than legend son!' their father snapped. 'With these elderly eyes, I myself have seen them one time in my life. Great big white beans, each the size of a man's fist. Lay hands on the *sese* bean – and the Mogbas will not dare touch us. To find them, you must go to Gbere. And that town has never before been reached from Ake.'

Awed by the prospect of attaining the unattainable, Kayode fell silent. However, his brother, who was plainly troubled, beckoned him out into the compound. The night sky was a perfect celestial hemisphere. Wispy clouds drifted beneath the moon. Wood smoke and the distinctive smell of palm wine hung in the air.

'*Aburo*,' said his brother, stressing his seniority with the customary title used for a younger sibling. 'Baba is right. This mission for the *sese* bean must be undertaken but Baba is too old to make such a long journey. One of us must go in his place. You are old enough to go alone.'

Smiling to himself at the expediency of his brother's argument, Kayode replied, as Yoruba custom dictated, with the deferential term of respect for addressing an elder sibling.

'*Egbon*, you are right, Baba is too old,' he said. 'But it is foolishness to propose that I go alone. Two will stand a better chance of success. As the eldest, you are expected to take our father's place, and together we will make this journey.'

His elder brother scowled at him. Due to the imminent birth of his first child, his elder brother had a valid reason to remain in Ake. However, with the very survival of the family in the balance, Kayode concluded that they could not entertain his brother's excuse.

It was he, the younger brother, and more than anyone else in his family, who possessed the confidence and the skills essential for survival in the rainforest – expertise acquired from his father, the woodcutters and the farmers of the forest. His domesticated sibling possessed no such comparable know-how. It was obvious that his brother hoped his inexperience of the rainforest would exclude him from such an arduous trek, but Kayode was not about to let him off. Po-faced and plainly in a huff, his brother turned and stomped back into the house. Following closely, Kayode halted in the doorway from where he addressed their father.

'Your sons will go to find the Bariba,' he said.

Through clenched teeth, his brother gave him a feeble smile. Their father pursed his lips.

'It will be a long and dangerous expedition, Kayode,' said their father.

'We will make it,' he replied.

'This journey has never been attempted by people living this far south,' their father cautioned.

'We have no choice – we must do something to save our family,' he replied.

In a low voice, their father said:

'The Bariba are renowned sorcerers and charm-makers. I once met a man who saw a high priest of the Bariba make himself invisible. And he also said that with ancient chants, herbs and potions, they could make dead men walk. Yes, I agree with you, Kayode, we have no choice.'

He sighed.

'You have mine and your mother's blessing for this journey,' said their father. 'I will find a buyer for the *oko egan* as demanded by the Mogbas after you are gone.'

Silence fell briefly before their father spoke again.

'Which way will you go, Kayode?'

'We'll follow the River Ogun north to Igbetti,' he replied. 'Then we'll trek east-of-north to Gbere. It will take us about three full moons, there and back.'

His brother's mouth fell open.

'It is forest nearly all the way, Kayode!' he exclaimed.

'Ah Ah, Taiwo, I am surprised at you,' their father said. 'Why do you think we are confident that your young brother will get you both safely there and safely back? Why do you think we call him the cat of the forest? Listen my sons. At first light I will speak to the Bale and the two-faced Mogbas. I will tell them that I have sent you south to a secret cove on the coast at Eko, where you will find plenty of cowrie shells. With good fortune, that should keep them off your trail.'

The wail of the hyenas signified the approach of dawn. Shortly after, Kayode heard the sheep making for the forest pastures. He lay on his back pondering the day ahead. His brother's unfamiliarity with the wilderness would certainly be an obstacle, even though he had been aware of his elder sibling's limitations when he proposed his participation. He knew, however, that in the dangerous domain of the rainforest two men stood a greater chance of success.

As the village began to stir he stepped outside to scrutinise the forest. The lightening sky was streaked with clouds. A diaphanous ground mist drifted in layers. Guinea fowl were scattered through the brushwood pecking for grass seed. Soon after sunrise his father departed for the intended meeting with the Bale and the Mogbas. Taking two sacks, he and his elder brother filled them with sun-dried meat, fish, dried black plums, a coil of rope, herbal medicines and ten strings of 'travelling cowries'. These were shells of the smallest variety, twenty of which had been threaded on twenty strings. After sorting out their provisions, he gave his brother a spear and a machete and stuffed his sling into his own bundle.

Awaiting their father, Kayode sat on his heels outside the forge while his brother squatted in the shade beneath the eaves. They had yet to begin the trek and he already felt worn-out. He knew he would need to keep a close eye on his half-hearted sibling. He prayed that *Oluwa* – God – would watch over them. To pass time, he traced the route to the *abura* bridge in the dirt, rising only to welcome their father on his return.

'Did they believe you, Baba?' he asked.

'Every word, Kayode,' said the old man.

'It is time for us to leave, Baba. We can spend only a short time with you. We have a long walk before us.'

'May *Oluwa* watch over you my beloved sons,' his mother said tearfully.

His brother embraced their parents. He solemnly did likewise. Apart from their parents, the blacksmith and the storyteller were the sole witnesses to their departure. He turned to go. A prickly heat ran down his spine. He was seized by dread at what lay ahead. Forcing himself forwards, he took one step, then another and another. His legs fell into a steady gait. Turning by the giant abura tree, he started down the earthy red track towards the river. A cooling breeze stirred.

'May *Oluwa* grant you success,' wafted into his ears.

Trailed by his brother and the howls of monkeys, Kayode headed southwards along the lush eastern bank of the River Ogun. Late in the afternoon, after making sure they were not being shadowed, they crossed the river. On the other side, they changed direction and headed northwards along the western bank . . .

21 October 1749

Hampered by sodden clothes and suffocating humidity, for the next ten days they stumbled blindly along vestiges of pathways through the sweltering rainforest. Dwarfed by colossal trees, lianas and ferns, they were surprised by the dimensions of the shrubs and mosses, the giant snails and the bird-sized, swallow-tailed butterflies.

In places the dense canopy prevented sunlight from reaching the ground, turning day into night. Every sound intensified Kayode's unease – from the staccato rapping of the woodpeckers to the squawks of quarrelling parrots. Menace also prowled in the undergrowth in the shape of the leopard, the rhinoceros and the boar.

Looking back at regular intervals, he checked to ensure his brother was not lagging too far behind. All his energies were being concentrated on hacking a passage through the labyrinth of lianas plummeting from the canopy far far above.

Treading cautiously in the dappled sunlight, he stepped over tentacular roots to avoid treading on the Gabon viper, a lethal coil of motionless muscle, typically buried in the layers of ground foliage. Fearing this snake from childhood, he knew that it possessed the longest fangs in the snake kingdom and that its venom, so deeply implanted, was fatal. Only the thought of the Mogbas, glorying in their ill-gotten gains, prevented him from turning back.

The rainforest eventually gave way to scrawny woodland, which in succession yielded to dry scorching savannah. Steering clear of a legion of ants, he halted in a grove of termite mounds and young flame trees, a safe distance from a family of elephants stripping the trees. He took a measured reconnaissance of the heat-hazed terrain yawning before them. Amid tussocky grasses and giant groundsel, swirling gusts lifted clouds of red dust, keeping them suspended like ghosts of the plain. Vultures circled portentously in the clear skies. Some distance ahead and shimmering in the flameless inferno was a copse of thorny trees, the eyrie of a solitary eagle.

The sprawling plain teemed with antelope, buffalo, giraffe, zebra, wild dogs, hyenas, rhinoceros and elephants. He suspected that the leopard, the cheetah and the lion could be lying in wait in the tall grass. On horseback he and his brother would be safe from the big cats, whereas on foot, they were certain prey. A sudden movement caught his eye. A huge grey bull elephant tossed his head at them. His mouth dried. Scenting threat, the heavily scarred giant took a few steps in their direction, lifted his trunk and trumpeted. He shuddered. His brother gasped. The route across the savannah was plainly closed to them.

'Too risky to walk across,' he said.

His brother's face lit up.

'Shall we turn back?' he asked, eagerly.

Dismissing his brother's sudden enthusiasm to return to Ake, he waved his arm in an arc.

'We go around,' he said.

His brother groaned.

Skirting the savannah, they set off for the western bank of the Ogun River. Kayode knew the locale was the domain of harmful parasitic flies. For protection from sleeping sickness and malaria, he rubbed his mother's herbal balm deep into his brother's exposed skin and then into his own. After so many nights dozing fitfully in trees, followed by hours spent scorching leeches off their bodies with burning embers, they halted and camped to get a full night of sleep. He reckoned they were about three days walk from the gates of the royal city of Oyo, the imperial seat of the Alafin.

A crimson sun was setting. In the twilight, his brother leaned against a trunk gazing across the river in the direction of Oyo.

'Can we not at least beg the Alafin?' his brother asked, earnestly.

'*Egbon*. That would be very unwise.'

'Why is that?'

'His silver-tongued Majesty will take the life of anyone who withholds Sango's Tribute.'

'The Alafin's a crook,' his brother snapped, angrily.

This caused him to smile at his brother, who had stayed obedient to the Alafin and his dictates. Thus to hear an insult directed at the divine personage meant that his elder brother was, at long last, beginning to question the compliant traditions of the Yoruba towards their earthly King. He slumped down against a tree to wait for daylight. Apart from the glimpse of a mamba caught in the firelight, the night passed without incident.

November 18 1749

It happened after daybreak. They were nearly two full moons from Ake. High above the Ogun River, Kayode lay sprawled on a boulder watching his brother buff his teeth with a chewing stick. With seemingly little prospect of danger, a warm agreeable day promised peace. His eyes drifted lazily along the line of palm trees arching gracefully over the gorge-pools, below the terraced waterfalls. Wading through the shallows, storks waited for lungfish. Vermillion throated birds hovered within the multitude of flowers.

'Ssshhh,' he whispered, sitting bolt upright. 'What's that?'

Dropping on his belly to investigate, his brother thrust his head through the undergrowth. Almost instantly, he shot backwards quivering and goggle-eyed, his mouth opening and closing like a fish.

'What's out there?' Kayode asked. 'What did you see?'

A hoarse whisper came from his brother's mouth.

'*Funfun, funfun* – White, white,' he said repetitively, waving his hand at the bushes. 'Whitelings. Two men with white faces speaking in a strange tongue. It is *Elegbara*! – The Devil!'

'What are you babbling about? Let me take a look,' Kayode whispered. Warily he poked his head through the bushes.

Every sinew and muscle stiffened at the unearthly image that met his eyes. In a clearing stood two white-skinned men, urinating against a tree. One was tall with a black patch over his eye. Thickset and scarlet-faced, the other retained a long reedy pipe between his lips. In spite of the heat, the pair were clad from head to foot in wide brimmed hats and strange tight garments. A coiled whip and machete dangled from their waistbands. Long iron sticks were slung across their backs. Quaking with disbelief, he slithered backwards.

'What kind of tongue are they using?' his brother asked.

'Devil-talk,' he whispered tersely. 'Baba knew a fisherman who told him about some white men. They had arrived in a big big boat at Ebute Metta, near the mouth of the Ogun.'

'What happened?'

'After setting fire to the village, they made prisoners of the villagers.'

'Where did they take them?'

'Don't know.'

Crawling into the undergrowth, Kayode took another look. The white men had finished relieving themselves. Fumbling with their garments, they strolled away chattering. Trailed by his brother, he shadowed them to their camp. It was sited in a clearing a short distance from the man-groved shallows of the river.

Bounded by brushwood, the glade was overlooked by two giant *abura* trees, with a smaller one standing alone on the riverbank. At the heart of the camp, a table had been erected under a tree next to which sat a large wooden box. A row of beehives was appended beneath a thick branch, about ten feet above the table. Bordering the hives was a line of garments drying in the sun. Keeping close to the ground with his brother, he circled the camp until he arrived at a fern-thicket – not more than a whisper from the table.

He felt a gentle tap on his shoulder. His brother pointed at the *abura* tree facing them. At the foot of the trunk, he counted thirty sullen black men and women squatting in chains. A movement by the river caught his eye.

'Look,' he whispered.

By the water's edge, a brace of sedan chairs sat side by side. Two glistening young black men were washing the mud-encrusted chairs. Iron bands were fastened around their necks from which four in-capacitating spikes projected. Though angered by what he saw, he was utterly powerless. He could muster only a whisper.

'*Eru,*' he said.

'Slaves?' his brother asked.

Craning his neck above the ferns, Kayode sized up the camp. The first two whitelings had been joined by ten more. One sat with his iron stick trained on the two washing the sedan chairs. The others sat around the table against which leaned a cluster of iron sticks. Several picked up long clay pipes and stuck them between their lips. Then they deposited fire into the cups at the end. One put a short black pipe to his mouth and started to blow. Soon, to the trill of his pipe, song and laughter echoed through the canopy of the forest, while the huddled prisoners sat watching through the clammy heat of the day.

A prisoner cried out for water in the Yoruba language. Belching loudly, a pot-bellied man left the table. He ambled darkly across to the captives. Hauling the culprit to his feet, he kicked him hard in the groin. The prisoner shrieked, toppled like a tree and crashed face-first into the dirt. Not satisfied with the result, Potbelly hauled his whimpering victim onto his feet and punched him full in the face. The prisoner collapsed, lay still and fell silent. Turning to his companions, Potbelly dispensed a toothless grin. Kayode shook his head.

'What are they doing with slaves?' his brother asked.

Before he could reply, a horrific scream disturbed the clearing. Slithering rapidly below the ferns to the river, Kayode made for the source of the heartrending howl.

Hanging by her wrists from ropes slung over the bough of a tree on the riverbank was a bare-breasted girl of about twenty. From where he lay, her lithe physique and firm breasts were evident to him, as was her tight black hair. There her beauty dangled, swaying slightly, her body glistening with sweat. A goatee-bearded man stepped in front of her. Kayode held his breath. In the bright sunlight, the stunted man looked as callous as a machete. Suddenly kicking out, he sent her spiralling wildly. Arresting her motion as she swung back, he unsheathed his cutlass in one smooth action. One hand opened her thigh; the other rammed his cutlass hard up into her. Stepping back, he abandoned his blade inside her. Emitting an agonising scream, her body juddered violently. A bloody river gushed down her legs, drowning the hilt. Her head crashed onto her chest. Her fluids pumped to the tempo of her spasms into a spreading pool. A funereal wail rose from the prisoners. Stifling a gasp, his brother buried his face in the ground.

'Why?' he asked.

His eyes brimming with tears, Kayode turned away.

'She rejected him,' he replied.

'But he can just take her?'

'A slave cannot refuse.'

'I will mash up his balls,' snarled his brother.

Heavyhearted, Kayode watched her body cut down and tossed into the river. Her corpse spun fleetingly on the surface of the fast running current and then sank. Wiping his cheeks and raising his eyes to the skies, he pleaded:

'*Oluwa* – God, why did you not come to her aid?'

He turned back. Something inside him had changed. An icy hate hardened his resolve . He knew what he must do.

'We will free them,' he said.

'You're crazy, Kayode. There are twelve of them and two of us.'

'We cannot stand by and do nothing. They know not how many we number and will not be expecting us. *Egbon*, surprise walks with us.'

His brother fell silent. As far as Kayode was concerned, death was the conspicuous companion of the Yoruba. The actions of the Mogbas, who brought conflict and death into the life of his village, more than equalled the atrocities committed by soldiers in battle. He, like others, accepted the Mogbas as an essential component of the Yoruba tradition. But the action of this white-skinned man had sickened him like nothing before. Now he was bent on revenge.

'Here is how we shall free them,' he said quietly.

'Tell me,' said his brother.

'When the camp is sleeping, I will crawl to that *abura* and seek out the Yoruba.'

'But we are outnumbered?'

'So are the white men.'

'By what?'

'Bees.'

'Bees? I see no bees.'

He pointed at the *abura* tree.

'See the line of hives under that branch over there?'

His brother brightened up.

'Bees!' he exclaimed.

'Killer bees,' said Kayode. 'I have been watching those hives. Those bees are very very active.'

'Can you hit the hives with your sling?'

'I cannot miss,' he bragged. 'I'll crack those hives. The bees will break out and sting anyone flecked with honey.

Extracting a leather pouch of honey from his sack, he said:

'*Egbon*, gather a pile of pebbles and dip them in honey. Then we will begin. Those bees will inflict true agony. Many stings will kill a man. How many bees do you think inhabit the hives?'

'Countless,' his brother replied.

'I'm sure that the three by that *abura* tree are Yoruba,' he said. 'This night I will acquaint them with my plan.'

His brother scowled.

'Plan?' he asked.

'*Egbon*, I will crawl to the other side of the clearing,' he said, 'and signal you from that tree beyond them.'

'Signal?'

'The cry of the hyena will be the signal that I'm about to attack the hives,' he said. 'When the first hive is down, start throwing fistfuls of pebbles at the white men. Chaos will break out. Take the prisoners down to the river. I will meet you there. Now let's eat.'

He sucked a mango and looked at his brother, his face buried in a green coconut husk. After a lifetime of dodging responsibility, he thought, the ordeals of this trek have changed him. His confidence has grown.

Its heat exhausted, the sun was sinking and splattering crimson and tangerine streaks across a turquoise sky. White-headed parrots were roosting noisily in the trees. The aroma of suckling pig entered their nostrils.

'Smells good,' said his brother, licking his lips. 'The whitelings eat well.'

'*Egbon,* they eat for the last time!'

Circling the dark encampment through the undergrowth on his belly, Kayode arrived at the foot of the *abura* tree. Manoeuvring himself soundlessly over the loam, he arrived behind the three prisoners he knew were Yoruba.

'*Akin ee ku gbe* – brave men don't die in vain,' he whispered.

Chains rattled amid sharp intakes of breath. A whisper shot through the dark.

'Who is that,' a voice said in Yoruba.

'A friend who has come to set you free.'

'How do we know you are not working for the white men?'

Irritated by the suggestion, he took a deep breath before answering.

'Tears filled my eyes when they killed our sister this day.'

'You saw that?'

'My brother and I watched from the forest. We cannot stand by and see them kill you as well.'

The captives huddled in whispered counsel. The forest rang with the screams of monkeys and the rowdy activities of the slavers. Then the bushes rustled. A voice came through the dark.

'What do you want us to do?'

'Nothing. We will come to get you. I leave you until then.'

'We are desperate my friend,' urged the voice. 'Come back quick.'

Kayode returned to his brother. Everything was ready. He gave his brother a leaf-parcel filled with a brackish paste made from crushed *oguna* leaves.

'*Egbon,* rub this into your skin. It will stop the bees stinging you.'

A low bright moon cast long eerie shadows about the clearing. Slipping into the undergrowth with his sling, he slithered on his belly keeping well inside the darkest shadows. Crickets set his nerves on edge. Disturbing grunts from the forest accelerated his heartbeat. About fifty paces away, the slavers stood around a fire warming themselves. At the foot of the tree, the prisoners gathered together for warmth. Reaching the opposite side of the tree, he cupped his hands and imitated the cry of the hyena. Swivelling around with fright, the slavers reached for their iron sticks.

Spinning his sling, he let fly at the largest hive. It split open splaying infuriated inhabitants across the table. He heard the honeyed-pebbles, hurled by his brother, showering the table and the slavers. The insects sought their revenge. Brushing away the angered assailants with their hands, the slavers frantically flailed about. Rocks and pebbles flew alternately until nearly all of the nests had been ruptured.

Animal noises were superseded by the screams of slavers soaring into the canopy, before being stifled by the frenzied insects cramming their mouths. From behind a plum bush, he saw his brother take hold of a prisoner, yank him onto his feet and haul him towards the river. Still attached to the endless chain the prisoners followed in his brother's wake. The goatee-bearded man put an iron stick against his shoulder. A loud crack rang out. Fire spat from the end. The last prisoner screamed, flung his hands up and fell, to be dragged down to the river by his companions. Kayode was propelled into action. Stepping from behind the bush, he hurled his spear and pinned the bearded man to a tree. There he stayed, spattered with honey, alive, bleeding and transfixed, while his tongue, swollen and poisoned by an untold number of stings, slowly choked him to death.

Machete in hand, Kayode walked into the fire-lit clearing. White men were even now swiping wildly at a dense cloud of bees. Stepping across to the wooden chest and flinging back the lid, he gasped – it was crammed with cowry shells. Hearing approaching voices, he ducked down behind the chest. Two white men stormed into the camp – one was Potbelly. Loathing catapulted Kayode onto his feet. He flung his machete. It struck his quarry with a sickening thud. Potbelly crashed to the ground. His comrades fled. Nine white men lay dead or dying. Three had fled. Retrieving his blood-smeared weapons, he headed for the riverbank.

Making sure his brother and the captives were safe beside the water's edge, he returned to the clearing. Dragging the heavy wooden chest the short distance to the bend in the river near a lone mango tree, he dug a hole in the moonlight. Lining the cavity with banana leaves, he emptied the contents of the chest into it. Burying the cowries and camouflaging the site with foliage, he flung the chest into the river. A poor man knelt to offer gratitude to all the deities of the Yoruba. A rich man arose from his prayers – harbouring the kind of confidence that unexpected wealth bestows.

Slipping back to the river, he found his brother squatting anxiously on a large rock.

'I was worried for you, Kayode? Are the whitelings dead?'

He looked edgily around.

'*Egbon*, we must be gone from here,' he said. 'Three white men escaped into the forest. It is not safe to stay here.'

'The prisoners are still chained together,' his brother said.

Gleefully holding up a long iron key, Kayode thrust it into the padlock.

'I took this,' he said. 'I have seen how they use it.'

Twisting the key in the heavy lock, the hook fell open. Uttering thanks in unfamiliar tongues and with heartfelt gestures, the liberated men and women melted into the darkness – leaving a woman of about twenty and the dead man. Hurriedly they buried the corpse. Kayode was impatient.

'We must go. We must go,' he insisted.

'Wait, Kayode,' said his brother. 'What about this woman? Her name is Asabi. She is from the village of Pategi in the far north-east. She cannot find her way back to her village alone.'

At first sight he felt his blood rise. In the moonlight, he made out beguiling features ravaged by hurt. Between high cheekbones, scorn played on her lips. Clearly intent to go with them and eager to be gone, she stepped onto the track and looked intently at him. Moved by her resolve and certain they could not abandon her, he nodded.

'Let us go then,' he said quietly.

She fell in behind him. For a considerable distance he walked in silence at a fast pace along the riverbank. She begged to rest. Reminding her of the bearded one, he turned north and marched into the night.

In the early dawn, with the sun melting the mist from the landscape, Kayode found a track winding uphill through the tall grasses. Below to the east was the river meandering through the palm bush. On the marshy riverbank, great white birds searched for prey, holding their wings wide open. Though waves of fatigue washed through his body, he still marvelled at the cunning of the birds – for where the water was too deep they took flight and attacked from the air.

Towards the end of the day, he found a fissure in the face of a rocky embankment some distance along the trail. After checking that it was free of snakes, he flung his sack and weapons inside.

'My eyes scream for sleep,' his brother mumbled, slumping to the ground.

Sprinkling jumeke leaves across the entrance of the cave, Kayode cast a length of material on the ground for the woman.

'Sleep, Asabi,' he said.

'*Adupe* – thank you,' she replied softly.

She lay down. Pulling the cloth over her, his hand brushed her skin. Her eyes flicked open.

'*O daro* – good night,' he whispered.

'*O daro*,' she said, closing her eyes.

Settling down nearby, he lay back gazing through the entrance at the dark starry night. He drifted off to the serenade of crickets.

At daybreak, the woman's exhausted condition was evident. Kayode counselled that they rest inside the cave for the next few days. On a fire by the cave entrance that first night, his brother roasted bush pig and sweet potato. Mollified by kindness and the strength a full belly bestows, the woman rose to give them an account of her capture.

'White men stormed into my village,' she said. 'Soon all the houses were in flames.'

Pressing a stick into her shoulder, she emulated the invaders with their iron sticks.

'Fire spat from the end of the long stick. People fell all over the place. I saw that when people fell, they were dead or dying. All those still alive were seized, even the babies! They killed the Bale. I was dragged by the bearded one into the forest. He forced himself into me again and again.'

Discomfited, Kayode dropped his eyes.

'Did they not spare anyone?' he asked.

'Only the ones they took prisoner. The rest they butchered like cattle.'

Lifting his head, he eyed her thoughtfully.

'Does it not comfort you to know,' he asked, softly, 'that the bearded one met his death in great agony?'

'Huh,' she said, tossing her head.

Grimacing, she sat down, her lips quivering with anger.

'The woman he killed was my best friend in the village,' she said.'

Now I see how deep is your wound, he thought. Death had stalked her tracks from the moment she was kidnapped. When her best friend was killed in the rainforest, the last link with her village was severed. The barbarous spectacle of her friend being scythed internally came flooding back to Kayode. Sympathy engulfed him.

Burying her face in her hands, the woman lay down. She was soon asleep.

In the early morning, he sat by the cave entrance eating rose apples. Groaning softly, the woman opened her eyes. Smiling at her, he proffered an apple.

'How you feel?' he asked.

'My family is dead, Kayode. How do you think I feel?' she asked, indignantly, cold-shouldering his offering. 'Slaughtered by the same white men who escaped. I carry a poison deep inside me. The white men will pay for what they have done.'

'Which ones will you kill?' he asked, facetiously. 'The three white men you seek escaped into the forest. How will you recognise them among other white men?'

'White men are cruel,' she replied. 'I will kill them all. As long as I live, I will sleep with no man. I will carry no child into this heartless world. I sleep only with hate.'

She paused. Her eyes filled with tears.

'I am lost with no family,' she said, her voice breaking. 'Without you and your brother, I am friendless in this dangerous forest.'

His brother woke up.

'*E'karo* – good morning, Kayode.'

'*E'karo*,' he replied. '*Egbon*, we have the cowries we need.'

His brother frowned.

'How? Where?'

'Remember that big chest next to the table in the white men's camp?'

His brother nodded. Although they were alone, Kayode spoke in a whisper.

'It was filled with cowries.'

Raising his arms, his brother cried out.

'*Ori* – the god of fate – has answered my prayers.'

Kayode smiled.

'I buried them,' he said. 'Now we seek only the *sese* bean.'

'But we can satisfy the Mogbas' demands for cowries,' his brother exclaimed. 'Why do we still need to track down this boring *sese* bean?'

His brother's attitude irritated him. Shaking his head with incredulity, he simply sighed.

'*Egbon*, we have to seek out the *sese* bean,' he said. 'The sight of it alone will lawfully force the Mogbas to retrieve the thunderbolt. That way we sever the stranglehold they have on our people. And we will not have to forfeit any cowries. But we have been lucky, so far. Luck is like the cowrie – it soon runs out. *Egbon*, we must press on.'

Bearing in mind what he knew of her experience at the hands of white men, Kayode addressed the woman with all the sensitivity he could muster.

'Woman,' he said. 'The forest trembles with danger. You cannot walk alone. Your village lives no more. Walk with us to Gbere and back to Ake. There we will tell the Bale of your plight. We are sure he will help you. We cannot carry you and we cannot leave you behind. When we walk, you will walk and keep up with us.'

A crimson-tailed hawk wheeled into view. Cool refreshing breezes gusted through the cave. Slowly uncoiling, the woman rose to her feet. In suspense, he held his breath. Proudly erect she stood, her eyes dark and lucid. Deprived of womanly company since leaving Ake, his eyes probed every tuck, crease and crevice of her sensuous physique. But for the cloth fastened at her waist she was naked. Her torso was scored by unsightly wheals and across her small breasts, the floggings had composed a hideous design. It was evident to him that the lash had not broken her. The flogging blisters will heal, he thought. But the white men have also wounded her deep inside.

'I will do like you say,' she replied softly. 'I will walk when you walk. I will sleep when you sleep. I will eat when you eat. Do not let the fact that I am a woman make you think that I am weak. Forget not that among the Yoruba, it is the women who break their backs sweating in the fields. It is the women who walk the big big distances to fetch water. We pound the *gari*, cook the food and take care of the children. I am strong because of it. I need no man to carry me.'

Silence settled on the cave. Striding to the entrance, she stayed for a moment with her back to him. Glancing in his direction, she returned and sat back down. He grinned at his brother.

He found it hard to keep his eyes off her. His brother appeared similarly mesmerised. We need a cook, he thought. Yoruba women were renowned as cooks and for carrying similar loads to men. He liked her courage. An extra pair of hands would lighten their load and ease their journey.

His brother tactfully broke the silence.

'It is still cold. Let us be gone.'

Dividing up the food and possessions, Kayode handed the woman and his brother a sack each. Lifting hers onto her head, she walked hands free and easily over the rough terrain, whereas he and his brother carried theirs awkwardly over their shoulders. For some distance, he led them alongside the river. A little later he branched off upward into the hills. He was making for the busy market town of Shepeteri and then northwards to the Bariba . . .

Flagellum Dei

The Scourge of God

Those who are the favourers of companies suggest, that if the Trade must be allowed, and the Christian Scheme of enlarging the flock cannot well be carried on without it, that then it seems necessary and better for the Publick that some rich and powerful Set of Men should have such exclusive Powers to encourage and enable the subsisting of forts and garisons, to awe the natives and preserve the Trade from being engrossed by our dangerous Rivals here, the Dutch; which, as we relinquish, falls an acquisition to them, and renders all precarious; they could also bring (as an exclusive Company) foreign Markets to their own Price.

JOHN ATKINS,
Surgeon of the Royal Navy.
5 February 1720

Cape Tres Puntas, Coast of Guinea
28 January 1750, 06.00 hrs

'Land Ho! Land Ho!'

The cry startled the starboard watch of the Royal African Company's barque, the *Pelican*. Tools crashed onto holystoned decks.

'Where away?'

'Two points on the larboard bow.'

By the larboard rails, First Officer Thomas Wimborne raised his telescope to peer at his first sight of land through the morning mist. Dropping his scope, Wimborne groaned as the captain appeared on deck. A fresh northerly gusted through the weathered shrouds of the barque. At the break of the poop, the master mariner stood muttering to himself about the 'great glory of God' and the 'magnificent spectacle of landfall' after two months on the high seas. It was his thirteenth voyage in command of the *Pelican*.

'By the mark ten. Sand an' shells,' shouted the carpenter.

Sniffing the air, the captain declared:

'Cape Tres Puntas, Mister Wimborne. I first shipped here as Mate with Captain Wilson.'

Wimborne feigned the interest expected of a subordinate.

'Were you seeking slaves on that occasion, sir?'

'Pirates, Mister Wimborne.'

Fixing his eyes on the looming coastline, the captain was terse.

'I'd say we're about a hundred cables off,' he said.

'Aye sir.'

'Never forget, Mister Wimborne, slavery is our business.'

Wimborne scrutinised the forty-eight year old master mariner, the gruff bearded legend of the Royal African Company. His sunken eyes gave rise to crow's feet from the murk of countless watches. Ebenezer Blunt was a sallow-skinned seafarer, weathered by the elements and tempered by the seas. He was the eldest son of Captain Thomas Blunt, late of His Majesty's Ship, *Encounter*. According to the ship's grapevine, it was from his father that Blunt junior acquired that habit called brutality. In April 1718, his father had been despatched on a mission by Captain Woodes Rogers, Governor of the Bahamas, tasking him to arrest buccaneers in their stronghold on the Bahamas. While a cabin boy, Blunt junior witnessed cannons raking the fleeing vessels with grapeshot during his father's dramatic pursuit of the pirates. Nineteen captured pirates were keelhauled and twenty-two were forced to walk the plank – the rest were charged with piracy. At the trial's end, his father sang *I'll swing nearer to thee*. The young Blunt was compelled to watch the eight buccaneers strangling slowly in the morning breeze.

In the sailing master's judgment, Captain Blunt had more than justified the trust and confidence placed in him during the commissions entrusted to him by the Royal African Company. Due to the frequent revolts on England's slave plantations, the price of sugar had risen alarmingly. The crisis was reducing the profits of the Company. Following consultations at the beginning of 1749, the Principal Shareholders had resolved that profits must be increased. Blunt was given command of the *Pelican*, a three-masted, square-rigged barque of one hundred and twenty feet in length, thirty-two feet beam and a crew of seventy men. He was given explicit orders to extend the Company's interests to the east along the coast of Guinea. The aristocratic Principals then called at the coffee houses off Fleet Street and whispered words into powerful ears. In turn, they utilised their connections and notified the Prime Minister, Henry Pelham. Thus a frigate, the *Resolution*, was ordered to escort the *Pelican*, for the greater protection of the vital transactions of the slave trade.

A sudden gust drenched the poop deck in salty spray. The twenty-five gun *Pelican* groaned as she beat her way up the channel on a broad reach. Through spray, Wimborne made out a vast, dense, sloping forest divided by a terraced waterfall materialising below a stone fortress perched on the cliff top.

'Connu's Castle,' the captain growled. 'I'll have all hands on deck, Mister Wimborne.'

He relayed the orders to Pobjoy, the Second Officer.

'Watch below,' yelled Pobjoy. 'All hands on deck. All hands on deck.'

The larboard watch stumbled out on deck to join the starboard watch.

'By the mark six. Sandy bottom,' shouted the carpenter.

'Lay a course, Mister Wimborne,' said the captain, 'to stand off about four cables in the bay of Cape Tres Puntas, between the two outer points. That'll be plenty of water. I'll have us anchor. Bow and kedge, Mister. Bow and kedge. Got it?'

'Aye aye sir,' he replied.

'By the mark ten,' shouted the carpenter. 'Sand an' shells.'

The wind shifted to blow from astern. The *Pelican* was running free. With no alteration of course and speed, Wimborne knew that she was headed for a lee shore.

'Mr Graceforth, drop t'gallants and bear up if you please,' he said.

Spitting out a lump of shuruttu, the sailing-master replied.

'Aye, Mister Wimborne,' he said. 'Lee braces. Lee braces. Steady there helmsman. Steady as she goes.'

The *Pelican* began losing way.

'By the mark five,' shouted the carpenter. 'Sandy bottom.'

By noon, the *Pelican* was anchored in the wooded bay. Wimborne scanned the anchorage. In parts, mangroves combined in tracts and their long spiralling branches spanked the water, as foam surfed gently up the shore of white sand. At the eastern end of the harbour, a long jetty tilted at a crazy angle. Following the stormy crossing of the Atlantic Ocean, he was soothed by the tranquillity of the haven.

'Drop that there kedge, Mister Wimborne,' said the captain, 'and pay out ample catenary.'

Wimborne relayed his orders to the deck crew. A splash told him that the anchor was on its way down to the bottom.

'By the mark four. Sandy bottom,' shouted the carpenter.

The *Pelican* came to rest. Cannon fire was discharged from the castle.

'Prime the six-pounder if you please, Mister Pobjoy,' said the captain, 'and return salute.'

'Aye, aye sir.'

Wimborne scanned the natural harbour. He ignored the crack of the *Pelican's* six-pounder. Close to the cockeyed jetty, two barques flying the Dutch and English ensigns lay at anchor. Having scrubbed the barnacles off her bottom, the crew of a third vessel, a heeled Danishman, were overhauling the standing and running gear. There was no sign on the horizon of the *Pelican's* escort, the second-rate frigate, the *Resolution*. Of one hundred guns, she was on an Admiralty-ordered Commission for the Suppression of Pirates on the coast of Guinea. Having escorted the *Pelican* as far as the Guinea coast, the *Resolution* had sailed to the west to ascertain the proximity of pirate activity. The two vessels were scheduled to link up at Connu's Castle.

Under the noonday sun, the sandy bottom could be clearly seen below schools of red snapper. He shaded his eyes. On a rocky outcrop halfway across the bay, turtles basked in the sun. The anchorage echoed with the chatter of sweaty careening gangs, cursing and swearing as they toiled. Heading out from the shore was a canoe, making its way unswervingly through the breakers towards the *Pelican*.

'John Connu's man,' sniffed the captain.

'Begging your pardon, sir,' he asked, 'who is this Connu fellow?'

'Connu's the law around here, Mister Wimborne,' replied the captain, without so much as a glance in his direction. 'As a rule, the nigger kings and chiefs are the sole middlemen. They sell all the slaves. Connu is different. He may not be a king or a chief but he is the principal cabiceer around these parts. Controls the territory, has a private army and sells everything from water to slaves. Even the local chiefs are scared of him. He is pricey. But all we need from him is water and intelligence on that pirate Rogers.'

Turning to his cabin boy, the captain snapped.

'Fetch my pistols, boy.'

The tousled lad returned with a slim rectangular box of polished mahogany. Flipping open the container lined with maroon velvet, the captain extracted two walnut-handled Robert Wogdon pistols. Sighting the gruesome epigram inside the lid, Wimborne scowled.

Hail Wogdon. Patron of that leaden death.

Waving his pistols about, the captain began musing about his 'faithful disciples and righteous instruments of The Lord' that had 'converted many a heathen.'

Rowed by twenty men standing at their paddles, the eighteen-foot canoe was dexterously manoeuvred alongside. Three black men scrambled up the *Pelican's* Jacob's ladder. Setting foot on deck, their eyes scanned the vessel suspiciously from stem to stern. Wimborne overheard the cabin boy's whisper.

'They're black as coal, Mister Graceforth.'

'And twice as dirty, no doubt,' replied the sailing master. 'Don't trust them.'

Extending his *okyeame poma* – a long, gold-headed cane – for inspection, the headman who was swathed in a cerise cloth, approached the officers standing by the mainmast. Engraved into the top of his cane were the words 'John Connu'.

'Attee ho,' said Connu's envoy, snootily, as if he were addressing an inferior.

'And how do you do,' the captain replied, disingenuously. 'I want water. And I want to see your Master.'

Brandishing a bony index finger, Connu's envoy was emphatic.

'Ounce of gold for water,' he said.

Furnishing a slight unenthusiastic bow, the captain accepted the envoy's price.

'You want me Massa? *Fabra Fabra* – Come Come.'

Turning to the Second Officer, the captain gave orders.

'If we're not back by nightfall, Mister Pobjoy, you'll lead an armed escort up to the castle to negotiate our release. It would be better if the *Resolution* were here before then.'

Aye, sir.' replied the Second Officer.

On face value, Wimborne had initially regarded the Second Officer, William Pobjoy, to be a sedulous, respectful officer. But at thirty-six years of age, his soft cheeks, lively dark eyes and black ponytail contradicted the truth of him. Pobjoy had confided that he had signed on the *Pelican* on account of the captain's reputation for securing large profits on the coast of Guinea. As far as Wimborne could see, the Second Officer had little adjustment to make to fit into the captain's distasteful way of doing things.

In his eyes, Pobjoy had clearly grasped from an early age that there was more to life than pilfering on the streets of the East End of London. Thus, from his own account, he clawed and slashed his way out of the squalor of Spitalfields. At fourteen, he signed up as a cabin boy on a barque of the East India Company. Working his way through a number of vessels, he was eventually made boatswain. Worming his way into the confidence of a navigation officer, he contrived instruction in the mysteries of navigation. Scraping through navigation and seamanship examinations, he attained the rank of Third Officer with the East India Company. In the ten years since gaining his ticket, Pobjoy terrorised the swindlers and pickpockets manning the vessels of the Company. In dire need to quit England's shores due to a predicament with the Excise men and an affair of the heart, he slipped into the service of the Royal African Company as a Second Officer. Off watch and drunk one night, he boasted that he was 'assembled without a heart'.

'Mister Graceforth, take one or two tenders, some men and casks for water,' said the captain. 'Mister Wimborne will accompany me with an escort of four armed seamen. We will ride with you as far as the jetty. Replenish the casks and wait for me there. We will continue up to the castle to parley with Connu. Is that clear?'

'Aye aye sir,' replied the sailing master.

Laden with ten men and the empty water casks, the *Pelican's* tender was barely able to keep up with the canoe. On the stern thwart, the captain nudged him. Jabbing a finger at the twenty rowers paddling to a high vocal harmony, he asked:

' 'Tis a strange sight, aye, Mister Wimborne?'

'I venture so, sir.'

Rolling his eyes with exasperation, the captain snapped:

'A feckless reply, sir!'

'I merely answered your question, sir.'

Leaping onto the lopsided jetty, the captain scrutinised the rainforest and the fortress. Following a snarl at the sailing master to be about his wits, he said:

'Let's be on our way, Mister Wimborne.'

Ahead of four seamen, Wimborne trailed the captain up the steep twisting footpath leading to Connu's castle. Arriving at the top of the rocky path, steps had been chiselled out of the rock. On the topmost step, surrounded by men wielding swords, short pikes and muskets, stood the legendary John Connu. Wimborne shivered. Connu was of huge dimensions. About fifty, pitch-black with a bull neck, he had big black eyes, large ears and a sullen countenance. Dressed in a red cotton sleeveless jerkin, he wore baggy white silk breeches tied at the ankles. A dagger tucked into a belt of woven kente cloth completed his piratical appearance. Fanning banana leaves above his head, two men fended off the flies. All his men wore hats, tie-dyed shirts, breeches and wrappers or loincloths of indigo. The big man himself was bald and bareheaded. Dangling from the thick gold chain around his neck was a rosette-patterned *akrafokonmu* – the solid gold pectoral disc of a soul-washer.

'*Attee ho* – hello, Captain white man,' said Connu, coldly. 'Gold for water.'

Tossing a small leather pouch into his waiting palm, the captain responded.

'*Attee ho*, Captain Connu, an ounce of gold for Duty.'

Pocketing the pouch without scrutiny, Connu proceeded to look over the seamen off the *Pelican*.

'*Praam Praam* – Good Good,' he said, at the conclusion of his inspection. 'Come eat cockracoo.'

The invitation sounded very much like an order to Wimborne's ears. Connu led them below the main portcullis, through a passage beneath a set of meurtieres and a secondary portcullis, to emerge in a bright stifling outer bailey.

'Ye gods,' Wimborne gasped, turning to look at the four ashen-faced seamen who had halted.

Beside piles of human skulls, twelve tightly bound white men sat sweating and trembling under a blistering sun. Standing over them were four black guards, armed with muskets and machetes. Their black locks were threaded with gold flakes and precious stones. They were naked but for a cloth circling the hips, pulled between the thighs and fastened below the belly button. Pausing in his stride, the captain was trenchant.

'Mister Wimborne?'

'Aye, sir?'

'Hold your tongue there, sir,' said the captain, scathingly. ''Tis nothing that concerns us. 'Twould be better for us if you kept your fright to yourself.'

'Aye aye, Captain Blunt.'

Averting his eyes from the captives, his gaze settled on the footpath on which he stood. It was constituted almost entirely of buried skulls, stretching from the main gate, disappearing inside the castle. He gulped.

The inner sanctum of Connu's citadel boasted an inner bailey and stone keep, well protected by gun-loops, embrasures and loopholes. At each corner was a square turret with small windows, which on the lower level were mere slits. The first floor was reached by a steep staircase leading up to the forebuilding at the side of a great tower. Crenallations topped the lofty walls of the keep. Machicolations had been erected at intervals along the perimeter of the vast building boasting fifty cannons. According to their host, the slaves were housed in dungeons set deep below large iron grates in the middle of the inner bailey.

Following Connu up a flight of steps, they arrived on the first floor of the forebuilding that also housed the garrison quarters and the wellhead. On the second floor, they passed the armoury before entering the Great Hall. Through the doorway of an adjoining room, Wimborne caught sight of the solar, complete with a four-poster and garde-robe. Entering the Great

Hall, Connu's stature grew visibly. A heavy refectory table surrounded by chairs dominated the room. The walls were lined with Danish tapestries of coloured tessellations. All the windows had been opened wide, admitting the clement breeze that cooled the grand chamber continuously.

Dropping onto a baroque chair, edged in gold, with a matching foot-stool, Connu indicated seats to the two officers and four seamen. Two men took positions either side of him. Primed to address his host, the captain remained on his feet.

'Your Excellency, His Grace, the Duke of Chandois, Principal Share-holder of the Royal African Company, extends his felicitations to your great personage. He has been angered by reports received about the activities of Israel Rogers the pirate. He has lost many ships an' . . . '

An irascible Connu interrupted the captain's monologue.

'Eat first then we palava,' he muttered gruffly.

Judiciously, the captain relented. Another testing moment had passed. Wimborne sighed inaudibly. Lifting a silver-lined skull containing a light brown liquid, Connu tersely introduced the fare.

'Slabbersauce and rice,' he said. 'Taste good.'

During the peculiar repast, Wimborne received an account about the fortress from the interpreter. Formerly known as Fredericksburg, Connu's Castle was built for slave trading by the Danes around 1690. The Danish power had abandoned the fort when they found it uneconomical to maintain supplies. They transferred their interests to the Cape Coast.

John Connu was the fourth son of a poor fisherman from the village of Inkoranza on the Tano River. He was a servant, pilot and tracker for the slave-trading garrison, until he became a cabiceer. Under Danish instruction, he learned to clean and fire the cannon, flintlock musket and pistol. Following the decamping of the Danes, Connu took possession of the deserted castle. Outside its precincts, he built a trading post called Connu's Town.

There was a lull in the conversation at the table. His captain secured the attention of their host.

'Captain Connu,' he said, 'I could not help noticing the *brinnee* – white men – in the courtyard.'

Connu's countenance darkened. Wimborne's heart thumped.

'Them *panyarred* – kidnapped – off Englishman, Captain white man,' said Connu, brusquely. 'Mister Captain Rutley of the *Portobello Star* refuse to pay my man ounce of gold for Duty. I take my people down to jetty and seize twelve of his men with water casks. The Mate get in my way so I broke his head. Mister Captain Rutley not get his *brinnee* back 'til Duty is paid. By God I am king here. I want payment for water and the trouble in collecting it.'

Exceedingly alarmed, Wimborne felt a sudden desire to relieve himself. He hurriedly left the chamber. Hastening to the courtyard, he was anxious to speak with the hostages off the *Portobello Star*. He baulked at the spectacle that met his eyes. Saturated with sweat, the twelve seamen were now like ghosts on life's edge – certain their Captain's failure to disburse gold would result in enslavement or death. Contemptuous of his presence, the guards drifted together to glare at him over the heads of the hostages. A prisoner called out to him.

'For the love of sweet Jesus, Mister, I hail from Plymouth,' he cried. 'You cannot leave us in this godforsaken place.'

A guard brought down his musket butt on the head of the hostage. Silence in the courtyard between white men was clearly part of the punishment. In an effort to hearten the hostages, he threw them a weak smile and hastened back inside the Great Hall. The big man had just raised the silver-lined skull and thrust it at his captain.

'Drink punch, Captain white man!' Connu snapped.

His captain's face drained of colour. Wimborne held his breath.

'I said drink, Captain,' said Connu, testily. 'I put lime, water, brandy an' sugar.'

Closing his eyes and taking a swig of the liquor, his captain speedily passed it across. Following his mouthful, Wimborne smiled. A formula worthy of note, he thought.

Lifting the skull to eye-level, Connu erupted with laughter.

'His head Dutch, Captain,' he said. 'I get angry with him, so he lose his head. Now he stays with me for good.'

Connu leaned threateningly closer to his captain. Wimborne promptly downed another mouthful.

'Them men sit in yard 'til I get gold, Captain white man.'

'Your consent to proffer a few words, Captain Blunt?' asked Wimborne.

'Permission granted, Mister Wimborne.'

Rising to his feet, he turned to their fractious host.

'About Rogers, Captain Connu,' he said. 'His Grace, the Duke of Chandois, has been much angered by reports received about the activities of Israel Rogers. The Duke seeks Intelligence about this pirate who has struck much panic into our traders.'

Following a significant pause, Connu grinned.

'The Intelligence you want cost gold – then I search my head.'

Tossing a small pouch onto the table, his captain was terse.

'Half ounce for what you know,' he said.

'You understand business, Captain.'

No sooner had his hand closed on the pouch, then Connu became obliging.

'I heard from my canoes that Rogers is along the coast of Ouidah. He chased and took two Englishmen. He hanged some men and chopped others into pieces. The rest them dead – them kickatavoo.'

Captain Blunt recoiled.

'Has he indeed. We shall attend to the rogue presently and . . .'

Seven buxom women entered the Great Hall, curtailing the captain's irate response. Wimborne smiled to himself. For this salt-seasoned captain, he thought, the bodily proximity of compliant women speaks louder than the Company's commission.

'Ye Gods,' cried a sailor.

'I'll take two.'

'Me first laddie.'

'Can we take 'em with us?'

Rounding on his crew, the captain snapped.

'Avast there you scurvy jackanapes. Belay that prattle. Save it for the foc'sle.'

Except for gold necklaces, ivory bangles and a slender piece of cloth covering their groins, the women were virtually naked. Voluptuous breasts captivated them all. Wimborne felt himself hardening. But his want was curbed by the unsavoury thought of the two months of deprivation quivering inside the filthy breeches of each seaman. The fantasies of the gawping sailors were broken by Connu's voice.

'My white friends, I give you dashee o' bombo.'

Lecherous comments burst from the seamen.

'Mister Wimborne, despatch a message to Mr Pobjoy,' his captain ordered, 'that no escort will be required. Our business ashore has yet to be concluded. Graceforth is to remain by the jetty. Take the men and wait in the quadrangle. I am confident that while you pass the time, you will no doubt find a chamber in which you can amuse yourself, as can the men.'

His captain's inference was unequivocal – he and the crew were in line for bombo as well. Trying to appear as if he was leaving the gathering for more consequential dealings, the master mariner cut a farcical figure striding across the Great Hall behind the largest pair of breasts.

3 February 1750: 11.00 hrs

Peering at the sail on the horizon through his telescope, Wimborne released an audible sigh.

'"Tis an English man-o-war,' he said. 'Compliments to the captain, bo'sun. Inform him that the *Resolution* is hull up.'

Soon the warship was clearly visible. Elbowing his way through the deck crew, the captain halted beside him with his telescope.

'How'd she wind Mister Wimborne?'

Turning his scope on the distant man-o-war, he replied confidently.

'Nearly end on, sir.'

'Aye 'tis the *Resolution*,' the captain said, dropping his scope. 'If you please, Mister Wimborne, you will accompany me in the cutter to pay our respects to Captain Sykes.'

Pointing at a man who the previous night had had his left hand nailed to the mainmast for stealing food, Wimborne raised the subject of his liberation.

'Permission to release Cooper, sir?'

The pinned seaman was anxiously watching his blood trickling down the mast onto the deck into a congealing pool. To prevent the nail from slicing through his palm, he had twisted himself into a bizarre pose to keep his bodily weight off his hand. Mumbling incoherently, his face had turned a deathly grey. His bloated hand was almost unrecognisable. Without so much as a glance at the suffering man, the captain turned to examine the approaching warship. Wimborne persevered.

'He'll die if he stays hooked up much longer, sir,' he said.

'A no good rascal that one,' replied the captain. 'He's either drunk or stealing. Before he set his sights on that there cheese, he should have considered the penalty.'

'If he lives he may well lose the use of his hand,' Wimborne retorted. 'And if he dies we will be a man short, sir.

'If he dies? If he dies?' roared the captain. 'We'll pick up another no good murderous thug before the day is out. Plenty hereabouts. Nay, Mister Wimborne. Inform Pobjoy that I want the scoundrel to endure a while longer. Free him and clap him in irons when the *Resolution* has anchored. The blighter can serve as a warning to the other debauched rascals that if they pilfer, they can expect no mercy from me. And Mister Wimborne, if he loses the use of his hand, he will be more diligent with the other – or he will lose that one as well.'

To pursue the matter would be a waste of time, Wimborne thought.

'Aye aye, sir,' he replied, coldly.

'And lower the cutter, Mister Wimborne.'

Cupping his hands, he yelled:

'Raise a crew, bo'sun. Lower the cutter and stand by.'

Sailing into the bay and turning smartly into the wind, the *Resolution* dropped anchor. Perched in the cutter, Wimborne was compelled to listen to his captain's grubby account about a woman he had bedded on the Guinea coast. Before long, only the sound of oars clunking rhythmically against the rowlocks echoed in the anchorage. Suddenly ear-splitting howls rang out from the *Pelican*. Knowing they were from the seaman whose hand had been nailed to the mast, Wimborne closed his eyes and put a hand to his brow. As the cutter drew beneath the gilded stern of the warship, he rose gladly to his feet.

'Oars,' he commanded.

'I'll wager that Captain Sykes,' said his captain, 'has not heard about Rogers and his seizure of English merchantmen.'

'Then we shall happily acquaint him with the facts, sir. Though I very much suspect he already knows.'

Annoyed by his remark, his captain's face withered into a scowl. Dodging any riposte, Wimborne scrambled up the Jacob's ladder and set foot on the deck of the frigate. On the deck a row of smartly dressed seamen stood at attention. In keeping with the old salts of His Majesty's Navy, there was a good number of tarred pigtails in evidence. He gazed wondrously at the three towering masts, divided into three sections, rising inexorably into the sky. Why three? Deducing that the topmasts and topgallants could be struck and lowered to the deck in stormy weather, he marvelled at the innovation. His eyes drifted down to the honour guard of sailors and marines – the regulation salute for a visiting commander. His captain, for whom the ritual was being performed, stood conceitedly at ease basking in the tribute.

Attended by his officers, the portly Captain Douglas Sykes, with a monstrous pustule on his right cheek, strutted towards them along the *Resolution's* spotless decks. He was a stony-faced officer with twinkling dark eyes that were almost buried by bushy eyebrows. In full dress uniform, the colour of which had been chosen by King George himself, he wore an embroidered gold-lace waistcoat beneath a navy blue frock coat with elaborate white lace cuffs. A shoulder-length wig crowned his head, on top of which sat a three-cornered hat adorned with a purple silk cockade. He looked a plump nautical fop at play.

Wimborne was well aware of the naval commander's exploits. As First Lieutenant, Douglas Sykes had sailed around the world with Captain George Anson in 1740. Reputed to be not only a naval peacock, he was also a strict disciplinarian. During that historic voyage he acquired his reputation for brutality. Sentencing five seamen to one hundred lashes each for contriving to steal the ship's tender for the purpose of deserting to a nearby coral island, he then had them hanged from the main yard-arm. Throughout the prolonged tortuous procedure, it was said that Sykes stayed doggedly on deck. Notwithstanding reports about the severity of his regime, the Lords of the Admiralty had nonetheless seen fit to reward him for his loyalty to Captain Anson. Thus he was given command of the *Resolution*. The commander's cruelty at sea was matched sufficiently by his conduct ashore – he had allegedly killed his wife by flinging her against a wall during an argument.

Ending the inspection of the honour guard with his captain, the naval commander turned to him.

'It is undeniably pleasing to meet up with *you* again, Mister Wimborne.'

Delivering a convivial smile, Wimborne gave him a polite bow.

'The pleasure is mine, Captain Sykes,' he purred.

'My compliments to your Principals, Captain Blunt,' said the naval commander. 'I fear I have a disturbing report for you.'

'And what might that be?' his captain asked, almost nonchalantly.

Motioning along the deck, the naval commander turned sociable.

'We shall be more comfortable in my quarters, Ebenezer,' he replied. 'I have wine fresh from Madeira, rum from the Indies and a fair brandy. You too should be in on this, Mister Wimborne.'

'The honour is mine, Captain Sykes.'

'I trust you did not have too much trouble with Messrs Connu and company, Mister Wimborne?' the naval commander asked.

'Nay sir, but Captain Rutley of the *Portobello Star* has . . . '

'There is nothing we can do for him, Mister Wimborne,' said the naval commander, abruptly. 'These people have their own laws by which we must abide if we want to do business with them.'

Halting momentarily, the captains proceeded to scan the bay.

'John Connu is a reasonable man in his own black-hearted way,' the naval commander continued. 'Provided that he gets paid for his wood, water and whatever else, you will get no trouble from him. Some Masters think his brain is as black as his skin. After refusing to pay for his wood and water, they then try to enforce their thieving with musket power. Only to find that Connu has more men, more muskets plus a fortress crammed with cannons.'

Hearing the resigned sigh from his captain, Wimborne smiled to himself.

'Belay your sympathy, Ebenezer, Rutley will pay up,' said the naval commander. 'He always does. The old scoundrel has tried that dodge down the coast. He usually gets away with it. This time however he has met his match in Connu. That scallywag harbours a malevolent temper. He will kill Rutley's men if he does not get his gold. That is if he has not already chopped off their heads.'

Stroking his neck and then smoothing his uniform, Wimborne stepped over the threshold into the stately confines of the Great Cabin.

It was a large, well-ventilated, polished mahogany-panelled cabin. Through the ornate, open windows under the poop, Wimborne held an unobstructed view of the harbour with Connu's Castle perched atop the headland. While decanting fortified wine into three goblets, the naval commander was straight-faced.

'I say 'tis an opportune moment to turn that pirate Rogers' woman into a hempen widow.'

'Aye, Douglas, that it is,' his captain replied.

Clasping his goblet, Wimborne made himself comfortable beside a cherry wood table. The commanders opted for armchairs on opposite sides of a small card table.

'What disagreeable intelligence do you bear, Douglas?'

Dispensing a knowing smile, the naval commander replied.

'It seems that rascal Rogers has been causing mayhem down the coast.'

Given the expression of the naval commander, Wimborne was convinced that he was already aware of the pirate's activities. At the disappointment on his captain's face, he stifled his glee.

'No doubt you will be vigilant to the extreme, Ebenezer,' said the naval commander, 'when you sail with your cargo. 'Tis a bad business. Merchantmen have been losing their gold, ivory and slave cargoes, which Rogers sells off to the Portuguese. Worse still, each vessel seized by that infernal nuisance furnishes him with more cannon and muskets. He grows ever stronger. Why, the cut-throat has even sacked two English merchantmen near Cape Coast. My orders are to put an end to his antics.'

'Aye, Douglas, I know,' muttered his captain, glancing at his fob watch.

The naval commander thumped the card table. Wimborne jumped.

''Tis an insult,' roared the naval commander. 'The brazen rogue has been boasting that he doesn't give a fiddle for King George's Navy. That he intends to go wherever he pleases.'

'The bloodthirsty traitor!' his captain snarled. 'And the blackguard now has a greater price on his head.'

'He doesn't give tuppence for it,' said the naval commander.

'Is that so?'

'Aye.'

'Where is the vagabond now?' his captain asked, casually.

In the game of one-up-man-ship played between commanders, Wimborne knew that his captain was struggling to justify, to himself, the half-ounce of gold he had paid to Connu for intelligence on the whereabouts of the pirate. It had also become exceedingly clear to him that the naval commander had acquired matching information without any disbursement.

'He's holed up in a secluded bay west of Cape Coast below Phipps' Tower,' said the naval commander. ''Tis a mere three-quarter mile on land from here. Forty leagues by sea. 'Tis a trifle. If the *Resolution* sails tomorrow afternoon on the ebb, God willing, we shall be there by first light on Thursday. Ebenezer, we'll surprise him in the cove and stuff his tail 'tween his legs. That'll teach the rogue to have more respect for His Majesty's Navy.'

'Aye, Douglas,' said his captain, half-heartedly.

For the time being, Wimborne remained in attendance at the whim of his captain. Invigorated by an excess of Madeira and brandy, the commanders chortled their way through the afternoon. The crews of their respective vessels awaited their orders. At the change of watch, Wimborne was finishing his second goblet when the somewhat inebriated naval commander merrily thumped the wing of his chair.

'What with Connu's uncouth victuals, Ebenezer,' he said, 'I'll wager you hanker for the delectation of salt beef and boiled potato.'

'Aye, Douglas, 'tis some time since I tasted the like. A storm swept my beef overboard in the Bay of Biscay.'

'In this god-forsaken wilderness,' said the naval commander, 'the food of the nigger leaves much to be desired. It gives me flatulence and worsens my gout.'

''Tis difficult to outdo good English fare,' he said.

'Will you take supper with us, Ebenezer?'

'Gladly, Douglas.'

'And Mister Wimborne?'

Following a conspicuous hesitation, his captain consented.

'Aye, he'd best stay,' he said.

At eight bells, supper was served in the Great Cabin. Wimborne settled himself at the table in a shadowy corner of the cabin. Captain Sykes sat beside his captain, whose customary boorish behaviour was decidedly contradicted by his present agreeable conduct. The pair sank into muted conversation. Sitting on the other side of his captain and looking thoroughly out of sorts due to an excess of liquor was Parson Samuel Merriweather. Beside the cleric was Francis Rutley, Master of the barque *Portobello Star*, accompanied by two landowners who had taken passage with him for the purpose of buying slaves. Squire Christian Brigstocke was a pale, drawn and dissolute aristocrat in his early forties, but whose conversation nevertheless betrayed a shrewd intelligence. In his late forties and dressed to an inch of his life was Squire Benjamin Ogden, a dark-hued Jew. He was refined and gangling, with a gentle composure and a tendency for fondling his gold-lacquered cane. After surveying his companions, Wimborne frowned slightly. This motley clique, he thought, look exceedingly like pirates themselves.

Clattering plates arrested his reflections. The cook and his assistants served up cold roast beef and potato for supper. The sight of English fare, last seen before the Bay of Biscay, fired Wimborne's appetite. But his hunger for the roast ritual was curbed by his curiosity in the intrigues of the two commanders. Thus he spent the repast picking at his plate and keeping a close watch on the conspirators. Affectedly forking a hunk of beef, Brigstocke's voice held more than a trace of ridicule.

'I ask you, sirs,' he posed, 'is not our civilisation decidedly more progressive than that of the nigger?'

Daintily dabbing his lips with his napkin, Squire Benjamin Ogden responded.

'John Connu may be a barbarian but he owns too much power,' he said. 'The scoundrel is too free, has a monopoly on prices and dominates the trade on this part of the coast.'

'Aye, that he does,' agreed Brigstocke.

Wimborne recalled how his captain had been permitted to speak only with Connu's consent. He knew it could be fairly said that the big man, who had obliged his captain to drink a somewhat unholy concoction, had intrigued him. His captain had not enjoyed the humiliation at the hands of John Connu in the presence of an inferior officer. Akin to profit, he thought, resentment can be a profound motivator. Accordingly at this moment in the Great Cabin, the looks exchanged between the two commanders warned him to be vigilant. Were they about to unveil their strategy? Would he be able to stomach the consequence of their scheming?

'Fiddlesticks,' said the naval commander, unequivocally. 'You don't have to barter with the likes of Connu. Why on the Grain Coast, the Merchants around Cape Mesurado have been taking what they want for years. I see no reason why the practice should not be extended to these parts. But be careful gentlemen. Do not forget that there are many Masters sailing under the English flag who will have no truck with your kind. It very much depends on how you proceed.'

Picking up his long goose-bone pipe, Brigstocke cleared his throat and addressed the table.

'Gentlemen, Ogden and I have estates in Kelvington in the county of Yorkshire,' he said. 'We are also in sugar with plantations on the West Indian island of Pertigua. And we represent an English syndicate who wish to crop out those middlemen-cabiceers on this part of the coast.'

At last they have dished out the fundamentals, thought Wimborne.

'Not ahead of time,' said the Master of the *Portobello* Star, his cheeks bloated with beef.

'Of late,' continued Brigstocke, 'the amalgamation of pirates and slave prices hiked up by the cabiceers have all had a detrimental effect on our profits. Because of the escalating tariffs, some of England's largest estates stand at the very gates of bankruptcy. For a case in point, Randolph Fleming is the richest man in all Pertigua, yet even his Augustfields estate outside the city of York teeters on the edge of impoverishment, because his tropical estate on Pertigua suffers from a shortage of slaves. You can therefore deduce, gentlemen, that the prosperity of his estate in York-shire depends on the profits from his West Indian estate. The Cinder-field Estate is another instance. With fifty thousand acres in and around the Forest of Dean, and because of the current crisis regarding sugar, the Estate has laid off eighty of its two hundred workers. Were that condition allowed to continue unabated, the unemployed toll would spread like a plague across all England – which would doubtless signal a corresponding upsurge in vagrancy, idleness and thievery. Gentlemen, there is no estate worthy of being called such, in England or the West Indies, which does not depend on slaves in one way or another.'

At those words Wimborne comprehended the strategy. His captain and the naval commander were the vanguard of a scheme to radically increase profits. By utilising a pioneering policy, they were set on doubling the number of slaves on every ship already engaged in the trade. Never mind the crush that would ensue from packing their human cargo even tighter together and the increase in fatalities that would result. He raised his eyes. Through the open windows of the poop, the bickering between the gulls over slops thrown from the deck turned to conflict. A stentorian fart from his captain echoed around the cabin.

'There's dung not far behind that, sir,' said the naval commander.

Laughter rang around the cabin. Irritated by the anal humour, Wim-borne set his face and pressed his lips together. His nose twitching from the fetid donation, Squire Ogden curtailed the jollity by raising his voice.

'I concur with Brigstocke's analysis and predictions,' he said. 'Pray, continue Christian.'

Brigstocke paused. Wimborne narrowed his eyes with curiosity. Packing his pipe with hemp, Brigstocke put it between his lips, and then pulled out a small card coated with phosphorus and a wood splinter dipped in sulphur. Drawing the splinter across the paper, it flickered into flame, which he put to the bowl of his pipe. Sucking in deeply and letting out a long stream of smoke, the aristocrat's face turned scarlet, after which he began to speak.

'Gentlemen, I have to tell you that Interlopers who will have no truck with the cabiceers have crept in to contend for a share of the market. Their pernicious activities undermine the privileges of our Letters Patent. The Interlopers apprehend the niggers themselves, avoiding the tariff of the cabiceers and thus obtaining a greater profit at auction. It has become imperative that we must act likewise or else we risk our livelihoods. If we take no action now, there will be corresponding privation for much of England's gentry, their estates and farm workers.'

Following Brigstocke's revelation, a hush descended on Wimborne's ears. The frigate groaned as she turned with the outgoing tide. Vying with the bellow from the change of watch above his head were the mournful cries of gulls. Dispensing a tot of brandy into a goblet, the naval commander broke the silence.

'As you all know, gentlemen, the *Resolution* is here officially on a Commission for the Suppression of Pirates on the coast of Guinea. I am also under orders to render you any assistance I can while I lay off this coast.'

'Your support will be invaluable, Captain Sykes,' said Brigstocke.

'I am in agreement with Brigstocke,' said his captain.

Raising his eyebrows, Wimborne cast his eyes derisively over the figure of Captain Blunt, who now addressed the table.

'My Principal, His Grace the Duke of Chandois, has lost much revenue because of these Interlopers,' he said. 'Between 1741 and 1749 Barbados wanted annually nine thousand niggers, Pertigua ten thousand, Jamaica seventeen thousand and the Leeward Islands collectively bought ten thousand from the Royal African Company. In each of those eight years we imported about eighteen thousand, leaving a shortfall of twenty-eight thousand which were trafficked by interlopers.'

'The filching blackguards are bleeding the Exchequer dry,' said the naval commander, 'which perhaps accounts indirectly for the paltriness of my pay.'

'Aye.' the Parson mumbled.

Wimborne was particularly attentive when Brigstocke rose to continue.

'Gentlemen, expensive slaves mean exorbitant prices for sugar. This successively affects everything that necessitates sugar, thus converting the profit margins to our detriment. Because there is much at stake, I say we are obliged to take decisive action by badgering the cabiceers to cut them out. Not to put too fine a point on it, gentlemen, we are therefore obligated to plunder slaves from the hinterland ourselves.'

'An imaginative and courageous stratagem, sir,' said the naval commander. 'It would be commendable to shave the privateer's cupidity and carry off a share for England. But pray tell me, sir, why abduct niggers from the backwoods? Why, with a company of seasoned marines we can snatch whom we please from around these parts.'

Swaying from the influence of hemp, Brigstocke was scornful.

'And confront the hotspur of the cabiceers on his home territory?' he asked. 'Take John Connu?'

Sitting bolt upright, Wimborne provided a courteous warning.

'That would be an injudicious exploit, sir,' he said. 'He has a sizeable army, equipped with flintlocks and cannon. With those arms, most probably weapons of English construction, Connu's men might well give a good account of themselves.'

Throwing a disdainful look at him, his captain voiced his opinion.

'I think our Mister Wimborne might even have a point.'

'In my judgment,' said the Parson, 'Mister Wimborne does indeed have a point.'

Steadying himself on the lip of the table, Brigstocke addressed the naval commander.

'In order to subdue these barbarous Kingdoms we need the Redcoats, Captain Sykes,' he said. 'At present it is not the policy of King George's government to secure territory on the coast of Guinea. No need, when there is profit aplenty in the people themselves. Without a substantial company of Redcoats, the only way to take John Connu is to deplete his gold reserves. Make no transactions with him for slaves or anything else, bar water. Gradually he will become superfluous. No need for this practice to apply to French or Dutch vessels. England's merchantmen have nigh on a monopoly of the trade along these coasts. Nay, Captain Sykes. By initiating an action in the unsuspecting backwoods, we avoid unnecessary bloodshed. When slave caravans escorting niggers from inland tribes pass through villages on the coast, they will pay us no heed. That germane truth, gentlemen, is to our great advantage. Unless their Kings have formed a pact, niggers from one tribe will never fight for niggers from another.'

Our peoples are more alike than unlike, thought Wimborne. How similar are England's quarrels with the Welsh, Irish and Scottish separatists.

Striking the gimballed dining table with his fist and upending a silver candelabrum, the Master of the *Portobello Star*, who had lately suffered a panyarring, was adamant.

'We must act now,' he urged. 'John Hawkins would have singed his beard. We should do likewise. Gentlemen, I propose we establish an association, nay, a joint-stock company, with the sole intention of breaking the garrotte of the cabiceers and their agents.'

Wimborne did not miss the deliberate look exchanged between the naval commander and his captain. And he knew why the pair looked so smug. The joint-stock company proposal by the Master of the *Portobello Star* had to all intents and purposes laid the cornerstone of their strategy. They were set to shatter the established way of doing business along the Slave Coast. Though it was against his better nature, he was intrigued to be sitting in such close proximity to the men responsible for the change of direction of an entire trade by surreptitiously tugging at strings that twisted lives out of shape.

'The members of the joint-stock company will not barter with the cabiceers,' said the Master of the *Portobello Star*. 'They will instead carry Letters Patent allowing the bearer to seize niggers without let or hindrance. This coast is lawless, but by force we will make the Law and promulgate a fresh way of conducting business. Slowly but surely the niggers will come to respect and abide by our Law. I have no doubt we shall prevail. At present, we have here a force large enough to prosecute our mission and deter any detractors. I suggest we employ that force. Gentlemen, in the spirit of John Hawkins, I further propose the formation of the Honourable Company of Guinea Venturers.'

Clinking glasses and pledges criss-crossed the table. Following the pronouncement, Wimborne observed the satisfaction on the visages of the two commanders. A streamlet of Madeira dribbled down his captain's chin and dripped onto his uniform.

'A capital contrivance,' his captain roared. 'Hold hard and fast, I say. Hold hard and fast.'

Closing his eyes briefly, Wimborne could still picture the last shipment of slaves, pleading and crying with hurt, who without cause had incurred his captain's wrath. With a greater number of slaves on board, the *Pelican's* regime would turn considerably bloodier. Consequently he could not share in the high spirits that enveloped the Great Cabin.

'Let us commit ourselves to a Christian campaign, gentlemen,' said the Parson, 'by bringing the light of the Lord to shine down on these heathens.'

Now I understand the rationale for your presence here, thought Wimborne. Under the banner of the Church, you furnish them with the moral justification for any action they choose.

The naval commander rose to bring the proceedings to a close.

'I am with the Parson,' he said. 'Now is as fortuitous a time as any to christen our little enterprise. On the morrow the *Resolution* sails to seek out Israel Rogers. I shall again meet with you gentleman at Cape Coast and then I shall sail on to Ouidah.'

It was past midnight when the supper-conference ended in a clamour of intoxicated accord and confident expectations. Rising to depart from the precincts of the Great Cabin, Wimborne wondered what the price might ultimately be and who would pay it.

Wimborne had found the first voyage with his captain testing enough. That was when he first laid eyes upon a slave. He was filled with grief at the thought of that petrified creature, squatting in the scuppers of the *Pelican*. At the time, his own ambitions facilitated a blind eye sufficient to draw a veil over the collaborating cruelties of slavery – until the day he arrived on the wild shores of Badagri, when right before his eyes a slave was beheaded for attempting to escape. Under a bright tropical sun, he had been splattered with blood and drenched with conscience. The thought of an innocent being imprisoned for no offence was sufficiently horrible. Slavery was infinitely worse. Having had his eyes finally prised open, he now saw the Slave Trade as the definitive sin. As an outcome of the formation of the Honourable Company of Guinea Venturers, he knew his previous torments would pale into insignificance. On this his second voyage with the *Pelican*, he made a pledge to himself.

'At the end of this voyage,' he said to himself, 'I vow never again to set foot on a slaver.'

At thirty-four years of age, the blue-eyed, fresh-faced Wimborne was a moderate, carrying a small scar on his chin stemming from a sword duel. He had acquired the wound in the halcyon days of his youth – when defending a harried farm worker, he had trounced the bullying son of the Lord-lieutenant of the County of Surrey. The exploit earned him the uncertain epithet of libertarian. Though he considered himself principled and cultured, in all honesty he believed he was simply the heir of intemperance and luck.

Born Thomas Fitzgerald Wimborne, the scion of a rich land-owning Surrey family, he received a stuffy classical education at Christchurch School. Notwithstanding his father's wish for him to pursue a career in law, he opted for a yearlong course at Smith's Nautical Academy in Brightlingsea, Essex. Passing out of the Academy, he secured an apprenticeship with the Anglo India Company on barques transporting cargoes of silk, sisal, gold and spices.

Fourteen years later, he signed on as Second Mate in the employ of the East India Company, a prosperous well-established institution. Because they were reputed to receive an excellent regular stipend with large bonuses, its officers were known for prolonged service. Hence promotion in the service of the Company was gallingly slow. He felt destined to remain a Second Mate, certain that he would be 'fodder for the maggots' long before he was appointed captain. Casting his eyes around for better prospects, he sought opportunity in the burgeoning trade in slaves through a sailing notice of the Royal African Company – a gilt-edged company of England's mercantile marine. Its two hundred and forty-nine ships were engaged entirely in exporting slaves from the coast of Guinea. He knew the trade was a proven route for speedy promotion and for amassing a substantial sum. His fortunes improved significantly after the Mate of the Royal African Company vessel, the *Pelican*, was washed overboard in a following sea in the Bay of Biscay. Despite the reservations of his parents regarding a seafaring life and his participation in an obnoxious trade, he signed on the *Pelican* as First Officer.

From the beginning his relationship with Ebenezer Blunt was thorny. At their first encounter on the poop deck, the master mariner strutted around him like a popinjay before getting underway with a taunt.

'So you think you are up to serving as my Mate?'

'At your service, Captain Blunt, sir.'

The captain halted.

'It was undoubtedly too big, Mister Wimborne.'

He frowned.

'What was, sir?'

'The silver spoon you sucked from birth, sir.'

'I do not believe, sir, that the quality of a spoon will prevent me from the diligent execution of my duties.'

'Enlighten me, Mister Wimborne. Why would a dandy from fancy circumstances like you think he'd be fit to be a ship's officer?'

'Because, sir, he had passed the rigorous examinations in navigation and seamanship with a pass mark of ninety-four per cent.'

'Is that so?'

'That is so, Captain Blunt.'

'Well, Mister Wimborne, don't let your ninety-four per cent deceive you into thinking you know it all.'

'I am confident I do not know it all, sir. I was short by six per cent.'

'I've encountered your kind before, Mister Wimborne. You hail from a breed who have not the backbone for the grind of long watches and who skulk into lofty positions through connections. The Examiners, who in all probability attended school with your father, liked your swanky ways and marked your papers up because of it. I daresay they expect the likes of your kind to make captain ahead of the likes of mine. Let me tell you, Mister Wimborne, I came not with your good fortune. Unfortunately for you, it is the likes of me who is deemed fit to be master of this here vessel. Perform your duties with alacrity and diligence, maintain a tight ship and keep your nose clean. I am not persuaded by your kind, Mister Wimborne. Don't you go forgetting that.'

'I shall keep your philosophy very much in mind, Captain Blunt,' he replied, straight-faced. 'I can see that you are an officer who has reflected most deeply on the iniquitous apparatus of the social order.'

The travesty in the Great Cabin left Wimborne feeling ill at ease. Under a bright moon on that hot airless night, he followed his orders to accompany the Parson to the *Pelican*. While the cutter was making way between the ships, he took stock of his grey-haired companion. A man of the cloth could surely not support doubling the number of slaves? On the slave decks alone, the crush would be unmanageable. How could a member of the clergy sanction it?

'I am somewhat perturbed, Parson,' he said quietly.

'Why, what ails thee, Mister Wimborne?'

'Are we right to do this?'

'If by that you mean, are we right to spread the word of God? I say we are right, Mister Wimborne.'

Frowning deeply, he shook his head.

'Nay Parson, that is not what is in my thoughts,' he said. 'Are we right to be trafficking human beings?'

'To transport these poor unfortunate heathens into God's light?' asked the Parson. 'Of course we should. And we have a God-given duty to do so.'

'We sell them for profit?'

'Like all and sundry they must pay their way,' the Parson replied, without hesitation, 'while we bring them closer to God.'

Fixing his eyes intently on the dark horizon, Wimborne wiped the sweat from his neck. Clearing his throat, he expressed his heart-felt unease.

'I cannot help but think, Parson,' he said, 'that in the somewhat cold light of history, the consequence of our endeavours on this coast might in one way or another come to rest on the heads of future generations.'

Stalled by Wimborne's comment, the Parson hesitated. Then, he was unswerving in his response.

'I doubt that,' he said. 'I must do God's work wherever I am sent.'

Cape Coast Castle

Principal fort and factory of the Royal African Company

10 February 1750

Mopping his face and neck, Wimborne gazed into the hot humid rain-forest from the crenallations of Cape Coast Castle. Screeching monkeys and the roar of elephants resounded through the mosquito-infested stretch of the Gold Coast. His eye was caught by a coast eagle wheeling in a virtuoso sweep over the forest canopy.

Summoned by his captain to breakfast with the Director General, he left the battlements and made his way to the stately dining room. Around the table were Captain Sykes, the commander of the *Resolution*, Francis Rutley, the Master of the *Portobello* Star, and Squires Brigstocke and Ogden. With his captain and the Director General, they were engrossed in a gory debate on the fate of the captured pirates. Taking the chair beside his captain, he took a closer look of the Director General who was lodged at the head of the table.

A slight sensitive character in his fifties, General Henry Tugwell owned watery-blue eyes, a shock of russet-red hair and a complexion so fair he scorched easily in the sun. Compatible with his position of Principal Factor of the Company's primary outpost, the man was salaried at three thousand pounds per annum – with the power of life or death over his subjects. Wimborne was intrigued by what he had learned about the powers invested in the Director General. On his authority, ships of the Company came to receive orders for further trade down the coast; factors were sent to the company's outlying forts and supercargoes were dispatched to board vessels, to collect the slaves and make up the accounts.

The day-to-day business of the Factory was conducted by the Director General's Council for Managing Affairs. This seemingly august body comprised thieves, murderers, convicted pirates and men press-ganged from the taverns of England. Roving the streets of England, these mostly

illiterate jobless men had lived from hand to mouth, whereas on the Cape
Coast, their white skin bought them a regular stipend and unaccustomed
status. They were otherwise known as 'white negroes', all of whom were
wholly enslaved to the rule of the Director General and the Company. At
salaries of between eighty and five hundred pounds per annum, they were
appointed as merchants, factors, artificers, writers and soldiers.

The *Pelican's* sailing master had informed Wimborne that these men
were disciplined by the severest regulations. Any contravention of the
Company's rules was punishable with several weeks or even months in
the dungeon. There, they suffered numerous drubbings and their salaries
reduced to a level sufficient only to buy canky bread – produced from
corn and water – palm wine, baked yam, palm oil and a little fish to keep
them from starving.

Such was the Director General's religious zeal, that for not attending
church on Sundays, they would receive twenty lashes of the rhino whip
or the wooden horse: a contraption whereby the victim, with hands tied
behind his back, was forced to sit astride the edges of two planks nailed
together which were in turn fixed to four tall legs. There the victim
would perch six feet above the ground, with twenty-five pound weights
tied to each foot for an indeterminate length of time dependent upon
the Director General's whim. Wimborne judged that the treatment of
these 'white negroes' almost matched in cruelty that received by the
slaves. Conspicuously, they were paid in Crackra, an artificial currency
that could only be spent at Cape Coast, thus preventing them from
purchasing items of food or buying their passage home to England
from passing traders.

Half-heartedly picking at his plate of dried beef and pork, cheese, canky
bread and salt butter, Wimborne noticed that the plates, silver knives
and cotton napkins bore the monogram of the South Sea Bubble
Company. Sitting back in due course with a goblet of palm wine, he
surveyed the table.

''Tis handsome indeed,' said his captain, 'to have done with the pirate
Israel Rogers.'

''Tis more of a pity that we lost his vessels,' said the commander.

'I'll purchase some of Rogers' men myself,' said the Director General.
'We shall try the rest. Since they are all demonstrably guilty, my men will
assemble a scaffold. We'll hang them after noon. That will put an end to

the matter. With Rogers gone, Howel Davis will be the only pirate of any consequence in these waters.'

'When he learns about the fate of Rogers,' said the commander, 'I wager he'll scuttle back to Brazil or the Indies.'

'I did hear that he is at present on the Grain Coast at Cape Mesurado,' said his captain.

'I reckon that is just idle talk,' replied the commander.

'Surely Davis will lay low around these parts?' said the master of the *Portobello* Star.

'Nay, Francis,' replied the commander. 'Davis will quit this coast the instant he learns that an English warship has arrived. I am certain he will lie in the darkest shadows of another coast, at least until the hue and cry has died down. You can be sure he will return when he feels it is safe to do so.'

'Thank God my duty in this infernal climate is nearly at an end,' groaned the Director General.

'How long have you endured here on this coast, General?' asked Squire Brigstocke.

'Twelve long years, sir,' the Director General replied. 'My constitution is not what it used to be. May God speed the arrival of my replacement on the *Dolphin*. I'm impatient to walk over the South Downs to taste again the ales of Sussex.'

'From where in Sussex do you come?' asked Squire Brigstocke.

'Little Dean, sir, about two miles east of the town of Brighton. I have two daughters there in the care of my dear sister. Their mother, bless her, died of consumption the first year I came out here. Happily I have Florence my buxom Confa to soothe me at night. Without her, my term here would have been insufferable with immutable melancholia.'

On the word 'buxom' Wimborne saw the commander's eyes sparkle.

'I commend your spunk and perseverance, sir,' said the commander, 'for having put up with the infinite discomfort and dangers of this God-forsaken province. But pray tell, sir, what is a Confa?'

The Director General chuckled with a gleam in his eye.

'A Confa is the woman of a white man,' he replied. 'She has rights and cannot be compelled to leave the country.'

'What if she were somehow compelled?' asked the commander.

'Then, sir, she would be a slave,' replied the Director General. 'You see as a Confa, she has rights to go where she pleases.'

'Continue, sir,' urged the commander.

'My Confa is mulatto,' said the Director General, 'progeny of a Dutchman and a nigger woman. I have been pleased to have had three children by her.'

'Begad, sir,' gasped his captain. 'How does your consequence appear?'

Wimborne smirked at his captain's reaction. Clearly unruffled by the question, the Director General answered calmly.

'As any other children, sir,' he said, 'though somewhat light-brown in colour.'

An awkward disturbing silence settled on the breakfast table.

'Do these children,' asked the master of the *Portobello* Star, 'acknowledge *you* as their father?'

Thumping the table with his fist, the Director General guffawed.

'Of course sir, what else?' he asked. 'I have recognised them and have been proud to care for them all their lives, sir. They have never wanted for the love of their father.'

Furtive grins and gasps of consternation greeted the Director General's avowal. And the impromptu conspiracy of silence that descended was heightened by indecipherable cries from the market, hot peppery aromas from the stalls and an altercation between animals in the rainforest. The air in the chamber had grown clammy. In echoing succession, eating knives clattered onto plates. As casually as he could manage, Wimborne scanned the expressions around the table. For these men, he thought, the notion of offspring from such a morganatic union is disturbingly grotesque. It was one thing for a white man to sow his seed inside the hot mindless body of a mulatto woman. But to recognise such children as his own was conduct unbecoming in decent English society. The Director General's avowed devotion to his tanned brood was bound to arouse prejudice in everyone present.

'That is all very well while you are here, sir,' said Brigstocke. 'But what do you intend to do with them once you return home to Sussex?'

'Why, they shall come with me of course. At home, they shall enjoy the benefits of English society and an English education.'

'And what of your mulatto woman?' asked the commander. 'You will leave her here, no doubt?'

A slight but evident pause followed. The Director General was adamant.

'I shall not,' he said.

'Will she not feel out of place in England?'

'You have two daughters, how will they feel?'

'Will it not be too cold for the mulattos?'

'Indeed! And what of your poor sister?'

'The local populace will be frightened of the mulattos, sir. Have you not considered that?'

Calmly raising his hand, the Director General said:

'I am confident that the good people of Little Dean shall take all my family to their hearts.'

Giving a sharp cough, Squire Ogden inquired:

'Are you certain of that, General?'

Wimborne suspected the General's expression reflected one who was far from convinced of the reception his family would receive on his return to England. Unhurriedly, the Director General rose to his feet. Taking his leave of the table plainly signalled a termination to the somewhat discomforting inquisition. The Director General himself managed the change of topic.

'Gentlemen, you shall meet them all at supper tonight,' he said. 'Right now, I should like to take you on a tour of the Company's holdings.'

Wimborne followed the Director General's party down to the quadrangle. Set flush with the ground were two large iron grates affording the sole source of light and ventilation for the slaves below.

'Gentlemen,' said the Director General, jerking his thumb upwards, 'come and inspect your cargo.'

Two guards pulled the ring attached to the grate, which groaned slowly open. Wimborne was instantly assaulted by the fetid odour of fear and filth filling every nook of the dank dungeon. Clouds of flies engulfed him, before settling to continue feasting on the sores and wounds of the slaves. Fanning flies away from his face and stepping warily onto the slippery stone steps, he descended into the gloom. When his eyes grew accustomed to the dark, he found himself dropping into a cavernous chamber. Little by little he made out the contours of human beings cramming the space. At the bottom the stink was such he felt faint.

'Bit dark ain't it?' asked Squire Ogden.

'We keep them in the dark to thwart escape,' said the Director General. 'At great cost we have learned that given the least opportunity they will bolt off.'

Shadowed by Squire Ogden, who was smothering his nose with his kerchief, Squire Brigstocke edged towards the steps.

'The stench down here is unspeakable, General,' he choked. 'We shall await you in the courtyard.'

'Turns your gentrified bellies, eh?' scoffed the master of the *Portobello Star*.

Ignoring his remark, the two men scuttled up the steps.

Wimborne scanned the dungeon. A network of rivulets trickled down the slimy rock walls. A meagre shaft of daylight from the far end of the dungeon barely penetrated the shadowy darkness. At the cost to the Company of a penny a day, slaves were chained to the walls and thus compelled to sit upright, while the rest lay head to head, chained in rows down the centre. Disturbed by the sight of a few white men chained up with the slaves, an instinct made him turn around. He could scarcely believe his eyes. The oppressive atmosphere was clearly having an adverse effect on the commander. Appearing to be fighting for breath, the executive officer stretched out his hand to steady himself, slumped against the wall and closed his eyes. 'Tis ironic, Wimborne thought, that in the dungeons of Cape Coast Castle where barbarity is axiomatic, the combative commander of the *Resolution* is about to swoon. Rushing to the aid of the flagging commander, his captain addressed his words to the Director General.

'If you please, General Tugwell,' his captain asked, 'will you be so good as to parade them in the courtyard?'

'As you wish, Captain,' replied the Director General.

Wimborne followed the four men up the steps. Out in the open air, temporarily blinded by the sun, he inhaled deep draughts. Whereas, the puce-faced commander of the *Resolution* leaned against a buttress gasping for air.

Overseers encircled the entrance of the dungeon. A row of musketed guards with fixed bayonets stood some yards behind them. Wimborne stayed by the opposite wall.

'Get them up and out!' the Director General barked.

At his command the overseers backed warily away from the entrance. Moments later, wincing in the intense sunlight, a man and a woman hobbled out onto the courtyard. To speed them up, an overseer sent his whip across the backs of the pair. Discharging a chilling screech, the woman hurled herself at a guard, whose bayonet punctured her abdomen stopping her forthwith. Shaken by her scream and closing his eyes momentarily, Wimborne swayed. With blood spraying out of a deep wound, she thrashed about until a cutlass was thrust several times through her heart. Wheezing and grunting with complaint, a podgy blacksmith set about separating her from her ankle-rings and the slave to which she was chained. Prising open the final link, he kicked the corpse aside. Squire Ogden shuddered and gasped.

'The woman deliberately ran into his blade.' he exclaimed.

'The niggers are at war with us, Squire Ogden,' said his captain. 'In the course of that war if they can't take your life – they take their own.'

Eventually the quadrangle echoed with the clatter of two hundred and sixty-two shackled slaves. Horrified by such an act of public suicide, Wimborne stayed behind the Director General. His other guests commenced their inspection of approved slaves. These were slaves who had had their right arm branded with the initials DC – the identifying symbol of the Duke of Chandois. His captain began to examine the teeth of slaves who looked wasted from the unwholesome diet of canky bread and water. Seizing a slave every now and then, he took the head in his huge hands to ascertain the expression in the eyes. Wrenching open the jaws and pulling back the lips, he took a good look at the gums. The technique used was one his captain said he used when inspecting the teeth of horses he was buying for his rigs. Throughout the entire procedure, Wimborne felt ill at ease. Following his sickening probe of half a dozen slaves, his captain sighed and shook his head.

'Blighters ain't broke yet,' he said.

'Nay, Ebenezer,' said the Director General. 'They require a good few more weeks before they are properly conditioned.'

'While we wait,' said his captain, 'we shall mount a raid into the backwoods to abduct our own slaves as agreed.'

The Director General grinned and began to stroll.

'Timely, sir, timely,' he said, 'we could do with a couple of hundred more.'

Having sufficiently recovered his poise, the commander of the *Resolution* posed a question Wimborne himself had been pondering on.

'When is a slave sufficiently conditioned, Ebenezer?' he asked.

'When a nigger no longer holds your eye with contempt,' his captain replied, 'and he bows his head when addressing a white man. Takes a bit of beating and starving to achieve results.'

Prompted by the captain's graphic answer, the Director General addressed the commander of the *Resolution*.

'The Royal African Company owns two hundred and forty-nine ships, Captain Sykes,' he said. 'We are renowned throughout the Indies for the condition of our slaves. We lose a handful at sea from illness, since the diseased ones are discarded back here in the factory. Individuals who are crippled are not worth a rush and we fling them overboard. There are those who fret incessantly, slip into melancholia and jump overboard. We lose them if the suicide-nets have not been spread securely along the ship's sides. Reminds me of a nigger who sighted a white shark, waited for the right moment and rushed headlong over the side. Somehow the blighter made it between the nets. He even managed an insolent wave at the ship's crew as the shark swam off with him. Just goes to show the extent of their determination.'

Arriving at a row of women, the Director General halted.

''Pon my soul,' he chuckled, 'methinks my hospitality has been some-what remiss. You have yet to sample the coastal delights. 'Tis an apposite moment to savour the fruits of the coast. Gentlemen, she can be admitted to your chambers which I have prepared for you here in the castle.'

A torrent of lewd comments burst from the squires. Stepping forwards and taking firm hold of the arm of a shapely young woman, his captain was candid.

''Tis fortunate the Parson ain't here,' he said. 'He'd want to bring the Lord's light to shine on God's children. That light won't penetrate where I'm taking this one, but my instrument will.'

Laughter rocked the lascivious gentlemen, who each in turn eagerly singled out a mate. Wimborne declined the offer. The Director General turned to an attending member of his Managing Council.

'Send word to the vessels of these gentlemen,' he said, 'they will be indisposed until at least nightfall.'

Wimborne shook his head.

In the late afternoon of the next day, Wimborne stepped outside the castle walls in the company of the Director General's party for an inspection of the town built by the Royal African Company. Entering Cape Coast Town through a gate set in the wall of a wooden stockade, he stepped into a lively market place. Hammering reverberated from the blacksmith's forge, where artisans were fashioning knives, spears and swords. Inside the dark interior, his eyes gradually adjusted to the faint light of pillar-fixed lanterns casting a sallow glow into a corner of the shop. Here, as sweat streamed down their bodies, three men in their early fifties with faces wrinkled by a life of hard labour, assembled thumbscrews, iron collars, leg chains and a variety of iron bonds.

Flickering shadows across the walls drew his attention to the forge proper. From piles of copper and tin, he watched wraithlike apprentices feeding fragments of the metals into a bronze-soup furnace set in the ground. Assisted by a score of underlings, Old Cracker, the cantankerous master craftsman, bellowed instructions while painstakingly pouring a bronze head. Lining the walls were finished bronze sculptures, plaques and sacred figures, apparently ordered by religious societies. Old Cracker, who was celebrated for his artistry all along the coast, had been fully trained and qualified by a bronze master in the town of Benin. Wimborne gained the distinct impression that Old Cracker's workshop was a grand seat of coastal tradition.

Managed entirely by women, who gave the newcomers a perfunctory look, the market throbbed with activity. As the visitors approached, naked children disappeared behind their mothers. Wimborne felt starkly white, for his skin contrasted dramatically with the black skins crowding around the stalls and hurrying around the marketplace. He was un-impressed by the sight of his captain brazenly lusting after the near-naked women roaming the market, particularly two pert-breasted willowy young girls who had caught his eye. Naked from the waist up, the adolescent girls were selling goats. Women sauntered by bearing huge loads in wicker-skeps on their heads. He thought it remarkable that it was the women who cultivated the land, pressed the palm oil and spun the cotton, after which they made the long trek to market with goods. Nursing mothers were suckling their infants, cooking food, threading necklaces and making ornaments, while glowing matriarchs sold fish, guinea fowl, venison and goat meat.

Small groups of old men sat or squatted in conversation, with some smoking reed-clay pipes. The sprightlier men were trained from a young age in war games, hunting, fishing and assembling huts and houses. From the Director General they learned that the young men were the warriors for the co-ordinated defence of the village and for attack when necessary. All smiles vanished as they drew near.

'I would have thought,' Brigstocke said scornfully, 'that the men would apply their energies to more constructive occupations than idling away in such slothful indulgence. 'Tis beyond belief that the womenfolk put up with such indolence.'

'I think your ignorance doth own a vast estate, sir,' said the Director General. ''Tis sheer hypocrisy to think that England is any different. In which province, sir, do men work harder than women? Is it not a woman's lot to bear the children, feed the family and support her husband? What you see, sir, are women going about the business of supporting their menfolk. Whereas man is the protector of woman the world over. That much, sir, can be found in the scriptures. 'Tis sanctioned by God.'

Following the Director General's idiosyncratic assertion, Wimborne caught Brigstocke's wink at Squire Ogden, who smiled. Halting at a stall, the Director General softened noticeably when he stopped beside the stallholder.

'Gentlemen,' he said. 'I give you my Confa, Florence.'

She was a strong beauty with ample lips, fine features, long, crinkled flaxen hair and light brown in complexion. He thought she had inherited the best traits of both her African and Dutch lineage. She was dressed in a wrap of yellow cloth draped over her shoulders and stopping inches from the dirt, and in the strong sunlight, the material scarcely concealed her buxom contours. Looking them over with an enigmatic smile, she addressed the Director General with a soft, sensuous, coastal accent.

'The General want me?' she asked.

The Director General blushed.

'Nay, Florence,' he said, 'I want you to bring my children this night.'

Giving the Director General a loving smile, the Confa replied.

'I will bring children to their Baba. First I must sell my goods.'

To Wimborne's surprise, the lothario in the Director General surfaced when his blue eyes sparkled. Taking off his tricorne he ran his fingers gracefully through his russet-red locks.

'Of course you must, Florence,' he said. 'I want to introduce these gentlemen to you. They have come all the way from England to visit us.'

Stepping eagerly forwards, his captain raised his tricorne.

'Delighted to make your acquaintance, Madam Florence,' he said.

Wimborne was irritated by her beamy smile at his captain.

'We shall have a feast tonight, Florence,' said the Director General. 'Bring women for our guests.'

Lowering her voice conspiratorially, the Confa turned amorous.

'I do like you want,' she breathed to the Director General, 'I will bring women for them.'

Jabbing a long slender finger at his captain, she was explicit.

'I will bring big big woman for him!'

Laughter engulfed the party. Bearing in mind his subordinate position, Wimborne grinned discreetly at his blushing captain. Upon a spirited parting and another captivating smile, the Confa turned back to her stall to continue trading in ivory, gold dust, gold chains and gobbets of gold for hair, wrists and ankles. At the end of her stall lay a large block of salt. Demand for the seasoning and food preservative was such that people trekked some tens of miles for just a cup.

That night they dined on salt pork and planned an armed incursion into the interior with the express purpose of 'kidnapping niggers'. Wimborne paid particular attention when his captain addressed the table.

'We shall not be buying slaves from the King of Ouidah on this occasion,' he said. 'Instead, we should allay his suspicions by paying our respects with a few trinkets. After which we shall sail and anchor off Badagri, and then trek up the Ogun River. We shall follow its course well into the interior before capturing the niggers.'

'Squire Ogden and I wish to accompany you on this expedition, Captain Blunt,' said Squire Brigstocke. 'We will buy a hundred from you, thus guaranteeing you a sale for your goods on the condition that they are delivered in good health to us in Pertigua. We will pay you a third in gold on this coast and settle our account when you land them in Jamestown.'

Thumping the table, his captain sealed the agreement with a handshake.

'Done, Brigstocke,' he said.

'I can furnish you with one officer and twenty Redcoats,' said the commander. 'And yourself, General Tugwell?'

A telling pause ensued, after which the Director General replied.

'The Royal African Company will be out of pocket,' he said, 'if it has to feed and clothe your slaves while they are here in Cape Coast Castle. Until they are handed over to you in Pertigua, it will therefore cost you tuppence a day per slave for board and lodging.'

From his neighbouring seat, Wimborne eavesdropped on the impromptu whispered conference between Squires Brigstocke and Ogden.

'We should agree,' said Brigstocke. 'We have nothing to lose. Not only do we cut out the steep cabiceer's commissions here on the coast of Guinea, we also dodge the auctioneer's commission in Pertigua. But best of all, we thwart Randolph Fleming whose presence hikes up prices.'

'You have a good point,' Ogden whispered. 'Fleming controls market prices utterly. And the old piker haunts every auction, as the Flemings always have.'

'Here on the coast of Guinea,' whispered Brigstocke, 'we buy slaves at a lower price. Whereas in Jamestown, Fleming will have to buy his slaves from us.'

Grinning mischievously, Brigstocke sat up from his whispered meeting.

'Times are hard and your price is somewhat onerous, General Tugwell,' he said. 'Nonetheless, my partner and I will stomach the board, lodging and transportation costs. But pray bear in mind sir, the locale you so eloquently refer to as a 'lodging' is in actuality, your odious dungeons.'

Laughter rippled across the chamber. Wimborne simply grinned.

'It is agreed then, Squires?' said the Director General.

'That it is, General,' said Brigstocke. 'Your hand on a gentlemen's agreement. And one more thing, sir. For a trek in this inhospitable climate, we are obliged to request sedan chairs and porters.

'Aye Squire, you will most certainly need chairs,' said the Director General, good-humouredly. 'Gentlemen, I shall provide you with enough chairs, slave-porters and muskets, and ten of my best soldiers who have much experience in the ways of the niggers. I shall select them myself.'

'Your hand on a commendable agreement, General Tugwell,' said Brigstocke. 'And Captain Sykes, what recompense will you require for the use of your legionnaires?'

Wimborne smiled to himself, for the moment naval commanders hankered after had arrived – the opportunity to amass capital.

The commander of the *Resolution* was candid.

'One hundred pounds in gold,' he said. 'In addition, a shilling per slave for every day.'

'Agreed,' said Brigstocke.

Unlike the sharing of a prize with the crew after the capture of a pirate vessel, Wimborne knew that the entire sum for slaving ventures was claimed solely by the commander of a naval vessel. The truth was that in these extra-curricular activities, the commander of a man-of-war fashioned his own code. Their exalted Lordships of the Admiralty conveniently chose to be ignorant of these enterprises.

''Tis agreed then, Squires,' said the Director General. 'You sail two days after the morrow. And may God go with you.'

The slave-raiding expedition, comprising the *Resolution*, the *Pelican* and the *Portobello Star*, sailed in an easterly direction along the lush tropical coast, bound for the Bay of Guinea. Wimborne diligently performed his watch-keeping duties. The first port of call was to be Ouidah, where respects would be paid to the King. If the winds were favourable, they should reach Badagri by June.

Homeland

Gbere: 28 February 1750

It had taken nearly four months. On a hot airless afternoon, ravenous, parched and exhausted, Kayode reached the town of Gbere with his brother and the woman. Within reach of their objective, his spirits soared as he walked along the crowded streets and alleyways.

It was the time of the Egugun Festival – a yearly occasion when the Yoruba remember the souls of dead relatives. Festivities had started in the morning, when the Alagbas – High Priests – directed processions of vibrantly clad celebrants through the streets to the house of the Bale. Like elsewhere in Yorubaland, they would dance until they received the Bale's blessings. The celebrants then returned with the Alagbas to their neighbourhoods in the town, to continue feasting and dancing until every street was alive with the sounds of revelry. The crowds were dispersing when Kayode and his companions entered Gbere. Three figures dressed in the shrouds of the dead were walking towards them. He backed instantly into an alleyway.

'It is an insult to pass them by with your heads uncovered,' he said. 'Cover your heads and remember they must not be touched.'

The shrouded figures passed by. Then the woman spoke.

'For the Egugun festival in Pategi,' she said, 'women spend days cooking food for the dead people. We serve the food to the men who work for the Alagba. The festival is a wonderful time for men, Kayode. It is just a big feast day for them. In my village for last year's Egugun festival, two hundred goats and hundreds of chickens were killed. Why are men worthy of so much?'

'It is the custom of our people, Asabi,' he replied, tersely. 'It is the tradition of the Yoruba. Women must not meddle when the dead have returned.'

He suddenly backed into a side alley. Led by medicine men with the sacred *ijimere* red monkey on a lead, shrouded figures were advancing down the main street. Some were dressed in shrouds similar to those worn to the grave by their dead relatives. Others were garbed in the feathers and skins of birds and animals. Gbere's citizens walked in carnival mood behind the shrouded figures.

'We must find the Alagba for this quarter of the town,' said Kayode.

'Why do we need a High Priest?' his brother asked. 'We come to find the Bariba?'

'We need an Alagba's help to find the Bariba,' he replied. 'Wait here.'

Stepping out of the alleyway, he joined the carnival procession with his companions. Providence was on their side – the parade was making for the seat of an Alagba. Shadowing the procession, they entered the crowded compound of the Alagba's house. Forcing a route through the gathering, Kayode worked his way onto the verandah of the long one-storied dwelling. Face to face with Alagba Ogundipe, a short, fat, kindly faced man, he speedily related his predicament. Eager to learn more, the High Priest invited him inside.

The Alagba reappeared a short time later with a grinning Kayode, who beckoned them into the house. A feast had been laid out in a room with a window opening onto the street. No sooner than the High Priest departed, they fell on an earthenware bowl full of chicken groundnut stew. While washing down the fare with water and palm wine, Egugun revellers danced past the window to song and drumbeat. In due course he recounted his conversation with the High Priest.

'Alagba Ogundipe has agreed to help us,' he said. 'At sunrise, he will send a tracker to guide us to the Bariba and the *sese* beans.'

'At last,' his brother sighed.

'Is it far, Kayode?' she asked.

'It will take all morning to get there, Asabi.'

'Do you think the Bariba will teach us how to make charms?' his brother asked.

'Alagba Ogundipe said the Bariba are a secretive people and very suspicious of strangers,' he replied. 'If they ask us to stay with them, it will be for a short time. His tracker will wait with us and bring us back to Gbere. The Alagba has kindly invited us to sleep here tonight.'

Narrowing his eyes with suspicion, his brother put a pertinent question.

'Why is this Alagba being so helpful?'

'Yes, Kayode, why?' she reiterated.

'Two reasons,' he said. 'Because the cowries I have paid him serve to remind him that he is on our side. And because he nurses ill will against the Alafin who he said is dying. His grievance began many years ago when the Alafin sent men to confiscate the land of the Alagba's father because of a debt arising from a failed harvest. The Alafin's men said that in accordance with ancient law, the family could all be enslaved due to the size of the debt. However, the Alagba's father was told that he was lucky, because he merely had to forfeit his land. Since the Alafin's decree, the Alagba's family have been made homeless and had to lodge in the blacksmith's forge. The Alagba was very sympathetic when I told him that our family had also sought refuge in the blacksmith's forge after Sango's visitation. This High Priest truly despises the Mogbas.'

'Why?' she asked.

The masqueraded head of a jackal shot through the open window. Kayode scowled.

'Is the Alagba here?' said a voice from under the mask.

'Can you see him?' Kayode asked, brusquely.

The jackal's head vanished.

'Why does the Alagba hate the Mogbas?' asked his brother.

'It was the Mogbas the Alafin sent to do his dirty work. A large portion of the cowries we owe the Mogbas flows into the hands of the Alafin. That is the penalty he exacts for Sango's visitation. After we have obtained the *sese* beans from the Bariba, the Alagba wants us to go with him to the Royal City of Oyo to witness the coronation of the new Alafin.'

He turned to Asabi. Her dark inscrutable eyes were fixed intently on him. What was that expression he saw in them? He could read not anything he could make sense of. She smiled at him for the first time since her rescue. He grinned back sheepishly at her. In the subsequent silence, he yawned and stretched himself out on a mat.

'We should sleep,' he said. 'If we can reach the Bariba tomorrow, we will soon begin our journey back to Ake.'

Despite being desperately in need of sleep, he felt restive. Rising stealthily, he crept past his sleeping companions and slipped out onto the verandah. The balmy night air afforded him time alone to ponder on a woman he found beguiling. Then he heard the soft tread of feet. Turning around, he saw her standing there – silent, remote – her aura drenching the shadows. He felt powerfully aroused. She must surely feel something too? Together they remained motionless beneath a lustrous moon, hearkening to the waning revels of the Egugun festival. Turning to him, she softened into a smile. He had the distinct feeling that some providential entity and the incomprehensible wheel of fate had thrown them together and was drawing them ever closer.

Early next morning, Kayode sighted a man shambling towards the Alagba's house. Even before the stranger had reached the threshold of the sunlit dwelling, he caught his odour. In his late twenties, the stranger bore haggard features as if in mourning, but his gap-toothed smile set the day alight.

'*E'karo* – good morning,' he said, in a deep friendly voice. 'My name is Olumide. Alagba Ogundipe sent me. I am his tracker.'

'*E'karo* Olumide,' said Kayode.

Rising with a broad smile, he was about to introduce himself and his companions, when the tracker set eyes on Asabi.

'*She* go with us, Kayode?' he asked.

'Asabi goes where we go,' he replied, and to make certain the tracker understood, he added, 'she's as strong as we.'

'She make we go slow!'

'She go where we go!'

Eyeing her up and down, the tracker's contempt for Asabi was apparent. Scowling menacingly at her antagonist, she said nothing.

'Keep up with us, woman,' the tracker snapped. 'We'll not stop to rest.'

'Put your feet up if you want!' she snapped. 'Point the way to us and go back to your little hut.'

'The Bariba chop off the heads of them they don't like, Kayode,' warned the tracker. 'When we reach the Bariba, they'll pack her off with the women.'

'We will abide by their customs,' Kayode replied.

'To be with my sisters is a privilege,' she retorted. 'Women feed the family, while men sit around cooking up conflict. What use is that?'

Mumbling an unintelligible riposte, the tracker pointed at a narrow track.

'We go this way, Kayode,' he said.

Through the rising heat of the morning, they followed the tracker through the arid bush, keeping an eye open for lions. Stopping from time to time, the man put his ear to the ground to listen for the vibrations of the rhinoceros. In the scorching heat of midday they arrived at the top of a bluff. The land sloped gently down to an expansive green plain on which nestled a cluster of huts and houses. Women pounded cassava root and children played. Of the men, there was no evidence. Arab mares and stallions, black-haired pigs, goats and broad-shouldered oxen roamed about in a fenced enclosure. Dogs, geese and chickens wandered freely.

'Wait here, Kayode,' said the tracker. 'I go and talk with the Bariba.'

'Go carefully,' said Kayode.

'In the town of the Bariba, Kayode,' said the tracker, 'it is better she keeps her mouth shut.'

Slumping to the ground, Asabi sat simmering darkly. A short distance away from her Kayode dropped with his brother. No one spoke. Hanging over them was the encounter with a people of sinister repute. By the time the tracker returned Kayode was sweating anxiously.

'They'll meet us?' he asked.

'They'll meet you. But they will speak only with the one who leads. That is you, Kayode. They'll speak with you alone.'

Turning to Asabi and his brother, he gave them a strained smile.

'Come,' he said. 'Let's step into the secretive realm of the Bariba.'

Nearing the bottom of the escarpment, he pointed at gnarled objects dangling from branches and swaying in the breeze.

'Fetishes,' said the tracker. 'They warn strangers to stay away.'

Kayode halted abruptly.

No more than twenty paces away, men wrapped in vermillion cloth wielding spears and short swords were advancing on them. Halting a spear's length away, a wiry elderly man stepped out from between the warriors. He was dressed in a maroon and sand striped *agbada* robe, topped by a matching *fela* hat. A small bony hand held a short sword; the other clasped an elephant-haired flywhisk. His overblown manner said he was the Bale of the town. Giving a somewhat obsequious bow, the tracker addressed the mayor.

'*E'kasan Oga* – good afternoon Master,' he said.

'*E'kasan*, Olumide,' replied the Bale. 'Why did you bring troublesome strangers to our town?'

'They have journeyed all the way from the village of Ake,' replied the tracker, 'far far to the south.'

Cuffing horse flies off his cheek, the Bale was curt.

'Never heard of that place!'

Kayode stepped forward.

'My name is Kayode,' he announced. 'We have trekked from Ake, the head village of the town of Abeokuta.'

Frowning with disbelief, the Bale challenged him.

'Ah ah, all the way from Abeokuta? That is not possible. The way is too dangerous and the wild animals fear no man. There are scores of bandits between here and there. It is said that white slavers take their caravans along it. Why do you think it is said that a caravan must have no less than twenty heavily armed warriors to be safe? Yet three of you claim to have made such a journey and survived? To mount such an expedition, you must have had a big big reason.'

Giving another respectful bow, the tracker interrupted.

'*Oga!*' he exclaimed. 'Kayode's house received a visitation from the great god, Sango.'

Raising his eyebrows somewhat distrustfully, the Bale swatted the air with his flywhisk and turned to Kayode.

'You're on a mission!' he exclaimed. 'I begin to understand why you have taken upon yourself such a perilous trek.'

Sweat was streaming down Kayode's neck.

'They seek the *sese* bean, *Oga!*' the tracker blurted out.

'I see,' the Bale said.

Handing his short sword to one of his men, the Bale circled Kayode for a closer inspection.

'You and you come with me,' he said, waving a hand at Kayode and the tracker. Pointing at Asabi and Taiwo, who had remained on the edge of the compound, the Bale continued.

'The woman should wait in the roundhouse with my senior wife. He must wait here.'

Flicking his flywhisk, the Bale turned and strode away with Kayode and the tracker in his wake.

In the Bale's residence, they were led through the sparsely furnished visitor's room that was attached to the exterior of the compound. Several petitioners languished in its confines, their disputes awaiting the judgement of the Bale. Crossing a large sun-baked courtyard, they passed women spreading peppers under the burning sun. A few goats were tethered in one corner, desultorily grazing on straw.

Entering a long rectangular building with numerous rooms, Kayode marvelled at the finely carved columns that confirmed the status of the owner. They were ushered into the house proper. He knew they were greatly privileged when they were shown into the Bale's sanctum – the family room – and invited to sit on a multi-coloured mat. Adorning one end of the large room were ebony and *sapele* sculptures of Sango and the mystical cult of the Bariba. At the opposite end, the Bale sat down on a finely carved ebony chair.

Looking around the room, Kayode noticed the ivory and stone *opon ayo* game boards, an ornate *sapele* wood chest and dark basalt libation bowls. As if to verify the importance of his host, ceremonial accoutrements of the Bariba were meticulously displayed along the entire length of the walls. At intervals, rich *asioke* hangings screened the doorways of the sleeping rooms. Beside the Bale, on a small table, sat two large wooden bowls of kola nuts and cashew nuts. Tossing cashews into his mouth, the Bale spoke.

'Tell me of the great Lord's visitation, Kayode,' he said, 'so that I may share and cherish this portentous occasion.'

While he recounted the tale of his family's impoverishment, the Bale picked his teeth and listened attentively. Following his account and a long disquieting silence, the old man cleared his throat and began to boast.

'Did you know that the Lord Sango's disloyal friends came here to the Bariba to acquire the art of *juju*, charm-making and bringing lightning onto the houses of their enemies? They made amends by becoming the first Mogbas and followers of Sango's traditions. The duty of a Mogba is to spread the legendary name of Sango and interpret his laws. It is only the Bariba who are blessed with the sacred antidote to Sango's visitations. Everyone, including the Mogbas, fear the Bariba. The Bariba fear no one.'

The Bale proceeded to tell him the story of Sango, the fourth king of the Yoruba. It was a chronicle he knew well, but he showed respect for the old man's age and hospitality by listening patiently. Rising to his feet at the end of his tale, the Bale gave him a smile of high regard.

'You have made an expedition beyond imagination, Kayode,' he said. 'A man who makes such a sacrifice esteems his flesh and blood above himself. In recognition of the courage you have shown in making such a trek, I yield to you the *sese* beans. Dwell with us awhile and we will teach you the art of crafting charms.'

Winning the praise of the leader of the Bariba filled him with gratitude.

He began taking out the strings of cowries from his sack. Raising his hand, the Bale was resolute.

'The Bariba need no payment, Kayode. We admire your endeavour and extend our hand in friendship.'

'On behalf of my kin, I thank you. I will never forget how you helped us in our time of need.'

For the next seven days, along with his brother, Kayode immersed himself in the sorcerous practices of the Bariba. How to make and lift a curse. How to spread suspicion, fear and conflict in an enemy camp. How to turn a person blind.

He was never really confident that he grasped the truth of their talents, or whether their dark practices actually worked. What he really wanted to see and understand was how they made a man invisible, as his father had said. It is strange, he thought, that no answer ever comes from anyone I ask. Then, the tracker said that they were to witness the bizarre event of a 'raising'.

According to the tracker, a young man had made a girl of twelve heavy with child, but had refused to accept responsibility for her condition. Furthermore, he had offended her family by boasting of his many conquests. Angered by what reached his ears, the girl's brother sought to redeem his family's honour. In a fight with the young man, the brother had been killed, thus depriving her family of the principal tiller of their land. Following his trial, the young man received the death sentence and the judgment was executed. The girl's family were not satisfied. Demanding that the two arms of justice – retribution and compensation – be fully exercised, they appealed to the Elders of the town council.

'He has paid with his life,' said the Elders.

'He has not given enough,' replied the grieving parents. 'Who will till our crops now that our son is dead?'

Re-examining the demand of the grieving parents, the Elders had decided that the dead man should not be left in his grave. Instead, he would be 'raised' to fulfil the demand for compensation. Recompense, they decided, would be satisfied by the dead man ploughing their land for a period of not less than three years as a replacement for the loss of their son. Since the dead needed no rest, he could therefore carry out the work of several men. The ground was thus prepared for the 'raising'.

By the light of the full moon, Kayode stood beside the tracker and his brother to watch the firelit event. Handing out copious measures of palm wine, the high priest's minions incited the warriors encircling the grave into an uproarious fervour. Clad from head to foot in a garment of scarlet feathers, the high priest stayed stone-still, a mamba draped around his neck and a bronze statuette of *ijimere* the red monkey on his head. Raising his arms, the deathly reptile swayed about, its fiercesome fangs glinting in the firelight. The high priest cried out.

'O *Elegbara*, your miserable servant awaits you. His wickedness has caused him to serve you by toiling in the light of evil time. *Elegbara*, your moment is at hand. Your servant is asleep – yet he hears it all. I beseech you to rouse your servant to fulfil your ancient curse.'

A cloud drifted over the moon, momentarily obscuring the proceedings. Moonlight came flooding back. Kayode shivered with fright. A tall figure with a featureless white mask and a hooded cloak of ebony-black feathers stood over the grave. The warriors howled.

Dropping to his knees, the high priest presented a long rhino whip to the masked figure.

'*Oga* – Master,' he cried.

Beating the grave with the whip, the masked figure chanted.

'*Omugo. Oku.* Fool. Dead One. Fool. Dead One,' he cried. 'Come forth from the sleep you have not enjoyed. Return to fulfil your ancient destiny. You can no longer sleep with the dark. *Dide. Dide.* Get up. Get up.'

'*Dide Dide. Dide Dide*,' the warriors intoned.

The drumbeat stopped abruptly – as did Kayode's heart. Silence reigned. A scrabbling noise came from inside the grave. Tightly gripping the tracker's arm, Kayode whispered hoarsely.

'The earth, it moves.'

Bit by bit the soil on the grave was being disturbed – from the inside. First came fingers, then a hand. Progressively, the head and upper torso sat up. Holding his breath, sweat deluged down Kayode's body. The corpse rose creakingly to its feet. Its skin was a deathly grey pallor and maggot-eaten cavities covered its body. Drumbeat drowned the cries of the warriors. The high priest turned to the corpse.

'Come.'

Eerily, the corpse shuffled after the high priest. Joining the animated procession leaving the graveside, Kayode pulled his brother close.

'*Egbon*, I cannot believe my own eyes,' he said. 'They must have built a secret cavity in the grave allowing him to breathe. Or else he was buried in a very shallow grave. He could not tunnel his way out if he had been properly put into the ground. To bring a man back from the other side? That is not possible.'

His brother gave him a weak, quizzical grin.

Seven days after the 'raising', they were summoned to a torch-lit ceremony in the family room of the Bale's house. At the end of a huge feast, arranging the sleeves of his *agbada* robe, the Bale rose solemnly to his feet.

'Kayode of the Sodeke family,' he said. 'We the Bariba, blood kinsfolk of the Yoruba, honour you. We offer tribute to your expedition in which you saved the woman from the white slavers – who will be ousted from our land. We pray to the gods of the Yoruba to grant you a safe return to the village of Ake. From whence you came may you return in peace, carrying these the sacred *sese* beans of the Bariba.'

Kayode glanced at his brother, whose eyes were wet. The Bale took two big white kidney-shaped beans, each the size of a man's fist, from a stack of leathery pulses. He prayed over each. It was an age before Kayode felt the silky-smooth pulses in the palms of his hands. His eyes welled with hot tears.

Next morning, they bade farewell to the Bale of the Bariba and set off in high spirits for Gbere. Not even the prospect of encountering lions could dampen Kayode's sense of achievement. Reaching Gbere in the heat of the afternoon, they made for the Alagba's house.

The Alagba repeated his invitation to them to accompany him to the enthronement of the new Alafin in the Royal City of Oyo. Accepting his invitation and thanking him for the use of his tracker, Kayode produced the *sese* beans. Delighted by Kayode's success, the Alagba offered prayers to Sopona – the god of suffering. With Asabi and his brother, Kayode watched the Alagba take a broom made from the stripped branches of the bamboo palm, fashion an effigy of the deity and smear it with camwood. Loudly cursing the Mogbas of Ake, the Alagba grasped the image, laid it on the ground and threw handfuls of hot parched corn and sesame seeds over it.

'What will happen?' his brother asked.

'Some Mogbas will develop the pox,' he said. 'Now he has seen the beans in our possession, the Alagba will help us openly. In fact, everyone will support us on sight of the *sese* beans.'

Two days later, with a light wind gusting from the southwest, they set out in the Alagba's caravan, bound for the city of Oyo. Travelling with the Alagba's cavalcade afforded benefits. First of all they were on horseback, which would take many suns and moons off the return journey to Ake. And secondly, the size of the armed escort discouraged bandits. Under a burning February sun, they cantered with the cavalcade over the hills and into the wilderness. On several occasions, they had to take refuge on the edge of the forest, to shelter from the dry dusty harmattan wind, or to avoid the warring militia of local kings.

'Those petty kings are manoeuvring for position before the new Alafin is sworn in,' the Alagba told them. 'We had best stay out of their sight.'

Kayode was content with the Alagba's strategy. He would not imperil their triumphant homecoming with the *sese* bean.

5 April 1750

At midday they entered the ancient royal city of Oyo with the dust-caked caravan of Alagba Ogundipe. The city was bursting with the fanfare and spectacle of a coronation. Kayode grinned warmly at Asabi and his brother. Trotting through streets that had been swept clean, they passed repaired and painted houses. Gangs of sweepers were stationed at intersections to clear horse dung off the tree-lined avenues. Ivory and *kakaki* trumpets publicised the occasion. The Alafin's special *ogidigbo* drums rumbled across the city.

Festooned with the flags of minor kings and the emblems of Yoruba clans and societies, Oyo was in festive mood. Men sported flamboyant *agbadas* and women were draped in dazzling parti-coloured *bubas* and extravagant *gele* headscarves. Giant statues carved by the celebrated sculptors of Oshogbo and bronze heads on plinths, from the artists of Benin, lined the route to the royal mausoleum known as the Bara.

'Each new Alafin,' the Alagba said, 'enters the Bara only twice – at his coronation and at his death.'

Standing to one side, they watched the new Alafin being escorted to the Bara at the centre of the ceremonial procession. At the front of the royal cortege were chanting ranks of white-robed Mogbas from all over Yorubaland. Following the priests was the Alafin's personal escort – the religious and civic dignitaries who would enter the Bara with him. Astride an ebony-black horse, the trim, princely Alafin dismounted at the grand steps and followed the High Priestess into the Bara. Rising onto his toes to get a better view, Kayode felt Asabi's hand slipping under his arm. A warm sensation surged through him. He turned to the Alagba.

'What happens inside the Bara?'

'The Alafin receives the divine authority to wear the crown of his ancestors,' the Alagba replied.

His brother's hand shot out.

'See that Mogba over there, Kayode.'

'Which one?'

'At the foot of the steps – the one with the pockmarked face.'

'*Oluwa* – God! It is the Mogba from Ake!'

Turning away to avoid being recognised, he whispered to his brother.

'That snake must not find us here,' he said. 'Baba told the Mogbas of

Ake that we were going south to the coast to search for cowries. If that wicked priest sees us this far north, he will soon guess that we have been to see the Bariba. Those wicked priests would surely kill us than let us arrive in Ake with the *sese* bean.'

'I seek your help, holy man.'

'Ask what you want of me, Kayode,' said the Alagba. 'You cannot let them take you here. What are your needs?'

'If we are to reach Ake ahead of them,' he said, 'we must leave at once. We require food and three horses. We have cowries . . . '

Raising his hand, the Alagba was adamant.

'I want no payment. I hate the Mogbas. Take the western road out of Oyo, as if you are heading for the Ogun River. That should confuse the devils. My tracker will show you the best route south. You will find food with my horses in the stables. Take what you want. Go now Kayode, before they see you. May the blessings of Oduduwa go with you all. Be gone my friends. Make haste. Make haste.'

Extricating themselves from the assembled throng, a sudden commotion in the crowd caused Kayode to look up. His eyes met those of the pockmarked Mogba. Recognition flooded into the face of his tormentor, who leapt to his feet and screamed at his fellow priests.

'In the name of Sango,' he cried, 'what are *you* doing here? Seize him. Seize him before he . . . '

At that instant like an earthly god, the Alafin emerged from the Bara to stand before the populace. Surging forwards, the crowd pressed the gesticulating Mogba back towards the Bara. Signalling to Kayode and his companions, the tracker forced a passage in the opposite direction.

'Stay by me,' he shouted.

Inside the vast communal stable the tracker swiftly extracted four horses and packed the saddlebags with provisions. They cantered out of Oyo in a westerly direction. Beyond the towering walls of the city, they broke into a gallop. For about five miles they rode hard in the tracker's wake until he came to a halt. Bidding them a warm-hearted farewell, the tracker pointed towards the southbound track.

Taking the lead, Kayode set a brisk pace. Week after week they trotted southwards. Day after day they cleaved and sweated their way through the chaotic palm bush. Arriving in the cooler, humid rainforest, they rode until they reached the River Ogun. Kayode was aiming for his hidden cache of cowries. In full flood, the Ogun made many trails impassable and forced them to find alternative routes. They needed to go as fast as humanly possible. Weary as they were, when the terrain was suitable Kayode cajoled them to ride through the night. Eventually they reached the spectacular curve of the Ogun River where he had buried the hoard. It took him no time to track down his marker – the mango tree, beneath whose spreading branches lay the treasure. Unearthing the cowries, they filled the saddlebags and pressed onwards. Kayode knew that in their haste they were leaving tracks that their pursuers could not miss.

For the next few days they continued on a southerly course with the sun behind them until at last they made camp high up on the forest slopes. That night, before feeding the horses and lighting a fire, Kayode scaled a lofty *abura* tree. Way below them out on the savannah he spotted the campfires of the Mogbas.

'They are about half a day's ride behind us,' he said. 'We will cross the river and continue down the western bank. We will leave fewer tracks in dry country. When we are closer to Ake, we will cross back again.'

'We should slow them down,' she muttered, almost as an aside.

'How?'

'Death traps.'

'*You* can make traps that kill?'

'Baba was a forester, Kayode. He taught me how to make and sow death traps. I will set them behind us as we ride.'

Early next morning, ready to depart before sunrise, he found her beside a tree looking intently into the shadowy valley. It was cold, dark and moonlit. The rank smell of rotting vegetation issued from the forest floor. Far below smoke rose from the Mogba's fires. A hyena cried in the distance. Grunting hogs rooted through the leaves.

'What can you see?' he asked.

In the muted light, he could feel her eyes probing his face for something only she could fathom. Turning away from him she continued her surveillance of the valley.

'I see the faces of my family,' she said, with a poignant note in her voice.

'We are also your people, Asabi. We, like you, are Yoruba.'

'But not my own flesh and blood, Kayode. I will never forgive the white men for what they have done.'

She turned back to him and her manner softened. Tentatively putting out her hand she touched his cheek.

'Thank you for saving me, Kayode.'

He held her dark eyes. His hand slid tenderly down her arm to her waiting hand, whereupon their fingers entwined. Her unexpected response all but overwhelmed him.

'We must be gone,' he whispered.

It was mid-morning when she set her first trap. With his brother as lookout, Kayode watched her hack down a great thorn bush. Taking out her sharp knife, she carefully removed the finger-length barbs from the branches. Hollowing out a finger deep shallow rectangular trench on the narrow track, she planted the thorns firmly in rows pointing upwards. Sprinkling soil over the thorns until they were completely buried, she masked her handiwork by tracing hoof prints across the surface of the trench with a twig. Stepping across to some red-tipped, short-thorn bushes, she enlisted Kayode's help.

'Chop down this bush, Kayode. But look out for the red tip of this thorn, it is very poisonous.'

Lifting the cut branches carefully, she laid them along the sides of her trench. There was a malicious gleam in her eye when she explained her plan.

'The horse that steps in this trench,' she said, 'will rear up and throw his rider who will fall onto the red tip thorns at the side of the trench. As the poison kills him slowly and painfully, he will thrash about for days. I think that will slow them down.'

Sheathing her machete and without a backward glance, she mounted her horse and cantered away. His blood ran cold. She had just calmly condemned a man or several men to death. Swallowing his dismay, he mounted his horse and trotted after her. His brother did likewise.

Kayode made his way along the wooded bank of the Ogun River until he found a bridge fashioned from two *abura* tree trunks. On foot they led their horses across and continued south. Asabi set more snares from time to time, each one more deadly than the last. Late one afternoon, on a rocky projection above the river, she halted to set a trap that she declared would be her most lethal. Raising a quizzical eyebrow at his brother, they dismounted and followed her. Close to the edge of the overhang she put a finger to her lips.

'Shhhh. Listen.'

'Listen to what?' he asked. 'All I hear is the river.'

'Open your ears,' she said.

Standing stock-still he listened as hard as he could.

'I can hear only the river,' he said.

'What are we listening for?' his brother asked.

'I don't know,' he replied. 'Only she can hear it.'

Striding away from the edge to nearby bushes, she cut a long forked stick and used it to lift a fallen leafy branch, below which lay a large flat rock. Giving him a mischievous grin, she prised up the rock. Underneath lay five dark grey snakes, each about an arm in length with a row of white spots on its back and a pale zigzag line on either side. Like a conjuror she said: 'Saw-scaled vipers!'

She let down the rock carefully. Kayode shuddered.

'The deadliest of all snakes, Kayode,' she said impassively. 'This is the reptile of nightmares.'

'Why have you disturbed them?' he asked, anxiously.

Grinning at him, she replied:

'To bid farewell.'

He frowned.

'Farewell to who?'

'I will gather these little fiends in this sack,' she said, 'and secrete the sack in the branches above the track fixed to a trip-line. They will drop onto any rider whose horse breaks the line. I say farewell to the Mogbas, Kayode. Snakes usually strike once. This viper strikes again and again and again. A man bitten over and over again will curse his own life before he loses it. And he will he lose it. Farewell I say.'

In this wilderness, where danger lurked behind every stump, he was awed by her self-belief. His objective was Ake and she was making it easier for them to beat the Mogbas back to the village. His brother's admiration for her could be heard in his hushed voice.

'The woman strides with the beasts of the forest.'

'*Egbon*, never let me forget,' he whispered, 'not ever to provoke the hidden side of this woman. We are lucky she rides with us.'

With bated breath and sweat seeping down his neck, he watched her use the forked stick to pin down each snake, deftly lift each one up and drop it into the sack. While she completed her deathly trap, he set up camp for the night with his brother.

They pressed on, day after day and week after week. To avoid delay or discovery, they dodged contact with the towns and villages they passed. Subsisting on the roots and rodents of the forest, they made agonizingly slow progress through the mangroves along the banks of the Ogun. Once or twice, he thought he heard the cries of the Mogbas blundering into one of her traps. On each occasion he would call a listening halt. Squawking parrots, trumpeting forest elephants and the chatter of monkeys made it impossible to be sure.

Arriving at the cataract where the Ogun merged with a smaller river, he reckoned they were about ten days ride from Ake. That night he insisted they camp above the waterfall. Over a heartening fire she roasted a bush rat. The forest pulsed with the sounds of mating animals. His eyes held hers in the flickering firelight. His brother's voice broke the spell.

'I can see Ake's faces when they see the *sese* bean,' he said. 'Our village will take you to her heart, Asabi.'

'The Mogbas will be plagued,' said Kayode. 'From this time forth they will interpret Sango's visitations more justly. Oduduwa has watched over us, but we must remain on our guard. It is still possible for the Mogbas to catch up with us. What my brother says is true, Asabi. Ake will take you to her bosom for saving the lives of her sons.'

She knelt down beside the fire and turned the rodent. His eyes wandered slowly down the curve of her body. He so wanted to tell her what he felt in his heart. His nerve failed him. Instead, he took her hand.

'I am forever in debt to you for my life, Asabi,' he said. 'Your traps have slowed them down. If not they would be upon us by now.'

She smiled warmly at him. Gently extracting her hand, she took the rat from the spit and pulled off a steaming leg. With barely veiled affection, she offered it to him.

'*Adupe,*' he breathed.

A further nine days of hard riding through the forest brought them to the liana bridge. Euphoria swept over them. Ake was now only a day's ride away.

Ake

They were exhausted by the time they reached the forested outskirts of Ake and the blacksmith's dwelling. Dismounting by the giant *abura*, they dropped to the ground. Kayode lay on his back and gazed through the massive branches to the blue sky beyond. He felt triumphant but was too weary to show it. Turning onto his side, he looked at Asabi who lay beside him blinking back tears.

He stretched out his hand. Taking hold of his wrist, she held it shy of her face and gently pushed it away. Turning onto her side to face him, she whispered.

'I reached twenty-one years at Oyo.'

He pulled her to her feet, put his arms around her waist and wheeled her around.

'Oluwa will bless that day, Asabi,' he cried. 'I too will cherish the day your mother gave you life.'

Lowering her to the ground, he pulled her into the blacksmith's stables. Inside, they found a corner where they buried the hoard of cowries under a pile of straw.

Suddenly the blacksmith crashed through the door.

'AAAiiiee!' he cried. 'Oluwa has watched over you and your brother, Kayode. People said you were dead. I said you would come back. Your return is going to kick the Mogbas in the teeth. Come my friend, let us go to the Bale's house.'

Drawing his friend closer, Kayode whispered.

'Not a word about the woman.'

Taking a good look at Asabi, the blacksmith turned and grinned at him.

'You have the *Ogo Elegbara*?' Kayode asked.

The blacksmith nodded.

'Hide it,' he whispered, 'and give it to me when I give a signal.'

The blacksmith bent down outside the forge. Extracting the carved stone effigy of the devil from a wooden box, he placed it into the bag hanging from his waist. Hoisting Kayode onto his broad shoulders, he set off for the Bale's house. Asabi and Taiwo fell in behind them.

Word of their return had clearly spread. Villagers twittering with excitement had gathered outside the Bale's residence. To rousing cheers, Kayode slipped down from the blacksmith's shoulders and skipped up the steps. In an embroidered *agbada* robe and *fela* hat, the Bale stood back from the topmost step with a chilly smile. Kayode grinned cheekily at the elderly official. Silence fell as the Bale stepped forward.

'Welcome home, Kayode,' he said coldly. 'We shall have a feast in your honour. Let us begin by settling the matter of the cowries. Have you Sango's tribute?'

Facing his audience, Kayode raised his voice.

'Let it be proclaimed,' he said, 'here in Ake, in the town of Abeokuta and in the court of the new Alafin at Oyo. In my hands I hold my answer to Sango's visitation.'

Lifting the *sese* bean above his head, he tossed it down the steps. The fabled corporeal representation of Sango bounced once and came to rest by the foot of the blacksmith.

'The *sese* bean!' the blacksmith exclaimed.

Awed gasps burst from the crowd.

'Oduduwa is great!'

'I have seen a miracle this day!'

'Kayode has done a great thing!'

The Bale bit his lip. Kayode smiled. He knew that, as a key officer of the Town Council, the Bale himself stood to receive a share of Sango's tribute. This knowledge made him doubt the sincerity of the Bale's subsequent words.

'You have honoured your family and your village, Kayode,' he said. 'And indeed your heroic act . . . '

To forestall the Bale's hollow song of praise, Kayode stepped forward and began to speak.

'I thank you, Bale, for the spirit with which you have received us,' he said. 'I want you my people to know a secret I have kept till this day. It was the Mogbas who set fire to the house of my family. They said it was Sango's doing. To counter Sango's visitation, we were forced to make a dangerous expedition to seek out the *sese* bean. In the course of our trek, we came across men with white skins who held many prisoners in shackles. We attacked the whitelings and released our people. The freed set out for their villages except for this woman. Her name is Asabi. You can see she is Yoruba. She could not find her way back to her village alone. Without her we would not have succeeded in our search for the Bariba.'

Citing the Bariba produced shrill gasps from his audience.

'She saved our lives many times,' he continued. 'And I say to you, but for her skilled efforts, we would not be standing before you this day.'

The Bale raised his arms.

'She is welcome to dwell here in Ake.'

Spontaneous applause broke out. Asabi gave a bashful smile.

'I have sent a boy to fetch your father from his *oko egan*, Kayode,' the Bale purred. 'I have also sent word to the *Agbalagbas* – the Council of Elders. They will want to hear your extraordinary account. I know they will be most interested to hear about the white men. Tell me, how did they look to you?'

'Like us but with white skins – like ghosts,' he replied. 'And they . . . '

A commotion burst forth from the rear of the crowd. The fat watchman yelled.

'The Mogbas have returned from the Alafin's coronation.'

Winking at his brother, Kayode whispered.

'Say nothing.'

A sweating, panting, wild-eyed pockmarked Mogba elbowed his way through the crowd. Behind him were two bitter-faced Mogbas, wearing shredded robes. Stepping discreetly behind the Bale, Kayode feigned innocence.

'They look in terrible condition,' he said.

The Bale exclaimed.

'Twelve of them journeyed to the coronation!'

'Perhaps they got lost in the forest,' Asabi sighed. 'It is a vast treacherous region.'

The three priests ground to a halt before the Bale.

'What has happened to you?' the Bale asked. 'Where are the rest of your companions?'

'*Oga* – Master,' replied the pockmarked Mogba. 'You recall that Kayode and his brother were said to have travelled to the coast to collect Sango's cowries?'

'Yes yes,' said the Bale, impatiently.

'We found him enjoying himself at the coronation in Oyo, far north of Ake. When he saw us, he fled . . . '

Kayode stepped out from behind the Bale.

'So the devil has returned,' snarled the Mogba. 'Children are father-less because of your doing. Why were you in Oyo when you should have been on the coast gathering Sango's cowries? You don't have them do you? I think not. The law is clear on this matter. Without Sango's tribute your family is dishonoured. Your farms are forfeit and you and your brother belong to us.'

Stooping to pick up the *sese* bean, Asabi mounted the steps and calmly gave it to the Bale. The Mogba's eyes bulged.

'W-what is that?' he stuttered. 'W-who brought that here? W-where did th-that come from?'

Disregarding the Mogba's bewilderment, the Bale delivered a terse proclamation.

'The *sese* bean has honourably satisfied the tribute for Sango's visitation,' he said. 'Kayode's family owe you nothing.'

The pockmarked Mogba threw the Bale an angry look. Then, reluctantly, he bowed, signalling his acceptance of Sango's ruling. The sacred bean was material evidence. Kayode knew that there was no appeal against the judgment. He winked at the blacksmith as agreed. In return, he felt the *Ogo Elegbara* being slipped into his hand. Masked by the blacksmith's frame, he poured nut oil onto the totemic idol. Raising the ghastly image above his head, he opened his arms and beseeched the heavens.

'I, Kayode of the Sodeke family,' he said, 'do solemnly swear that I shall never forgive the Mogba who set fire to our house. In the name of the great god, Sango . . . '

He thrust the idol at the three speechless priests.

'I hold you responsible for what has happened,' he cried. It was you who tried to destroy my family by stealing my father's sons and his land. I told you then that you did not understand the blood that binds my family. You have sharpened my sword. Now I will use it. This day I put on you a curse. Within seven dawns from this day, the wrath of *Elegbara* will strike at the heart of your flesh and blood. To that end, I pray that your loved ones are stolen from you.'

Throughout his speech, he noticed that the Bale and the Mogbas were not the only ones who looked aghast – his brother was also.

'You should not have done that, Kayode,' he said.

'Why not?'

'It was arrogant of you to lay a curse before you had talked it over with your own family.'

'I need tell no one. The Mogbas will think twice before accusing anyone again.'

'You drink at the high table of arrogance, Kayode,' he said softly. 'And that is your weakness. Arrogance will bring you to your knees and to your senses. Only then will you become master of yourself.'

He scowled at his brother. Laying a curse in public was a grave matter, for such affairs were usually conducted in the utmost secrecy. Although he had steered clear of condemning the sacred religion of the Sango oracle, he had nonetheless defied that tradition of secrecy. He would be on the lookout for any ill effects. All eyes, for the time being, would be closely scrutinising the wellbeing of the three Mogbas and their families. Accompanied by his brother and Asabi, he hurried back to the forge to celebrate the successful end of their mission.

16 June 1750

It was on the seventh dawn following his curse. The village was shaken by a cry from the fat watchman.

'*Ina! Ina!* – Fire! Fire!'

The blacksmith crashed headlong into the forge.

'White men! White men!' he screamed. 'White men are attacking the village!'

Snatching a spear and short sword, Kayode hurtled past the blacksmith out of the forge. Followed by his brother and Asabi, he sprinted towards the burning houses. From the opposite end of the village, he saw white men advancing with levelled iron sticks. Changing direction, he ran to the edge of forest and ducked inside the bushes. Not far away to his left, white men in red and blue uniforms were rounding up his friends and neighbours. To his right, fleeing villagers ran into a row of kneeling white men pointing iron sticks at them. Flashes and explosions spitting from the sticks filled the air with smoke. Men, women and children tumbled like felled trees, to lie groaning and twitching. The Bale's house was in flames. On the steps of his official residence, the Bale himself lay dead with three others. Emerging from the clouds of smoke, villagers hurled their spears. Four Redcoats fell. Another six hurled their spears. Two Redcoats crashed to the ground. But with their lethal weapons and surprise on their side, it was evident to Kayode that the white men would soon prevail.

'Oluwa! – God!' he breathed.

Burying his face in his hands, he raised his head. Lying powerless inside the bushes, flanked by his brother and Asabi, the village crumbled before their eyes. With tears in his eyes, he watched his dreams of times to come descend into ruin. Punching the ground with frustration, he was consumed with a desire to fight back. But they could not defeat the force and tactics of the white men. They boast awesome weapons, he thought. Spears and swords were no match for iron sticks that kill from a distance. No village could hold out against an attack like this. He must get his family to safety. They would return to punish the soldiers for what they had done.

'*Egbon*, stay where you are,' he whispered to his brother. 'There is nothing we can do here.'

'The white men possess such terrible weapons, Kayode. Your curse was powerful.'

'*Egbon*, your words are foolish. My curse had nothing to do with the appearance of the white men. I cursed three Mogbas – not the whole village.'

'These white devils, Kayode?' asked Asabi, quietly. 'Who are they? From where do they come?'

He shook his head and he shrugged his shoulders. Looking intently into her dark liquid eyes, a mixture of distress and affection gripped his heart.

The invaders were off the *Resolution*, the *Pelican* and the *Portobello Star*. They were commanded by Captain Blunt who carried his fêted Wogdon pistol. Reluctantly, First Officer Wimborne stayed close behind him. Pointing at a line of villagers, Captain Blunt screamed at his men.

'Fire.'

Several villagers were felled by the volley. Waving his Kinndt-fashioned blade about, the military commander of the *Resolution* sliced at the figure of a fleeing child. A hot pillar of blood spurted into Wimborne's face from the severed jugular. The body dropped, but the head rolled in the dirt until it came to rest at his feet. An involuntary retching seized Wimborne. Blithely kicking the head out-of-the-way, the military commander was flippant.

'Why, Captain Blunt,' he said, 'I do believe this lad has quite lost his head.'

His captain guffawed, then roared angrily at the soldiers firing indiscriminately.

'Wound 'em, you idiots,' he shouted. 'Niggers are worth nothing dead.'

Staggering away from the carnage to the shaded edge of the forest, Wimborne sought to calm his revulsion. He began a headcount of those who had been apprehended. It was then he realised that in this wild moment, free humans had become slaves.

Inside the bushes bordering the forest, Kayode whispered to his brother.

'*Egbon*, go back to the forge and find Baba and the blacksmith. Take the family to the giant *abura* tree. Asabi and I will stay here to see if we can help. We will join you to escape into the forest with the family.'

His brother was grave.

'*Aburo*, we will meet you by the *abura* tree,' he said. 'Be not too long, Kayode.'

Scrambling into the undergrowth, his brother disappeared.

Later that morning, anxiety for Kayode's wellbeing had reached fever pitch. Waiting with the family by the giant *abura* tree his brother Taiwo repeated over and over again.

'Kayode said he would join us here,' he said.

It was late in the day when he finally accepted that Kayode and Asabi must have been among those who had been kidnapped. *Be not too long.* His final words to Kayode thundered through his head. *Be not too long.* Sinking to his knees, he sobbed his eyes dry. *Be not too long.* In the subsequent days of fruitless rage and despair, he began to fear that Kayode's curse might be held responsible for the attack by white men.

One scorching afternoon, he attended the meeting held by the Council of Elders of Abeokuta, the seat of the *Agbalagbas*. They took a different view. He heard the *Agbalagbas* resolve that Kayode's curse could not be held liable. They judged that the attack was part of the plague sweeping through the region – the profitable trade of African Kings and cabiceers, who sold their own citizens to white men, who in turn trafficked them away across the Ocean.

'*Oyinbo, Oyinbo,*' cried the Agbalagbas. '*Afi okun se ona.*' – 'The white man, the white man, who makes of the ocean a highway.'

For countless new moons, Taiwo mounted a vigil at the place where Kayode and Asabi had last been seen. Fifty-two men, women and children from his village had been shackled and forced into the forest. He made certain that the talking drum broadcast the account of the attack by the white men. Travelling storytellers were speedily on their way, recounting tales of the whitelings who kidnapped people from the village of Ake before they had time to say goodbye.

Efuufu

Strong Wind

June 1750

The liquid notes of migrating swallows glancing off the waters of the Ogun River alerted Kayode. Raising his eyes in the morning breeze, the sight of black-headed seagulls screeching and drifting into the headwind confirmed his suspicions. We're on a march of no return, he thought. We have reached the coast. There are many more of us. Keeping count of the growing column he reckoned that, including those taken from villages deep in the interior, the slave caravan now totalled around four hundred and sixty.

From the moment he had been taken prisoner, escape never left his mind. Along with the column's other disconsolate souls, he had stumbled through the dry bush and staggered along the mangroved banks of the Ogun hugging the rainforest. Seething and sapped by the high humidity, he prayed for deliverance from the heavy wooden neck-yoke, linked to the next soul by an endless chain. Crippled by pangs of hunger, his craving for freedom was more acute than his lack of food.

Following days of slogging through the dark rainforest, the column staggered into coruscating sunlight. Salty air filled his nostrils. His instincts told him something terrible was about to happen.

'I can smell the sea,' he said. 'I think we are being taken away to . . . '

Without waiting to hear more, panic broke out. Caught unawares by the reaction, he remained stock-still. The rest scuttled in different directions – but the neck-yoke and endless chain prevented them. Firing a volley into the air, the Redcoats arrested all efforts to break the shackles with bare hands. Like the other prisoners, he dropped to his knees and cowered on the ground.

Following the restoration of order, Wimborne scrutinised his companions from the comfort of his sedan chair, borne by two slaves at either end. Sprawled in similar conveyances, Squires Brigstocke and Ogden were wreathed in the smoke from their hemp-filled clay pipes. The chairs had been supplied by the Director General, as had those carrying the military commander of the *Resolution*, Captain Blunt, Captain Rutley and the Parson. Having descended into bouts of melancholia through heavy drinking, the cleric leaned out of his chair to proffer advice to uncomprehending ears.

'Toil hard and the Lord will watch over thee,' he cried. 'Put your trust in Him. And He will preserve you from the dark pestilence that infests this place.'

Hogwash, thought Wimborne. This happens to be their homeland. To my eyes thus far they seem to have endured without our assistance.

' 'Twould be an inspired action,' said Ogden, 'if a body were to ram that flagon of Madeira down the hypocrite's pious throat.'

Why not ram two? Wimborne mused.

'We need the support of the Church, my friend,' said Brigstocke. 'The attendance by a man of the cloth furnishes us with a holy writ.'

Hampered by his neck-yoke, Kayode stumbled along, blinking from the glare of the morning sun. At last the column arrived on a rocky plateau overhanging the sweeping sandy bay of Badagri. Catching a glimpse of Asabi, his spirits lifted. And he held fast to her image, like a talisman of hope.

Following their return to Ake, he had hoped that in making friends with the villagers, Asabi would begin to erase the memory of the bloodshed she had witnessed in her short turbulent life. In those first few days, he had respected her wish to spend nearly all her time alone on the shores of Ake's lagoon. He had seen her once rising wet and naked from the water. She had caught him looking at her. There in the shadows of her grief, she had stood her ground like a lioness – frightened of nothing. He had smiled at her uncertainly. Bit by faltering bit, a new interest had seemed to shine out of the dark pools of her eyes. Two days later, he had asked her to spend a day on the banks of the river with him. She had hesitantly accepted. In the twilight of that day, he had roasted tilapia on the banks of the Ogun. There she had let him kiss her just the once before breaking awkwardly away. Knowing that she was not ready for the trust a union requires, he had not pressed his attentions. She needed to be loved unconditionally if she was to love again. His dreams were shattered when the white men attacked Ake.

Bound by a neck-yoke fostering a barely expressed and unconsummated love, he now stood on the shores of Badagri, prevented from any contact with her. An age apart, they were on the verge of a very uncertain future. He looked at the three ships at anchor, and despaired.

Stepping onto the sandy shore, Wimborne saw at once that the sheltered bay had long been a point for slave embarkation. Dense rainforest ran from the west along the brow of the shoreline. To the east the sandy expanse was littered with blackened hulks, rotting lengths of rope, rusty anchors, capstans, broken masts and spars. Sprouting like vegetables among the flotsam and jetsam were rusting manacles abandoned by slavers for over a century. Canoes skimmed back and forth like insects between the ships and the shore, conveying barrels of water, fruit, meat and mountains of canky bread. Down by the water's edge, grief-stricken prisoners bound for the *Portobello Star* were shuffling between two columns of sailors. Once unshackled, they were prodded through the shallows to board waiting canoes. A wailing baby was wrenched from his mother's arms and dumped into another canoe – to lie defenceless and screaming to no avail. With a growing sense of disquiet, he persevered with his supervision of the *Pelican's* cargo until he was accosted by the Parson.

'Before you dispatch them, Mister Wimborne,' he said. 'Allow me to bestow my benediction over those set to depart.'

'By all means, Parson,' he said.

Sighing resignedly, Wimborne leaned against a stack of hogsheads to watch what he thought was certain to be an intoxicated and amusing performance. Donning a discoloured black surplice, the Parson clambered onto a hogshead. Swaying drunkenly with his wisps of grey hair straggling in the wind, the Parson raised his crucifix.

'Hearken to me my children,' he said. 'Jesus saith suffer the little children to come unto me and I will give thee rest.'

Raising his face towards the sky, the Parson intoned.

'O Lord, bless thine flock who sail from this dark, ungodly province, so that they may be taught your word. Go now my children. It is done. The bell is rung, the book is closed and the candle is out.'

Thud. The preacher tumbled from the hogshead. Wimborne shook with stifled laughter. The sanctimonious fool, he thought. On his knees, the sand-coated clergyman was scrabbling about in the surf for his crucifix. Watching his antics with growing amusement were Squires Brigstocke and Ogden. As the cleric eventually swayed onto his feet, they shouted facetiously.

'Amen.'

Why is this drunk shouting in a baffling tongue and waving a bit of wood? Kayode wondered. The drunk suddenly crashed to the ground. He grinned at the other sniggering prisoners.

'A drunk is a drunk in any colour,' he murmured.

The sight of a white man fumbling on his knees was a dark reward. But the sight of his fellow prisoners sitting in canoes bobbing impotently on the surf, made his blood run cold. His turn to board arrived and he backed away. His temples were throbbing and his heart thundering against the walls of his chest – his rage touched the limits of his reason. Tears welled into his eyes. A whip propelled him through the breakers into a canoe.

A commotion by the water's edge made him turn around. Not more than thirty paces away, six prisoners were dashing towards the forest. When the leading pair disappeared between the trees, his spirits leapt. Musket fire burst from the guards standing along the shore. Three escapees crashed onto the sands. Fatally wounded, the fourth man kept crawling towards the forest. Striding up to the stricken prisoner, a black slave driver hacked off his arms. Moments later, a white slave driver severed the prisoner's neck. Raising the sand-caked face, the man flourished the head in the air with blood streaming down his arms, before tossing it into the surf. Swooping gulls with cruel orange beaks pecked out the eyes. Shaking uncontrollably, Kayode turned away with tears streaming down his cheeks.

Insensitive to the gruesome episode, Captains Blunt and Rutley and Squires Ogden and Brigstocke with the inebriated cleric in tow started along the sands for the *Pelican's* tender. Shaken by the incident, Wimborne walked behind them, listening to the Parson's justifying rationale.

'This breed have nothing in their lives and need to be led,' he said. 'I myself bear the burden of converting the heathen from the fetish and the graven image. To accomplish my mission, it is entirely necessary to remove the savages from this unhappy land. Of course while I am acting to save their souls, the Church also has to enlighten this black crop – thus they will be baptised and taught the word of God.'

Coughing diplomatically, Wimborne said quietly:

'They may already have their own deities, Parson.'

'Balderdash, Mister Wimborne,' replied the Parson. 'There is only one God. It is patently obvious that he has never visited this place.'

Rolling his eyes with disbelief, Wimborne retorted.

'No doubt, Parson,' he said, 'your black harvest will fill your pews and also increase the profits of the Royal African Company.'

'And not before time, Mister Wimborne,' said his captain. 'Especially now we know that we can sever the stranglehold of those grasping Kings and cabiceers. It might be prudent,' he added, with a glint in his eye, 'to continue buying a few slaves from them, at least for the time being.'

'Aye, it would be foolhardy to divest the Kings of their profits in a rush,' agreed Captain Rutley. 'My Principals nevertheless will be mightily pleased with the additional profit I have secured by means of this novel technique. I sail for Jamaica once this cargo has been conditioned at Cape Coast.'

'Won't take long to condition them,' said his captain. 'We sail for Cape Coast when our niggers are tight-packed and provisions squared away.'

Closing his eyes and sighing, Wimborne prayed beneath his breath.

'And may God have mercy on all who sail with you.'

'With this little haul,' said his captain, 'I think we might well have established quite a precedent on this coast.'

Chuckling loudly, Squires Ogden and Brigstocke boarded the tender. One sat fondling his cane, the other sat puffing his hemp-filled clay pipe, all the while laughing over their inspection and purchase of one hundred slaves. Pushed off into the surf, the laden craft was soon making for the *Resolution*. Perched in the prow, Brigstocke uncorked his brandy flask.

'A toast, gentlemen,' he cried, 'to the originating deed of the Honourable Company of Guinea Venturers.'

'Aye,' they replied.

Wimborne declined a swig.

Captain Sykes was awaiting them on the main deck of the *Resolution*.

'I see congratulations are in order, gentlemen,' he said. 'I trust you made up the numbers from your skirmish. The winds are with us and the tide is on the ebb. Let us get under way. The *Resolution* will escort you as far as Cape Coast Castle. There, Captain Blunt, I shall leave you to complete my commission. I intend to search for that other pirate, Howel Davis. I have a notion that he lurks somewhere to the west.'

'When Mister Wimborne has the niggers tight-packed and battened down,' said his captain, 'we shall signal with the six pounder and get under way.'

Giving a slight bow, Wimborne acknowledged his captain's wishes.

'A moment please, Captain Sykes,' said Squire Ogden, in a business-like voice. 'I think we agreed the sum of one hundred pounds in gold. And a shilling per slave per day.'

'Aye Squire Ogden, that we did,' said the naval commander, eagerly.

Passing his cane to his companion, Ogden handed the naval commander a leather pouch.

'Here is one hundred in gold, Captain,' he said. 'Squire Brigstocke and I have purchased one hundred slaves. By Captain Blunt's reckoning, it will take the *Pelican* six days to reach the Cape Coast. Six more days for your further protection, which amounts to thirty pounds. A further ten pounds, shall we say, for your diligence, making a total of forty pounds. Are we agreed, sir?'

Giving Ogden a spirited handshake, the naval commander beamed.

'Aye, Squire Ogden,' he replied. ''Tis agreed.'

Retrieving his cane, Ogden bowed and turned for the gangway.

'We bid you farewell until Cape Coast Castle then,' he said. 'And good sailing, Captain Sykes.'

The instant he stepped onto the *Pelican's* deck, the captain's face darkened.

'Keep a close eye on the niggers, Mister Wimborne,' he snarled.

You fool, Wimborne thought, what else would I be doing?

'I shall keep them surprisingly close to my eye, sir,' he replied.

'All the same, Mister Wimborne,' said the captain, 'don't be fooled. Niggers can appear docile, when they are really sullen and given to brooding. They can be sly and turn on you in a trice. Take no chances. Got it?'

'Aye, Captain Blunt,' he said, 'I will make certain the cargo is tight-packed.'

'After that, Mister Wimborne, signal the *Resolution*.'

'Aye aye, sir.'

The captain shouted for the sailing master.

'Mister Graceforth.'

'Aye, sir?'

'See the niggers get a weekly soaking. Make the blighters prance the jig for exercise. Got it?'

Stepping aside, the corpulent sailing master spat shuruttu tobacco over the lee rails.

'Aye aye, sir,' he replied, with a jaunty air and a glint in his eye. 'I'll have them prancing the jig fore and aft 'fore long.'

'Raise your anchor and get under way,' said the captain. 'Hoist your mainsails, t'gallants and staysails.'

'Aye, sir' replied the sailing master. 'Look lively there, bo'sun. Haul aft the foresail sheet. Mainsails, t'gallants and staysails.'

'Aye aye, Mister.'

The wind was blowing a fresh westerly in the early afternoon when Wimborne gave orders to fire the six-pounder – the signal agreed with the *Resolution*. With suicide-nets spread all round, the *Pelican* led the way. Shadowed by the *Portobello Star* and the *Resolution*, the convoy set course for Cape Coast Castle. From the sailing master, Wimborne learned the watch convention on slavers. The instant the cargo was loaded, together with the ship's watch, the slave-watch commenced – four hours on and four hours off. The watch consisted of five men, armed with muskets and cutlasses. Precise were the captain's orders: the sole responsibility of the slave-watch was to 'keep a close eye on the two hundred and fifty-nine niggers', who lay below, secured in tight-packed rows on the wet and stifling slave deck of the *Pelican*. Five cables off her larboard beam, the *Portobello Star* carried two hundred and six prisoners in similar conditions.

On the shadowy, cramped slave-deck of the *Pelican*, Kayode lay shivering in a pool of seawater. Permeating every crevice of the deck was the stench of vomit, faeces and terror. Looking up, he scowled at the strange arrangement of oak beams and the pitch-streaked underside of the *Pelican's* main deck through which he heard pounding feet and raised voices. As the creaking vessel made way into a swell, a groaning drifted down the rows of prisoners.

Whenever the ship rolled, his guts heaved. He closed his eyes to blot out the truth. Unless he escaped, he was set for a life not of his making. Ake was already a life's span away. Where was Asabi?

26 June 1750

Six days later, early on a bright morning, the *Pelican* dropped anchor in the roads before Cape Coast Castle. Wimborne gazed up from the deck at the vast promontory thrusting out like a breakwater and being pounded by powerful waves. Resting on the rocky outcrop was the impregnable castle with massive whitewashed, crenellated curtain walls. Jutting between the crenellations was a row of cannon, behind which were soldiers with muskets trained downwards. Assigned slave-disembarkation duties, Wimborne assembled the slaves in groups of ten and chained them together. In canoes, they were speedily transported through the surf to dock on sandy aprons at the base of the rocky headland. Floundering ashore, they were kicked and whipped into the precincts of the citadel.

Four hundred and sixty-five quaking slaves were lined up in the quadrangle and primed for branding with the letters DC – denoting them to be the property of the Duke of Chandois. Under his captain's orders, Wimborne was present to witness the official procedure for branding. Four guards pinned a slave to the ground. A hot branding iron was pressed firmly onto his right arm. The ghastly smell of blistering flesh and the screams of the slaves rattled his wits. Seeking relief, he looked fixedly into the skies craving deliverance. Once branded, the slaves were beaten down into the vaulted dungeons, to join the other two hundred and fifty-six already rotting inside its slimy confines.

Stinging from the whipping he had received in the quadrangle, Kayode sat on the steps of the dungeon tending his wounds. Peering into the murky interior, he made out walls of granite covered almost entirely with slimy moss. Raising his head, he gazed through the grates into a clear blue sky, as a bird soared freely and effortlessly upwards on warm updrafts. Looking back down into the gloom of the dungeon, he searched for Asabi. Inside the shadowy chamber, men, women and children were struggling for breathing space. Pitched battles were breaking out. Shouting in the Yoruba language, a deep voice rose above the turmoil in the gloom below.

'*Olorun wambe*,' cried the voice. '*Olorun wambe* – God exists. There is a god.'

Heralded by grumbling, a hush of sorts summarily came about.

'They call me Captain Tomba,' the voice continued.

Rising from the shadows, a broad-shouldered figure stepped into a shaft of light issuing from the ceiling.

'The white man is *Elegbara's* disciple,' said the big man. 'We are in the hands of devils and we're going to hell. We have a great fight before us. Open your ears. You must regain your strength. You cannot sleep sitting up. Lie on your side. Tuck into the one in front. This night when they bring food, eat everything they give you. Even if you don't feel hungry, eat it. And stop fighting.'

Slipping quietly down the steps, Kayode drew closer to the character who spoke with such confidence.

Good advice, he thought.

'Look to escape,' said the big man. 'The white men will not keep us here for long. They're taking us to another land. There they will sell us. We must break out from here. Or we will never see our children or our motherland again.'

From a dark corner burst an elderly voice tinged with unbridled hostility.

'How do you know so much, big boy?' asked the old man. 'How do you know we have not offended them? And that is why they have done this terrible thing to us?'

Whispers of agreement shot around the dungeon. Kayode was angered by the old man's questions.

'And how do you know they will not let us go after a few days?' said the old man. 'We should palava with them. I know I can make them understand that we have done them no wrong and we are not their enemy.'

Howls of derision greeted the old man's ideas.

An idiot, thought Kayode.

'Let me refresh your miserable memories,' said the big man, with a no-nonsense tone in his voice. 'But first open your eyes. The white men killed our people. We are their prisoners in our own land. You have all seen their awesome weapons. We are unarmed. Yet that fool wants us to believe that they will palava with us. Why should they? Ah Ah. Since they hold such powerful weapons, they need no talk. His ideas are as stupid as is he. I should know. I traded with the white men. Then they decided they would seize what they wanted without paying for it. One day they invited me to eat on their ship. After giving me food, they trussed me up in chains. Who gave these white men the authority to shackle us and make us prisoners? Did you not see the way they butchered our brother on the shore?'

'I saw it!' a woman shrieked.

'And chop off his head?' cried the big man.

'My brother!' wailed a grief-stricken voice.

'Only those twisted by *Elegbara* could do such evil,' shouted another.

'We have done nothing to be worthy of such brutality,' said the big man.

Pausing to size up his shadowy, gripped audience, the big man continued.

'Why would the white man arm himself with an *opa* he calls a musket,' he asked, 'put himself through perils sailing across the mother of oceans, trek vast distances through our rainforests, buy or kidnap our people and march and sail them all the way to this place? Why? To give us mangoes and bananas? Remember those who have been sold to the white men by the Alafin of Oyo and the King of Ouidah. No, my friends, the white men take us for profit. I have even heard that they cook and eat the people they don't sell. That is why nobody ever comes back.'

Gasps of revulsion reverberated around the dungeon.

'We must stay strong,' said the big man. 'Men and women of the Yoruba, this prison will be your last chance to flee. Sleep deeply and save your strength.'

'You can say what you want,' retorted the old man. 'During the light of day I will palava with the white men. You'll see how they deal with a heartfelt approach.'

Slumping into the niche beside Kayode, the big man sighed.

'So will you, my friend,' he retorted.

Plagued by fatigue, Kayode shut his eyes. On the brink of sleep Asabi drifted into his thoughts. From the outset, she was remote and quick-tempered; yet he felt that beneath her furious expression she desired affection. There was that night on the way back to Ake from the coronation of the Alafin of Oyo. As they had listened to the noises of the forest and the rush of the Ogun's waters, she had sat quietly staring into the fire, enigmatic and oblivious of her bodily appeal. He wondered if he would ever again feel her lips on his and see that particular look in her eyes?

Food arrived towards the end of the day. Slave drivers lifted the grate and screamed down into the dungeon.

'Get your black hides up here.'

At the top of the steps leading into the quadrangle, Kayode's ankle hoop was attached to the endless chain, one of the one hundred prisoners to be attached to it. There were seven such chains in all.

Directly ahead with levelled muskets were the crews of the *Pelican*, and the *Portobello Star* and the militia of Cape Coast Castle. Standing close by was a black female interpreter, who appeared to be indifferent to the proceedings. The cat, the boot and the bayonet kept order in the quadrangle while steering the prisoners to the food queue. Filing past a long trestle table, two canky rolls and half a coconut-shell of water were thrust into his outstretched hands. Although he kept an eye out for Asabi, he could not find her.

Stepping into the dining room of Cape Coast Castle, Wimborne scanned the company seated around the supper table. These were the men of the Guinea coast who traded in a new brand of mercantile treachery. Taking a seat next to the Parson, he felt he was at hand for what was the Last Supper. Despite his qualms, he appreciated even the present doubtful company, for in just over a fortnight he would again be exposed to the idiosyncrasies of his captain.

Two captains, two squires, a Parson and the Director General tucked into Irish roast pork, fresh English potatoes, parsnips and peas – apparently grown in the Castle garden. A tainted hunk of Stilton accompanied a fine brandy. Wimborne was all-ears when the Director General began to address his guests.

'Along the coast of Guinea,' he said, 'Cape Coast Castle is the largest and oldest among the Company's forts and factories. On the morrow, we will begin conditioning the slaves.'

'I wager that the slaves in your dungeons, General,' said his captain, 'will fetch the Company close to thirty thousand pounds.'

'A handsome sum indeed,' said the Director General, as if the amount was news to him.

'A tidy amount,' agreed Squire Brigstocke.

Startled by the sum that would be generated for the coffers of the Royal Africa Company, Wimborne thought that the salary of a ship's officer was a mere drop in the ocean.

'On the morrow we remove the women to condition them separately,' his captain chuckled.

He merely blinked at his captain's double entendre, but he squirmed at the thought of the man's hairy arms wrapped around any woman. Brigstocke winked at Ogden. Clutching a third glass of brandy in a shaky hand, the Parson posed a question.

'General Tugwell, do you perceive anything unusual about this consignment?'

They are slaves you simpleton, thought Wimborne. Is that not a sufficiently abnormal state?

'Nay, Parson,' replied the Director General. 'Those who are soldiers, who became prisoners of war before being sold to us know what to expect in our hands. Soldiers will, by and large, try to escape. The shipment presently in the dungeons have been for the most part abducted – a hotchpotch of farmers, foresters, fishermen and failures.'

The Parson poured himself another brandy before wobbling out a further query.

'Wo-won't they try to escape then?'

'They will indeed, Parson,' replied the Director General. 'These may not be soldiers and may appear docile. They may even cringe and cower. But therein lies the snare. Niggers will cut your throat if you so much as take your eyes off them for an instant.'

Rising to his feet, the Director General removed his dress coat. Rolling up his left sleeve, he displayed a gash across his bushy forearm.

'This was given me by one I bedded,' he said. 'I turned to close the shutters. In the twinkling of an eye, she seized my blade and slashed me. After the wound was dressed, I mounted her and made her pay for it. To make certain that her kind understood who was Master and as well to teach them that niggers must never strike a white man, I had her fed to the crocodiles. And I had all the slaves watch her being torn apart.'

Shuddering at the account of the gruesome execution, the Parson pressed home the question uppermost in Wimborne's head.

'Was that really necessary, General Tugwell?'

'You did right, General,' said his captain. 'I say we make a similar example on the morrow. Give one of them a taste of the cat. That should furnish them all with something to ponder on.'

'I'm with that,' said the master of the *Portobello Star*. ''Tis a long haul to Jamaica. A flogging will sharpen up their ways of thinking and attitudes.'

'Will that be necessary, General Tugwell?' Wimborne asked. 'Might we not lose a slave which will doubtless affect the Company's profits?'

'We'll lose many more, Mister Wimborne, if we don't dispense a salutary flogging to somebody,' the Director General answered firmly.

The earliest opportunity to 'make an example' arose the very next day. At breakfast with the Director General and his guests, Wimborne saw the charcoal-skinned interpreter approach the table.

'Massa, a foolish slave is asking to talk to the white men,' she said, as if she considered the petition shameful.

Dropping his fork onto his plate, the Director General snapped at the interpreter.

'Bring the snivelling wretch here,' he said. 'I will test his backbone.'

The interpreter flinched at the harshness of the Director General's response, and then shot out of the door as if fired from a musket. Wimborne looked at the Parson who was visibly turning grey.

'Wh-what do you intend, General?' asked the cleric.

'To finish this excellent breakfast and then make an example of him.'

'I sincerely hope, General, that the slave is not one Squire Ogden and I have already purchased,' said Brigstocke. 'Ours carry a star brand.'

'If he is, Squire Brigstocke,' said the Director General, 'I shall give you another in his stead.'

Giving a sharp knock, the interpreter walked into the room.

'Number twenty, General.'

An elderly chubby-faced man shuffled into the dining room. He was scantily clad in a frayed loincloth with DC branded on his arm. Secured by hand and leg irons and a heavy wooden neck-yoke, pride showed in his demeanour and shone sturdily from his black face. Wimborne felt ill at ease and lowered his eyes.

'What do you want?' snapped the Director General.

The interpreter speedily translated the Director General's challenge into the Yoruba language.

'I am the Bale of Ado,' the slave replied. 'I think your men made a big, big mistake when they entered my village, killed my people and took many prisoners. The people of Ado have never wronged you. Your men attacked the wrong village.'

The interpreter's translation had barely left her lips when the Director General, who had turned purple, raised his eyebrows and his voice.

'Avast there sambo. You call me Massa when you address to me. You think my men attacked the wrong village, do you? It bamboozles you as to why they attacked your village? I will tell you why. Because your village was in the wrong place, nigger – and so are you.'

Heeding the interpreter's translation of the Director General's invective, the sweating slave trembled. Wimborne looked doubtfully at the

Parson, who turned awkwardly away. Rising to his feet, the Director General bellowed for the captain of the guard.

'Secure this slave to the frame,' he said. 'A hundred lashes, if you please. Assemble them all in the quad. Make them watch. Should serve as a hard reminder for them to conform. Then move the women to the prison by the gate.'

Marching into the chamber, three guards bodily lifted the quaking slave and carried him out. Behind the Director General's party, Wimborne wandered into the courtyard where they were met by an assemblage of grim-faced slaves. With the sufferer spread-eagled against an upright rectangular frame, the whip-master laid the nine knotted tails across the exposed back. The ensuing scream was evidently not sufficiently deafening for the Director General. He bellowed at the whip-master.

'Lay it on there or take the nigger's place.'

Suitably rebuked, the whip-master backed away. Skipping forwards, he sent the whistling tails onto the fettered torso. Wimborne closed his eyes.

Amidst the congregated slaves, Kayode whispered to the big man.

'What did the old man do to earn such a flogging?' he asked.

Staring directly ahead, the big man was terse.

'He spoke.'

'What did he say?'

'Something the white men didn't want to hear.'

The flogging lasted a full half-hour. At the sight of the lacerated back, Wimborne's innards all but mutinied. A bucket of water was thrown over the shuddering slave, from under whom a stream bled across the flagstones.

'Cut him down,' said the Director General. 'Is the nigger still with us?'

A piteous groan dribbled from the slave.

'Aye, sir,' replied the whip-master, severing the bonds securing his wrists.

The slave slumped to the ground.

'Fling him in the dungeon,' said the Director General. 'Bring him to me when he has improved. And move the women.'

Reeling back to the dining room with the Director General's party for a luncheon of coast goose, Wimborne made his excuses and returned to the *Pelican*. His appetite lay somewhere out there on the bloodied flag-stones of the courtyard.

Following the orders of the Director General, Asabi was moved with the other women to a dry dusty prison above ground. It was set in the walls of the Castle, next to the forbidding and uncommonly tall and narrow Gate of No Return. Inside, she examined her surroundings. It was a rectangular, vaulted, coarse stone chamber about sixty feet in length, twenty feet wide and ten feet in height. Scattered over the craggy walls were sketchings of various gods and religious symbols, some of which she recognised. Also evident and clearly compiled over a lengthy period of time, were numerous scratchings of durations of imprisonment recorded by those incarcerated within its walls. For light and ventilation, a tiny window with iron bars was set high up in the wall at the farthest end, through which breakers and gulls could be heard.

Her eyes wandered over the two hundred and sixty women. Sinking to the floor below the window, she found herself beside a portly woman of about sixty with salt-streaked skin weeping quietly into her hands. Except for a frayed scrap of cloth tied around her waist, the woman was naked.

'Why is the water shaking your face so?' she asked.

Receiving a whimpered response, she put her arm around the woman's shoulders.

'My name is Asabi,' she said softly. 'What is yours?'

The distraught woman raised her head.

'Funke,' said the woman, gloomily, 'my name is Funke.'

'I do not know how long they will keep us in this place,' she said. 'You must preserve your strength and make an effort to escape.'

'I am fearful for my husband,' said the woman.

'Was he not also taken?' she asked.

The woman shook her head.

'I was visiting my sister's village when the white men attacked and dragged us into the forest,' she said. 'My husband stayed home in our village. I am afraid for him. He has a bad chest. He will take his last breath if he does not get the herbs I picked for him. I know not what has happened to my children.'

'I also have a man I yearn for,' she sighed.

'Your husband?' the woman asked.

'No, not even my lover yet.' she replied.

For a moment Asabi fell silent. Then she spoke of how she had been rescued from the hands of white slavers. The woman listened patiently. She told her how she had found the young men of her village overbearing. Like many men she had met, they treated women like inferiors. Then Kayode entered her life. The first sight of him had sent a rush through her. Before a union could begin the white men seized them. She also nursed a dilemma. Despite her feelings for him, she had been so brutally overpowered by the men who took her by force, it had affected her severely and raised a barrier against man.

'You bear the wounds in your eyes my child,' the woman said quietly. 'It will not be painless to let a man touch you again. Lose not your dreams, Asabi. A force in me makes me utter these words – an omen whispers in my head. Your destiny is to lie with him once more. The gods will bless your union with a child.'

Surveying the dungeon, Kayode sighed. The absence of the women substantially increased the space for the four hundred and sixty-one men. From the character of the comments circulating, it was evident that the flogging had killed off all notions of talking peace with the white men. That night, he found himself next to the big man.

'You see what happened to that ass?' he asked.

Before Kayode could reply, the big man rose to his feet.

'Now you understand why escape is the only way out,' he said. 'Listen to me. Once you are out, follow the coast to the west for about six days until you reach Connu's Castle. Seek out John Connu. If I'm not with you, tell him Captain Tomba has sent you. Join his militia and Connu will offer you protection. He fears not the white man. He has a big army and more iron *opas* than the whites. If you cannot escape and you want to stay alive, do nothing to provoke them. That does not mean they will leave you alone. They are of a breed that enjoys making people suffer. What you have just witnessed is but a little of what they can do . . . '

Kayode frowned.

'How do you know all this in such detail?' he asked.

'When I was trading with them, Kayode, I saw many ships come to buy slaves and carry them away across the sea. I met many captains. These very eyes have witnessed cruelty and bloodshed. I am ashamed to admit that I never hindered their trade. And they did not interfere with mine. I will be open with you Kayode – I was a cabiceer. If I don't say so now, the white men will tell you. You see my friend, I sold wood, water and slaves.'

The big man's candid disclosure caught him off guard. Unprepared for the shocking revelation that a man had enriched himself by selling his own people, he shook his head with disbelief. Though words were beyond him, revulsion was not. Whatever their status or circumstances might have been before they were captured, they had now been equalised by their confinement. Hating the big man would change nothing. Swallowing his antagonism, he delved further.

'Why did your men not save you?' he asked.

'The whites don't need cabiceers anymore,' said the big man. 'They get richer by cutting the cabiceers out of the trade. By kidnapping instead of buying, they make greater profits. I was reckless and foolish. I met them without my guards and walked into a trap. Once they had me in chains, they told me I was greedy and they did not need me any longer. That is why I am here. But I do not intend to stay for long.'

Kayode shifted closer to the big man, who began talking in a hushed voice about escape. By the time the guards arrived at feeding time, he was aching with hunger. He hurried to join the torch-lit line for his ration of canky bread and water. It was supplemented with two thin slices of boiled yam. But he did not wish to hear the interpreter's explanation for the extra handout.

'From the good Massa General,' she announced loudly.

'To help us forget the flogging,' he retorted.

Consistent with his plan, the big man tripped and flattened the trestle table, scattering yams and bread rolls all over the ground. In the confusion, the strewn food was snatched and secreted. The filched victuals were carried back to the dungeons, where speaking softly the big man began to flesh out the bones of his escape plan.

Approaching midnight, on his way back to the *Pelican*, Wimborne arrived at the guardhouse beside the main gate. He was obliged to wait for the gate to be unbolted. He stood to one side while a cheddar-accented guard-captain growled orders to the twelve heavy-eyed men of the night watch.

'Keep your eyes skinned on them niggers,' said the guard-captain.

'And don't you go trusting them women. They can give you a glad eye and then turn on you. No need to fret about niggers making a break. They'll never get beyond the grate. If any of them gives you trouble, drag him out and give him a right good thrashing out there in the courtyard.'

The guard-captain turned to Wimborne.

'Radcliffe, sir, Horace Radcliffe, at your service, Mister Wimborne. Returning to the *Pelican* are you, sir?'

'Aye, Mister Radcliffe, I am bound for my cot.'

'Then I bid you a good night, sir.'

Radcliffe signalled for the gate to be opened. Then snapping his fingers at two guards who were restraining a young slave, Radcliffe walked briskly away towards his quarters.

'Bring him!'

Wimborne had no illusions as to how the lad would be used. The gate was unfastened. Suddenly pandemonium erupted beneath his feet. The guardhouse door crashed open. A voice bellowed.

'Give 'em a right good pasting.'

Spilling out of the guardhouse, the guards scattered across the court-yard. Wimborne melted into the shadows. As the alarm bell sounded, Horace Radcliffe dashed out into the courtyard and ran towards the dungeon. Wimborne followed. The grate was lifted. Radcliffe charged down the steps followed by his men. Wimborne saw a muscular slave catch Radcliffe by the throat, twist his neck until it snapped. Snatching the keys to the main gate from Radcliffe's body, the slave bounded up the steps. Wimborne backed hastily away across the courtyard, as did the guards who panicked and left the grate wide open.

Taking refuge behind a buttress, Wimborne saw a guard lash out at the muscular slave as he leapt onto the courtyard. Catching hold of the whip, the slave yanked the guard off-balance. Strangling the guard with the whip, the slave retrieved a musket and sprinted for the main gate, followed by several escapees. At the wrought iron portals, the muscular slave swung the musket butt against the head of a sentry who slumped to the ground. Slaves began escaping through the open gate. Charging the muscular slave, the militia quickly overpowered their quarry. Ten slaves fled into the night before the main gate was slammed shut.

Wielding long pikes and bayoneted muskets, the guards forced the remaining slaves back down into the dungeons. Returning to the open grate, Wimborne looked down once again into the dark void. Illuminated by burning torches, he witnessed a sea of cowering faces. Meanwhile, the muscular slave had been pinned against the post of the main gate and was receiving a beating. Finally, he was bodily lifted, transported across the courtyard and hurled into the dungeons. Once more, the grate was locked fast. Shaken by what had taken place, Wimborne walked briskly through the main gate bound for the *Pelican* and a welcome cot.

Six white men had lost their lives. Noon of the following day saw the Director General chairing an enquiry into the incident. Wimborne was summoned as a material witness before the Court of Inquiry. By the time he arrived in the tense chamber, the tribunal had already decided that the crime of murder and attempting to escape merited the death penalty.

'As a rule it is the custom that two slaves are executed,' said the Director General, 'for every dead white man.'

'That will seriously deplete the Company's profits, General,' his captain protested.

'Aye, that it would,' agreed the master of the *Portobello Star*. 'I trust that no prisoner will be given any punishment that might result in permanent injury or death.'

Dispensing a cynical smile, the Director General pronounced his judgment.

'Very well, gentlemen,' he said. 'Every slave apprehended in the confines of the quadrangle will receive a flogging. But that big slave, the so-called Captain Tomba, is hereby sentenced to one hundred lashes of the cat.'

Dismayed by the severity of the sentence, Wimborne frowned. Unfortunately his captain noticed. Every day for one week thereafter, he was obliged to witness slaves being flogged, confined in the stocks with pepper rubbed into their eyes or being confined in the iron box. This particular punishment sickened him. He hated the terrifying theatricality of it all. The slave was ceremoniously bolted into an iron coffin. It was placed in close proximity to an open fire stoked to a blistering heat. Anguished screams from within caused him to shut his eyes in silent prayer. Standing by with a set jaw, the Director General determined the length of time suffered. At his signalled command, the box was hauled away from the fireside and unbolted. Before Wimborne's eyes the slave's skin literally erupted in blisters.

Kayode counted himself lucky. Losing his footing, he fell back down into the dungeons winded. By the time he had recovered, the soldiers at the entrance barred him from making a further attempt. His fall saved him from a flogging. Nonetheless, the 'conditioning' continued unabated for another seven days. The starvation diet and the cat-o-nine-tails upheld order in the dungeons of Cape Coast Castle.

July 10 1750

It felt like the middle of the night. Stung awake by the whip, Kayode was forced up the steps of the dungeon into the moonlit quadrangle. He stood among seven hundred and twenty-one prisoners, destined to board the *Pelican* or the *Portobello Star*. Looking up at the battlements where the castle's inhabitants were sneering down at them, a blood-red mist clouded his vision. By six in the morning, an orange sun was rising above the eastern hills. There was a guttural order given. The drivers began flogging the prisoners down to the shore. Soon, he found himself riding the waves in a canoe bound for the *Pelican*. Drawing up alongside the vessel, he caught sight of Asabi scrambling up the Jacob's ladder. His heart leapt. She was aboard the same ship.

To his left, he saw canoes on course for the *Portobello Star*, ferrying some now familiar faces. With a lump lodged in his throat, he scaled the Jacob's ladder and set foot on the wet teak deck. In the grief-stricken moments before he was forced below, he looked along the densely forested coastline of his motherland. Tears welled in his eyes. He longed to leap overboard and swim ashore. But hampered by his ankle-irons, he shuffled helplessly along the deck. Dropping down the companionway into the hold, he was chained to the deck.

Throughout the morning, he lay listening to the thud of bare feet, chains and shackles on the deck above his head. By midday, four hundred and twenty-three prisoners had been chained onto the same deck as himself.

'The *Pelican* awaits your orders, Captain Blunt,' said Wimborne.

'Are your niggers tight-packed, Mister Wimborne?'

'Tight-packed and battened down, sir.'

'The currents are with us, Mister Graceforth,' said the captain. 'We have a fair wind. Get her under way.'

'Aye aye, sir,' replied the sailing master, striding to the foc's'le-peak. 'Weigh anchor, bo'sun.'

'Aye,' yelled the bo'sun, from the capstan.

The *Pelican* was under way.

Wimborne found the Squires and the Parson against the poop rails. They were musing on the solitary figure of the Director General, who was himself watching the departing vessels from the crenellations of Cape Coast Castle.

'I wonder if England will welcome his nigger woman like he imagines?' asked Brigstocke. 'Indubitably, she will win him only the disapproval of his peers and keep him from good society. What say you, Mister Wimborne?'

'I suspect our Director General is a man of his word,' he said tactfully.

'The man does appear confident,' agreed Brigstocke.

'I wager Mistress Florence will not be the only name the 'good people' of Little Dean call her,' said Squire Ogden.

Mopping his brow, the Parson proffered his opinion.

'I own a high regard for the man's self-assurance,' he said, 'although it is providential for him that his service here is at an end. The man really does believe his dark-skinned family will find sanctuary in England. I am afraid that the Director General has been living for such a lengthy period on these shores that the sun has quite turned his head.'

'I for one am exceedingly content to be leaving these treacherous shores,' sighed Squire Ogden. ''Tis a primitive land and the air is vibrant with disease. What with the wild and dangerous beasts, 'tis truly perplexing that these niggers are not already all dead. In good spirit do we remove them from this land.'

'That is the mission of the Church, my friend,' said the Parson. 'To convert them so that they can join the Lord's Catholic flock. Though I daresay from the look of their evolution and society, 'tis abundantly clear why God has thus far neglected them.'

Rolling his eyes in exasperation, Brigstocke was candid.

'Fiddlesticks, Parson,' he said. 'Their predicament has nothing to do with your Holy Spirit. We came with muskets and cannons. The niggers carry short sword and spear. There is no equality in weaponry. That is why we take them at will. You would do well to remember that. You would also do well to remember that we have sailed to their land. Fortunately, they know not from whence we came. They also have no way of finding out. If you need to show gratitude to anyone, you should show it to men like Ebenezer Blunt who make it possible. You can help the niggers to join the flock as much as you like, Parson. But they will always remain at the bottom of the pile. We are infinitely superior, that is why we enslave them. That is also why God is on our side and not on theirs. Thanks to our trade, Parson, the Church gets its hallowed mitts on converts. We entrepreneurs, on the other hand, get rich.'

'I agree with Brigstocke,' said Squire Ogden. 'But methinks 'tis time to retire from this insufferable heat to the coolness of a cabin with a cot.'

'That it is,' agreed the Parson.

Bidding him good day, the three men went below.

'Set the slave watch if you please, Mister Wimborne,' the captain snapped. 'Prime the six pounder and signal the Director General.'

'Aye aye, sir.'

'Tallow your lead carpenter and sing out the bottom,' said the Second Officer.

'By the mark ten. San' an' mud,' yelled the carpenter. 'By the mark eleven. Mud an' shingle. By the mark fourteen. Shingle.'

Following the report from the signal-cannon, the Director General acknowledged their leave-taking from the ramparts of the fortress by raising his hat. From the poop, the captain bellowed at the sailing master.

'I want a full spread, Mister Graceforth,' he said.

'All hands look lively there,' shouted the sailing master, 'mainsails, staysails and t'gallants.'

Rounding on the Second Officer, the captain snarled:

'Prove the nets if you please, Mister Pobjoy. I want no suicides on this voyage.'

In turn, the Second Officer lambasted the deck crew.

'Avast there you hounds and prove them nets,' he said. 'Make sure you leave no gaps.'

'Inform the snivelling curs, Mister Pobjoy,' said the captain, 'that if a nigger finds his way through the nets, the scoundrel will be made to suffer like one.'

Taking a menacing step forward, the Second Officer turned to the crew.

'You hear that?' he screamed, 'you hear that? I want to see no daylight 'tween the seams.'

Wimborne thought the suicide nets stigmatised the *Pelican*. The netting was like a banner that invariably horrified merchantmen, who he knew would give her kind an uncommonly wide berth. In spite of this, the grand old lady was in her element, heading out to sea under a full sail bound for Pertigua.

Late one afternoon, Wimborne was pacing the deck. Fetid odours wafted up from the hatchways. The stink drew the attention of the lurking captain.

'Get some scoundrels to slop out the niggers, Mister Wimborne,' said the captain. 'There is no profit in any you find ailing. Fling them to the sharks. See they are exercised. Swill them in small batches on deck weekly.'

Smothering his nose with his monogrammed silk handkerchief and trying hard not to inhale, Wimborne stepped below into a chasm of despair. Disconcerted by the whispers darting about in the gloom, he trod gingerly over bodies groaning by the foot of the companionway. A near-naked carpet of black bodies obscured the deck. Men, women and children lay tight-packed, spoon-fashion, nose to neck. Overpowered by the unspeakable stench, he leaned against the bulkhead, closed his eyes and gasped orders to his deckhands.

'Soak them. Soak them,' he said, 'drench them all.'

Throughout the time Wimborne had served on the barque, he had grown increasingly aware of the captain's contempt for his concern for the wellbeing of the slaves. Now certain he had not the belly for the trade, he intended signing off when the *Pelican* returned to Spithead, England. He resolved to remain 'on the shore' until he found a berth on a common trading vessel. A few days earlier, he had had a significant exchange with the Second Officer.

'If you so believe that slaves are set upon without compunction,' the Second Officer had asked, 'why did you of your own accord sign on a slaver? And if you so disagree with this trade, why have you not opposed slavery itself?'

The gibe in the Second Officer's query pierced the veneer of his reformist credentials. On the *Pelican*, he dwelt close to a captain who harboured resentment, envy and distrust and whose most recent order to him confirmed it. It was not standard practice for officers of his rank to attend slaves below decks, but he was ordered to do so by a malicious captain who knew that he would find the conditions on the slave decks eminently disturbing. Indeed, he had been overwhelmed by the environment below. Having executed his assignment, he bolted up the companionway and retched over the gunwales. He then stood gulping huge quantities of clean fresh air.

After wiping his lips, he peered astern. A league away and likewise fringed by suicide-nets, the *Portobello Star*'s mainsail was snagging out. She was full and by when she turned to larboard and a south easterly course, homeward bound for Jamaica. Sharing shuruttu tobacco, the captain and the sailing master were jawing like chums at the poop rails, sizing up the *Portobello Star* until she was hull down.

'I daresay Rutley has made a handsome profit from this little venture,' said the captain. 'What with his share of the prize from that pirate Rogers and deducting the cabiceer's cut with our new method of procuring slaves.'

'Slaves have yet to pay for their lodging and protection,' the sailing master chuckled.

'They'll fetch a good return,' said the captain. 'I want you to examine the niggers for open wounds. Rub vinegar and gunpowder into cuts to stop infection. And Mister Graceforth, I want no slackers on this voyage. Make an example of any man who steps out of line. Got it?'

'I'll make them jump,' grinned the sailing master.

Graceforth had not long to wait. Wimborne was on duty with him when they happened on a seaman grumbling loudly.

'This fodder is fit only for niggers,' wailed the carpenter's mate. 'We ain't niggers. We're white men. We deserve to be treated like white men.'

Seizing him by the scruff of his neck, the sailing master hauled the man onto his feet until they were nose to nose.

'Avast there matey,' he growled, flinging the seaman down at the foot of the mainmast. 'Come and sing your mutinous moans to twenty-five lashes of the cat.'

Frowning at the harshness of the sentence, Wimborne exercised authority.

'Twenty-five lashes is too severe, Mister Graceforth. Reduce his rations instead.'

Faltering in his steps, the sailing master scratched his head.

'Aye, Mister Wimborne,' he said. 'I suppose cutting his rations might accomplish something.'

The captain unexpectedly appeared on deck.

'Belay that order, Mister Graceforth,' he said. 'Reduced rations will merely affect the blackguard's paunch, Mister Wimborne. Twenty-five lashes is insufficient for inciting mutiny. Nay, two hundred lashes is more fitting for a snivelling agitator. That will be far more instructive. I'll have all hands witness punishment, Mister Pobjoy.'

The Second Officer shouted.

'All hands on deck.'

'Prepare your ineffable, Mister Graceforth,' said the captain.

Dutifully, the sailing master walked away to fetch his paraphernalia.

Wimborne noticed the spring in his step. Graceforth had developed a particularly cruel instrument by dipping the last six inches of his lash in a ladle of light pitch, which rapidly hardened as it cooled. The formula added to the torment of the victim, for the stiffened tip peeled off the sufferer's skin in strips. Characteristically, the captain christened the end product 'Graceforth's ineffable.'

Stripped of his jerkin, the carpenter's quivering mate was laid face down across the deck. Ankles chained together, his legs were lashed to a post on the starboard side. His wrists were bound by a rope, the end of which was pulled through a pulley until he was stretched to his full length. It was made fast to a cleat. To intensify the stinging effect of the lash, a bucket of water was thrown over his body. The sailing master sent the hardened tip across the flabby back. It tore away a strip of skin – followed by a piercing scream. Tossing a willow chiv at the feet of the stony-faced captain, the tallyman sang out.

'One!'

The pile of chivs began to grow. When a violent spasm shook the man's frame, the pile had reached one hundred and ten. The *Pelican* no longer possessed a carpenter's mate. The flogging continued.

'One hundred and ninety-nine! Two hundred!'

The final chiv landed. Silently seething seamen stared spellbound at the body of their shipmate. Only the clatter of the sailing master squaring away his equipment could be heard. Blood was spattered across the gunwales. Pools of blood flowed into the scuppers. The man's back was a bloody mess. Down went the Second Officer's thumb. Unruffled by the proceedings, the captain bellowed his lack of sympathy.

'Square away the decks, bo'sun. I want them holystoned as white as a hound's tooth.'

Sewn up in sailcloth, the blood-soaked shroud was dropped unceremoniously over the side. For a while, the only sounds Wimborne could hear were holystones scouring the congealed blood off the deck.

'An extra tot o' rum,' shouted the sailing master, 'to the first man who fetches any nigger who steps out of line.'

Below decks, Kayode had been listening to the proceedings above his head. Though he could not understand the language, the belligerent voices and the anguished screams he fully understood – for a flogging was a flogging in any tongue. He whispered anxiously to the big man.

'If they savage each other in this way,' he asked, 'what they will do to us?'

A huge hand materialised from the shadows. It dangled before his eyes a tiny bag tightly lashed with cord.

'Gold dust, my friend,' the big man whispered, 'it will help you where you go. I give it to you, countryman. You seek not to judge me.'

Whispering his gratitude, Kayode secreted the unexpected bounty beneath his scrotum.

A cold easterly was blowing. The temperature dropped rapidly and the wind was howling from the stern. Wimborne gazed into the sky. Too much sail, he thought.

'Reef in, Mister Graceforth,' he said.

The captain stepped onto the poop deck. Spitting shuruttu over the gunwales, the sailing master set his jaw and waited.

'We have a tropical storm, Mister Graceforth,' said the captain. 'Staysails, t'gallants and jibs.'

Galvanised by the order, the sailing master shouted at the watch on deck.

'Reef in the main and mizzen you scurvy lubbers.'

Donning his weather cloak, Wimborne raised his eyes to the storm clouds gathering ominously in the leaden sky. The temperature was yet falling. A cold wind howled through the rigging. Lightning flashed dangerously close to the main topgallant mast and a thunderclap cracked with a splintering crescendo. The *Pelican* shuddered. Clouds ruptured and driving rain crashed onto her decks. Gigantic seas broke fore-and-aft. Surging along the decks, the seething, foaming torrent swept him off his feet. Drifting spume reduced the visibility. Knee-deep in water, he scanned the white horses gambolling atop the curling waves. A fine spray was drifting in sheets through the rigging. Struggling up a precipitous wave, the *Pelican* paused on the crest and plunged into the trough. Swept into the scuppers, he was soaked to the skin. The vessel rolled heavily to starboard. A dull thud from the bilges told him that the ballast had shifted. Rolling heavily to larboard, she righted herself and rolled uneasily again to starboard. Battered by the elements and flecked by the foam, the gulls cried above the raging wind. Clinging doggedly to the starboard gunwale, he looked around. Between the black clouds, fingers of sunlight eerily probed the waves, throwing a luminescent ghostly light onto the distant horizon. A league astern in the gale-force winds, an albatross sat almost motionless. From the poop, the captain screamed above the wind.

'Start pumping the bilges, bo'sun,' he cried, 'and level out that frigging ballast.'

Re-stowing the stone ballast in the heavy seas was an unenviable and dangerous undertaking. Wimborne felt sorry for the boatswain and six seamen, who were tasked to carry it out. The *Pelican* plunged into another trough.

On the slave deck, Kayode grew anxious.

'We have entered *Elegbara's* province,' he said. 'The sea gods must be very angry.'

'Rubbish,' said the big man, 'this is a storm. This ship will ride it out. It is good we sleep like so, locked together tight so we cannot easily be thrown about. Let me warn you, Kayode, bring no attention to yourself. They will make you regret it. Now they have begun to hurt each other, they will use any excuse to harm us.'

'But we give them no trouble?' he asked.

'Get it into your thick skull, Kayode. In the eyes of the whites, slaves are the colour of threat. Countryman, they flog us, kick us and starve us to terrify. That way they think we will not strike back.'

He fell silent. Rolling abruptly, the *Pelican* was shaken from stem to stern. Seawater gushed over her waist and down her hatchways. The deck was awash. Raising his head, he scoured the length of the deck for Asabi. She was nowhere to be seen. Glancing down at the cadaverous body beside him and then turning to the big man, he whispered.

'This old man he lies very still.'

'Never mind him,' said the big man, dismissively, 'he's not coming with us.'

From the instant he had been chained to the oak deck, the toothless old man had not stirred. Sprawled in a bizarre posture, his filthy loincloth had slipped past his bony knees and his eyes stared hopelessly into the distance. His dribbling wrinkled lips moved.

'I . . . have . . . a . . . vision,' the old man croaked. 'That . . . we cross . . . the big big waters . . . to build . . . .a land of . . . nightmares. We will not . . . ever return . . . to the land of our forefathers.'

His frail voice trailed off. In the faint light, Kayode scanned the half dozen faces gathered around the moribund figure. Simultaneously, he could virtually feel the old man's tenacity summoning his final dregs of energy, inching his way towards death's unfastened door. He was certain that no amount of encouragement or intimidation could force the old man back from the brink. In the mountainous seas, the wind began backing to the south-east. The change in direction threw the *Pelican* onto her beam-ends. An increase in wind speed preceded the line squalls, as gusts of freezing, salty air, howled along the slave deck. The dying man supplied all with a distraction. Hearing his failing words, Kayode felt as if he was being endowed with the responsibility of gathering vital testimony for evidence at some distant, inevitable trial.

A laboured laugh burst from the old man. Tears ran down the deep furrows of his haggard features. Then a skewed smile crossed his lips.

'Oduduwa has . . . been . . . kind . . . He . . . is . . . calling . . . me . . . away,' he rasped. 'These eyes shall . . . not see . . . the . . . joyless . . . day . . . when . . . this . . . voyage ends.'

The aged eyes rolled. His hoarse words grew fainter.

'Seize the wild, wild winds . . . my children. Pluck . . . the ripened fruits . . . and . . . reap . . . the . . . forgotten harvest.'

His weary lids closed. The huddle of faces around him wept. And the careworn figure was gone. From the corner of his eye, Kayode saw the big man wipe away a tear.

'Sleep, Kayode,' said the big man. 'The white devils won't trouble us while this tempest lasts. They will be too busy struggling with the ship.'

The gale raged for three days and nights. During this time no food was thrown down to them. Devoid of rations, Kayode ate live cockroaches and drank seawater. Saturated by sweat and saltwater and given the accumulation of salt in his belly, he had a vision. In his delirium, he beheld a mannish shadow resting on the frames and stringers along the vessel's starboard side. The shadow sighed. It then began wafting through a dark forest until it reached a vast, treeless tract of land. His heartbeat accelerated. A column of men, women and children snaked across the savannah from the villages, towns and cities of the Yoruba. Each one gripped a short sword in a bloody right hand. In the left hand they held a crucified figure affixed to a cross. Subsequently, flogged by faceless figures, thousands of chained slaves were hauling a monstrous cart that metamorphosed into an immeasurable plateau on which rested the corpses of destiny. Wading up to his knees among the bodies in the Abode of the Dead, he sympathised with the enslaved hordes who were staring through empty sockets into the ancient and mysterious Kingdom of the Yoruba. He screamed in anguish with the multitudes. The gods gave no answer. A thick pall of black smoke rose from a pyramid of burning bodies. Festooned in strands of elephant grass, a shimmering figure materialised above the pyre of cold flames. In his delirium he asked himself:

'Was it Sopona? Had the god of suffering slipped on board the ship?'

Shimmering and rustling in the sparse light, the apparition stayed pointing an accusing finger. He hid his face. The spirit drew nearer until it was hovering above his head. From its face a prodigious orifice slowly disgorged Asabi into a festering swamp. He awoke with a jolt. His teeth chattered and his body shook with fever. He felt a hand stroking his forehead as a soothing voice entered his ears.

'Be still boy,' the voice counselled. 'Shhh. Shhh. You be here boy. You be here.'

'I did not do enough to hinder the white men,' he whimpered. 'I did not do enough . . . '

'Be still boy,' said the voice. 'Be still.'

Closing his heavy lids, he drifted off.

Late next afternoon, two frigate birds sat high in the sky below tufts of downy clouds. The storm had cost the *Pelican* precious time. Pondering on his captain's options, Wimborne walked the poop deck. Due to the ferocity of a storm that had visibly unsettled the captain, the *Pelican* had lain helpless for three days. The weather had determined the course of events. Consequently, the barque had bowed to the true Master. On these occasions, he knew his captain felt powerless, a feeling that did not square with the gruff likes of him. Gazing aloft at where the main and mizzen t'gallants had snapped off, he dropped his eyes to the main deck. It was in complete disarray. Slave nets girdling the ship had been torn to shreds and the poles onto which they had been lashed were no longer in evidence. A great deal of time had been lost. Thus he approached the captain with caution when he stepped before the helm.

'The slaves have been drinking seawater and eating rats and roaches, sir,' he said. 'Permission to wash and give them fresh water.'

'Give 'em some food and plenty of fresh water, Mister Wimborne.'

'Aye aye, sir' he said.

Bestowing a sardonic grin, the captain jabbed his forefinger at the main deck.

'But permission to wash the niggers is granted, Mister Wimborne,' he said, 'only when all your storm clutterance festooning the ship has been squared away.'

'Aye aye, sir,' he said.

It will take a few days before the storm damage is cleared, he thought. Until then, the starved inhabitants of the slave deck would have to remain in squalor.

14 July 1750: 23.30 hrs

That night a frosty moon hovered above the horizon like a monarch's fingernail. It cast an opalescent light on the dark clouds that were welling up over the western limits. The storm will serve to remind them all, thought Wimborne, just how close and sudden, harrowing and formidable is the cruel silent space between life and death.

A breeze gossiped through the rigging. Tap, tap, tapping of blocks and tackles broke the ascending hush. Oblivious of the activity behind him, he gripped the stern rails of the poop deck with his legs braced apart.

'The captain's breed,' the sailing master had said, 'generate profits for the Royal African Company and for England.'

He had recounted to Wimborne the primary cause of the master mariner's capricious disposition. Captain Blunt had been greatly disturbed by the account of the Spaniard, Vincente de Escobedo, the first European to make the momentous discovery that:

'Beyond yon horizon layeth an ample abundance of horizons.'

Some five years before Columbus set sail on the caravel *Nina*, de Escobedo had sailed into an inlet of a large island. There he met with a people called the Arawaque. Not possessing the required representation in the Royal Spanish Court of Ferdinand and Isabella, the explorer was unsuccessful in obtaining the imperative *Carta Reconocimientto* – a document without which:

'You failed to see that which you claim to have seen.'

Thus, de Escobedo did not receive the recognition that went with his discovery of the island inhabited by the Arawaque, or indeed have any of his discoveries proofed. Because of his infinitely superior connections, Columbus received the credit due to de Escobedo. Drawing Wimborne closer, the Second Officer lowered his voice.

'You see sir, though he does not allude to it, Captain Blunt shares the resentment held by the Spaniard. As he sees it, men like de Escobedo were thwarted because of men with connections – gentlemen like you, Mister Wimborne.'

At the sound of four bells the boatswain had done his duty. Breaking away from directing the repair of ratlines and the manning of the bilge pumps, Wimborne started down the deck scouring the horizon. Streaks of silky daylight were breaking into the fervent hues of a rich tropical sunrise. The wind that had been backing easterly for the past hours gradually lessened. The freshening air bode a more clement day and better sailing conditions seemed assured. A husky voice grumbled up from the crew's quarters. Catching the whiff of something he did not like the sound of, Wimborne halted in his stride.

'The Old Man's a skunk of a seadog.'

'The feed 'e gives us ain't fit fer pigs.'

'Keep your blathering down before he whips out the cat an' gives you double rations.'

'Omens weren't good for this voyage. I sees a burning star in the sky the night 'fore we sailed. So I brought me rabbit's foot with me. 'Cos this here voyage is Blunt's thirteenth. And thirteen ain't a healthy number.'

Trying hard yet failing to identify the culprits from their voices alone, Wimborne stayed soundlessly attentive to the mutinous talk. These empty-headed buffoons are steeped in superstition and hampered by ignorance, he thought. He blamed the clairvoyants, the soothsayers and the fortune-tellers of England's seaports and villages, for peddling wares-of-dogma among the poor and illiterate.

He approached the captain on the forepeak.

'Can the watch be fed, Captain Blunt?'

Receiving no reply, he judged the man to be feigning deafness. He knew that his manner of command was autocratic. Aboard the *Pelican* his power was absolute. Wimborne owned a curious relationship with his captain. At sea, his captain was God. But it was he, Thomas Wimborne, who was the master in every sense. Not only could he navigate more accurately, he was also better acquainted with every seam and scarph joint on the *Pelican*, a vessel of three hundred and twenty tons burthen. He knew her sailing capabilities, strengths and vulnerabilities. His captain had forgotten most of these and did little to improve his understanding of them. In the critical area of handling men, he also believed his captain fell short. Most certainly, his captain's authority depended on an old saw: ' . . . that men harbour a fearful respect of those who hold naked power.'

Accordingly, his captain behaved as if his crew were a seafaring rabble to be exploited in the furtherance of his slaving ambitions. Knowing that grumbling stomachs make for disgruntled seamen, he restated his petition.

'Can I feed the watch, Captain Blunt?'

'Carry on, Mister Wimborne,' he growled.

16 July 1750

It was midday and stifling. Wimborne ordered the first twenty slaves on deck to be soaked and exercised. Draped over the rails, deckhands showed little interest in the morose laundry until the very last slave, a tall, shapely, ebony-black full-bosomed woman, stepped on deck. Rapt in her beguiling curves, the seamen began jeering and yelling lewd remarks.

Taking advantage of the sensuous distraction, an elderly man and woman holding hands hurried awkwardly for the larboard rails. Before anyone had moved, the pair scrambled over the side and through a gap in the suicide nets, vanishing beneath the waves leaving not a trace of their previous existence.

Swallowing hard and gawping with incredulity at the extreme sacrifice, Wimborne walked unsteadily to the gunwales, gazed into the waters and uttered a prayer. Wading into the eighteen remaining slaves with musket butts, the crew pummelled them into a squatting huddle. Bleeding profusely from a cut, a broad-shouldered slave punched a seaman clear across the deck. Purple-faced and spluttering, the captain screamed.

'Fetch me that nigger and attend to the nets.'

Strutting around the crouching slaves, the captain let fly.

'Strikes a white man does he? I will teach him who is God. I will show you what happens if a nigger lifts even a finger to a white man. I will make him suffer. Then I will hang him right before your black eyes.'

Snapping back his shoulders, the captain pronounced sentence.

'Fifty lashes and thumb screws if you please, Mister Graceforth,' he said. 'This nigger will never again strike a white man.'

Thus condemned, the slave was strung up by his wrists from the main yardarm. Wimborne's throat dried. Eighteen slaves and the *Pelican's* crew and officers were the exclusive witnesses to what happened next. Fifty lashes were applied. Then a hangman's noose was dropped around the neck of the half-conscious slave. Taking up the slack, the six-man crew heaved. The slave rose up onto his toes. Fingering the palpitating abdomen of his petrified victim, the captain turned around with a twinkle in his eye and grinned.

'Forget the screws, Mister Graceforth,' he said. 'I have a different scheme. I think this one has been belly-worshipping.'

Grasping his sword handle, the captain drew a finger lovingly along its shining edge. Wimborne glanced anxiously at the Second Officer, who looked impassively back at him. Turning back to the unfolding drama, he was aware of the sailing master by the hatch coaming, eyeing the episode with morbid curiosity.

Placing the tip of the sword at the top of the victim's pulsing ribcage, the captain turned with an evil grin. A queasy sensation crept into Wimborne's gut. Turning to the six-man pulling crew, the captain jerked his thumb upwards. Trotting backwards with the rope, they yanked the victim high into the air. The blade sliced the belly open from top to bottom. Out gushed a bloody porridge. Twitching and groaning, the disembowelled slave swung back and forth with his entrails convulsing above the deck. Strangling in the fresh breeze, a trail of blood along the deck defined the full extent of his pendular motion.

Flecked with blood, some slaves fell to the deck in sheer terror. A handful stood gawping at the horrifying spectacle. The Second Officer remained deadpan. Ambling across the deck with his hands behind him, the sailing master perused the gory handiwork. Steadying himself on the gunwales, Wimborne retched quietly over the side. Wiping his blade on his cabin boy's jerkin and his blood-spattered face on his own sleeve, the captain gave orders to the sailing master.

'Shark bait, Mister Graceforth,' he said. 'Leave him dangling until I say cut him down. He will serve as an *aide memoire*. Splice the mainbrace. Break out the pipes. Sort out that big-bosomed wench the men were gawking at. Drag her to my cabin after supper with some rope. We have a long passage ahead of us. A man must sow his seed to tone his muscles.'

'Aye aye, sir,' the sailing master said, giving a roguish grin.

The captain turned to the Second Officer.

'Log it, Mister Pobjoy,' he said. 'Slave number thirty-four died while attempting to escape.'

The Second Officer grinned slyly at the captain.

'Aye aye, sir,' he replied.

'Get them niggers below,' the Second Officer shouted at the deck watch, 'and throw them some feed. We'll soak them tomorrow.'

'Aye aye, Mister Pobjoy,' replied the bo'sun.

Following supper, the sailing master hauled the woman to the doorway of the captain's cabin as ordered. Through a chink in the bulkhead of his adjoining cabin, Wimborne witnessed the proceedings. Kicking the door shut, the captain took stock of his victim, who stood rooted with fright.

Despite her debasement, Wimborne could see the contempt in her eyes. Suddenly, the captain slapped her face, hard. Wimborne winced. She screamed and collapsed onto the cot, sobbing hysterically with blood pouring from her nose. Sitting astride her chest and uncoiling the rope, the sweating mariner lashed her wrists together. Up on deck, the carousing crew were jigging to the trill and tremolo of the hornpipes. The stamp and bellow of revelry rose to a pitch.

Rolling her onto her stomach, the captain secured her bound wrists to a hook fixed to the bulkhead. Forcing her thighs apart and spreading her legs, he secured them in position by tying her feet to iron rings fixed to the deck. Panting heavily, he ripped off the fragment of cloth concealing her nook and slumped into his chair to examine her pinioned frame. Steadying himself against the roll of the barque, he unfastened his breeches and began masturbating. Then splaying her buttocks apart, he thrust frenziedly back and forth. In moments, with a laboured grunt he collapsed onto her back. She shrieked. Jerking himself out of her, the sweaty captain fell back into his chair panting. Wimborne clenched his fists. Incredibly, the captain sat masturbating, set for another foray. Wimborne could look no longer. At the change of the midnight watch, he heard the captain yell for the Second Officer.

''Tis your turn, Mister Pobjoy,' he said. 'A prime lay waits for you in my cabin. Take her to yours. Afterwards, give Graceforth his turn.'

'Aye aye, Captain sir,' said Pobjoy. 'And Mister Wimborne, sir?'

'Our nautical popinjay would have no appetite for her kind,' the captain replied. 'He'd want milky-white skin in silken knickerbockers to get it up. Nay, Mister Pobjoy, he can wrist himself in his cot.'

Slumping gladly onto his cot, Wimborne leaned back against the bulkhead and groaned. Signing on the *Pelican* was an endeavour of his own making, and he felt trapped in his station as a transporter of slaves. He knew what the company's articles expected of him. But he was in no doubt that fornicating with that half-conscious woman was not part of his assignment. With a long resigned sigh, he left his cabin and made his way on deck to fill his lungs with fresher air.

Augustfields, Yorkshire

England

August 1750

The great-great-great grandson of Sir William Ampleforth Fleming, Randolph Fleming, had inherited a fortune, which included the Yorkshire estate of twenty-two thousand acres surrounding the mansion house of Augustfields. Like his ancestors, he was Magistrate for the District of Marchington. In the West Indian archipelago of Pertigua, he was owner of Turtle Island on which stood the Beaumaris Great House. As well, he owned the China Lights plantation, comprising three thousand acres, and five hundred acres south of Crab Mountain on Little Pertigua.

Subsequent to his great-great-great grandfather's flight from the Puritans in 1616, his family acquired the motto: *Deus est meum perfugium* – God is my refuge.

If truth be told, he was not an ardent Catholic. Nonetheless, he was, in his own way, true to his faith and in times of trouble, he sought solace in the arms of the Catholic Church.

Looking younger than his fifty-one years, he was straight and stout with big brown eyes, a round head and long bushy sideburns. When she was barely twenty, he had married Elizabeth Seymour. The daughter of a ship owner and the mother of their fifteen-year-old son, Matthew, his spirited wife had made and kept him a very contented man.

Submerged in the murk of a dreary afternoon, the peace of Augustfields was broken by the arrival of a horse-backed courier. Fleming examined the delivered letter. From the handwritten address he knew it was from his close friend Harry Blake. An instinct told him that the missive brought untimely news.

Blake's Coffeehouse,
Eastcheap,
London.

August 10th, 1750

My Dear Randolph – Further to my last letter, I fear that matters have deteriorated. The latest figures in the Shipping Journal confirm our worst fears. It would appear that shipping losses overall have had a dire effect on sugar imports. The market is forty percent down. It is imperative that something be done.

I spent a joyous evening in the company of the Prime Minister yester night at his club. I thought you should know that I did meet in his party a John Harrison Esquire, the inventor of the marine chronometer. He is a carpenter by trade, a very clever gentleman and agreeable, though he was for the most part quiet. I am led to believe that his invention, once approved by the Admiralty, will bring about accurate navigation. If that be true, then it would suit our trade splendidly considering our need for speedy shipping deliveries and prediction of arrivals. Pelham is in good spirits, and I understand that the cause of his pleasure being most certainly the recent votes in Parliament, which have all gone his way. The Whigs are loyal at present. I took the opportunity to converse with him over the nature of our concerns. He gave me his assurance that his government would be interested in any thoughts we may have on a curative.

For that reason, it is a matter of great urgency that the Cartel convenes while we have the ear of the Prime Minister. Your presence is urgently required. I shall inform the Secretary that you will attend at midday on August 25th. We shall be meeting at my Eastcheap coffee-house.

We did so enjoy our last visit to Augustfields.

Our love to dear Elizabeth.

Your loyal friend,

Harry.

Strolling down the oak-panelled gallery, Randolph Fleming paused appreciatively before the long looking glass to smooth the creases of his embroidered satin waistcoat, knee-length breeches and cream silk stockings. Smiling to himself at the resilience of his family through times gone by, he entered the panelled library. Even in the month of August, the room was redolent with wood smoke from the fires of winter. His eyes wandered around the softly lit chamber. Dear Harry, he thought, would that half the men in the kingdom were as trusty as you.

A maidservant had lit the Italian oil lamp and the polished table shone under its glow. Despite the elegant pieces of furniture, the library was sombre. A gust of air rattled the windowpanes. The clatter of hooves on the carriage-drive drew his attention. Through the great window, he saw a liveried courier galloping away.

Elizabeth burst excitedly into the library waving an opened letter. He smiled. At thirty-seven, she was disarmingly pretty and green-eyed, with that almost translucent skin of the redhead. And she was English, very English, with the delicate familiarity of an English garden. He treasured the grace and sophistication she had brought to Augustfields.

''Tis another courier, Randolph,' she said. 'The King is going to review the Duke's Regiment at York Barracks next week. Following the review he is giving a banquet to which we have received a personal invitation. Is that not perfectly delightful? I shall wear my . . . '

Raising his hand, he curtailed her sentence.

'I'm afraid I have to disappoint you, Bess,' he said. 'I have received a communication from our dear friend Harry Blake. Here, read it for yourself, my dear. We shall be leaving for London this night.'

Taking a seat by the window, she read his letter. Looking up at him, he saw the unease in her eyes.

'Is it not possible that dear Harry exaggerates?' she asked.

'We cannot take that risk,' he said softly, 'our prospects depend on it.'

'Unquestionably,' she replied, 'I shall instruct the servants to pack our baggage. I shall as well send word to my sister Emma to expect us. We shall lodge with her. And of course Matthew shall travel with us. It will be his first visit to London. It will excite the boy so.'

Though worried by Blake's letter, he gave her a reassuring smile.

London

The carriage rumbled through the streets of London. Fleming smiled dotingly on his wife and son chattering excitedly about the unfamiliar sights. Gazing out of the window, he too was soon engrossed in the activity on the pavements. The crisis on the West Indian plantations was evident on the streets. Criers with news-sheets were shouting about the latest shortages of sugar. Determined to keep up with the escalating state of affairs, he stopped the carriage to buy one. Frowning deeply, he read an account regarding the French capture of an English slave convoy off the colony of Saint Lucia. In a fierce action, HMS *Incredible* was sunk and the *Invincible* had been fired and grounded, with the loss of twenty sailors. We must act decisively to put an end to this affront, he thought.

The sugar crisis was deepening daily. In the western approaches of the English Channel, warships displaying no flag had attacked an English sugar convoy. France had been suspected of committing the outrage. He liked to believe that it was a backlash from King George's War, which had ended two years previously. That bitter conflict had pitted Prussia, France and Spain against Austria and England. France had fought on the losing side. Nettled by the defeat, a number of French captains continued to harry English merchant vessels. Attacks by buccaneers on English slave convoys had also intensified in the past year. Fresh slave rebellions on English sugar plantations had further reduced the flow of sugar. On London's dining tables and in her drawing rooms and kitchens, the revolts had rendered the sweetener a scarce commodity.

Sighing thoughtfully, he was turning over the news-sheet when an article caught his eye. At a meeting in an Eastcheap coffeehouse in the City of London, Members of the West Indies Sugar Cartel had demanded action from the Prime Minister. Reports of that meeting revealed that under orders couriered from Downing Street, their Lordships at the Admiralty were commanded to devise a comprehensive response.

Rumbling along the toll road heading towards the Piccadilly home of his wife's sister, they passed by the sprawling scaffolded site of the new British Museum. Nine days before, he had set out with his wife and son from Augustfields. They were now passing the costermongers of Seven Dials, who were hawking counterfeited Josiah Wedgwood buttons, Maiden Blush apples, oranges and vegetables from handcarts and street stands. Plying their timeless trade, smiling harlots lurked in the doorways. Hansom cabs clattered on the cobblestones down Saint Martin's Lane.

Turning onto Pall Mall, the carriage slowed along the genteel thoroughfare of fashionable showrooms. Confirming the class of the neighbourhood, elegantly dressed ladies strolled into view, escorted by dandies with flamboyant knots, tightly clutching the hilt of their sword canes. The sight of the rich raised his spirits. This is London at its finest, he thought.

It had been a warm day and the light was fading. Grimy-faced men wielding long cumbersome poles were tending the oil-burning street lamps.

'Are those men paid just to light the lamps, Father?' his son asked.

'Lamplighters,' he said, smiling affectionately. 'We are in the world's greatest city, Matthew, so the streets must be well lit. It would not do to leave the populace of this great city to the mercy of footpads at night.'

'London sits at the very heart of our Empire,' exclaimed his wife. 'She must be shown off to the world by day and by night.'

The bells of St Mary's struck seven. Hard by Dover Street off Piccadilly, they turned into the carriage drive of Hardwicke House, the grand five-storey Georgian residence of Peter Sackville, Emma's husband.

They were shown into the blue withdrawing room to be welcomed by the Sackvilles. At first sight, Fleming thought that his sister-in-law's blushes matched her bois-de-rôse brocaded silk robe. She bestowed her greetings and smiles like royalty dispensing largesse. In spite of her evident sociable spirits, he nevertheless thought she seemed remote. Dressed in a black silk coat, knee-length breeches and white stockings, her husband waited with a fixed smile. He could feel the tension passing between the couple.

'Dear sister Elizabeth, what joy it is to see you,' said Emma. ''Tis a pity that it has to be under such worrying conditions. I trust your journey was without incident?'

Elizabeth sighed and then replied.

'It was a wearisome journey, dear sister,' she said. 'Randolph was summoned in such haste we had little time to pack any sweetmeats. Ten days ago we took delivery of a consignment of sugar from our estates in Pertigua. In our haste, we managed to snatch a mere quintal as we departed.'

'A quintal indeed?' said Emma. ''Tis a handsome quantity and most welcome news.'

She turned to her husband as if she had just remembered his presence.

'Is it not so, Peter?' she asked, frostily.

Without waiting for his reply, she continued.

'Sugar is in such short supply, Elizabeth. I fear the populace may take to the streets at any moment. Profiteering is rife, sugar thieves and footpads abound in the city. We keep the sugar under a stout lock in Peter's study.'

Turning to her nephew and not pausing for breath, Emma effervesced.

'My oh my, how you have grown Matthew,' she said. 'You are quite the young man now. Your cousins will hardly recognise you.'

Smiling shyly, Matthew responded.

'Thank you, Aunt Emma,' he said. 'It is my first time in London. I have seen the lamplighters and the phaeton carriages and the King's Dragoons.'

Chuckling at his son's enthusiasm, Fleming made his excuses to the ladies and followed his brother-in-law out of the room.

Elizabeth examined the countenance of her sister, as she gave directions to a manservant.

'Tell the girls that I want them to come here,' said Emma, 'and instruct cook to prepare supper for the children.'

'As you wish, ma'am.'

'I trust all is well at Augustfields, dearest Elizabeth?' asked Emma.

'Indeed, Emma, indeed. And we have thus far been enjoying a splendid summer. Before Harry Blake's correspondence, we had planned to attend the King's review of the Duke's Regiment at York Barracks. Then we were going to banquet with the King – at his personal invitation, of course. But this dreadful sugar crisis has put paid to all that. We now await the harvest. After that we plan to return to Pertigua. Randolph believes that the prevailing conditions warrant our return to the islands as soon as possible, for we are short of slaves. Not to mention that some of them persist in foolish acts of sabotage, which has considerably reduced our profits. We cannot afford to lose the revenue . . . '

The appearance of her adolescent nieces stopped her in mid-flow. Amid shrieks of delight, the two girls curtsied and greeted her simultaneously.

'Welcome to London, Aunt Elizabeth,' they said. 'And welcome to our house.'

Charmed by the mannerly improvement in her nieces, she smiled broadly.

'Why thank you, girls,' she replied, 'your welcome is most enchanting.'

'You remember your cousin Matthew?' asked Emma. 'He will be staying with us for a few days. You are to take care of him while he is in London. Go with your cousins to the parlour, Matthew.'

Chattering excitedly, the cousins left the room. The instant the door closed, her sister's face clouded over.

'Dear sister,' said Emma, lowering her voice, 'I fear that all is not well between my husband and myself.'

Gently taking Emma's hand, Elizabeth spoke softly.

'What ails thee, dear sister?'

'Peter has lost a fortune as a result of the sugar crisis,' Emma whispered. 'And his losses have opened an abyss between us . . . '

In the library, Fleming and Peter Sackville were comfortably ensconced, with port in hand. From an analysis of the sheets of intelligence forwarded by the West Indies Sugar Cartel, Sackville delivered a report on the dire state of the sugar markets. As he listened to the inventory of problems, Fleming scrutinised the troubled man.

Tall, pale and athletic, Sackville spent a great deal of time pursuing his business interests in London's gentlemen's clubs and coffeehouses. By all accounts, his otherwise undistinguished appearance had surprisingly captivated Emma at first sight. Fleming recalled when his sister-in-law had first told him how warm and considerate she had found Sackville to be. Bequeathed a substantial sum by his father, Sackville invested heavily in sugar. It seemed that his finances had been hammered in the current sugar crisis. The shipping companies and West Indian plantations in which he had invested had been among those hardest hit by piracy and slave rebellions. Sackville was now staring at financial ruin.

'Dividends from my shares in shipping and sugar have fallen drastically,' Sackville said. 'I am poorer by ten thousand guineas, Randolph. Bingley, my broker, tells me that I should invest in another commodity altogether, unless sugar recovers quickly enough to make good my losses. We shall meet my broker at Blake's this night. After some refreshments I propose we leave for Eastcheap. I trust that meets with your approval, Randolph?'

'Certainly, Peter, but it ails me to hear of your misfortune. Nevertheless, it would be a flawed venture to divest yourself of your remaining shares. My advice would be to expand your holdings and . . . '

'Increase them, Randolph?' Is that not a preposterous notion in the current state of affairs? As it is my losses threaten my marriage. To buy more shares would, I fear, initiate the prospect of an unseemly public separation. Emma would first have me flailed. Unless, that is, you have a proposition to remedy my situation?'

'Believe me when I say I am grieved to hear of your circumstances. Pray God they may be short-lived. Nonetheless Peter, I want you to listen carefully and hear me out. I am in possession of a scheme that should increase our stock of slaves and our profits. While we are about it, we can reform the trade by excising the French, the interlopers and the freebooters. This is how I see it.

'Firstly, there would be a lowering of slave tariffs on the coast of Guinea by the issuing of Letters Patent to English vessels for the legal abduction of slaves. Simultaneously, the practice of buying slaves from the Kings and cabiceers would be scaled down. Secondly, the number of English ships plying the coast of Guinea would be doubled or even tripled. Thirdly, His Majesty's Navy would be required to maintain a continuous presence along that coast under the pretext of a Commission for the Suppression of Pirates, similar to the mission His Majesty's Ship *Resolution* is presently embarked upon. Naval captains must be confident that the Admiralty would turn a blind eye should they find space aboard their vessels for shipping a few slaves. Finally, to counteract the accusations of cruelty which the trade in slaves has attracted, certain Churchmen will be prevailed upon to provide spiritual justification for these measures.'

With a smile, he concluded his advice.

'I think that should allay all our fears, Peter. Would you not agree?'

His brother-in-law sighed.

'An indubitably fine stratagem, Randolph. You have clearly given it much consideration. I am certain Emma will be heartened by your plan, as will the Cartel. With the support of the Church, I cannot see that the League Against the Importation of Negroes can pose a threat. I shall fetch my hat and cane. We leave for Eastcheap at once.'

Awaiting his brother-in-law, he thought back to when he first learned about the League Against the Importation of Negroes from the Coast of Guinea. During his very last visit to London at Purvis and Purvis, his Jermyn Street shirt maker, he chanced upon a Bertrand de La Fontaine, an agreeable Frenchman in his early forties. Grandson of the renowned storyteller, Jean de La Fontaine, he was a wine importer from the Champagne region. He recalled how the haughty airs in the Frenchman's manner were reflected in his Gallic nose and framed by the long black curls of a powdered horsehair wig. Having time to spare, he accepted the Frenchman's invitation for refreshments at his club where he made known his trade in sugar. At that, the Frenchman had been impatient to acquaint him with intelligence regarding certain 'Christian men of conscience' who were hostile to his trade. As a corollary these men had founded the League. Fleming had been scathing.

'What Englishmen should have on their minds,' he had said, 'are England's interests!'

'Perhaps, Monsieur Fleming,' replied the Frenchman calmly. 'You should meet with these Christians. And maybe even the creature of their arguments? Say the word, Monsieur, and I will arrange it. I am acquainted with a Monsieur Beecham and his enchanting wife. They were unhappily without progeny and to my surprise adopted a child from the Indies. That child is now a man. I myself have met this, how you say it, nigger. He is clothed just like us. *Exactement.* He speaks with much eloquence against the trade. And he brings credible light to bear on the cruelty he says people of his skin suffer. He also says that he himself is proof of a person who is able to do more than just cut cane. I am not altogether persuaded by this League, Monsieur. But I think that if it were not so, how you say, visible, perhaps your trade would secure more support?'

Moreover, the Frenchman had divulged a disconcerting discourse he was party to in the libertarian salon of Lady Anne Reynolds, Countess of Windermere. Disturbingly, the views expressed were sympathetic to the philosophy of the League Against the Importation of Negroes from the Coast of Guinea.

If handled judiciously, thought Fleming, the League should pose few problems. And if the Cartel follows my advice, losses in sugar will soon be overtaken by profit. Nevertheless, he had felt persuaded to meet with the men of conscience when he was next in London. He was beginning to look upon the League with more than mild curiosity.

It was dark and gone nine-thirty. Rattling along Eastcheap in the City of London, the carriage halted outside Blake's Coffeehouse. Stepping onto the pavement of the congested street, Fleming eyed the building. It was a brick-built establishment with huge window frames which held a myriad of crown glass panes. Opening the door, they were assaulted by the pungent whiff of coffee and tobacco and the hubbub from the crowded smoke-filled rooms. Lit by oil lamps and candles and linked by arches, the ground floor contained three large chambers. There was an assortment of tables and upholstered banquettes. These were filled by bewigged Members of the West Indies Sugar Cartel, dressed in expensive brightly coloured silk coats, waistcoats and breeches. In the cellars lay the Chinese Room, where moneyed gentry smoked opium and played for high stakes at the mah-jongg tables. Blake's was famed for this dimly lit sanctum, set aside for patrons with an interest in toasting their good fortune in the shipping markets or drowning their losses. Aficionados simply came to chase the dragon.

Waiters jumped to the snap of the maitre d'hotel. Messenger boys scurried about delivering commodity reports and maritime intelligence. Stopping at the table of a tousled-haired plump gentleman glued to a plain-covered book, Sackville bent down.

'What is the work that commands your attention so, my friend?'

Raising his head, the gentleman grinned.

'Scandal, dear boy, scandal,' he said. 'I have the talk of all London in my hands.'

'Mister Bingley. May I present my brother-in-law, Squire Randolph Fleming.'

'Delighted to make your acquaintance, Squire Fleming,' said the broker, rising to his feet.

Giving a slight bow, Fleming asked:

'May one ask the name of the work and its author?'

'Fanny Hill penned by a certain John Cleland,' replied the broker, sitting back down. 'I have one of only two hundred copies. It seems that the author was imprisoned for debt. In return for being bailed out of Newgate by a printer friend, he agreed to write this lewd novel.'

'And how do you find his work, Mister Bingley?' Fleming asked. 'Is it anything near as bawdy as I have been led to believe?'

'It is everything they say it is, Squire Fleming,' the broker replied, with a lustful grin. 'Inspired. Magnificently obscene.'

'I look forward to reading it.' Sackville interjected.

'And so you shall, Peter,' the broker said, beckoning to a waiter and giving a wayward grin. 'You can borrow this one when I am finished with it. A large pot of coffee, waiter. Not forgetting a bowl of sugar and a porringer of molasses.'

The waiter promptly returned bearing a steaming pot of coffee and sweeteners. Behind the waiter stood a tall man with a refined bearing. He was distinctive in his powdered tie wig and toupet-black ribbon solitaire. Smiling and rising to his feet, Fleming greeted the proprietor of the coffeehouse, Harry Blake.

'My dear Randolph,' said Blake, 'many thanks for attending at such short notice.'

'We came the instant we received your communication, Harry,' he replied. 'An impressive gathering I might say. I see everyone is here.'

'Everyone, except the Duke of Chandois who will be addressing the Cartel,' replied Blake, and then lowering his voice. 'The word is that he has lost fifty thousand guineas due to the state of the market.'

'A princely sum,' said Sackville. 'Does he not have Pelham's ear, Randolph?'

'I believe he enjoys the confidence of the Prime Minister,' Fleming replied. 'We shall need his connections to effect the strategy I have in mind.'

'What is the nature of this scheme of yours, Randolph?' asked Blake.

'Be seated, Harry,' said Fleming. 'Let me acquaint you with the particulars. I shall need your help to sell it to the Members.'

At ten-thirty, the Duke of Chandois swept into the coffeehouse at the head of a fashionably clad entourage. With a flamboyant display of consequence, he took his seat at a reserved table adjacent to Fleming's.

'I am heartened by your presence, Squire Fleming. We live in troubled times.'

'We do indeed,' he replied. 'No doubt Your Grace will be interested to hear my scheme for a remedial course of action? I think it should resolve our present difficulties and even turn a little profit.'

'Sounds intriguing, Squire Fleming. Pray tell me what is this proposal of yours?'

'At the outset, Your Grace, let me say that to facilitate my plan we will need to make use of your connections.'

Leaning towards him, the Duke beckoned him to continue. He began to lay out his ideas at the end of which the aristocrat looked up approvingly.

'Indeed?' he asked.

Deeming the nobleman's response to be that of interest, he spoke quietly to the Principal Shareholder of the Royal African Company. Subsequent to revealing the finer points of his proposal, they sat back and drank a toast to a gentlemen's agreement.

'I shall commend it to the Members myself, Squire Fleming,' said the Duke, standing up to raise his hand and his voice.

'Honourable Members, Honourable Members.'

The commotion in the coffeehouse subsided.

'Honourable Members,' said the Duke. 'It is well known that Frenchie harasses our vessels on the high seas. He plays havoc with our trade in the Indies and in the Atlantic. I am confident you will agree that this is an undisguised threat to England's mercantile interests and consequently to ours.'

'Pelham sleeps,' yelled a voice.

'But with whom?' cried another.

Laughter flooded the coffeehouse.

'As I see it slave prices are too high,' said the Duke. 'Interlopers contend for a share of our profits. Pirates never lag far behind. In addition, slaves on our plantations persist in acts of sabotage, constantly rebelling against their masters. They seem to have forgotten the reason why we transported them all the way to the Indies – at a great cost to ourselves I might add. They also seem to have eradicated from their minds who it is that feeds, clothes and furnishes them with dwellings. The result being that sugar production has dropped by forty percent.'

Employing a hard edge to his voice, the Duke was forthright.

'The time has come to strip the hair of the dog,' he said. 'What say you?'

'Shame on Pelham and his government,' an angry voice yelled.

The Members howled agreement. The Duke shouted above the uproar.

'Gentlemen, gentlemen,' he cried. 'Squire Fleming has outlined a course of action to me which I believe will indisputably transform this regretful state of affairs. I think it is worthy of your consideration. With your concurrence I shall put his proposed line of action to the Prime Minister. Honourable Members, I give you Squire Fleming.'

The biting aroma of coffee and opium pervaded the coffeehouse. Fleming rose to his feet to outline his plan. His hushed audience hung on his every word. All that could be heard was the shuffle of feet and the clink of fine china.

Mid Atlantic: August 24 1750, 12.00 hrs

Wimborne was pacing the main deck, deep in thought. The watch were grumpily holystoning the decks, effecting repairs and feeding the slaves. Close to midday, the captain spoke to the Second Officer on the poop.

'Mister Pobjoy,' he said, 'I want a word with that cabiceer who titles himself Captain Tomba. You know, the big one who reckons himself. Fetch him here. General Tugwell forewarned me about that one.'

'Aye aye, sir,' replied the Second Officer.

A sense of foreboding filled Wimborne. He leaned over the gunwales. His eye was caught by a lone albatross sitting on the water, scooping scraps thrown from the *Pelican*. The large web-footed seabird suddenly ran over the surface flapping its wings, leapt into the brisk headwind, soared high into the air and out of sight.

Returning with the cabiceer, who was a striking, surly-faced, broad-shouldered character, the Second Officer kicked the big slave onto his knees.

'So you are the illustrious Captain Tomba?' asked the captain, derisively.

'Yes Massa,' replied the cabiceer, submissively. 'They call me Captain Tomba.'

Taking hold and twisting the cabiceer's ear, the captain said: 'Now see here nigger. I'm called Captain Blunt because I get to the point.'

The cabiceer remained silent with his gaze fixed ahead. Impatiently, the captain snarled at him.

'I am the Captain. You're a Captain, Mister Tomba. Are you a Captain as well, Mister Pobjoy?'

'Nay, Captain Blunt,' said the Second Officer. 'I am not. And I would not call myself Captain if I were not.'

''Tis not healthy for a vessel to have two masters,' said the captain. 'Is it Mister Wimborne?'

'Nay, sir,' he replied, half-heartedly.

'T'will lead to . . . ' said the captain.

'Confusion!' cried the Second Officer.

'Aye, that it will,' agreed the captain. 'What shall we do with this here sham Captain, Mister Pobjoy?'

'Strip him of his bogus rank, sir.'

'Are you a Captain?' shouted Blunt, 'or are you slave number forty-eight?'

The cabiceer hesitated and then, dropping his eyes to the deck, answered.

'They call me slave forty-eight, Massa.'

'How right you are,' the captain said. 'We shall hear no more of your Captain Tomba business. Got it?'

'I got it, Massa.'

'That is how we get results, Mister Wimborne,' said the captain.

Giving a disingenuous bow, Wimborne smiled to himself. The old seadog, he thought, has been outwitted by the cabiceer's expeditious acquiescence. But he was horribly aware that this master mariner was bound to modify his tactics.

'Slave forty-eight,' said the captain, 'you must suffer a forfeit for impersonating an officer aboard my ship. I know you have gold hidden hereabouts. You were a top cabiceer and amassed plenty of gold. General Tugwell reckons you would smuggle it aboard my ship. If you hand it over here and now, the voyage will go easy for you. If you keep it hidden, you'll be dead before you reach Pertigua.'

The captain spat over the leeward gunwales, turned back to the cabiceer and waited for an answer. From a blank stare, slave number forty-eight broke his silence.

'You want gold, Captain? I get you gold. I get it. I get.'

Following the cabiceer to the slave deck, the Second Officer recovered an ounce bag of gold. In this instance, Wimborne thought, the Captain's greed has overcome his sadistic nature. Surrendering the gold had probably saved the cabiceer's life.

Jonas Guinea

1 September 1750

It was a light silky evening. Starlings were flocking in the plane trees. At six o'clock, Fleming's horse-drawn carriage halted in front of a large house on the Highway, a thriving mercantile artery running alongside the River Thames. Having journeyed from Piccadilly, they had arrived at the Deptford Creek home of the evangelist, Thomas Beecham Esquire. Dressed and cloaked *à la mode*, he stepped down from the carriage and gazed up at the ivy-covered red brick residence. Accompanied by the Frenchman, Bertrand de La Fontaine, he had come to meet the founder members of the League Against the Importation of Negroes from the Coast of Guinea. It was a fledgling organisation as yet, with little or no influence, but he knew that could change. He was thus nominated by the Duke of Chandois to make enquiries about the League and report back to the West Indies Sugar Cartel. The Frenchman had readily agreed to effect an introduction.

The large double-fronted detached Georgian residence was set back from the pavement. Bricked steps lead up to a bottle green door with an ornamental sanctuary ring. Lifting the weighty iron hoop, Fleming let it fall twice in rapid succession. He could scarcely conceal his surprise when a smiling young black servant complete with scratch wig opened the door.

'We have an appointment with your master.'

'May I have your names please, sir?' the servant asked, politely.

'Squire Fleming and Monsieur de La Fontaine.'

Taken aback at the servant's tutored accent and manners, it struck him that he was the first black man he had ever encountered who was not a slave.

'Will you please follow me, gentlemen.'

'*Oui*,' said de La Fontaine, '*après vous*.'

Towards the end of a candle-lit passage they entered a well-appointed drawing room. Seated around a card table were three wigged gentlemen, sipping tea and playing the card game *paille maille*. Close to the fireplace on a giltwood daybed lay a plump well-dressed woman, fanning away the heat radiating from the logs in the hearth. Rising to her feet with the gentlemen, she greeted them with a bashful smile. Having by now taken in the pristine orderliness of the dwelling, he was certain that she was responsible.

It was a large room evenly punctuated by French windows with aquamarine blue silk damask on the walls, at the windows and on the upholstery. Adorning the polished oak floor was an Exeter carpet with Rococo scrolls and floral motifs. Mirror-backed girandoles were affixed either side of the fireplace. Above the mantelpiece sat a large mirror bordered by a carved, painted wood frame. Fleming was clearly inside the residence of a very prosperous man.

A small pallid gentleman in his fifties stepped forward. Before the man uttered a word, he knew him to be the evangelist, Thomas Beecham, founder of the League Against the Importation of Negroes from the Coast of Guinea.

'It is a pleasure to meet you, Squire Fleming,' said the smiling evangelist. 'I trust your journey was not too tiresome? The beggars hereabouts do trouble one so. Squire, may I introduce my wife, Alice.'

Taking the hand of the evangelist's wife, he bowed respectfully.

'It is indeed my pleasure to make your acquaintance, Mistress Beecham,' he purred.

'Delighted, Squire Fleming, truly delighted,' she replied, graciously.

The evangelist next presented Ezra Drinkwater, a dark-skinned Jew and banker whose visage was utterly inscrutable. Then he was introduced to the Secretary of the League, Reverend Nicholas Whitehouse, a gangly character of about sixty with a formal reserve.

'A glass of Madeira, Squire Fleming?' enquired Mistress Beecham. 'Before you arrived, my husband was quite inspiring and persuasive on the subject of rights for the negroes. What say you, Squire?'

Giving a slight bow, he answered.

'A glass of Madeira would be very agreeable, ma'am,' he said. 'As for the rights of negroes. I cannot see that any useful purpose will be served by handing out rights to their kind. Similarly, no useful purpose would be served by giving rights to the beggars and the idle vagrants on the streets of London. Rights are for those who have a use for them.'

An awkward silence fell on the room. Handing him and the French-man a glass of Madeira, Mistress Beecham returned to her daybed from where she posed her next question.

'Surely, Squire Fleming?' she asked. 'Should they not have the right to live as they please?'

Taking a seat by the card table, he answered her with a question.

'Who will look after them, ma'am?' he asked. 'Why, on the coast of Guinea they exist in a state of complete anarchy. Lacking any semblance of law, they have no discernible order. They are continually fighting and dispatching each other without compunction. The kings sell us their prisoners for profit. Otherwise, they themselves put them to the spear and all manner of cruelties and executions. We, on the other hand, take them and care for them on our plantations in the Indies. I might add, they are also taught the scriptures and brought closer to God. If it were not for the white man, they would remain in the depths of darkness and ignorance anchored by a great deal of superstition.'

With the veneer of a smile, Mistress Beecham delved further.

'I did hear that a number of slaves were abducted rather than pur-chased,' she said. 'Would you know anything about that, Squire Fleming?'

Irritated by her obvious knowledge, Fleming responded with patronising assurances.

'You've been most maliciously informed, Mistress Beecham,' he said. 'English traders make no inroads whatsoever into the interior. Our merchants effect their transactions there or thereabouts on the foreshore.'

Throughout his response, her eyes narrowed and probed his face. This woman is privy to some consequential source of intelligence, he thought.

'I see,' she said, holding his gaze.

Reverend Whitehouse changed the subject tactfully.

'We are Methodists, Squire Fleming,' he said. 'May I inquire your persuasion, sir?'

'I am of the Catholic faith, sir,' he replied. 'My ancestors suffered greatly for the Catholic religion, when the Puritans burnt many at the stake. I fervently hope, Reverend Whitehouse, that we have learned much from those terrible times. I also pray that our respective Churches will at least grow closer on this issue of slavery.'

The door opened. A slim elegant black man entered the room. Fleming was mesmerised. Of medium height with fine features, he was dressed in a three-quarter length black coat, black shoes and silver buckles – the common garb of a secretary. Rising to his feet, the evangelist made a presentation.

'Squire Fleming,' he said, 'allow me to introduce my secretary, Jonas Guinea Esquire.'

Bowing politely, the secretary extended his hand. Surprised by his innate confidence, Fleming hesitated noticeably before shaking the proffered black hand.

'It is a pleasure to meet you, Squire Fleming,' the secretary said genially.

'It is undeniably a surprise to meet you, Guinea,' he replied, coldly. 'We were expounding on the virtues of shipping negroes to the Indies. I am of the opinion that they enjoy a better life in that climate. What say you?'

The Frenchman coughed with discomfiture at Fleming's intended *faux pas*, whereas the secretary appeared unruffled.

'Would that not depend on whether they were first asked if they wanted to leave their motherland, sir?' he said. 'Furthermore, sir, one also needs to consider whether they are happy with the conditions they meet in the Indies?'

Resuming his seat, he felt a distinct chill in the atmosphere. A glance at the evangelist and his friends told him that they did not share his outlook. Giving the secretary an insipid smile, he answered him.

'Unlike yourself, Mister Secretary,' he said, 'they have not had the benefit of an English education and consequently remain ignorant. Would you not agree, therefore, that negroes can learn a great deal from the white man?'

'That is indeed true, Squire Fleming,' said the secretary. 'It would as well be reasonable to suggest that they can learn from all peoples. But why, sir, do they have to learn any of these lessons in the Indies? Could they not learn as much on the coast of Guinea? If indeed, as we are told, the instruction they receive on the plantations consists of cutting a daily quota of cane, I daresay they could as well presumably grow that cane on the coast of Guinea.'

Bridling at the accuracy of the rejoinder, Fleming gave the secretary a closer scrutiny. The evangelist, in contrast, chuckled and clapped his hands.

'My secretary has you there, Squire Fleming,' said Beecham. 'If schooling is the plantation owner's prime motivation, why could these people not be taught the scriptures and anything else in situ, so to speak?'

'Aye, Squire Fleming,' said Reverend Whitehouse. 'And if it has never been properly determined whether they wished to leave their homeland, then surely it follows that they have undoubtedly been compelled to do so?'

Imparting a benign smile, Fleming posed a question.

'Have any of you actually voyaged to the coast of Guinea?' he asked.

Shaking their heads sheepishly, including the priest, the gathering fell silent. Given their acknowledged ignorance, he sat confidently upright.

'That being so, then you are not familiar with the state of affairs in that dark inhospitable territory,' he said firmly. 'Well let me acquaint you with the conditions you will find, should you ever care to visit. The negroes live in dire poverty. They wander around utterly naked. Women suckle their babies at the breast – in full view of all. Children attend no school and the adults cannot read or write. What will astound you is the fact that they have no written texts. I ask you seriously where would the civilised world be without books?'

'I believe that knowledge on the coast of Guinea is lodged in an oral tradition, Squire Fleming,' said the secretary, politely. 'Would you not concede that in England, citizens who can read or write are in a minority?'

Studiously ignoring the secretary's question, he sustained his line of reasoning.

'The negroes do not busy themselves in any industry,' he said, 'and the menfolk sleep all day. They have no civilisation. As I see it, we have a duty to Our Lord to spread his word and to civilise others.'

The secretary responded without hesitation.

'With great respect, Squire Fleming,' he replied, softly, 'when I look down the Highway I see little civilisation. For the most part I see people who are more often than not illiterate, a poverty-stricken people at the bottom of the social order. People who scratch a living, while others relieve them of the few possessions they have.'

Exasperated by the secretary's deft argument, he changed tack.

'And how came you to be here in England, Guinea?' he asked.

'Captain Somerset brought me here from the Indies when I was twelve years old,' the secretary replied. 'At the onset of his sickness, he informed me that he had granted me manumission in his last will and testament. Before he passed away, the Captain helped me to find a position with Mister Beecham, who in good time became my guardian. I have lived here for the past eleven years. I was tutored by George Prebble Esquire and cared for by Mistress Beecham. My master supplies the finest tackle to ships on the River Thames. The vessels, Squire, trade in American tobacco, slaves from the coast of Guinea, silks and spices from India. As Secretary, I have had occasion to witness the trade in slaves on American vessels anchored in the roads at Gravesend. I am of the opinion that the trade is in decline, Squire. Profits grow smaller every year. I should indeed be glad of your opinion on the subject, sir.'

Rankled by the secretary's succinct précis of the Atlantic slave trade, his response was brusque.

'We experience a mere hiccup in our fortunes at present,' he said. 'But I am happy to inform you, Master Secretary, it is of no real consequence. You can be sure that England's merchants will take steps to remedy the situation.'

Fleming turned to the evangelist.

'Mister Beecham, gentlemen and, of course, Mistress Alice,' he said. 'What do you think would happen if England were to prematurely end her participation in the slave trade? Have you considered what the consequences would be on employment in the kingdom? The end result would be catastrophic, for the trade supports a profusion of dependent companies. Your chandlery enterprise would suffer adverse effects, since the number of ships putting into Gravesend would dwindle disastrously . . . '

The banker's pained expression did not go unobserved by Fleming. By mentioning the consequences for ships chandlers if the slave trade were proscribed, he had deliberately put his finger on the libertarian's dilemma – the Achilles' heel of the supposedly tolerant – Conscience or Profit? He knew that the difficulty for the evangelist lay in the balancing of his financial interests in the profit-making vessels lying at Gravesend against the thought, sight or knowledge of manacled human beings.

'I tell you gentleman, England needs the trade,' he said, returning to the subject matter. 'And in England's commercial affairs, there cannot be room for too many like Guinea here.'

Mistress Beecham flung a stern look in his direction. With a telling sigh, the evangelist rose to his feet and walked to the French windows overlooking his gardens.

'Your words trouble me, Squire,' said Beecham. 'At present, our League lobbies for the ending of slavery in England. We cannot believe that the colour of a man's skin should invalidate the most inalienable of human rights, that of being a free person in England. Moreover, Squire, I am certain we will absorb whatever effect the cessation of the trade has on our account.'

The evangelist's words reverberated around the room. Closing his eyes, the banker muttered to himself.

'I am disturbed, Squire Fleming,' said Reverend Whitehouse, 'to find myself on the opposite side to yourself. You hold information about the Guinea coast and the Indies of which we are not in possession. If the slaves cannot be freed, can we not reach an accommodation as to how they can be better treated and their conditions improved?'

Caught unawares by what was clearly an olive branch, Fleming twisted in his chair.

'You will agree that all men must work to earn a living, Reverend Whitehouse?' he asked. 'Only if our negroes labour in the canefields can we provide them with excellent shelters, food and protection. The Church meanwhile generously furnishes them with religious instruction. All things considered, gentlemen, our negroes have more than they had on the coast of Guinea. We are not heartless men. Plantation owners also strive for better conditions. An increase in productivity will bring an increase in profits. Better conditions will naturally follow. Gentlemen, the trade works towards the same end with your League. I trust you would agree that my reasoning makes sound economic sense, Monsieur de la Fontaine?'

The Frenchman fidgeted, and then provided an answer shrouded in diplomacy.

'It is generally true that greater production will result in an increase in profits,' he said. 'But Monsieur Fleming, I am a guest in your country. And as such I am not in a position to comment on England's affairs.'

'And such a fine guest you are, Monsieur de la Fontaine,' said Mistress Beecham. 'When do you plan a return to the Indies, Squire Fleming? Your plantation requires your attention no doubt?'

He was irked by the discourse, principally because of his inability to provide a morally credible argument to justify the trade in slaves.

'I shall return after the harvest is in on my Yorkshire estate, ma'am,' he said. 'I shall travel with my family who I might add, treat the negroes with a great deal of kindness. Negroes in Pertigua are very happy at their labours.'

He caught the mischievous glint in her eye. Clapping her hands, she spoke excitedly.

'Why Jonas, you hailed from Pertigua!' she exclaimed. 'Do tell us what you remember of that island?'

All heads turned to look at the secretary, who looked as if he was about to answer her question. Feeling the blood draining from his body, Fleming held his breath. The look in her eye said she warmed to his discomfort, though her voice was silken when she spoke.

'Perhaps though,' she said, 'that can wait for another occasion. We must not weary Squire Fleming with what he already knows so well.'

From the instant he had expressed scorn for the notion of 'rights for negroes,' Fleming knew he had fallen in her estimation. Nonetheless, she smiled at him with no discernible trace of ill feeling.

'Squire Fleming and Monsieur de la Fontaine,' she asked, 'you shall both of course honour us with your company at our supper table?'

'You are most kind, ma'am,' he replied.

'But of course,' said de la Fontaine. '*Merci*, Madame.'

Supper was served in a warm and genial candle-lit burgundy-toned dining room. Fleming sat down to a table of cold meats, boiled potatoes and roast parsnips, apple tart, brandy sauce and cream. In the course of the repast, the evangelist furnished him with the history and philosophy of the League Against the Importation of Negroes.

'Five years ago, a strange and unexpected event took place on my doorstep,' said Beecham. 'Alice, Ezra and myself were having supper when someone started pounding on the front door. The door was opened. Wearing only a loincloth and terrified out of his wits, a negro tumbled into the hall. He was cut and bleeding, from all manner of gashes on his neck, his trunk and his legs.'

'I was horrified at the state of the poor wretch,' said Mistress Beecham. 'No human being should suffer such brutality. The marks all over him showed he had been severely flogged. I sent a servant for hot water to clean him up and instructed cook to make him some hot broth. You would not believe the way he fell upon the food cook placed before him. The man was starving.'

'He was a runaway,' said Ezra Drinkwater, 'and his broken fetters testified to that fact. A hue and cry had evidently been raised, for in a few moments men with muskets and dogs were hammering on the front door.'

'I attended the door myself,' said Beecham. 'It was the Tipstaff from the Assizes. He demanded the return of the runaway whom, it transpired, had escaped off a slaver moored midstream at Rotherhithe. Producing a writ for Instant Possession, we had no choice. We had to give up our runaway, who had the appearance of someone near-demented with fear.'

The table was cleared. A decanter of port was passed clockwise. Beecham sipped Madeira. De la Fontaine rubbed his gums with snuff. From a small silver casket, Reverend Whitehouse tapped a mound of snuff onto the back of his hand and sniffed. The bells of St George-in-the-East struck nine. Shaking his head, the evangelist lowered his glass. Looking intently at him he continued.

'For as long as I draw breath, Squire Fleming,' he said, 'as they dragged that poor man away, I shall never forget the terror in his eyes. The Tipstaff's men had barely stepped onto the street, when to the utter consternation of all, he snatched a dagger from one of his captors and stabbed himself right through the heart. Instantly dead he fell and his blood drenched his captors. The terror inducing him to take his own life in such a manner gave me sufficient cause to consider the issue of slavery in its entirety.'

Frowning deeply, Mistress Beecham quietly added:

'We witnessed an atrocity,' she said.

'An act of such consummate desperation naturally commanded my attention,' said the evangelist. 'Henceforth, I resolved to discover the whereabouts of runaways on the streets of London. It did not take me long. I found them in Wapping, Whitechapel and Spitalfields. Like poor whites, the blacks live in much squalor and moral degradation. My secretary visits them regularly in Whitechapel.'

'I find your account disquieting, Mister Beecham,' said Fleming.

Turning to the secretary, he asked:

'Are there any freemen among them, Master Guinea? If so, how came they to be enjoying the liberty to roam the streets of London unrestrained?'

'Many of them are freemen, Squire,' replied the secretary, without hesitation. 'Some attained freedom when their masters were finished with them and threw them out onto the streets. Others received manumission and instant destitution on the death of their masters.'

'How are they received by the white populace?' he asked.

'Reasonably well from what I have encountered, sir,' the secretary replied. 'Some poor white people have shown them much kindness, Squire. Perhaps because they are also poor and derive no benefit whatso-ever from the trade.'

'And what do these people do, Mister Secretary,' Fleming asked, 'for gainful employment?'

'Some work as seamen, some as domestics,' replied the secretary.

'Others as valets and street singers. Those who cannot find employment have to beg for a living.'

'My point is, Mister Secretary,' he interrupted. 'I do not think that they should be in England under any circumstances.'

'With my deepest respects, Squire Fleming,' said the secretary. 'I do not think that negroes can be blamed for being here at all. It would do well to remember, sir, that it was English men who brought them here in the first place. Perhaps, Squire, your objections should properly be put to these English men, since they are the ones who have thrown their negroes onto the streets.'

'Touché,' cried Mistress Beecham.

'You have to admit, Squire Fleming, that my secretary has a fair point,' said Beecham. 'Besides, they could hardly have thrown themselves onto the streets. They roam the streets because of the actions of English men. I see no attempt being made to curb this influx. Indeed, I frequently hear that even members of His Majesty's Government, let alone the aristocracy and the gentry, are importing negroes. Only last week did I read in *The Gazetteer* that Sir Joshua Reynolds himself has acquired the newest modish accessory, a black pageboy.'

Fleming was irritated by the amusement of his hostess at his expense, and by the disclosure of Joshua Reynolds's acquisition of a black servant. Until now, he had never really taken note of the presence of black people on England's streets. Nor had it occurred to him that their presence in England was a direct consequence of the trade in which he was busily engaged.

'How many claim relief under the Poor Law, Master Guinea?' he enquired. 'Perhaps they hasten to England because they have heard of the benefits available under that Act?'

'Nay Squire, that is not so,' replied the secretary. 'For those who are already here, it is their belief that the Poor Law grants a subsidy to those who want to work, but cannot because of circumstances beyond their control. I am sure you would agree, sir, that they are not responsible for the position they find themselves in, or for being in England. To answer your question, sir, I know of only two who have managed to obtain poor relief. Besides, Squire Fleming, they prefer to work when they can find employment.'

He responded with a conspicuous note of sarcasm in his voice.

'They do, do they?'

'All this would be unnecessary Squire, if the trade were outlawed in

England,' said Beecham. 'I believe on England's shores all men must be free men. The extreme sacrifice of our runaway caused me to pursue a notion. Were we to obtain another runaway, we would test the Statute at the King's Bench. We would seek to obtain a ruling that slavery was not legal in England. To that point, we have sworn to petition for an end to the trade on England's shores. A few days after the suicide of that poor wretch, in October of 1739, I set out to meet John Wesley at the church in Aldersgate Street. There I spoke with the great man and the Reverend Whitehouse. To them, I proposed the formation of a League Against the Importation of Negroes. And that, Squire, was the significant issue that inaugurated our little League.'

Nodding politely, Fleming addressed the evangelist.

'I am indeed grateful to you for acquainting me with the history of your League, sir.'

Following supper, he was thankful the conversation once again grew congenial.

'I met John Wesley at Oxford,' said Reverend Whitehouse. 'I was a member of his Holy Club.'

'Holy Club?' he asked. 'How then came you to be called Methodists?'

'We were a group of devout students, Squire Fleming,' replied Reverend Whitehouse, 'who pledged ourselves to a well-regulated attendance at Holy Communion and Bible readings. We also committed ourselves to visiting those poor souls in prison with some regularity. On account of our methodical ways, our fellow students derisively called us Methodists. They also mocked us with unflattering names, like Bible Bigots. And they ended up calling us the Holy Club. We were not offended, Squire, owing to the fact that most of those who scorned our practices were renowned hypocrites.'

Adjourning to the drawing room, they continued the discourse in front of a blazing hearth. And along with the other gentlemen, Fleming savoured the fine brandy that their generous host produced.

It was time to depart. He thanked Beecham and his wife for an illuminating evening. Half-heartedly, he expressed his gratitude to the secretary for the light he had shone on the question of black people on the streets of London. Accepting his host's entreaties to visit again soon, he took his leave of the evangelist's home with misgivings.

He had a great deal to think about. This League could become a problem for the West Indies Sugar Cartel, a fact he would report to the Duke of Chandois. But he did not like the look of the morrow in the guise of Jonas Guinea. He hoped never to see such a man arise in Pertigua. He felt distinctly ill at ease when he and the Frenchman stepped out into the night to go down the steps to a waiting carriage. For despite the whiteness of his skin, he held the distinct impression that under the roof of the evangelist, Thomas Beecham, he had been the outsider.

Atlantic Ocean: 13 September 1750, 0800 hrs

For over a week the *Pelican* had been becalmed in the horse latitudes. Bad-tempered men of the watch scrubbed the deck and sorted out the rope and sail lockers. Constantly mopping his face and neck, Wimborne paced the poop deck in the sapping heat. A flaccid mainsail displayed the frustrating slowness of the *Pelican's* progress. On the morning of September the thirteenth, the wind-strength changed decisively. A fresh westerly coursed through her rigging and she moaned as a lively breeze filled her sails. On a starboard tack and close-hauled, she surged forth, creaking and groaning in a quickening sea.

In the afternoon, the arrival of a swordfish provided the ship's company with a welcome distraction. It was the first time Wimborne had laid eyes on such an extraordinary creature. The blue-grey scaleless fish was about fifteen feet long, with a flattened sword and dorsal fin protruding above the water. The captain, who had previously encountered sword-fish, remained watching the slaves who were being soaked and exercised before the foremast. To the trill of the hornpipe, the screech of the fiddle and the sting of the lash, malnourished slaves were grumpily hopping up and down.

Wimborne grew aware of unintelligible grumbling from the captain. He turned to look over the slaves. One caught his attention. The man had striking features, a sinewy frame and a quiet dignity about him. Despite the malnourishment and putrid conditions below decks, he thought, that one appears to have survived better than the rest. He was certain that the hostility in the man's eyes would draw the captain's attention before long. The master mariner's subsequent demand was accordingly unsurprising.

'What's the number of that nigger, Mister Wimborne?' he asked.

'Two hundred and twelve, sir.'

'I see you know your friends, Mister Wimborne,' the captain sneered. 'I expect you know his capabilities as well? Got me thinking that you might also know why he is so ignorant?'

The Second Officer smirked.

'How do you mean, sir?' Wimborne asked, 'for he speaks not our tongue.'

'You might know for instance,' asked the captain, ignoring his reference to language, 'why niggers know nothing of navigation? Without which, they will not be finding their way back to the coast of Guinea, even if they were given a fully manned, fully equipped ship-of-the-line, minus officers of course.'

The captain's crude judgements infuriated him. On this vessel, he thought, slaves are not the only ignoramuses aboard.

'Navigation and astronomy are an utter mystery to the crew as well, sir,' he countered. 'Likewise not one of them can read or write or work the vessel without officers to direct their efforts.'

'There is a difference, Mister Wimborne,' retorted the captain. 'The scurvy crew as you call them, have the brains but do not want to learn. They are simply shiftless, womanising blackguards. Whereas, the nigger's brain is not fully developed. He lacks the cerebral capability to absorb or comprehend the mechanics of instruction. Or are you saying that the nigger is as knowledgeable as yourself, Mister Wimborne?'

It was true he commiserated with the slaves. And that he did what he could to alleviate the unearthly conditions on the slave deck. But as liberal as he believed he was, he could not bring himself to admit that a slave was his intellectual equal.

'Nay, sir, I do not,' he said.

'Fetch that nigger, Mister Wimborne,' the captain snapped. 'Fetch your number two hundred and twelve.'

'Aye, sir.'

He returned with the slave. The captain addressed him in English.

'Mister Wimborne here thinks you are as intelligent as himself,' said the captain. 'Perhaps then you can show me how you would make use of this.'

Giving a twisted smile to all, the captain passed his octant to the slave. As he examined the strange instrument, the slave held it upside down. Wimborne could see that although he did not comprehend the white man's tongue, he certainly knew that he was being played for a fool. Shaking his head with bafflement, the slave guardedly returned the octant. Delighted by the verification of his opinion, the captain was unequivocal.

'As you can well see, Mister Wimborne,' he said. 'Your protégé is incapable of demonstrating even a methodical approach. He does not own the requisite acumen with which to fathom its technicalities. A nigger's wits, Mister Wimborne, are comprehensively inferior to those of a white man. Never ever forget that.'

Unconvinced that the demonstration provided evidence of anything consequential, Wimborne nevertheless replied courteously.

'I shall keep that very much in mind, sir,' he said.

Wimborne winced as the Second Officer kicked the slave back down the companionway. It is useless to cross swords with this captain, he thought. For as master, the man held the power of God Almighty over all for the duration of the passage.

'What is our position, Mister Wimborne?' asked the captain.

'I was about to take a sight, Captain,' he replied. 'Mister Pobjoy has the corrections at hand.'

The captain barked at him.

'Fix our position, Mister Wimborne.'

'Aye aye,' sir.

Striding to the poop rails with the Second Officer in tow, he peered through the telescope of the filtered octant at the darkened image of the sun. In a smooth steady action he brought the sun's lower limb down until it kissed the horizon.

'Mark,' he said.

The Second Officer logged the precise moment from the ship's clock. He read out the altitude off the arc. The Second Officer logged the degrees and minutes in the Sight Book.

'Corrections if you please, Mister Pobjoy,' he said.

'Aye aye, sir,' replied the Second Officer.

To each of the requested corrections, the Second Officer read out a set of figures. After applying each in turn, Wimborne opened Brown's Nautical Tables to find the zenith distance and declination of the sun. Straightening up, he briefly checked the latitude on which the *Pelican* was sailing. He then approached the captain.

'I have us in Latitude, seventeen degrees and forty minutes North, sir.'

For the first time on the voyage, the captain smiled at him.

'Hmmm. A few days from Pertigua. What do you recommend, Mister Wimborne?'

'To make landfall, sir, we should dead reckon from here on in,' he replied. 'Just now sir, we should steer south-west by south.'

'See to it, Mister Wimborne.'

'Helmsman, steer southwest by south,' Wimborne ordered.

'Southwest by south, sir,' replied the helmsman.

The *Pelican* had been at sea for two months and four days. Late on a balmy afternoon a crimson sun grazed the horizon. A welcome cry fell down from the masthead.

'Land Ho. Land Ho.'

'Where away?' shouted Wimborne.

'Two points on the larboard bow, sir.'

Four leagues off the larboard bow lay the Three Apostles – three giant, craggy pillars of granite glistening in the evening sun. Bleached-white and guano-covered, they rose over one hundred feet out of the sea. Even from that distance, he made out black-headed gulls circling the three peaks on which many a vessel had foundered. Several miles south of the shipping hazard, he made out the green mountains of Pertigua. Thankful for the sight of salvation, he closed his eyes and sighed. It had felt an eternity at sea and the vision of land was an immense relief. There were few on board whose company he had enjoyed and his voyage, in many senses, had been a solitary one. Thus he eagerly anticipated the invitations to soirées in Drake House, where he could mingle with the class of cultured company he enjoyed.

'I'll wager the *Swallow* has not docked as yet,' said the captain. 'Old Grant would have run through the same storm.'

'Aye, I wonder how many niggers he has shipped?' asked the Second Officer.

'If he's shipped more niggers than the *Pelican*,' replied the captain, 'I wager they'll be in a right sickly condition.'

'Aye that would be true, Captain Blunt, sir,' agreed the Second Officer.

'I'll have us anchor in the roads before Jamestown this night, Mister Wimborne,' said the captain. 'We'll make harbour in the morning. Got it?'

'Aye aye sir,' he replied.

Kayode heeded the masthead cry. The report that land had been sighted echoed around the stifling slave deck. Surrounded by his fellow captives, Kayode sensed a palpable dread of the terrors this strange new land might hold. There were frantic whispers voicing queries that no one could answer. From the shadows sprang the booming voice of the big man.

'Countrymen, we are here,' Tomba declared.

'Where?'

'Which land is this?'

'Will they eat us?'

'We will work as slaves in this place,' said Tomba.

'How do you know?'

'The ones you sold to the white men, Tomba. Is this the hell to which they were sent?'

The challenge caused Kayode to think about the big man's situation. He had shattered many lives. Thereafter he would have to live his days with the part he had played in the selling of his own people. Rising quietly to his feet, the big man shrugged his shoulders and turned his back on his tormentors and the ugly truth.

In deepening twilight, Wimborne took a bearing of the green pinnacle of Pertigua, the lofty Mount James. In total darkness, minus her main and mizzen t'gallants, the *Pelican* dropped anchor in the roads off Jamestown, the capital of the island.

Jamestown

Pertigua

At first light, heads bowed, the slaves shuffled down the groaning gangplank of the *Pelican*. In keeping with his orders, Wimborne had moored the vessel in the Careenage in Jamestown's deepwater harbour. Daylight progressively unveiled the misty Caribbean landscape. Scarcely a breath of air stirred in the port. The temperature was already starting to climb. Wiping sweat off his brow, he took a wide-ranging look around the sheltered horseshoe-shaped anchorage. Circling seagulls plunged into the pale blue waters to pluck the sprats that abounded in the warm coastal stream of the island. Straining at her mooring ropes from the offshore breeze, the barque listed to larboard under the gross weight of slaves. Leaning over the rails beside the captain, he watched the slaves plod sullenly down the gangplank.

'Have you seen that squirming preacher, Mister Wimborne?'

'Dead drunk in his cot, sir. He shan't be returning with us to England.'

Thrusting his hand at the slaves obstructing the gangplank, the captain barked at the sailing master.

'See to them idlers, Mister Graceforth.'

'Aye aye, sir.'

Chuckling to himself, the captain turned to the Second Officer.

'Given that they've had a taste of what's to come, Mister Pobjoy, the blighters ain't so uppity.'

'Aye, sir,' said the Second Officer. 'No doubt they will apply themselves with more diligence in the canefields.'

Lowering his voice, the captain asked:

'How many did we lose?'

Being the officer responsible for logging casualties, the Second Officer fumbled in his pocket and produced a crumpled casualty list.

'Ten jumped, seven died of heartache and thirteen died trying to escape, sir,' the Second Officer replied. 'We lost thirty in all. We have three hundred and ninety-three niggers who are sound in body and mind. The ones who went mad have, thank God, wheedled themselves overboard.'

Believing the casualty figures to be wholly mendacious, Wimborne did not miss the signal that supported his suspicions – the sly wink the captain gave the Second Officer.

Wimborne knew the casualty list was a charade of the trade. He had witnessed the harsh punishments and the deaths that generally followed. Death was the penalty for striking a white man and the antidote for illness. The condemned man, woman or child was often used as bait when the vessel was sailing through shark-infested waters. With a bowline tied around the victim's waist, Wimborne had watched as one was dangled over the stern, shy of the water. The ensuing tug-of-war between the frenzied great white and the crew was their entertainment. With rows of teeth embedded in his body, the victim's terror was such that his eyeballs almost burst out of his sockets. Wimborne thought, death is constantly beckoning. For women who refused the sexual attentions of white men, death was a certainty. The casualty list comprised suicides and homicides, all of which were logged by the Second Officer as 'died while trying to escape'.

The loss of only thirty slaves proved the *Pelican's* passage had been exceedingly successful. A loss of thirteen per cent. The average loss among West Indiamen was between fifteen and twenty-five percent. Nonetheless, the monetary value of the *Pelican's* cargo would be finally determined at auction in Sho'town, on the western side of the harbour.

Watching the slaves shambling helplessly down the gangplank, Wimborne felt tainted. In his mind's eye, he could see the fired homes and villages from which they had been plucked. He had partaken in an armed action that had resulted in downright kidnapping. And he was certain his mother would say that he had contributed to a moral felony, whereas his father would point a finger at the price of his aspiration. He knew that ambition was something for which he could not be rebuked or punished, at least not under the laws of England. The gospel truth was that he had transgressed his own moral standards. Tears welled into his eyes and he gazed intently out to sea. Desperate for solitude, he returned to the deserted poop deck from where he surveyed the island to which he had helped transport a consignment of broken-hearted souls.

Shuffling feet and the clatter of chains fractured the stillness of the harbour. From the direction of the wharves and warehouses, a pristine, solitary soprano wafted high over the masts of the assembled vessels. He was transfixed by a lament imbued with a terrible sadness:

> I have heard the last of the lion,
> For submission, I have prayed,
> I have sailed an awesome journey,
> I have come to be a slave.

The Second Officer joined him at the rails.

'What mantra was that?' he asked, with his back to the junior officer, determined that not a soul would catch sight of the grief in his eyes.

'Father Clement's Homage to the Slave,' came the reply.

'A strange tribute,' he muttered.

Following the melodic homage, bedlam returned to the harbour when the slave drivers cracked their whips.

'Kick 'em down,' shouted the superintendent.

'Get your black backside on that there quay.'

'Look lively there now. I'll tan your black hide if you don't.'

Wimborne turned around. On the gangplank stood the slave who had been ridiculed by the captain for his ignorance of the octant. He pondered briefly on his fate. He wondered to which plantation this man would be enslaved for the rest of his natural life. Gazing along the shore, he surveyed the slopes bordering the harbour and the buildings surrounding the green acres of the Savannah. In the centre of the horseshoe-shaped harbour stood Drake House, a palatial white building serving as the island's seat of government. Once more, his eyes dropped to the *Pelican's* gangplank still disgorging a black column that was now snaking along the quayside.

At the foot of the gangplank the captain was deep in conversation with the Chief Tally Clerk. Squires Brigstocke and Ogden were occupied identifying slaves bearing their star brand. Clad in white breeches, jerkins and black tricornes, the tally clerks set about the task of checking the cargo against the ship's bill of lading.

Dallying close by, in stark contrast to the clerks, were a number of unrestrained black men, clad in threadbare jerkins, sweat-stained breeches and floppy brimmed hats. Strikingly conspicuous by their smiles, these were the men of the infamous Mongoose Gang. They had entered the island as slaves, but due to expert tracking skills, they were signed up as members of a rudimentary law enforcement unit founded by the island's authorities and plantation owners. They were tasked to track down slaves escaping while the ships were discharging. The smiling shifty-looking characters, with nothing to do but keep an eye on the manacled slaves, lounged against the wall beneath the eaves of an open shed.

Crossing the quayside from the *Pelican* and scrambling up a grassy embankment, Wimborne stepped onto the partially cobbled Promenade Road. On the other side of the wide thoroughfare, women in voluminous crinolines perched in open carriages, fluttering fans like the wings of humming birds. Behind them stood slave boys in crimson jackets and powdered wigs, clutching umbrellas to screen their mistresses from the strong sunlight. Husbands stood alongside, waiting to perform an examination of the newly transported slaves. The strident tones of a redheaded woman brought Wimborne to a halt.

'Oh my. Look at that pretty little thing,' said the woman. 'Georgie dear, I want that one over there to tend me in my chamber.'

Dutifully stepping down from the carriage, her husband's gloved hand pointed at a shapely girl of about sixteen years.

'That one?' he asked.

'And make sure she has strong teeth and goodly sparkling eyes,' said the woman. 'Scrubbed and properly dressed, she will be very presentable.'

'Then she shall be yours my dear,' replied the husband. 'See to it Craddock.'

'I'll follow them to Sho'town for the auction, Mister Henshaw,' replied his overseer.

'Not a penny above twenty-five guineas,' the husband snapped. 'I put you on notice, Craddock, every penny over twenty-five guineas will be deducted from your pay.'

Hindered by the rusty iron bonds, Kayode stumbled down the gang-plank and set foot on the island of Pertigua. Stiff, aching and bewildered from want of light and lack of movement, his lips were cracked from the salty air and scarcity of fresh water and his skin was streaked white with salt residue. Given the gruesome conditions on the slave deck, the island's air smelled fresh and sweet. He prayed that Asabi was still alive.

On land once more, he searched for her among the throng. With his back to the warehouses, he surveyed the harbour. Turning around, he narrowed his eyes and scrutinised the overseers.

Baba was right, he thought, the white men are going to keep us in this place forever, I must get away. Even if he could break away, how would he get back to Ake?

He wanted to lash out at the overseers, but the musket was a deathly reminder as to who was in control. A tall hook-nosed white man cracked his lash above his head and bellowed.

'Get going!'

The air was beset with whips. Shrieks and curses followed. The column of leaden legs shuffled forward. Six abreast, three hundred and ninety-three slaves trudged sullenly away from the *Pelican*. Elephant ears and palm bayonets swayed in the gentle wind of the afternoon. Under a bright blue sky, swathes of vegetation, palmettos and brightly coloured shrubs jostled for space along the roadside.

Ordered to witness the sale of the *Pelican's* slaves, Wimborne tailed the column along Promenade Road, hugging the contour of the horseshoe-shaped harbour. Smiling white faces peered from the carriages. Stacking barrels of molasses at the side of the road, slaves stole furtive looks from beneath cowed heads. Shuffling and jangling the length of the waterfront, the procession presented an unmitigated picture of despair. Gritting his teeth and shaking his head with remorse, Wimborne walked on.

In Sho'town, the slave column came to a halt before the Auction House. Slipping past a throng of whites on horseback, in carriages and on foot, Wimborne entered the lattice-windowed long rectangular wooden shed. He stopped just inside the door. Moments later, the slaves were whipped towards a low sawdust-covered platform at the far end of the shed. Positioned near the centre, a stout plank lay across two sawn trunks. Nearly knocking him off his feet, buyers stampeded into the shed and formed a ring around the plank. Bracing himself, Wimborne stayed by the door.

'They are going to sell us,' Tomba hissed, to those around him. 'Farewell, Kayode. We will not meet again. Pass it on.'

Kayode's mouth fell open. The big man's startling revelation shot down the line. A loud groan soared into the air. Over the heads of the spirited buyers, a hoary, grey-bearded white man caught his attention. Watching the proceedings from the door and standing close to the troubled officer off the *Pelican*, the white man held a black tricorne in his hand. Their eyes met and both were held in a steady gaze. A warm unwavering smile materialised on the elderly, wrinkled white face. Given his hopeless position and having never before been smiled at by a white man, he could only stare lamely back. The old man nodded at him. Uncertainly, he nodded back. Then the old white man was gone. From that momentary contact, he clutched onto a flicker of hope. It was a brief respite only. Tomba grasped his arm.

'Never forget the land of your birth, Kayode,' he said. 'Remember your people. Never forget your language. You must escape. Remember . . . '

A whip terminated Tomba's sentence. An overseer raised his fist.

'Hold your tongue nigger,' he snarled.

'Damaged goods,' someone yelled.

The overseer dropped his fist. At auction it was essential that goods were sold in the best of health and undamaged. Striding out into the cleared space, the auctioneer raised his arms.

'Me Lords, Ladies and Gentlemen,' he said. 'The goods in this sale are off the *Pelican*, a well-found vessel of the Royal African Company. She arrived this instant with a cargo of three hundred men and ninety-three women. The utmost care has been taken to keep them free from the slightest danger of being infected with the small-pox. All the slaves off the said vessel are strong and in the finest bodily condition. Further-more, Captain Ebenezer Blunt, of the said Company, testifies that his slaves from the coast of Guinea are free of all impediments. Accordingly, these slaves may be legally sold here at the Auction House. In attendance to witness this auction is Mister Wimborne, the First Officer of the said vessel.'

Signalling to an assistant, the auctioneer spun around, extracted six slaves and led them to the plank. His hawkish assistants prodded them along the thick piece of wood. A hush fell throughout the shed. Bidders began a close inspection of the human merchandise. A small procession caught Wimborne's eye. Sashaying across the floor was a bullish, richly dressed character. Overseers walked deferentially by his side taking notes. From his supercilious mien, and the employ of his gold-tipped cane to single out the slave he desired, he was clearly a person of consequence.

'There goes Randolph Fleming,' said Brigstocke, above the furore. 'I'll wager he knows not the purpose of our venture to the coast of Guinea.'

'Then indeed you have lost your stake my friend,' said Ogden. 'The night before we departed, I advised him that we were bound for Guinea to procure our own slaves from the source. Naturally I forgot to tell him that we would be buying them at cost price. I also neglected to say that we would be selling them on the open market for profit, thus making ourselves, in effect, producers. For once we have stolen a march on him. Henceforth, he will probably do likewise, lest he remain a purchaser. It is good business based on sound principles.'

Following the buyer's examination of the slaves on the plank, the auctioneer rang his bell. Leaping forward and seizing the ankle of the nearest slave, he shouted.

'Who'll gimme twenty-five guineas for this strong young buck.'

Up shot the hand of Frederick Bradshaw, the owner of the Tamarind Trees plantation.

'I'll give you twenty-five,' he said, 'so long as he keeps his bucking to his own kind. And he don't buck my wife.'

Laughter shook the Auction House.

'Ave you seen his wife?' shouted a voice. 'Slave would turn her down.'

A peal of laughter raised the bidding spirits. Bradshaw was outbid and the auction gathered pace. The sale continued interminably throughout the afternoon. One terrified black face blurred into the next. A hundred slaves had been sold by the auctioneer's gavel, when Wimborne saw the slave with the octant pushed into view. A sea of white faces surged towards the plank. White men prodded his skin and pulled his lips, his hair, his nose and his vital parts. Wimborne's head was bursting.

This man may not comprehend the English language, he thought, but he must know what it all means.

It seemed mere moments before the man was sold to Bradshaw for the sum of thirty-two guineas. He felt a strange empathy with this man and was moved by his sale.

To Wimborne's astonishment the sum total of the auction was fourteen thousand four hundred pounds for the Royal African Company. He was forced to admit that his captain's ruthlessness had turned a profit.

Hauled out of the Auction House by an overseer, Kayode was man-handled onto a cart drawn by two greys. A scrawny girl of about sixteen lay weeping in the opposite corner. Pulling his knees up, he tucked them under his chin. Looking down, he saw that the ankle-irons had chafed his skin raw and blood was trickling over his feet.

Pitched into the cart, a young woman crashed into the wooden partition separating them from the driver. Straightening herself out, she sat up. He found himself gazing into Asabi's dark eyes. His mouth fell open and his eyes bulged. He shook his head and put a finger to his lips. Stretching his foot out, he gently made contact with hers, skin to skin. Her presence raised his spirits. He could see that she was astonished to see that he had also survived. It is a miracle, he thought. Not only had they sailed on the same ship, but they had also become the property of the same owner.

Striding out of the Auction House, a surly Frederick Bradshaw climbed onto the passenger seat. Slamming shut the tailgate, the chisel-jawed, olive-skinned overseer leapt onto the driving seat, flicked the reins and started off along the Promenade Road. By a bridge on the western perimeter of Jamestown, the cart turned towards a mountain. Skirting the base of the mountain and a high plateau giving rise to a plunging waterfall, the cart rattled past a signboard. A short while later, the greys were trotting through tall open gates onto a gravelled carriage-drive. They came to a standstill outside an enormous residence. At the sight of the Palladian villa fronted by white Corinthian columns, Kayode's eyes strained with his disbelief. Asabi's expression mirrored his own. In the sweltering afternoon sun he examined the extraordinary structure. Stepping onto the drive, Bradshaw muttered over his shoulder and strode into the Great House.

The door crashed open. Her father stomped into the pale yellow drawing room. Faith raised her eyes without emotion. Giving her not so much as a glance, he strode across the room. She remained quietly at the table working on the plantation's accounts. With one hand behind him and the other resting on a papier-mâché globe of the known world, he gazed out of the big windows bordered by fringed ivory silk curtains.

'You should venture out more often, Faith,' he said. 'It cannot not profit a soul to rot away in such discontent. Squire Fleming has kindly sent an invitation. You will accompany your mother and I to supper at China Lights.'

Knowing what lay behind her father's words, she glowered at him. Of late, the extent of his desire to marry her off had become not only intolerable but also unseemly.

'And which feeble entity am I to meet on this splendid occasion, Father?'

Her taunt was transparent. She hoped it was. Scarcely weeks had elapsed since her father's last marriage-promoting effort had fallen foul of the grave. Before the hastily convened wedding ceremony had even begun, her rich elderly bridegroom collapsed and died on the steps of the chapel. Ever since then she had rarely exchanged a word with her father.

There was a knock at the door.

'Come,' he snapped.

Propelled by the overseer, Kayode crashed into the drawing room. Picking himself up off the floor, he came face to face with his owner – Frederick Bradshaw. His heart thumped and he began to sweat. Before him stood a tall thin man with barely discernible lips set in a narrow face. His tapered grey eyes betrayed a certain malevolence. Stepping up to him, the planter grasped his balls in his hand and squeezed. Throbbing with agony, Kayode felt the man's stale breath rasp his face as cold grey eyes bored into his head.

'Me, Massa Bradshaw,' the planter said. Jabbing a finger at the woman sitting at the table behind him, he snarled. 'Missy Bradshaw.'

Through mists of pain, Kayode looked at Faith. Pale with soft features, her jet-black hair was wound up into a knot shaped like a bun. She presented a dark and gloomy figure, dressed entirely in black, she sat witnessing his humiliation with complete indifference. Following her cool scrutiny of his body, she raised her eyes to his face. Throwing a contemptuous look at her, he dropped his eyes to the floor. Raising his head with a finger, the planter again pointed at Faith and pulled a finger across his own throat, signifying she was forbidden territory. On the verge of passing out from the excruciating pain, the planter suddenly let him go. Collapsing onto the floorboards, he lay there doubled up. His tormenter stood over him clicking his tongue.

'*Olorun* has forsaken me,' he mumbled, beneath his breath in the Yoruba language. 'I must not forget Tomba's words. I will never forget.'

Hauling him to his feet, the planter shoved him hard. Thrust into the wall he crashed to the floor. Unfurling a whip, the planter laid it across his back.

'Get this scum out of here, Mister Ferrers,' the planter shouted. 'And make sure you teach him our ways. His name will be Jacob.'

Ferrers hesitated.

'We already have a Jacob, Mister Bradshaw,' he said weakly.

'Now we have two,' snapped the planter. 'Send in the women.'

'Right away, Mister Bradshaw.'

Seizing him by the scruff of his neck, Ferrers marched him out of the house and across a courtyard. He caught sight of Asabi being pushed into the house. Gripping his neck, the overseer thrust him towards a long windowless shed. Pulling the door open, the overseer shoved him inside.

'Jacob,' he shouted, kicking the door shut.

Men and women scrambled about the floor retrieving vegetables knocked over by his violent entry. Sullenly, they went back to peeling a mound of sweet potatoes. Rising shakily to his feet, he looked sheepishly around. A long trestle table ran halfway down the centre of the otherwise spartan shed. Lit by oil-lamps and candles, the place reeked of fish, rum, sweat and sorrow. Perched in an odd position at the table, scraping scales off red snapper, an old man spoke in the Yoruba tongue.

'Welcome to the Slop House, boy,' said the old man, perfunctorily. 'What's your name?'

'Kayode of the Sodeke family from the village of Ake,' he replied, proudly.

The old man laughed at him.

'Boy you is now Jacob Bradshaw from the nightmare of the Tamarind Trees plantation,' he said. 'Accept the name the master has given you, boy. He name me Moses Bradshaw. Everyone called Bradshaw around here. At last count, there was one hundred and thirty-three Bradshaws.'

'How long will he keep us here?' he asked.

'Forever, boy, forever,' said the old man. 'You will never see your village again. Get it into your head boy. You will never again see your Baba and Iya. No escape from here, boy. If you get off this plantation and off this island, which way is Ake?'

The old man's words hurt. Despair washed through him. A fever started burning deep inside his head.

'I shall be the first,' he muttered to himself, 'to escape and make it back to my village.'

'Now if you be thinking 'bout escape, Jacob', said the old man, tersely, 'you will have to speak and understand the white man's tongue. Them call it English. I will teach you this English to help you get by. Now eat to save your strength.'

Pulling himself upright, the old man pushed a battered cup of rum towards him. Picking up a bowl of boiled potato and fish heads, he placed it on the table in front of him.

'*Adupe* – thank you,' he said.

'Say your name and say *adupe* in English,' the old man instructed. 'You say, J.a..c.o.b and t.h.a.n.k y o u. Say it, boy.'

'Ja..c.o.b,' he repeated hesitantly. 't.h.a.n.k y o u.'

'I will help you, Jacob,' said the old man in Yoruba. 'After you finish work, you sleep in my house 'til you build a chattel house. At night I will teach you all I know 'bout the white man's language.'

'When do we work?' he asked.

'From can-see-light,' the old man replied, 'to can-see-dark.'

He was glad to be in the company of the kindly old man. Following the brutalising ocean passage, the gentle sociable exchange brought him a little relief.

'Where do we work?' he asked, apprehensively.

'I work in the Slop House,' said the old man. 'Them plan to work you to death in them canefields with my friend Ol' Bones in the First Gang. A fine one Ol' Bones. He called Ol' Bones 'cos he been cutting cane a long, long time. Stick close to him in them fields until you pick things up. If you gives no trouble, Mister Bradshaw might even train you as a mason, smith or carpenter.'

'I do not think that I want the sort of luck,' he said, 'that brings me into contact with him.'

Tears started rolling down his cheeks.

'*Kilo kini nse oe*? – What is the matter with you?' asked the old man. 'Why is the water shaking your face so?'

'I see many people dangling along the road,' he replied, despondently. 'They will all be dead by now.'

'If them were hanging along Promenade Road,' said the old man. 'It mean them tried to escape together, so them hang together. That's plantation law. Them were lucky. Them only tried to escape. If them had taken part in an uprising, them would have been roasted alive. On this island it is not against the law for a white man to kill his slave. Slaves are his property. You can't kill property, like you can't kill a chair. Don't you go trying your luck. I know you have lost your family. We all have. But you must have hope.'

He frowned.

'Hope in what?' he asked, sincerely.

'Hope in the work of the Good Lord,' replied the old man. 'He works in mysterious ways. We must have faith in his justice. One big day is coming when he will come down from heaven to set us free.'

'Who is this Good Lord?' he asked. 'I know of Sango, Oya, Erinle, Orisa Oko, Ifa, Oro, Sopona and many more. I have never heard of this Good Lord. Sango visits somebody in Ake because they have sinned. That is the custom of the Yoruba.'

'So what?' asked the old man.

'What sins have we committed for us to become slaves?' he asked. 'Surely the Good Lord would not have to set us free if he had not allowed us to become slaves? Should we not try to free ourselves and give the Good Lord some help?'

'In time you will understand,' the old man said dispiritedly. 'You're young and still feverish with foolish ideas of escape. That thinking will die in time. Round here, young Jacob, time is something you have no need to worry about. You now living slow time boy. You got plenty of time. Plenty of time.'

'How long have you been here?' he asked.

'With Massa Bradshaw or here on Pertigua?'

'On this island.'

' 'Bout thirty years,' the old man replied.

Although defiance was still feebly present, Jacob could see that the old man was essentially resigned to his fate – breaking out was something that he had long since relegated to a dream.

I must find out all this old man knows of this island and its white people, he thought. I will never submit like him.

Darkness was falling. The chirp of crickets echoed through the Slop House. He last heard them in Ake. The memory brought a lump to his throat. The conch wailed. It signalled the end of the working day. The long shed was bathed in the dismal light of oil lamps and candles. A child in frayed breeches walked about with a taper lighting candles. He narrowed his eyes. Men and women were spilling into the shed displaying bruises and abrasions. They slumped onto the benches around the long trestle table. A young man burst into the shed bearing unsightly facial welts and an ugly gash across the bridge of his nose. Between bouts of coughing and spewing bloody saliva and mucus onto the floor, he held a cotton wad soaked in salt water over his nose. Two women sat comforting a young woman sobbing hysterically in a corner. Jacob frowned at Moses.

'That woman work in the Second Gang,' the old man explained. 'Been 'bout two months since she was taken into canefield by two overseers.'

'Why does she weep?'

'Mama Jezebel told her something bad.'

'Who is Mama Jezebel?'

'Them buy her in Ijebu Ode on the coast of Guinea,' the old man replied. 'She look after women heavy with child. Mama Jezebel knows everything about babies. Using herbs alone, she can bring baby out, stop baby coming and stop bleeding. And when them white doctors scratch them heads cos them don't know what to do, the white women yell for Mama Jezebel. Ever since that young woman was sullied, her man has not come near her.'

Jacob easily identified the lover – the young man who had burst angrily into the Slop House. Sitting away from her, he was contorted with rage and vowing loudly to kill Ferrers.

'Let us pray,' said the old man.

A few bent their heads in prayer. The majority began to eat.

'O Lord we thank thee for the food we eat,' the old man intoned. 'And we . . . '

A chorus of voices cut the prayer short.

'Amen,' they cried.

Raising his hand and his voice above the following uproar, the old man was kind.

'Let we welcome Jacob and Eliza,' he announced, 'who them buy in the Auction House today.'

Drained smiles and jaded voices greeted them. Rum flowed. Some gave them scraps of food and others touched them out of sympathy. Although the kind attention failed to raise his spirits, it nevertheless helped to lessen his ache. He turned to Eliza. Her prominent cheek-bones bore three long scars, converging to a point at the corner of her mouth. Knowing them to be the ethnic marks of the Yagba, the most north-easterly of the Yoruba peoples, he addressed her in Yoruba.

'In the big house,' he asked, 'did you see a woman called Asabi?'

'Yes,' she replied.

'What happened to her?'

'The big white man's wife want her,' said the girl, wiping away her tears. 'She live and work in the Great House. I know not what name them give her.'

Jacob fell silent.

Inside the fine confines of the Great House, Asabi had been marched into the washhouse by Widdecombe the housekeeper. Despite the forceful handling of the white woman, she retained her composure. Scrubbed and rinsed, she was crammed into a cotton dress. Shackles had ended her liberty on the coast of Guinea, now she felt imprisoned in cloth. Alongside the girl from the cart, she was marched onto the verandah and thrust before the Mistress. In the flickering light of the oil lamp, she stole a glance at the Mistress. Lying on a wicker daybed, the sour-faced deity lowered her glass. Breathing a languid sigh, she cracked an icy smile and stabbed a finger at her.

'Does she speak any English, Widdecombe?'

'A few words, ma'am.'

'She shall be called Florence,' said the Mistress, 'and attend my daughter and myself.'

Turning her attention to the girl, the Mistress once more pronounced sentence. 'We'll call her Ruby,' she said. She shall be employed *servus servorum*. The slave of the house slaves.'

The housekeeper frowned.

'In other words, Widdecombe, she is yours to do with as you wish,' said the Mistress. 'Florence, on the other hand, shall serve at table tonight. Teach her how to turn my bed, tidy up my bedchamber and lay out my gown for supper. Make it clear that I want no swearing, stealing, shirking or sneaking out to sleep with field slaves.'

'Yes Ma'am,' said the housekeeper. 'Thank you, Ma'am. Come, Florence and you Ruby.'

Elegbara is in this woman, Florence thought.

She was hustled away from her first audience with the Mistress of the Great House. The housekeeper put her to work at once, scrubbing floors, dusting and polishing. On the stroke of eight, as directed, she stood by the wall when the plantation owner entered the wood-panelled dining room. His wife, daughter and the housekeeper followed. A sense of dread assaulted her. She shook. No matter what, I must keep away from this man and never smile in his presence. In anticipation of his orders, she walked to the door.

He snapped his fingers. She began serving the supper of cold cress soup, wild pig, roast potatoes and a dessert of trifle. Though she could not understand the tongue, she knew the conversation was about her. Throughout the meal she felt his eyes conducting a systematic exploration of her body. Ignoring her husband's evident interest, his wife picked up a glass of gin.

'Florence may be scarred,' she said, 'but she is nonetheless a lissom and pretty little thing. Good teeth and gums too.'

Wolfing down a wodge of trifle, the housekeeper responded.

'I agree, ma'am, she is very presentable.'

In a voice edged with hostility, the Mistress issued a directive.

'You will instruct your charge, Widdecombe, on the regulations regarding house slaves,' she said. 'Particularly that one about associating with field slaves. Make sure she understands the consequences should she transgress any of them.'

'I shall keep her on a very tight rein, ma'am,' said the housekeeper.

Florence felt the daughter's eyes sizing her up.

'Scars?' she asked.

'Across her breasts and her back,' replied the housekeeper. 'But she is strong. She will give good service for a goodly number of years.'

'How did she come by these scars?' the daughter asked.

'Does that matter?' her mother snapped. 'What should be of greater importance to you is her acquiescence. The labours the niggers are put to ensures that you have food on your platter and clothing on your back.'

Turning to his daughter, the plantation owner growled.

'Our slaves are lawfully owned young lady,' he said. 'A right good thrashing keeps their kind in line. Did you not see the hate in the eyes of that last slave? I named him Jacob. I will sort him out. Or would you have the likes of him lording it in this Great House while we cut the cane? Soon you will be joining those reformists.'

Florence could not miss the fury that flickered in the daughter's eyes.

After supper, the family and the housekeeper retired to the drawing room. When they eventually went to bed, Florence followed her Mistress to her bedchamber. Having completed her duties, she was making her way down the stairs, when the drunken planter stopped her, turned her forcibly around and pushed her back up the stairs. On the landing, he shoved her in the opposite direction to his wife's quarters. Kicking her inside his own bedchamber and barring the door, he thrust his arm at the bed.

'Get them clothes off an' get your black hide on that.'

Although she understood only a few words of his language, she fully understood his intentions. She wanted to live. Having endured the lust of white men before, she knew what she must do. Grunting excitedly he lumbered on top of her, prised her legs open and rammed himself in. His hot foul breath rasped her face. Gritting her teeth she prayed to the gods of the Yoruba.

In the Slop House, Jacob was watching the herbalist tending the injuries of the cane cutters. Those with lovers and families then headed for their chattel houses. Rising clumsily from the table, Moses beckoned to him.

'Come back-a-yard and meet the people.'

Jacob scowled at the cause of the old man's odd posture – his left leg was devoid of a foot. Laying his unbending, footless leg along the bench, he leant back for balance. Upright, he stood on one able foot and a wooden crutch. Noticing the grimace on his face, the old man explained.

'It happened when I escaped a good while back. Them catch me on Mister Greenwood's plantation in Sun Valley. A house nigger caught me fishing. He run to tell his Massa, who sent the Mongoose Gang with their dogs. Them dogs trained to hate slaves. Them catch me up in an orange grove. I climb tree to keep away from them big teeth. Them dogs hate slaves so bad. Them even tried to climb up the tree.'

'The Mongoose Gang?'

'You see them blacks in the harbour with no chains?'

'I see them.'

'In return for a fine chattel house, plenty food and liberty,' said the old man, 'them turncoats is freed by the plantation owners to join the Mongoose Gang. Them is trained as trackers and gets paid for every slave them tracks down. Nothing fills their bellies like when them is chasing black skin. Them sniff your backside – them never give up. When ship arrives with slaves, them fall on the harbour ready to hunt down them who run away. The traitors tied me behind a horse and dragged me from the orange grove through the canefields 'til them get me back here. I was mighty cut up by then.'

Pausing for a sip of rum, the old man carried on.

'Mister Bradshaw tell Ferrers to chastise me. Come sunrise, Ferrers paraded the slaves in the yard to watch. Overseers lash my leg to a log and held me down. Ferrers chop off my foot with an axe. Holding up my foot, he says this is what happens to runaways who get caught. He toss my bleeding foot into the fire right in front of my very eyes. He burn my stump with a red-hot iron and push it into the salt bucket. I never know pain so bad. I cry and cry for many months. Ahhh, the hate I have for that devil Ferrers . . . '

As they sat in silence, Jacob thought about the brutal amputation that had left an able-bodied man mutilated for life. Lowering his voice, he asked:

'What is a house nigger?'

The old man turned visibly contemptuous.

'House niggers live and work in the Great House,' he snarled. 'Them not allowed to mix with we. Massa trusts them. We don't!'

'So Asabi is a house nigger,' he muttered, almost to himself.

'Who is Asabi?' the old man asked.

'My woman,' he said proudly.

'I been told your woman called Florence,' the old man said, 'and she's to be a house nigger.'

'House nigger or not, I trust her.'

'Follow your nose, Jacob, but watch where you stick it. There are some around here who them give more food to turn traitor.'

'I will say few words and watch where I put my feet,' he said. 'If she is a house nigger, what are we?'

'Field niggers,' replied the old man. 'We're not allowed to enter the Great House, 'cos them don't trust we. House niggers hardly ever try to escape, while field niggers are constantly dying to break out. But mostly them just die.'

Later that night the slaves congregated around the fire in the barracoon. He followed the hobbling old man into the gathering. The camaraderie displayed towards him on this his first night brought tears to his eyes.

'These are the very last tears,' he said, 'that I will ever shed on this terrible island.'

The old man said nothing, but gazed at him momentarily and then turned his hoary eyes to the night sky and muttered to himself. The moon drifted from behind the clouds. The land was bathed in light but for the vast shadow of Orange Mountain.

'Share my house, Jacob,' said the old man, quietly. 'Come, we must sleep.'

Alone with his apprehension, Asabi drifted into his thoughts. Trying hard to envision where she might be, he longed to be with her again.

The conch sounded at dawn. Opening his eyes, he saw the old man shaking him awake with a chewing stick in his mouth.

'Come Jacob, we go to the Slop House for porridge 'fore line-up.

'Not hungry.'

'If you not eat now, you not eat till midday. It's not good to cut cane on empty belly. Come, you will eat.'

Rising groggily to his feet, Jacob staggered after him.

Chaos reigned around the Slop House. Musket-wielding overseers wandered about. In the barracoon, slaves were gulping down mouthfuls of porridge. Sitting on a cask, sweating and panting from physical exertion was Woodham Ferrers, the head overseer. His whip lay on the ground beside him. Hanging by the wrists from an iron frame was his victim, blood oozing from numerous lacerations.

'Cut the villain down,' shouted Ferrers. 'That flogging should cure his greed. I said one bowl of porridge. That thief was caught with two. Give him some water and get him out to them fields. He will sweat with no rations today.'

'I'll seize that whip and he'll suffer someday,' Jacob muttered.

'All you'll hold this day, young man, is a machete,' the old man said tersely. 'You'll cut cane or Ferrers will cut you. Stay well away from that devil. Never meet his eyes. Else he think you have no respect. As you is a slave, it follows that you're being aggressive. That one is heartless.'

'Line-up,' shouted an overseer.

A frantic scramble followed the order.

'First Gang,' shouted the lead male slave.

Hobbling quickly, the old man slipped into the First Gang line-up. Following him closely, Jacob fell into a row of sullen, embittered men.

'Second Gang,' shouted the lead slave woman.

Pregnant and breast-feeding women fell into the line behind her.

'Third Gang,' shouted an elderly woman.

Children and elderly slaves lined up behind her. Three work gangs snaked across the torch-lit yard. Inside the First Gang, the old man tapped the shoulder of the man in front of him.

'Countryman,' he said.

A sinewy figure of about forty turned around. His furrowed face broke into a smile.

'This is Jacob,' said the old man. 'Jacob meet up with Ol'Bones.'

'My name is Foluso,' Ol'Bones said in Yoruba. 'Folks round here call me Ol' Bones, on account of my bones.'

Ol'Bones paused, and then he grinned and added:

'Them old.'

Jacob smiled warmly at him.

'Stay close to me, countryman,' said Ol' Bones. 'I will change English into Yoruba, till you can speak the white man's language. Okay?'

'T.h.a.n.k y.o.u,' said Jacob.

Ol' Bones grinned.

'Who teach you that?' he asked. 'I see you know the white man's tongue already. Did them give you language lessons while resting in the ship on the way here from Guinea?'

The three men laughed soundlessly. With the count completed, the old man bade them farewell and hobbled back to the Slop House.

By first light the three gangs, comprising eighty-three males and thirty-seven females, were lined up and ready. Jacob looked up. The upper limb of a scarlet saffron sun crept above the junction of earth and sky. A fresh steady breeze came from the south-east. Cockerels crowed the advent of the new day and hens were pecking hungrily for grain. Ol' Bones brought him back to the ugly present.

'Men work the First Gang,' he said. 'Them sow and cut the cane and slave at the mill house. Women work the Second Gang. Them weed the canefields and carry the cane to the carts. Children and the elderly work the Third Gang. Them feed the animals, cut firewood and look after Bradshaw's kitchen gardens. We work every day except half of Saturday and Sunday. When Ferrers wants to be really cruel, we work all seven days. This day we work above Dolphin Bay, countryman. A three mile walk there and a three mile walk back.'

Jacob's spirits plummeted. Ferrers blew his whistle.

'Get going!' he shouted.

One hundred and twenty slaves shuffled slowly out of the dark yard. Several overseers followed on horseback. Others carrying muskets sat in a cart, closely trailed by another cart filled with machetes.

'When we pass Ferrers, look not at him,' whispered Ol' Bones. 'Keep your eyes down.'

Drawing level with Ferrers, despite the advice, Jacob was tempted to look up at the overseer, to find himself staring into his menacing grey eyes.

'Damn your hide you arrogant nigger,' yelled Ferrers. 'You look no white man in his eyes.'

A searing pain tore across his back before he even heard the crack of the whip. Dropping his eyes and smarting with agony he staggered on by, knowing this overseer could cause him any amount of suffering. Ferrers yelled at the column.

'Dolphin Bay,' he shouted. 'And you had better cut more cane than you did yesterday.'

'Yes, Massa,' shouted the gangs.

Summoning his resources, Jacob began to walk the rugged distance to Dolphin Bay. The column trudged along Liberty Lane. His hackles rose at the sight of the horse-backed overseers trotting alongside. The trek had just begun. His legs were already leaden. Bass chords suddenly sang out the first line of a song. Raising their voices, the gangs sent the chorus echoing down the rows of cane lining the route. Riding up to the lead singer, Ferrers snarled.

'Croon a faster melody boy.'

'What does he mean?' Jacob asked.

'Sing faster,' whispered Ol' Bones.

At the redoubled tempo, Jacob felt the steps of the slave gangs quicken.

Before he had made his first cut, Jacob already felt an instinctive loathing for the spindly green stalks, ten to twenty feet high, bearing sword-shaped long rustling leaves, which waved innocently in the breeze.

'So this is sugar cane,' he said. 'Why do they worship it so much?'

'It is their God,' said Ol' Bones, 'and makes white men fat and rich.'

'How?'

'In the Mill House we turn cane into sugar,' said Ol' Bones. 'Them English crave sugar. Them take sugar in ships back to England and sell it. It fetches much gold and makes them rich. The English worship religion, but their God, my friend, is gold.'

Pointing at the acres of fully-grown cane, Ol' Bones was unemotional.

'That cane not yet cut,' he said. 'This day we start here above Dolphin Bay. By the time we have cut it all the way back to the Great House, another crop will have grown again above the Bay. We start over again. We live to cut cane and make children, who will be sold. And then, when them owners have squeezed out of us the last drop of sweet sap, we die for nothing.'

Jacob spirits fell. It was five o'clock in the morning. Daylight was filtering across a mother-of-pearl sky. By the time he stumbled into the seemingly boundless field overlooking Dolphin Bay, his legs were aching, he was out of breath and his throat was parched. He looked from one side of the field to the other. So this is the devil they call Farthest Field.

'Get your machetes and jump to it you lazy niggers,' Ferrers shouted. 'Get your backs into some grind. You'd better cut more than you did yesterday.'

Hastening back to the cart, Jacob pulled out a machete and followed Ol' Bones into the canefield. Soon all he could hear was the crack of the whip and the thud of the machete. Women scurried among the cane cutters, ferrying the cuts to the waiting carts. The sun leapt up from the horizon showering them with shards of gold and vermillion. The temperature began to rise. Jacob started hacking haphazardly at the cane. Ol' Bones stopped him.

'Chop like so, Jacob,' he explained, kind-heartedly, 'and chop no faster than me, 'cos pit vipers nest in this here field. Stay close to me, boy, 'cos I can smell a snake by sound of its coils. Snakes in this field are very poisonous. If you is bitten and you by me, you stay on this here earth. If not, you instantly on the road to them pearly gates. I knows how to kill the poison. And watch out for a big black centipede, like so.'

He approximated a gap of half an arm's length with his hands, before continuing.

'Its bite don't kill, but the pain them give you so bad you wish you dead. Come Jacob, let's cut cane.'

The sun climbed into a clear blue sky. Sweat cascaded down Jacob's body. His back, arms and legs screamed with agony.

'Here Jacob, chew *obi* – kola nut – and cane,' said Ol' Bones. 'Cane and *obi* juice give you energy. The first week is agony. *Obi* ease the pain and help your body make a friend of pain. *Obi* give you strength.'

'T.h.a.n.k y.o.u,' said Jacob, before reverting back into Yoruba.

'Has anyone ever escaped and never been captured?'

Drawing back in feigned surprise, Ol' Bones cast a quizzical eye over him and smiled.

'Runaways head for them mountains,' he said. 'White men who chase them deep into them mountains never come back. So them overseers will do anything to stop you reaching them mountains. And believe me boy, when I say do anything, I mean everything.'

'Not if we outwit them,' Jacob said.

As they toiled, Ol' Bones recounted the torments and challenges facing a runaway.

It was midday when the wail of the conch blared out the break for feeding time. Canecutters walked shakily to the cart for a ration of bread and water. Jacob flopped down next to Ol' Bones to eat. A fight broke out. Two young men were circling each other in the freshly cut portion of the field. One was a bull with thick biceps, and the other was a pretty boy, nimble of foot and agile. Before the giant had budged a muscle, pretty boy kicked him hard in the groin. Big bull grunted, his eyes rolled and he exhaled a prolonged groan as he sank slowly onto his knees. He endeavoured to speak just before his face hit the dirt with a distinct thud.

'Haul the blighters off to the rack,' an overseer shouted at the slaves closest to the pair.

'What is the rack?'

'Watch.'

It was a method of punishment employed in the field. The two men were dragged to two separate posts and laced to the uprights. Their hands cuffed in front of them, a rope was passed in between the handcuffs and pulled around a second post, set in front of them, until their arms strained in the sockets. The rivals were left in that excruciating position for the remainder of the break. They had been brawling over a woman. The voice of Ol' Bones broke his concentration.

'That is why it is difficult to cook up an escape, Jacob,' he said, heaving a sigh. 'We don't work together, cos we're too busy fighting each other.'

Engrossed in the activities surrounding the rack, Jacob said nothing. The woman at the centre of the quarrel was compelled to stand before her suffering rivals. She was shapely and vulnerable. So much so that moments later, together with a hatchet-faced overseer, Ferrers proceeded to shove the woman into the canefield until they were out of sight. Clenching his fists with fury, he whispered to Ol' Bones.

'She goes like a sheep?' he asked. 'Why does she not struggle?'

'Remember what I told you,' said Ol' Bones, 'about them who escaped and never recaptured?'

'Yes?'

'Them make plans and wait for a lucky break,' said Ol' Bones. 'Like them, if she put up no struggle, she will live another day and get another chance. Boy, she too is waiting for a lucky break.'

One hour went by. Two grinning overseers sauntered out of the canefield. Her hands lashed behind her, a silent seething woman stumbled along behind them with her eyes averted. The women ran to her aid. The canecutters kept their distance, partly out of empathy, but mostly because white men had sullied her. Ol' Bones told him that she would be regarded as unclean until the men forgot. The conch ended the food break and any further chat. All through that long afternoon, Jacob angrily chopped down stalk after stalk.

A blood-red sun kissed the horizon. The conch wailed the end of the working day. Struggling out of Farthest Field, every bone in Jacob's body protested. Ol' Bones helped him back to the cart into which he tossed his machete, before merging with the line-up on Liberty Lane.

'Machetes accounted for,' an overseer shouted.

'Count 'em,' shouted Ferrers.

An overseer kicked the gang into a single file. He then walked slowly back up the line counting them.

'We got 'em all,' he shouted.

'Chain 'em,' barked Ferrers.

The end of the endless chain was passed through the iron ring attached to Jacob's ankle. Threaded through the iron ring of each slave, both ends were then padlocked together. On the tailboard of the cart, the pair who had suffered the rack lay writhing and groaning in a semi-conscious state with blood oozing from shoulder blades where the skin had broken. Behind the cart, women supported the violated woman.

'Now see here you idle niggers,' Ferrers said, 'this day you filled barely twenty-five carts. You'd better fill twenty-six on the morrow, else some of you will get a taste the cat.

'Yes Massa,' cried one hundred and twenty exhausted voices.

Mounting his horse, Ferrers cracked his whip.

'Get going you lazy niggers,' he shouted.

The column shuffled forwards. Churning with agony and rage, Jacob staggered the three miles back to the Slop House. By the time the endless chain was removed, it was pitch black. Virtually carrying him to the chattel house, Ol' Bones laid him out on the boards. Through mists of slumber, he heard a soft voice.

'Only way to escape is by planning, young buck,' Ol' Bones said. 'Never ever forget that.'

'I will not forget,' he mumbled, before crashing into sleep.

Some time later he awoke to find himself gazing up into the dark moist eyes of Moses, who chuckled and spoke in Yoruba.

'Wake up Jacob, now you eat. Your time to quit this life is yet to be. The dark comes before the light. Something tells me that destiny will bash your door. Eat, drink and gather strength. I give you plenty *obi* to ease your pain.'

From dawn till dusk under the plantation's exacting regime, Jacob sweated in the canefields. Night after night Moses began his lessons by counselling him against running away, and then proceeded to teach him the English language. The days drifted into weeks.

Late one Saturday afternoon, he was on the verandah when the old man, who knew more than most about the island, began relating what he knew of Pertigua. Quoting from the wealth of information inside his elderly head, he reckoned that in 1750, Pertigua had around fifteen thousand whites and over one hundred and eighty thousand slaves. Though staggered both by the figures and by the old man's detailed knowledge of them, he wondered how accurate they were. The ratio of slaves to whites had been steadily increasing in recent times. Faced with the rising slave numbers, said the old man, the plantation owners called for more overseers, craftsmen and indentured servants for extra security. Their agents responded by sending press-gangs into the taverns of England.

Ferrers had apparently been a victim of this practice. The old man was already at Tamarind Trees when Ferrers first arrived. He told the old man that he'd been abducted in a drunken state outside the Prospect of Whitby public house, next to London's Wapping Wall. Dumped in the hold of the barque, *Evening Star*, he was shipped to Pertigua. Fifty guineas was paid for the eighteen-year-old, who arrived on the plantation ostensibly as an indentured servant. It was not long before the angry young novice saw that, despite his debased status on the plantation, his white skin held power.

Ferrers began life on Pertigua, sweating and lodging with the slaves and cutting cane on the plantation. In almost every respect, he had been a slave. It was an experience from which he never recovered. During those first gruelling years, he survived, like the slaves, on starvation rations. After serving the term of three indentured years, he was granted the customary three acres of land awarded to new supervisors. From the beginning of his life as an overseer, in addition to a wage, he was rewarded with the power of life and death over the slaves, a two-bedroom bungalow and a slave woman upon whom he could force himself nightly and change at will.

'On account of his slaving in the canefields, Ferrers grow to be a very resentful man,' said Moses. 'So angry is he for being kidnapped and crammed with hate for being whipped, that he flogs slaves mercilessly for the floggings he got. I heard him tell one of his mates that it was his ways that helped turn the plantation into profit. I think that what he said was true 'cos after three seasons as a field overseer, he were made head overseer. The number of overseers rise to thirty-five. Slaves grow from fifty to one hundred and twenty. Believe it or not, Jacob, 'cos the plantation owners needed more slaves, them start breeding slaves on this here island. Them call it Pickaninny Farm. It is down in the parish of Dorset.'

Pulling a face and downing some rum, Jacob urged the old man to tell him more.

'I was shipped to this here island as a young man,' said Moses. 'Pickaninny Farm had been up and running for a while. Them select muscular men who them considered sturdy and silent. Them send us to the Farm where we were forced to fuck strong passive women for the purpose of making strong humble children.'

'Fucking is better than cutting cane, Moses.'

'The babies were sold at birth, Jacob!'

'Sold at birth?'

'Men and women were sorted and match up like cattle. I was the bull reared for his seed.'

'That is truly wicked.'

'I father ten children, then I ran into big trouble.'

'Your seed dried up?'

'I said no to a big fat white woman.'

'What did she want?'

'To take me to her cot!'

'And you refused to get into it?'

'She was the supervisor, Jacob. She look like a pig.'

'What did she do?'

'I was given twenty-four lashes and clapped in the stocks. To stop me talking or eating, a long flat iron was strapped above my tongue. I was left like that for three days. It was a long lingering agony. On the fourth day, the iron was pulled from my mouth. I was spread-eagled to the iron frame. A thin strip of wet hide was tied around my balls and I was left under the sun. As the hide dry out, it started strangling my balls. That was when truth bash my wits. The words screamed through my head – I am a slave. I am a slave. I am a slave. *That* was the truth, Jacob. I screamed until I see my own bleeding soul. When she was satisfied with my cries for mercy, she set me free. After I was healthy and strong again, I give her everything I got to make her happy.'

Clenching his teeth and closing his eyes, Jacob opened them on the old man with a higher regard.

April 1751

One bright Sunday morning, Jacob was digging over his vegetable garden when he saw the plantation owner's daughter enter the Oval gardens with Florence in her wake. Easing off work, it took all his strength not to shout out to her. It was the first time he had seen her since they had arrived on the Tamarind Trees plantation. Dressed in a black ankle-length dress with pinafore, she appeared stiff and remote, one hand behind her back and the other carrying a basket of vegetables. Overjoyed by the mere sight of her, he leaned on his shovel to watch her progress. Given the direction in which they were heading, he soon realised that they were making for his allotment, a square rod of land given to all slaves to supplement their meagre diet. To avoid incurring the wrath of the white woman, he resumed digging. Moments later he heard her white voice at the opposite end of his plot.

'Wait here, Florence.'

The white woman walked towards him alone.

'What do you grow there, Jacob?' she asked, softly.

Straightening up, he beheld the eyes that had watched him being assaulted in the drawing room of the Great House. Contrary to the counsel of Ol'Bones on 'holding the eyes' of whites, he sustained his gaze.

'Sweet potatoes and beans, Missy Bradshaw.'

Though he could not be certain, he thought he caught the trace of a smile.

'Come here, Jacob,' she said. 'I have a task I want you to perform.'

Dropping his shovel, he took a step towards her. Though her eyes at first appeared cold, they softened when she smiled. Otherwise, she remained the prim woman he had been warned off by her father.

'What do you want me to do, Missy Bradshaw?'

'This night, Jacob, I want you to report to the summer-house,' she said. 'You are to wash and you are not to tell a soul. Is that clear?'

'Yes, Missy Bradshaw.'

Without turning around she waved a hand at Florence.

'This house slave will bring you to me,' she said. 'Is that understood?'

The close proximity of Florence strongly affected him. He found her nearness almost unbearable. Nonetheless, she looked back at him through a mask he could not interpret.

'Yes, Missy Bradshaw,' he replied.

'If my father ever learns of this matter,' said the white woman sharply, 'you shall both pay with your lives.'

'Yes Missy Bradshaw,' they said together.

'Be sure that remains so,' she retorted.

Having taken seriously her father's threat with regard to what would happen to him if he went anywhere near her, sweat gushed down his temples and his heart beat furiously. How could he refuse her summons to meet her alone? He glanced at Florence. She stared fixedly at the ground.

Turning abruptly, the white woman snapped:

'Come, Florence.'

With his heartbeat quietening down, he watched Florence until she entered the Great House. After seven long months, he thought, the mere sight of her stirs me. Her image charged through his head. At least she was alive and outwardly unhurt. Despite his wretched situation, he ached for her.

On the brink of nightfall, harmonies began drifting from the barracoon. Jacob sat close to the fire in front of the chattel house. Dressed in sleeveless jerkin and breeches and all set for his summons to the summer-house, he sat listening to Moses furnishing him with the gossip from the Slop House. Florence appeared quietly out of the dark. He grinned at her. She spoke softly.

'Are you ready Jacob?'

'No,' he said, rising to his feet.

'Good luck, boy,' said the old man, all but beneath his breath.

Florence turned and walked away. He followed her. On that balmy half-mooned evening amid palm trees rustling in the dark, he fumbled for and found her fingers. Hand in hand they strolled beside the slave-hewn lake, breathlessly whispering their feelings for each other. Behind a screen of yucca plants, coconut palms, paw-paw trees and bougainvillaea, he drew her towards him and took her face in his hands.

'I thirst for you my beloved,' he whispered.

'You are eternally in my thoughts,' she breathed.

The touch of her sultry skin intensified his craving. Her cheeks were cool to his touch. Sliding his hand lovingly down her shoulder, he slipped it down over her breast. Taking her into his embrace, he felt her breathing quicken. Her lips responded to his and her hot tears wet his cheeks. Drawing back from her, he gazed into her eyes.

'My beloved,' he whispered.

Kissing her once more with a searching intensity, her tongue tasted fresh and sweet. Wanting to lay down with her skin to skin, he longed to kiss the breasts he had seen bared, long ago in another existence in Ake. But the white woman was waiting for him in the summer-house, so they must not linger. The instant they sighted the windows of the summer-house, their hands parted. In silence, they walked the remaining distance to the white octagonal building.

'Watch yourself, Jacob, she can be spiteful.'

'Her father warned me off her, yet how can I defy her?'

'You cannot. Her father has gone away with his wife for a week. If the daughter wants to see you on your own . . . '

'That is what I fear.'

'I will come to you when I can,' she said, abruptly changing the subject.

'Come soon.'

The moon slid behind a cloud. He felt her fingers caress his cheeks as her open mouth pressed down on his lips. Pulling back from her momentarily, he whispered:

'I plan to break out. I swear to take you with me.'

Given her soft intake of breath, the darkness could not hide her shocked surprise.

'Break out, Jacob,' she whispered. 'I promise to go with you. Go now. We must not keep that bitch waiting too long.'

Heartened by her vow, he let her go reluctantly. A few short strides and she was swallowed up by the night.

Mounting the steps of the moonlit building, he suddenly felt very alone. Although the front door was faintly ajar, he knocked softly. Silence answered him. He pushed the door. It creaked slowly open. With considerable unease, he tiptoed into the hushed interior. A vestige of lavender entered his nostrils. An owl hooted. He quaked. Candlelight was spilling out of a doorway at the far end of the passage. He stopped abruptly. His heart thumped. Steeling himself and breathing shallowly, he called out softly.

'Missy Bradshaw?'

Her voice shot down the passageway.

'Jacob?'

'It is me, Missy Bradshaw.'

'Bolt the door and come here.'

'Yes, Missy Bradshaw.'

Treading soundlessly down the passage he arrived in the doorway of a large bedchamber. Set in two free-standing, silver-gilt holders, the chamber was lit by tall candles casting a soft shadowy glow. Rich tapestries adorned the walls and simple white muslin hung languidly over the painted shutters. A mosquito net splayed down from the ceiling, encircling a carved mahogany four-poster. There she lay beneath the linen with a half-smile, her black hair swept back off her face and her bare arms lying on top of the coverlet. His eyes fell on her covered shape. His breathing deepened and his heart faltered. Swallowing hard, sweat streamed down his temples and the nape of his neck. He stayed transfixed in the doorway until he heard her voice.

'Come here,' she said quietly.

He took a tentative step inside the mosquito net. Her finger beckoned him on.

'My father does not know that you stand beside my cot, Jacob. If you make me happy, he will never find out. Come closer.'

Lifting one foot, he took a leaden step nearer to the four-poster.

'Do you know why I sent for you, Jacob?'

Her question unsettled him. Hearing not a trace of authority in her voice, his throat dried. Her voice instead was gentle, causing him to look directly at her, only to meet the feverish intensity in her eyes. Her breathing was heaving with desire as her hand slid up his thigh. The first signs of betrayal stirred in his groin. Flinging aside the coverlet, she exposed her large pink breasts crowned by dark engorged nipples. Her pink nakedness and shock of dark curly hair squashed any illusion as to what she wanted. Recollection of the penalty for the prohibited contact compelled him to pull away, just as he felt a tug at his breeches.

'Off with them.'

Fumbling his clothes off, he stood before her naked. Taking his hand, she placed it firmly on the moistness between her thighs. He attempted to pull away, until he felt her nails sink into his arm. She prohibited his retreat with a command.

'Down.'

Gulping with mortification and kneeling down, he touched the top of her curly mound with his lips. She gasped and then forced his head further down.

'Lick me.'

Under duress he touched her with the tip of his tongue. She groaned and pushed her quivering hips against his tongue. She peaked, and he felt the tremors of her thighs on his cheeks. Sitting up breathless, she pulled him onto the four-poster, pushed him onto his back, and then straddled him. Incredibly, and in spite of his reluctance, he had risen. Taking him in her hand, she rose up on her knees and sank slowly down. Her hair tumbled over her breasts. She began to rise and fall. He stayed almost motionless watching her rising excitement. Her back arched un–expectedly and she discharged a lengthy cry. Following the series of convulsions that shook her body, she crashed down onto him shuddering and instantly surrendered to sleep.

Daring not to budge, he lay beneath her staring into the apex of the mosquito net and fuming at his helplessness. She lay above him softly snoring, with his very black existence in her small white hands. He cursed his subjection.

He had slept with only two women in his life. Both had been Yoruba and a consequence of his choice. Similarly then, as now, he had been on the lookout for their fathers. In the village of Ake, had he been discovered, Yoruba custom would have merely demanded that he take the girl as his wife. All he would have lost was a young man's freedom in exchange for the responsibilities of family life. But he would still be free. As the slave of this white woman, death would be no illusion if he failed to please her. He knew her father would not even consider the idea that he had had no choice but to comply with her orders.

If I make her happy, he thought, she could give me a plot for my house. With a dwelling of my own, I can meet Florence away from prying eyes. During the course of the night, she awoke him on three further occasions to satisfy her lust. At the first streaks of daylight she stirred and opened her eyes.

'Did you sleep, Jacob?' she asked, softly.

'I stay awake to keep watch, Missy Bradshaw.'

'No one will lay a hand on you here, for only I come to this house – it is my refuge. Do not fret, Jacob, my father has journeyed to Jamestown.'

'Can I ask something, Missy Bradshaw?'

'Yes, Jacob.'

'I want to build a house, Missy Bradshaw,' he said warily.

'Yes?' she asked.

'I will need a plot to build on, Missy Bradshaw.'

Throwing on her floral Indian gown, she sauntered over to the window and gazed out. He grew apprehensive. Had he said too much? Had he been too familiar? Beyond her, the sky was streaked with orange and yellows and the deep blue Caribbean Sea was starting to shimmer. The shrill birdsong and the rising heat said it was going to be another scorching April day. At length she turned around and faced him with a calculating smile.

'A chattel house is an attractive thought, Jacob,' she said. 'I shall ponder on it.'

'I have to join the First Gang, Missy Bradshaw.'

'You will not cut cane this day, Jacob.'

As if by some mysterious command, her Indian gown fell open to reveal a shock of dark curly hair. Sinking onto the four-poster, she rolled onto her back and pulled him onto her.

'Ferrers can do without you this day,' she sighed. 'My needs comes first.'

With her nails digging into his buttocks, he slowly entered. She groaned.

Long after midday, she awoke and fetched a tray bearing china plates and silver cutlery emblazoned with the falcon-crest of her family. He gave her a hesitant smile. From the parlour, she produced an oval silver platter upon which lay a broiled chicken and a roast ham, with boiled potatoes filling an ornate porcelain tureen. To sweeten the flavour of the meat, there was a silver sauceboat filled with berries cooked in syrup. Picking indifferently at her food with a fork, he ate ravenously with his hands. The more he devoured, the more she proffered. Finally, she tendered a hunk of cheese, red grapes and a flagon of light rum. There he stayed until sunset, when she sent him away with a word of warning.

'Not a word to anyone about this, Jacob,' she said. 'I am content with you. I shall send for you again. Remember I can have you removed from the First Gang.'

'To send me where, Missy Bradshaw?'

'Why to no gang at all,' she said breezily. 'I can have you trained as a gardener, a carpenter, a mason or anything else I want. That depends on whether you keep me happy. Otherwise, I can make your life extremely unpleasant. I advise you to keep me content, Jacob. Now go. I will send for you when I want you again.'

Stepping out of the summer-house, he headed for the chattel house. Stripped of his manhood by a woman who had forced him to sleep with her angered him. The reward for his services was his continued existence and the leftovers of his feast in the bag over his shoulder. By some means he made it back to the chattel house. There he found the old man on the steps with tears in his eyes swigging a bottle of Jack-iron rum.

'I sit all night,' Moses sobbed. 'I sit and fret for you.'

'Grieve not old man,' he said. 'I will never forget the tears you shed for me this day.'

'People round here vanish if you blink,' said Moses. 'If you don't see a body for one whole day, he has been sold or he is dead.'

He became keenly aware of the old man's eyes again, and the hurt that bled from them. Moved by the old man's solicitude, he placed a reassuring hand around his bony shoulders.

12 June 1751

During her father's absences in the month of May, Faith Bradshaw sent for him, twice. By his third visit, Jacob realised that, intriguingly, the frenzy that had initially characterised her demands, seemed to be tiring, to be replaced by a deeper, graceful, more comforting intercourse. A new enquiry was emanating from her eyes into his being and humanity, rather than at the blackness of him. It was as if she really wanted to understand him and his life on the coast of Guinea. But while she craved carnal pleasure, he yearned for freedom.

The source of Faith Bradshaw's hunger for bodily relations lay in her emotionally barren upbringing. She was the only child of a gin-soaked mother and a stern, combative, Catholic father, who had got rich from slavery long before her birth in the Great House of the Tamarind Trees plantation. On her arrival, she was bundled into the arms of a glacial wet-nurse, to spend the rest of her vulnerable years under the tongue of a starchy Northumbrian governess who believed that physical contact was a sin. Following a tutored schooling, she was kept occupied managing the accounts of the plantation. Emerging from years of adolescent and maidenly loneliness, she was withdrawn and frosty. She became partner-less at balls and garden parties, given that the bucks of Pertigua made clear their preference for *femmes fatales*.

Many months had passed since the timely demise of her last, aged suitor. Restless and physically frustrated, she finally yielded to temptation and resolved to take advantage of the power she possessed over her father's slaves. Her decision coincided with the advent of Jacob. A few days after he had been introduced onto the plantation, aglow with excitement, she invited her friend Rose to luncheon at her summer-house.

'I have seen him,' she gushed.

'But have you seen it?' Rose giggled. 'Is it as firm as the rest of him? My slave's is almost brutal.'

'He pants like a wild black stallion,' she said. 'He has a fine powerful body. An intriguing tempest rages in his eyes. And there is a heady vivacity about his person.'

'There are many like him. Why him in particular?'

'His attitude and the look he gave me,' she said. 'He needs breaking in.'

'What look did he give you?'

'One of arrant hostility.'

'Hostility?'

'In the drawing room when he first arrived,' she replied. 'That slave is consumed with arrogance. But I shall break him.'

It was a warm June evening. Jacob was chatting with Moses and Ol' Bones on the moonlit verandah of the chattel house. Florence appeared in a gingham dress and a basket in her hand. Sitting cockily upright, Ol' Bones grinned.

'You want me, Princess?' he asked.

Shifting his left stump to make himself comfortable against a pillar, Moses laughed.

'She got no use for them old bag of bones,' he said.

'The bitch sent me to fetch you, Jacob,' she said, raising the basket. 'I steal snapper and bread from the Great House for you.'

Smiling at the suggestive signals passing between his companions, Jacob stood up and stepped off the verandah.

'Share my fish between you countrymen, I must go.'

'Watch your backside boy,' laughed Moses.

'And your front,' Ol' Bones added.

Clasping her hand in front of his trusted friends, they made for the lake beneath a silvery moon. Halting on a grassy apron by the water's edge under a flowering hibiscus, he kissed her neck lovingly. In a string of kisses, he moved onto her cheeks and then his lips met hers. Her heart pounded against his chest and his hunger intensified.

'To escape this hell is all I think about.'

'You're a dream believer. I see it in you when we found the cowries of the white slavers in that chest.'

'What is a dream believer?' he enquired

'Someone who makes things happen.'

'What are the others?'

A gaggle of ducks crash-landed on the moonlit, mirrored surface. Turning to look at the waters, she breathed:

'Just dreamers.'

For what seemed a lifetime, he held her close.

'Do what you must to do,' she whispered, 'I will go with you when you break out. And when you have put up your house, I will lie with you.'

She turned to go back to the big house. He mounted the steps for his fourth visit.

The front door was slightly ajar. Gently pushing it open, he stepped inside. He trod lightly towards the candlelight spilling into the passageway. Stepping into the bedchamber, he experienced the rare scent of oranges. By the window, on a George II walnut lowboy, were platters of meat, chicken, potatoes and fruit. To the side were two flagons, one of water and one of rum. His eyes shifted to the four-poster. There she lay, dark-eyed and sultry, her jet-black hair framing her pale face and a playful finger toying inside her parted lips. He hoped she would not see that he was aroused. The means to fulfil his dream of escape with Florence lay before him in the planter's daughter, who drew back the bed linen sufficient to reveal her breasts.

'Come, Jacob.'

Stripping off his clothes, he lay down beside her.

'I want you, Jacob,' she said tenderly.

Sliding her hand down his groin, she took him in her hand, rose onto her knees and straddled him. Lust blazed from her eyes. Sinking down, she groaned as he crossed her threshold. As if intent on shaking off something, her fervour grew rapacious and frenzied, until she bellowed a long agonising cry, igniting his hunger. Utterly out of control, without uncoupling and with Florence filling his head, he turned her on her back and almost instantly shuddered. In the ensuing moments of gratifying descent, she clung to him tightly and gradually she fell deeply asleep.

Annoyed with himself for yielding, he rolled onto his back and lay staring at the ceiling of murals depicting titillating panels of cavorting nymphs and shepherdesses. Eventually, he too fell asleep.

The questioning began in the early hours of the morning.

'From where do you come, Jacob?'

'The village of Ake on the coast of Guinea, Mistress Faith,' he replied.

'I know not anything of that coast,' she said sympathetically, 'you must tell me all about your land and your people.'

At first, he was uncertain whether it was a request, an order or a new class of torment. Following a faltering pause, he told her about his family and the people of Ake. She was visibly moved when he spoke of the attack on his village by men off the *Pelican*, the forced march through the rainforest, the dungeons of Cape Coast Castle, the ocean crossing and his sale in the Auction House.

'Now I am your slave,' he concluded matter-of-factly.

'Would you not agree that your people fare better here in Pertigua?'

'Why do you say that, Mistress Faith?'

'Here your people are fed and are better protected,' she said. 'I am told that in your land you are stricken by scores of wars and dangerous animals?'

Her words riled him. But with his slave status very much at the vanguard of his thoughts, he selected his words carefully.

'In my land I was free, Mistress Faith,' he said. 'It is true my people fight many wars. We also make peace. The wild animals live in the forest and hardly ever come into my village. But the men who kidnapped me, killed my people and carried me here were white. What protection do I have from them?'

Faith felt ashamed. Her mind raced back to an exchange she had recently held with her friend, Rose Greenwood. On a glorious day arched by a turquoise sky, they had gone riding through the woodland and cane–fields of the Greenwood plantation. In the heat of midday they had stopped to water their mounts. By the water's edge her friend had casually recounted a sickening incident.

'One of our runaways has suffered a field amputation,' she had said.

'What did they hack off?'

'His left foot.'

'Blessed Mary, Mother of God. I am horrified at what we are doing.'

'Don't be so ridiculous, Faith. They were heathens who spent a goodly measure of time despatching each other in the most ungodly ways.'

'While we're about it, tell me who gave us the right to turn them into slaves?'

'Might is our right, for are we not infinitely superior?' Rose had asked. 'As I see it, our Christian duty is to civilise those less fortunate and weaker than ourselves. Through slavery, we advance civilisation. We transport them to Pertigua away from poverty and disease. Here we feed and clothe them, for which in return they must earn their keep.'

'Go to any plantation and take a good look at the misery there,' Faith had retorted. 'For at the end of the attenuated road you speak of, you and

I are slave owners. We are the direct beneficiaries from the horrors being perpetrated on the coast of Guinea, as well as, in case you have forgotten, here in Pertigua. And what is more, it allows us to live in the comfort to which we have grown so accustomed.'

'Why, Faith, I do believe that your lust for this slave has conquered your judgment,' Rose had said, mockingly. 'And I do detect that you are in danger of combining with the reformists on the plight of the niggers. Have we not been tutored by some of England's greatest minds that they are a lesser species? If I did not know you better, I might think that you were more concerned for them than your own kind.'

'What, me a reformist?' she had asked. 'You are indeed mistaken. Hear me out, Rose. We took it upon ourselves to leave our shores and make mischief in foreign lands. And speaking of the trade, to put it succinctly, Rose, we steal people, whether we buy or kidnap them. Even if they were of a lower species, they are still human, which makes them very much like us. What I am saying is that our power stems from the fact that we carry the musket and cannon.'

'You should hear yourself, Faith,' Rose had said. 'You sound like an abolitionist. You would not have such ease were we not superior. Slavery is sanctioned by our Church, or are you now of the opinion that our clergy, our merchants and their bankers are misguided to endorse or finance such activities? Abolitionists are not to be trusted and ought to be locked up, for they are determined to demolish our way of life utterly. My great-great-great grandmother all but died reaching these shores with the *Lady Margaret* expedition. As governess to the Fleming family, Emma Chapman helped turn these islands into the tropical haven we so enjoy. She would twirl in her grave were she to hear your words. Where would our kind be without slavery?'

She awoke, with a start, from her reflections. The truth was hideous. Her eyes fell onto the body next to hers. A wild fury seized her.

'Get up, Jacob, and get out.'

Tears were streaming down her cheeks when she screamed.

'Get out! Get out!'

Leaping off the four-poster and scampering into his breeches, Jacob shot out of the bedchamber. He fled down the steps, with his heart beating horribly. Was it something I said? he thought. He knew that she could invent a slur for any punishment she wanted – disfigurement, amputation, being skinned alive, hanged or sold to another plantation or even another island. He would lose Florence. Covered with sweat and distraught, he panted into the chattel house and collided with Moses.

'Why are you fretting, Jacob?'

Gulping down two mouthfuls of rum, he answered.

'She's spitting blood, Moses.'

'What she say?'

'She ask about my village and how I came to be here. What I said sent her into a rage.'

'That's the white way,' sighed the old man with a wry smile. 'Get it into your head and learn quickly boy. She don't want to judge the actions of her people through your eyes. She wants to hear how she helped you by bringing you to civilisation. And how she saved you by taking you to her cot.'

'What do I do?'

'Stay well out of sight.'

A nerve-wracking day turned into two, and then into a week. Being constantly on the alert for an angry white woman sapped his energy. She could spare his life or end it at will. In the following days, he sweated despairingly in the canefields. At night he slept fitfully, awakening from nightmares bathed in sweat – he had been sold and was being carted away in chains, with a screaming Florence looking on. Tossing and turning for the best part of each night, he woke up exhausted at day-break. Worse still, since he had been ordered from the summer-house, Florence seemed to have disappeared. The sight of anyone suffering punishment struck terror into him.

Early one Sunday morning, he was roused by a deep white voice.

'Jacob.'

Looking aghast at Moses, despair gripped his gut. Convinced his end had come, he dressed at snail's pace to eke out the time he thought was left of his existence. Entrusting his few possessions to Moses to share out with Florence and Ol' Bones, he stepped into the sunlight. Leaning against the tamarind tree was a stocky white man in a black dress coat with a black tricorne on his head. About sixty years of age with deep-set eyes and a grey beard, the face seemed startlingly familiar. Frowning deeply, he narrowed his eyes. Was it not at the Auction House where he had first laid eyes on this white face? Yes yes. Those were the very features that had caused the first smile he had ever given to a white man. There had been such incentive in the white man's smile that he had been induced to return it.

'Greensleeves,' the old man said cheerily. 'Nathan Greensleeves at your service, Jacob.'

Why would a white man speak to me this way?

'Calm yourself, Jacob,' said Greensleeves. 'Mistress Faith sent me. I have come to help thee find a site for your chattel house.'

His thoughts raced: what really lies behind this white man's kind approach? Can I trust him? Does it mean that the white woman is keeping her promise, despite her anger?

'I will go with you, Mister Greensleeves,' he replied guardedly.

'Right, young Jacob,' said Greensleeves, 'come and we will find thee a fitting plot.'

Side by side they walked, during which time he learned that the white man performed a variety of tasks for the planter's daughter. Surely then he must have her confidence? His conduct said he did, for he made directly for a glade under a spreading breadfruit tree. The site was conveniently out of the sight of the Great House and a discreet distance from the other chattel houses. Time alone with Florence loomed large. He was overjoyed. If pleasing the white woman is the penalty I have to pay to see my woman, he thought, I'll give her everything. He had to confess that his feelings towards the white woman were changing. A new mood was watering down the hate he had held for her. At this moment, he was not sure what he felt. Despite his existing uncertainties, he gave the white man a broad smile.

'I thank you, Mister Greensleeves.'

'I will help thee whenever I can, Jacob.'

Given this change in his otherwise gloomy fortunes, the dread that had been eating into him for the past days began to slip away. Slumping down at the foot of the tree, the white man rested against the trunk and crossed his legs. He did likewise. A barely credible thought stole into his head – a black man and a white man sitting side by side, without whips, without pain, without hate. A gust of warm heartening air wafted through the clearing. Suddenly there was a new rich yellowness in the light of the rising sun. He had a site for his chattel house. Briefly, he felt his world was at peace.

'I will give you seeds for your plot, Jacob. The soil on this island is rich. You can grow anything you want in it. I will show you.'

'And I will learn quickly, Mister Greensleeves.'

'Mistress Bradshaw wants you to have the timber you need,' said Greensleeves. 'Now you will let me know, Jacob, what you will be wanting for your shelter?'

'I thank you, Mister Greensleeves,' he said. 'I will ask you for what I need.'

He ran all the way back to the chattel house to tell of his good luck. Following his account, Moses had much to say about Greensleeves.

'For 'bout forty years, Greensleeves has been the key propagator for many of the plantations,' said the old man. 'Before Faith was born, Bradshaw was away in Jamestown a lot in them days. Sometimes he would not come back for weeks at a time. Them were all young then. The sun shone on their lives. Day after day, he left his hot-blooded wife Katherine by herself with gin under the hot sun. After fondling the cane shoots in his nursery, Greensleeves would come and caress Katherine and give it to her good. I was right in this here chattel house when she was with child. Bradshaw was gone most of that year. The bugger never figured it out. But all his slaves know that Greensleeves is the blood-father of Faith.'

'Bradshaw must be blind!' Jacob exclaimed.

'That devil is deaf and dumb as well. Greensleeves knows that his daughter is very sad. He wants her to be happy. So he helps you to please her.'

'You think she knows he is her father?'

'She not know but them is very close. Always have been.'

'And Bradshaw doesn't know?'

'Nope,' said Moses. 'Bradshaw's head was up his arse when Green-sleeves hand 'tween his wife's legs.'

Jacob chuckled. That afternoon and for the rest of his free day he planned his chattel house – a minute space with covered verandah, within which he would secrete the gold dust given him by Captain Tomba.

The instant Jacob obtained his plot, Woodham Ferrers kept a close eye on him. In the subsequent hot punishing weeks, as well as sweating in the canefields, Jacob began to build his chattel house under the suspicious eyes of the overseer, who was never far away. For his part, Jacob kept the overseer in his sight at all times.

By the first week of July, Jacob had finished his chattel house. On a platform set on stones two feet off the ground, he built a habitat for himself and his small number of possessions. Excavating a hole in a wooden upright, he stuffed the tiny bag of gold dust into the cavity and filled it with mud. Carefully wiping the pillar, no trace of his handiwork was evident.

Ol' Bones and Moses appeared that night to visit his chattel house. After serving them rice and fish, they swigged rum from his cracked Waterford bottle. He pulled out a cane pipe and filled it with weed. Accepting the offering, Moses beamed and lit the pipe. Ol' Bones passed Jacob a folded yellowed paper. Spreading it out, he found himself staring at a sketch of the island, with its bays, inlets and surrounding islands. It had been compiled over many years from what Ol' Bones had seen, as well as scraps of information provided by recaptured runaways. Taking the candle closer to the drawing, Jacob traced the route they would take once they were off the plantation. Sitting back, he began picking his teeth thoughtfully.

'Moses think the rainy season is the best time to go,' said Ol' Bones.

Sitting bolt upright, Jacob pulled the toothpick slowly out of his mouth.

'When you say go, you do mean break out?' he asked.

'It will be a long hard trek and a hard hard climb, Jacob,' said Ol' Bones.

'When is the rainy season?'

'September to November,' replied Ol' Bones.

'Why is that a good time?'

'Rain make it hard for dogs to smell your backside,' chuckled Ol' Bones. 'If we cross river in flood and them follow, them drown in the digee current.'

The two old hands chuckled. Jacob frowned. Moses explained.

'When I escaped,' he said, 'I run all night 'cos of them pitiless dogs. Them hellhounds bite plenty of black backsides. On the second night, the dogs catch up with me. I swim quick quick across the river. I look back to see the hounds in the river struggling to hell. I see them being carried away crying for mercy. So I give them plenty of mercy like them gives we. Picking up some big spikey rocks, I throw them at the beasts. I hit one boof and he go under to dog hell and don't come back up. River go whoosh, and the two hounds go same way. I stand on the riverbank, jumping up and down, busting my sides. Overseers stand on other bank and watch their slave-killers dying. Them get very angry and shoot at my backside. I get out of there quick, and the overseers shout:

'Nigger, we're coming back with more dogs.'

'I shout back, whitey, your killers have gone to join the rest in hell. And when you get there, them will sink their teeth into your big fat white bottom.'

The two men chuckled. Jacob's thoughts returned to his plans for escape.

'Our passage may well be flooded in the rainy season,' he asked. 'What if we need a boat to go by sea?'

'It will take gold, luck or both,' said Ol' Bones, 'if the seller can be trusted to sell you a seaworthy boat.'

'We'll break out in November,' Jacob announced, calmly. 'In four months we'll have all we need – weapons, food and water. We must make contact with the runaways in the mountains. Is that possible?'

Glancing uneasily at each other at first, the two men turned their eyes on him. Clearing his throat, Ol' Bones answered.

'We'll warn them in Lake Disappointment,' he said quietly. 'To do that, we talk to the Hungan who is like a Mogba on this island. He leaves his body in a dream to talk to the runaways hiding in Lake Disappointment. The Hungan can even talk to the Mogbas on the coast of Guinea. You follow the Hungan out of his body in the same dream, Jacob. You cross to the land of rootless spirits and talk to the runaways 'bout your plans.'

He scowled. How can anyone talk in a dream? These two have had too much sun. Or have they been slaves too long? Maybe the brutality on this plantation has shrunk their heads and their senses.

'Let me tell you about the white man's spirit world, Jacob,' said Ol' Bones quietly. 'Take Bradshaw. He is Roman Catholic.'

'Roman what?' he asked.

'A Roman Catholic,' Ol' Bones repeated. 'Bradshaw worships the Virgin Mary.'

'Bradshaw worships a virgin?' he asked. 'Why?'

Moses laughed.

'She's a new breed of virgin,' said Ol' Bones, 'who give birth to a baby boy called Jesus.'

Were his ears deceiving him?

'A virgin have baby boy called Je-sus?' he asked.

'Jesus, Son of God,' said Ol' Bones emphatically. 'God is like *Oluwa*.'

'A virgin give birth?' he asked. 'Not possible.'

'Mister Bradshaw worships in a big house called Catholic Church,' said Ol' Bones. 'Cos we his property, we worship in the same house as him. But this night belong to we. This night we worship voodoo.'

'Voodoo?' he asked, frowning. 'Who is voodoo?'

'Voodoo belong to slaves,' said Ol' Bones. 'God of voodoo called Papa Goodwill. Only the Hungan has the gift to get in touch with Papa Goodwill. He is not easy to reach, that is why we are still slaves. Hungan said slaves should believe only in Papa Goodwill, 'cos he is the only God who can save us. White priest say we slaves 'cos we sinners. I myself don't know what I did wrong. White priest says, believe in the Virgin Mary and we will be saved.'

Rubbish, thought Jacob, I don't believe in any of it.

'If this Virgin Mary be on our side and we is slaves,' he asked hesitantly, 'and she is also on the white man's side, but he is free – whose side do you think she is truly on?'

A fleeting quizzical look passed between his companions, who then broke into a quiet fit of laughter.

'Why has Papa Goodwill not come to free us before now?' he asked.

'Before Papa Goodwill reveals himself and his great works,' replied Ol' Bones, 'we sing redemption song and pass through many revelations until we is clean. Papa Goodwill himself is the final revelation. After we leave this life, we go to the Promised Land where we is born again and come back clean. If you do not worship Papa Goodwill, you go straight to hell where you burn in big big fire. 'Til the day of final revelation when Goodwill shows himself, we worship Iwa.'

On hearing a familiar name, Jacob readily responded.

'Iwa is a powerful spirit,' he said.

'Iwa will set us free, but we must take a gift,' said Ol' Bones.

'What gift must we give Iwa?' he asked.

'Hungan tell us when we meet for mass,' replied Ol' Bones. 'He put *juju*, Catholic prayers and Latin words into his big pot, he mash it up and out fall voodoo. Bradshaw must never catch you talking about voodoo or he will cut out your tongue. If a slave give away plans to overseers, the Hungan turn him into zombie.'

'Zombie?' he exclaimed.

'Zombie is a body with no soul,' said Moses. 'Like Ol' Bones say, slave law say a slave who betrays us will be killed. After a few days, the Hungan hold a mass and bring him back from the dead. The dead one is then a zombie. After that, the zombie work for the Hungan. All through the day, the Hungan hide the zombie and only bring him out at night to cut cane. The cuttings of the zombie are left in Farthest Field. Second Gang pick up cuttings of First Gang during long hot day. It makes it look like the First Gang cut much cane.'

Spellbound as he was by what they said, Jacob believed not a word. It is not possible to come back from the dead, he thought. However, since the map belongs to Ol' Bones, it would be unwise to reject his beliefs. Discharging a weary sigh, Moses, the older man, rose unsteadily onto his crutches.

'Countrymen, I go back to my house,' he said. 'Mass too far for me one foot.'

'Come Jacob,' said Ol' Bones, 'we go to voodoo mass.'

The instant they left the chattel house, he grew uneasy. Under a watery moon, they set off through the canefields for Dolphin Bay and the disturbing realm of Voodoo.

Pointing to the southwest, Ol' Bones said:

'We go that way. Follow me, Jacob, and do everything I do. When we get to the crossroads, I will carry out a ritual to learn the location of the mass.'

At the junction, he followed Ol' Bones to the centre of the junction and knelt down. Following his sign of the cross, the old man produced a small leather gourd filled with sanctified juniper oil. Pouring the oil onto the road, it splashed unswervingly to the northwest. Emitting a fiendish cackle, Ol' Bones ended his ceremony by touching the top of each road with his right foot.

'This I do or danger walk with us,' he said. 'A while back, an overseer tried to stalk us and disappeared. His mates now too frightened to want to know.'

Throwing anxious glances around, the old man pressed on. Though Jacob was clamouring for answers, he stayed silent and fell in behind his companion. They entered a dark and dense wooded region. All he could hear were rustling trees, barking dogs and the steady thud of the old man's steps. Some distance ahead, a fire-lit clearing came into view through a row of flaming immortel trees. The old man quickened his steps. Some distance later they entered a glade. A group of worshippers was gathered around the fire, chanting in Latin from the repetitive texts taught by the local Catholic priest. As the voodoo rites eerily resonated through the darkness, shadows like haunting silhouettes flittered over the foliage in the flame light. Sweat was trickling down his neck. Jacob felt his hackles rise. Beckoning him into the pentagonal-shaped assembly and pointing his finger at a bizarre visage, the old man whispered hoarsely.

'The Queen!'

Dressed in a red cloak, her face was painted with vertical red and white stripes. Round-faced and rotund, she held a skull in one hand. Jacob shivered. Kneeling before her was a row of voodoo devotees with bowed heads. Beside her stood the Hungan – a wiry, balding voodoo priest in a black cloak. In his left hand, he held a long silver knife. A pit viper hung from his right. Muttering unintelligibly, she poured drops of an oily libation from the skull onto the hair of each devotee. Alongside Ol' Bones, he joined the queue, knelt down and waited his turn.

'She do cleansing,' whispered Ol' Bones. 'We must be clean to meet Baron Septem, who is Goodwill's servant. Septem will be here this very night.'

Soon, she had sent droplets of the sacred oil onto the head of Ol' Bones. Pausing before Jacob, she instantly sprang back with alarm.

'Holy Mary,' cried the Queen, 'Mother of Our Blessed Papa Goodwill. Ah Ah. 'O-me-O. You is the Captain. You come at last.'

A sparkling fine black powder began spewing from the mouth of the priest.

'Hallelujah,' cried the Hungan.

All eyes tracked the powder. The fine particles drifted over the assembly. He felt the tension rising in the clearing. In moments he was covered by the black dust, settling inexplicably and solely on his shoulders. The devotees cried out and threw handfuls of parched rice over him.

What did it all mean? Why had the Queen called him the Captain?

Arms yanked him out of the pentagon. Drums began to throb. The devotees danced him around the pentagon three times. Pressed onto his knees by the Queen, she trickled the bile of a freshly slaughtered chicken over his head. When the squelchy mass landed on his scalp, his nostrils smarted from the stink. Bending down, the Queen inscribed the sign of the cross in the dirt. She straightened up and raised her voice.

'O mighty Papa Goodwill,' she cried. 'Bless Jacob your forgotten son who has been found by we. Make his arm strong, for surely he will need it.'

Devotees snatched pieces of dried salted plantain from a wooden bowl. Smiling at the assembly, the Queen thrust upon him a calabash of goat's blood mixed with ground obi and scrapings of sanctified salt.

'Drink,' she said. 'This is my blood.'

Blood spilled over his tongue. Blood entered his gullet. Queasiness gripped his belly. Had the devotees who were now swaying rhythmically behind the Queen not distracted him, he would have vomited.

'Hallelujah, Amen,' they chanted. 'Hallelujah, Amen. Hallelujah, Amen.'

Rejoining Ol' Bones at the side of the pentagon, he sat cross-legged.

'What does it all mean?' he asked.

'That you have been accepted by the island's High Council of voodoo,' said Ol' Bones. 'Everyone here has taken a bloody oath to help you with whatever you have to carry out.'

Talking drums echoed across the island to gossip into the ears of the drum-listeners. By daybreak, all the voodoo worshippers on the island would know about the judgment of the mass held near Tamarind Trees.

'Now we wait for Baron Septem,' said Ol' Bones.

Seven white-robed women suddenly appeared.

'Hounsis disciples,' whispered Ol' Bones. 'Them dance for the Queen.'

In a trancelike state, the disciples entered the pentagon and began to shuffle and reel. By the light of the fire, Jacob made out an ornately carved wooden bench on which the words HOLY SEE were scrawled in birdlime across the back. Worshippers repeatedly chanted a bizarre mishmash of Yoruba, Latin and Catholic prayers. Drums throbbed hypnotically into the night. Two devotees led a ram before the bench. The disciples scattered. The voodoo priest calmly placed the pit viper on the haunches of the now quivering ram. Slithering up to the neck, the snake struck. Yelping horribly and staggering, the ram halted and groaned, sank to its knees and fell dead. Slitting the ram's throat, the voodoo priest held the animal firmly while its blood pumped into a white-daubed calabash. The drums climbed to a higher pitch. The dance steps of the disciples took on a lustful flavour. Jacob's heart pounded. The Queen raised her arms.

'Stop,' she screamed.

The drums and chanting stopped at once. Dogs ceased barking and the rustle of the cane stopped. Silence came out of his mouth when Jacob tried to speak to the old man. Sound was no more. Even the hum of the earth had died.

Mumbling unintelligibly, the Queen raised the blood-filled calabash above her head and lowered it to the ground. Something flew from her hand into the fire. Bursting into red and saffron smoke, the vapours coalesced into a lofty, faceless figure. With yellow sockets for eyes and a backwards-curving horn rising from its forehead, a silvery aura completed the apparition. Before this ghastly image the Queen and the devotees prostrated themselves. The ecstatic kneeling congregation chanted:

'Welcome Baron Septem, servant of Papa Goodwill.'

Whispering through the fields came the distinctive swish of the breeze. Dogs began to bark. Leaves stirred with the chirp of crickets and sound was restored. The Queen rose to her feet. The shimmering figure of Baron Septem turned eerily from left to right.

'He look for Hoodoo,' whispered Ol' Bones.

Nervously glancing around the gathering, Jacob frowned.

'Who?' he asked.

'Hoodoo is someone or something who makes bad luck,' whispered Ol' Bones. 'They're not welcome at voodoo mass.'

Jacob caught the sign passed between Baron Septem and the Queen. From the edge of the clearing the choir, in white cotton habits, began singing Gregorian chants. One by one, the worshippers stepped forward and whispered their petitions to the Queen, who repeated each supplication to Baron Septem.

'Baron Septem will take each plea to Papa Goodwill,' whispered Ol' Bones.

Jacob remained silent.

'Tell her what you want, Jacob,' urged Ol' Bones.

'I will,' he said.

Twelve petitioners were seen before Jacob. Stepping up to the Queen when his turn came, he put his lips to her ear.

'I plan to break out of the plantation,' he whispered. 'I want to talk with the runaways in the mountains. I have gold.'

Anxiously, he watched her eyes searching his face for what felt an age. She turned and engaged Baron Septem in voiceless dialogue. Moments later, she turned back to him:

'It is all set,' she said. 'You go with the Hungan and meet them runaways. Gold first, then you leave your body here and go. When mass ends, the Hungan talk about escape. Sit down here.'

Under the piercing gaze of Baron Septem, he tendered half of his gold dust to the Queen. He sat cross-legged before her in the dirt. Dispensing half a coconut shell filled with a dark liquid, the voodoo priest pointed up at the heavens.

'Drink,' he said. 'You cannot talk up there. To talk you must think. Just think.'

He was suddenly seized with convulsions. Frenziedly writhing and twisting about, he felt powerful hands pinning him firmly to the ground. Eyes wide open, he felt himself deserting his body and soaring effortlessly upward. Waiting for him in the starry heavens were Baron Septem and the Hungan. Unbelievably, he could see the stars through the ethereal form of the Hungan. From a great height, he looked down at the voodoo mass. Beside the fire stood the Queen and her worshippers, close to his lifeless body sprawled in the dirt. Grasping the Hungan's outstretched hand, they began to glide. Soaring over the Great House of Tamarind Trees and Mount James, they were soon above marshland.

High above the swamps of Lake Disappointment, a spirit form materialised. Wafting closer, the silvery pupils of the apparition gazed unswervingly at him. Uncannily, he found himself understanding the thoughts coming from it.

'My name is Samuel,' thought the spirit. 'I left a life of hell behind on the plantation.'

Samuel had escaped over five years before from the China Lights plantation of Randolph Fleming. Through the spirit's thoughts, he ascertained the location of Freetown, the runaway settlement at Lake Disappointment.

'When you break out, take food, plenty, plenty food, water, rope and machete,' said the spirit. 'You come. I wait. When you reach Lake Disappointment, don't trust Elijah. I go now. I tell you don't trust Elijah.'

Following that forewarning the spirit vanished. Together with the Hungan and Baron Septem, they descended to the voodoo ceremonies where he woke up with a jolt. Gazing about, his head was thumping. Nothing had changed. The horned figure of Baron Septem remained steadfastly in evidence, as did the Queen. How could he leave his body? Had he been drugged? Had he truly met Samuel? Who was Elijah?

'We talk when mass finish,' said the Hungan.

Raising her arms, the Queen cried out at the still rising moon. A furious wind whirled around Baron Septem. The assembled fell face first into the dirt.

'Don't look,' whispered Ol' Bones. 'You must not look.'

All heads bowed to the ground. Minutes passed. Mysteriously, as if freed by an unspoken command, the assembled raised their heads simultaneously. Jacob did likewise. Baron Septem had vanished. Raising her arms, the Queen cried out.

'Go now my people. Go. This mass is at an end.'

Before heading back to the plantations, the devotees kicked dirt over the fire until it fizzled out.

'Come, we must talk,' said the Hungan.

Mystified and perturbed, Jacob followed Ol' Bones and the priest into the darkness, away from the pentagonal-shaped assembly and through the canefields near Dolphin Bay. Smoke rose wispily into the night sky behind them.

Striding silently behind the two men through the rustling cane, Jacob's thoughts revolved around a single issue: what difference would a voodoo priest make to an undisciplined runaway stronghold? In the village of Ake, he had witnessed the powerful effect the *juju* man had on warriors before battle. With potions, incantations and ritual, the *juju* man roused the fighters into a potently heightened state, ready to enter battle with the daring of giants. On Pertigua, the voodoo priest performed much the same function. It is necessary that I take this man with me, he thought.

Eventually the priest halted beneath a breadfruit tree. From there, Jacob could see figures silhouetted by oil lamps in the windows of the Tamarind Trees Great House.

'When I step foot on this bloody island, I think of only one thing,' he said.

'What is that, countryman?' growled the Hungan.

'Breaking out,' he replied.

He saw the priest stiffen in the sparse light.

'You have a plan?'

'We are going to break out. You come?'

'Who go with you?'

'Ol' Bones and Florence.'

The priest recoiled as if he had been struck across the face.

'*She* from the Great House?'

'Why not?'

'You trust she?'

'Every breath she takes.'

'You sweet on she?'

He chuckled. Laughing quietly, Ol' Bones added:

'He trusts her with his life. I do with mine.'

'She's a house nigger?'

'We will not go without her.'

A short pause followed his declaration. He felt the priest's hand on his shoulder.

'Count me in, Jacob,' the Hungan growled. 'I make good voodoo in them mountains.'

Without pausing for breath, Jacob outlined his plans when they would break out, what supplies they would take and the route they would follow. He turned to the priest.

'You still with us?' he asked.

'I'm with you, Jacob,' replied the Hungan, with a marked tremor in his voice. 'I know you would come. I know you would come one day.'

'How?' he asked.

'Voodoo,' replied the Hungan, tersely.

Indifferent to his curiosity, the priest turned sniffily away and strode off into the night. Jacob frowned. He knew the shrouded world of the supernatural was a prohibited domain to outsiders. Although he wanted to know more, the brusqueness of the priest's manner counselled him to probe no further. On his way back to the chattel house, he plagued Ol' Bones with questions.

'How was Baron Septem conjured? Who was the one called Samuel? Had he heard about the one called Elijah?'

To all his queries, Ol' Bones responded with a shrug of his shoulders.

Lying on his verandah that night, he gazed into the sky. Any way I look at it, he thought, it is not possible for a man to leave his body behind and wander through the heavens to meet with another. No matter what happens, I won't forget the name Elijah.

Stepping into his musty abode, he lit a candle. Then he heard a footfall on the verandah. Florence opened the door. His heart leapt.

'Quick,' he said, pulling her inside.

Closing the door quietly and turning to face her, he grinned.

'My angel has come at last.'

Her sparkling dark eyes lit up the chattel house.

'I have come, Jacob,' she said sweetly. 'What a fine home you have made.'

Her embrace overwhelmed him with a tender longing. He held her at arms length, to look at her – it was as if he were seeing her for the very first time. With moist eyes he whispered:

'*Iyawomi* – my woman.'

Her wet eyes lifted.

'I love you,' she said softly.

He stroked her cheek.

'I love you, Florence.'

A slender finger traced the contour of his lips. He kissed around her neck, till at last his lips reached her ear.

'I will never let them hurt you,' he whispered.

Dreamily, they slid down onto the straw-filled pallet.

'*Iyawomi*,' he whispered again.

Her lips brushed his shoulders, neck and ears. Lovingly taking off her clothes, she moved about to assist him. In his excitement he fumbled with the fastenings of her pinafore dress. Touching the scars across her breasts, he saw the want in her eyes. Baring her skin until she was utterly naked, she was as charged as he. She reached out for him, her eyes dark, intense and inviting. The heat in him rose. He entered her. They were gripped entirely by a slow luscious rhythm. Her back arched. She smothered her mouth with her hand. He let out a muffled cry and shook as his strength ebbed away. Resting his head between her breasts, his heavy breathing gradually lessened. Interlocked they lay, fulfilled and heavy-eyed after the long-awaited consummation.

In the early hours of the morning, she spoke about the barbaric incidents suffered by the slaves of the Great House. Although she said almost nothing about her own wellbeing, he noted the rage in her voice. He told her about the voodoo mass and his escape plans. Her smile heartened him. He had not seen her smile that way before.

Slipping out of his house before dawn, she made her way back to the Great House.

It was hot, clammy and airless on the first day of August. The Great House resounded with preparations for the yearly Tamarind Trees Summer Ball. A half-day break for the field slaves had been awarded. Around midday the First Gang was ordered to down machetes. Cut, drained and bleeding, Jacob struggled back to the Slop House for his bowl of corn porridge. Then, he headed for his chattel house. About to enter his dwelling, an instinct made him turn. Florence was standing in the shade of the breadfruit tree. She comes in daylight? His heart beat hard as she walked towards him. Taking her by the waist when she reached him, he drew her inside and close until their noses touched. Her lips were quivering when she raised her eyes.

'Kiss me,' she whispered.

Smoothing her mouth with a finger, he touched his lips lightly onto hers.

'I have hungered for you,' he whispered, with a quake in his voice.

An amorous look crept into her eyes.

'I think only of you,' she said. 'We must flee from this wicked place.'

'You put yourself in great danger coming here.'

'Vex not, Jacob. That bitch sent me to tell you to expect her here this night.'

'But she goes to the ball?' he asked. 'How then can she be here?'

'She'll drink and dance and make it look good,' she replied dispassionately. 'The instant her father staggers to his cot, she'll come here.'

'And her mother?'

'She'll be too drunk to notice.'

'The woman is rich, yet she is miserable,' he said.

A strange look entered her dark eyes.

'Make her happy, Jacob. She'll help us escape,' she said. 'I heard her tell her best friend, Rose, that she sweet on you. But Rose do nothing to help you if that spiteful bitch turn on you. That dizzy Rose eats food enough to support an insect. She faint all the time. And she turn scarlet if a man smiles at her. I don't know how she ever got married. That bitch tell Rose you're first man to make her happy. Mistress nasty Bradshaw is a fine friend when she has her way. She's a snake in the grass when she don't.'

The sun was low over the horizon when Jacob left his house with Ol' Bones. Making sure they were not being followed, they scuttled into the giant rhododendron opposite the Great House. Lying on their bellies in the flowering shrub, they watched landaus, phaetons, curricles and carriages drawing up on the grand carriage-drive for the Summer Ball. Cone-shaped corseted women passed sideways through the main door of the Great House. They stifled their laughter. White men swaggered around in florid coats and waistcoats. Ol' Bones was mocking.

'Them strut about like cockerels,' he said.

Poking his head through the foliage, Jacob was confronted by a bizarre spectacle. The guests, men and women, wore bright red lips and porcelain-plate complexions. He shook his head.

'They wear death masks,' he said.

In sight of the festivities on the opposite side of the lawn, a trembling slave hung by his thumbs from the frame. None of the guests appeared to notice. Shaking his head sadly, he whispered.

'They are a heartless people.'

The figure of Faith Bradshaw caught his eye, dressed in a low-cut gown of coloured brocade with silver trimming. She stood graciously welcoming guests alongside her parents.

A black lacquered carriage emblazoned with a golden crest clattered to a halt. Stepping smartly forward, a costumed house slave pulled the door open. Clad in a saffron and crimson embroidered coat, a bullish figure descended like a deity onto the drive. Squeals of delight burst from the assembled guests.

So *this* is the wicked Mister Fleming, he thought, the owner of Turtle Island and China Lights plantation.

Greeting her guests with a munificent smile, Faith Bradshaw nonetheless felt uneasy. She possessed a terrible secret and the weight of possible discovery lay upon her. Raising her voice to disguise her anxiety, she declared:

'Why father, the richest man in all Pertigua has come to our Summer Ball with his charming wife, Mistress Elizabeth.'

Knowing he was needled by Fleming's wealth, bearing and dynastic sophistication and, seeing him flush with irritation, gave her immense satisfaction.

'The witch tries to outclass everyone,' he said hoarsely, 'with her ample cleavage and voluminous acreage of sleeves and lavish trimmings.'

'We give a Ball, Father!' she countered sharply. 'A woman is supposed to flaunt her best at such occasions. I think she looks splendid. And there are not many here who can match her.'

'Keep your voices down!' her mother snapped. 'Oh my. Here comes a most noble and welcome guest.'

Out of a green and yellow phaeton stepped the island's Governor, Sir Anthony Ashleigh, and his wife. Bringing up the rear was a stylish black landau with admirable lines, bearing the proprietor of Tradewinds, the island's leading sugar-refining factory. The podgy proprietor helped his buxom companion down from the carriage. As Faith expected, her father immediately engaged the proprietor in a tiresome dialogue on the sugar prices. She beckoned to a house slave.

'Tell the musicians that I wish them to begin their performance at once,' she said.

Moments later the chamber orchestra struck up with a sonata by Henry Purcell. As she had intended, the musical interruption terminated her father's discourse. He turned for the main door in the company of Fleming and the Governor.

'And right glad am I to see you Governor and you also Squire Fleming,' her father said. 'I trust you were not inconvenienced by the posse in pursuit of the two runaways from Harmony Hall?'

'We encountered no posse, nor did we see two strolling niggers,' replied Fleming. 'Gone a week, have they not? I fancy that they will be beyond reach by now.'

'I did hear that two runaways were apprehended in Sun Valley,' said the Governor. 'The blockheads could string up only one nigger, because the other took to his heels.'

'There goes another recruit for the runaways,' said the proprietor of Tradewinds. 'Must be a small army of them in the mountains by now? Mark my words, there will come a time when we will have to force them out.'

'I think not, Squire,' Faith interjected, 'for it would be a very costly exercise indeed. In the first instance, would it not be more productive if the energies of our militia were better spent putting an end to the escapes? Besides, why risk the lives of white men clearing slaves out of the treacherous swamps in the mountains? Runaways hardly affect our lives here. Come sir, no doubt you would agree, slaves are a poor subject for such a grand occasion.'

At her calculated termination of his discussion, her father's look of barbed surprise was camouflaged by a chilly smile.

'Aye, Mistress Faith, slaves are indeed a poor subject this night,' said her father, waving his hand at the house. 'Shall we, gentlemen?'

Jacob was sickened by the opulence of the festivities. The brilliant white-stuccoed façade of the Great House was garlanded by tropical blossoms and bedecked with ribbons. Scuttling between the guests were bewigged house slaves, wearing garnet satin jackets and pale stockings. Darkness fell to the strains of a chamber orchestra. Slipping out of the rhododendron he bade farewell to Ol' Bones and walked away from the merriment.

Back in the flimsy refuge of his chattel house, he sat down to wait. A little after midnight he heard the swish of skirts. Faith stepped inside the candle-lit chattel house. A flowery fragrance followed her.

'I have pined for you, Jacob,' she said. 'We have the night before us.'

In silence, he rolled out the straw-filled pallet. Her eyes never left him as she disrobed. Turning his back to her, he stripped off his jerkin. She gasped. Stretching out her hand she touched lightly the welts across his back. He winced. Drawing back from him, he saw the fire in her eyes.

'Who did this to you?'

'Ferrers. He wants me dead.'

'Oh he does, does he? We shall see about that. I could weave another Bayeux Tapestry with all the people who loathe him.'

Anger crossed her face and her eyes flashed as she spoke.

'Ferrers is scum. The stench of death haunts his person. His name matches his cunning ways. I shall make him pay for this.'

Taking a step forward, she embraced him. She behaves differently this night, he thought. She acts more like a woman tempting her lover – bashful yet expectant. Her hands stroked his cheeks. Her soft tongue was inside his mouth. She pulled him down onto her.

'Come,' she whispered, 'let me help you forget. Draw closer, my love.'

Touching her skin, her urges stirred his own. Kindled by her wetness and the desire that issued from it, he thrust gently as she passionately reached her peak, her hand stifling her cries. He felt her nails digging into his buttocks and pulling him into the core of her. He shuddered and lay there panting for some time. Gathering his thoughts, he selected his words carefully.

'Can I say something to you?'

'You have my ear, Jacob.'

He quietly recounted the torments occurring daily on the plantation and the threat posed by the two men who hated him most – her father and his sadistic overseer, Woodham Ferrers. He hoped to draw on her compassion. By the time he ended his account with the bullwhip and the outlandish implements of torture, she looked ashen and haunted. Lowering his voice, he added that she should believe he was dead if ever she heard that he was missing. For what seemed an eternity, she remained silent, and then posed a startling question.

'Where will you go, Jacob?'

Stunned by the question, he sat up. Uncertain as to how much to divulge, he kept his thoughts to himself. But her next words left him in no doubt.

'Have you thought about the mountains, Jacob?'

'I never stop thinking about them.'

'Have you thought about fleeing to the mountains?'

Her question rendered him speechless. Was it a trick? Confessing to the daughter of the plantation owner that I am planning to break out, he thought, is a gamble with my life. If she changed her mind, he would be hung. Ferrers would ensure a slow death. If he stayed on the plantation he would die anyway, except that it might take a little longer.

'Breaking out is all I think about. I live for escape. I was born without fetters. I hunger to be free again. I have been planning to make a break. I must get as far away from here as I can.'

The silence that fell between them was like the gravid hush that takes place after an earthquake. Slowly tracing a bead of sweat down his nose and onto his lips, she raised his chin and gazed into his eyes.

'We will have to trust each other, Jacob,' she said quietly. 'When I say trust I mean trust. You are right, Jacob. You will die if you remain here. And believe me, Jacob, I do not want your death in my heart or on my conscience. Now let us speak of your escape.'

'Doubt,' he said abruptly.

'Doubt?' she asked.

'Trust sleeps not easy with doubt,' he said. 'As long as you have no doubt about helping me, I will trust you. So, I trust you not to change your mind about helping me escape.'

She smiled. I love his steadfastness, I love his warmth and I admire his fortitude, she thought. He was like no man she had ever met. He wanted for little. The dandies and bullies of Jamestown were brash and insensitive. This man took nothing for granted. He had changed her outlook and her life.

A life dependent on plantation slavery no longer lay easily with her. This one-time stranger from the coast of Guinea had seen to that. Through him she had learned about the animals, the plants and the character of the humans on these islands. Inadvertently, he had revealed much to her about herself. She had taught him to read and write. He had taken to poetry with an unbridled affection. She treasured the few verses he had written. She liked the way in which he spoke and how his lips gave birth to a wry smile at the end of a long sentence. She loved him. The thought of an end to their encounters filled her with grief. She had no option. She must let go of him – if he was to stay alive.

'You must go,' she said quietly, 'and I will go with you.'

The blood rushed to his head. His jaw fell open. What you ask is not possible, he thought. A white woman with runaways in the mountains would be judged to have been kidnapped. He could see the massed ranks of English regiments in hot pursuit. Chilling descriptions of them would foster such loathing among Jamestown's whites that a simple hunt would turn into a persecution without restraint. A result the other runaways would not thank him for. And then there were those who would hate her white skin being amongst them. A white woman living and sleeping with a runaway in the mountains was unacceptable, for black and for white. Plucking a greasy bone out of the cooking pot, he thrust it at her.

'You eat pig trotter?' he asked.

She shrank back with revulsion. He tossed his filthy breeches onto the pallet beside her.

'You would wear no more silk or ride in carriage,' he said. 'You would wear cotton and use your legs like us.'

Trying hard to conceal her aversion, she lifted his breeches with two delicate fingers and tossed the garment aside.

'I will cope,' she said weakly.

'You'll sleep in the forest and the swamp,' he said, 'with rats and poisonous snakes. And you'll have to shit in the bush.'

She paled at his catalogue of terrors and indignities. The fingers of dawn crept into the chattel house. A cock crowed. Sitting down beside her, he spoke to her quietly.

'How would you feel,' he asked, 'being among people whose friends have been beaten to death or hanged on the orders of your father and his overseers?'

He saw the anguish in her tearful look. Closing her eyes, she took a deep breath.

'If you go, Jacob,' she said, 'there is nothing left for me here that I care for. I want to help you. I am trying to understand what you have suffered. You have opened my eyes. I am filled with horror at what has happened to your people. I am not the one who licensed slavery, Jacob. I am not the one. And as for living among your people, I know not how I would conduct myself in the presence of those who have reason to hate the colour of my skin.'

Rising shakily from the pallet, she began to dress.

'I understand it might be a problem,' she said, 'but I would like you to give it some thought.'

'That will not happen,' he replied unequivocally. 'If you run away with me the hunt will be massive. They will call out the army and call in the Mongoose Gang to track down the white Princess kidnapped by runaways.'

He saw her falter.

'There you have a point, Jacob,' she said. 'Father would not rest because mother would not let him. I shall remain here. But through my man, Nathan Greensleeves, we can meet from time to time. Slavery will not last forever.'

'Someone will get blamed for my escape,' he said.

'Don't worry, Jacob,' she said. 'Ferrers will be held entirely responsible. He will be accused of neglect of duty. I shall see to it. As to your escape, I shall seek the help of Nathan Greensleeves.'

'Mister Greensleeves found a fine place for my chattel house,' he said. 'I thank you.'

She walked away from him, hesitated at the door and gave him a tentative smile.

'He did well for us both, Jacob,' she said. 'I shall harness his talents again. Put your trust in him. He is dear to me. A man who never falters. He will be of great help to us both.'

Many plantation mistresses sleep with their slaves, he thought. She had gone much further and wanted to be the woman of a slave. Behind the backs of her own people, she was helping his escape. He hoped and prayed she would go on doing so.

5 October 1751

It was a cold dawn with a light breeze. A slate-grey sky promised another scorching day. The First Gang was at morning line-up. Jacob slipped into the row of sullen men. Suddenly he was seized by the neck and kicked in the buttocks. Staggering out of the line in agony, he spun around eyes blazing. Taking a step back with menace, Ferrers flicked out his whip and left it snaking along the ground behind him. The overseer was goading him. A desire to live made him stay his ground.

'You used good judgment there nigger,' Ferrers sneered, slowly furling up his whip. 'I ain't going to cut you this time. You've been liberated. You ain't cutting cane no more. Mister Bradshaw wants you to learn carpentry.'

His spirits soared. By the violent way he was singled out, it was clear that the overseer had been tempting him to lash out and spoil this opportunity. Ol' Bones winked. Faith Bradshaw had kept her promise. Carpentry would enable him to move about more easily to advance his escape plan. Ferrers was scornful.

'Why would Mister Bradshaw think you're good with your hands?' he asked. 'Is it because you've been fondling the lusty Mistress Faith. You'd best be careful there nigger. If Mister Bradshaw ever finds out, he'll cut your black hide to pieces. Report to the carpenter in the kitchen garden. Keep your wits about you nigger. You don't fool me. You're trouble. I said so the minute I laid eyes on your black hide. I know you're going cause me a great deal of trouble.'

'You are right, Mister Ferrers,' said Jacob impulsively. 'Anything you say, Mister Ferrers. I go and find the carpenter, Mister Ferrers.'

Backing onto a broad terrace, the Great House overlooked the rose garden. On a lower level lay the vast kitchen garden, designed in the tradition of the parterre. The beds were filled with a cornucopia of indigenous vegetables. Striding along the row of banana trees, he found the carpenter, a stocky middle-aged man, staking out an area at the far end of the garden. His cheeks bore the marks of the Yoruba, his eyes twinkled youthfully and his smile held the sun in it.

'So you be Jacob? Them call me Sunshine. Them say you keen to learn 'bout wood? What you know 'bout wood, Jacob?'

'It grows,' he replied, frivolously. 'And with the help of water or tools, it grows into a tree or shack. I will learn quickly, Sunshine. It's better than breaking my balls in the fields.'

Chuckling loudly, the carpenter slapped his back.

'You do fine. I teach you all I know. Over there we build a vegetable outhouse for that pig Bradshaw. We build off the ground like so, 'cos of the rats. You got that?'

He nodded. The carpenter set him to work digging the first of eight deep holes for the foundation posts. The Great House gradually came to life as they toiled. It was mid-morning when he saw a white woman striding towards them, followed by a smartly clad house slave. For the moments before she reached them, he doubled his work-rate.

'Good morning, Sunshine,' she said.

The breathless carpenter stopped working to greet her.

'A good morning to you, Mistress Widdecombe.'

'I will send food for you and this slave,' she said disdainfully.

'Jacob, Mistress Widdecombe,' replied the carpenter politely, 'his name is Jacob.'

Raising his head, Jacob met the frosty eyes of the woman he had seen only from a distance since arriving on the plantation. At close quarters, she was stony-faced and condescending.

'This house slave,' the housekeeper said, waving her hand over her shoulder, 'will bring food to you.'

Florence stepped out from behind the housekeeper. The sight of her aroused him. Dressed in a black dress with a high-necked collar, she seemed extremely remote. Not a trace of recognition showed in her sad dark eyes. Since they had arrived he had never seen her in such close proximity to the Great House.

'Thank you, Mistress Widdecombe,' said the carpenter.

'See that you build a stout outhouse, Sunshine. I want no holes left for the rats. Come Florence.'

The housekeeper strode back to the Great House with Florence closely on her heels. Concentrating his thoughts on her, Jacob prayed that she would look back. The woman I knew in Ake will turn and look back, he thought. Reaching the house and about to enter, she turned around. He smiled. Some hours later, she returned with a small bundle and placed it on the ground behind the carpenter.

'Mistress Widdecombe said to give this to you.'

Sunshine turned around to get hold of the bundle. Over the carpenter's head, she smiled and mouthed 'this night' at him. Jacob caught sight of

Faith Bradshaw striding through the flower gardens towards them. His smile dissolved. Florence turned around to look for the reason. Gathering herself, she started back for the Great House, passing her mistress with bowed head. Halting beside the banana trees, Faith Bradshaw beckoned to him. He approached her with his heart thumping wildly. She raised her eyebrows. His thoughts raced through the catalogue of crimes he could have committed.

'What did that slave girl say to you, Jacob?'

'She brings food and water, Mistress Faith. Thank you for keeping your word.'

She blushed shyly.

'I simply told my father that you had built a stout chattel house. That you were good with your hands. And my word you do have remarkable hands. I should know. And at my request that you should be trained as a carpenter, he agreed to your transfer from the canefields.'

She dropped her voice to a whisper.

'Expect me the night of the morrow.'

'Yes, Mistress Faith.'

Watching her retreating figure, he fervently hoped that she had not yet begun to suspect his feelings for Florence. Wiping the sweat from his neck, he resumed digging.

He toiled through the afternoon. Suddenly there was a horrific scream followed by painful cries. Certain it came from the barracoon, he dropped his pickaxe.

'Keep digging, Jacob,' snapped the carpenter. 'You work with wood now. Your business is the outhouse. You heard nothing out there.'

Annoyed by the rebuke, he was going back to digging when he caught the carpenter's expression. His mentor was breathing heavily with rage in his eyes. His bald head was lined with beads of sweat, and his tribal marks accentuated his dark scowl and pursed lips. Soon, the carpenter's pick was striking the ground with a furious intensity. Raising his pick above his head, Jacob struck the ground, hard. The piteous cries were fading into intermittent groans. As if intense concentration would obliterate the truth, the carpenter kept his head down. By nightfall, all eight foundation posts had been sunk. Thoroughly exhausted and picking up their tools, they headed for the Slop House.

As they stepped into the barracoon, Jacob beheld the nightmare of the enslaved man – a torso propped up in a pool of blood. The man had suffered paring. His arms and legs had been hacked off and tourniquets had been applied to prolong his agony. Though his eyes were shut, the man groaned weakly as his life-blood flowed inaudibly from his stumps. Quivering with fury, Jacob closed his eyes briefly on the gory spectacle. With tears flowing down his fleshy cheeks, the carpenter was indignant.

'Them take life without mercy.' he cried.

Jacob drew the carpenter away.

'Come, Sunshine, if we linger here we'll finish up like him.'

Entering the Slop House that night, he could almost touch the anger enveloping the long shed. He found Moses in heated in conversation with Ol' Bones. Plonking himself down beside them, he listened to the account of why the man had suffered paring.

'His name Jacob, like you,' said Ol' Bones. 'This Jacob fella see Ferrers pushing his woman into Farthest Field. Grabbing a spade, he comes up from behind. Boof, he hit his big thick head. Ferrers drop like a tree. Overseers hold this Jacob down. Ferrers wake up with one big thump in his head. He tell poor this Jacob that he lose his arms and legs.'

Swearing that one day he would have Ferrers dangling from a rope, Jacob left the Slop House. On his way back to his chattel house he renewed his vow to escape.

Close to midnight, Florence came by his chattel house as she had promised. Breathing heavily, she was clearly distressed. Raising a weak smile, she gave him a loaf of bread and half a roasted chicken. A dark look crossed her face.

'That spiteful bitch asked me to which men I have been giving myself. I told her to nobody. She says that slave women sleep around.'

'Did she say more?' he asked.

'Had I seen you. I said that I didn't talk to field slaves. The bitch told me to stay that way.'

Putting his arms around her shoulders, he drew her gently to him. Faith Bradshaw is on the lookout, he thought. The desire of Bradshaw's daughter was a subject they never broached. He knew why Florence never manifested jealousy. Survival was her primary aim, she had once said, after which escape was her next priority. Jealousy lay at the very end of her long list of grievances.

She had to be back in the Great House before first light. That knowledge heightened his sense of urgency. Again and again they kissed and soon they had passed beyond captivity into a realm of their own making. Despite the risks, he treasured these moments. On a plantation, he thought, the house slave is the border between the whites and the field slave. But they would do anything to stop them becoming friends. Divide and rule made for a successful plantation. They were breaking all the rules.

Given there were more male than female slaves at Tamarind Trees, a male without a mate might feel compelled to denounce another. In similar vein, a white Mistress, accomplished at doing nothing, might easily become eaten up with jealousy because of her slave's affections for another slave. In the incestuous confines of a sugar plantation, physical attraction was a tempting and hazardous affair. Thus the precautions he was taking for their escape had to be founded on certainty. Their lives depended on it.

The cock crowed. Having agreed to meet him in two days, Florence started out for the Great House. Unease beset her in the cold morning air. Nearing the house, she was passing by the long gooseberry hedge when an owl hooted. She jumped with fright. Panting lightly, she crossed the terrace and trod lightly up to the back entrance. Quietly opening the door she had left unbolted, she stepped inside. Avoiding the loose floorboards, her heart thumped as she tiptoed up the three flights of creaky stairs. Candlelight spilled out from beneath the door of her previously darkened bedchamber. Seized by a sudden panic, she pushed the door open. Perched on her cot was Faith Bradshaw, breathing deeply and quietly seething. Her heart stopped. Sweat streamed down her neck. Bizarrely, she still noted the stark difference of her owner's Indian gown against the bleak walls of her meagrely furnished bedchamber.

'Shut the door! Where have you been skulking?'

Speedily closing the door, she cast her eyes down.

'I shall speak bluntly. With whom did you sleep?'

Such was her terror she barely heard her own reply.

'I slept in the house of a field slave.'

Her fuming tormenter shot onto her booted feet.

'I said who did you sleep with slut! Not where?'

She stayed silent.

'All right then. To which field slave does the chattel house inside which you slept belong? I want your answer this instant.'

From somewhere in the bowels of the Great House came the pendulous resonance of a chiming clock. In the hush of dawn, it sounded loud and all pervading. The strip of sacking over the open narrow casement window lifted in the breeze, admitting the first streaks of daylight. She was trapped. If the bitch raises her voice and wakes the house, she thought, her father will enter this fight. At the best of times he is cruel. If he hears that I have been sleeping with Jacob, he will invent a lingering death for both of us. Fighting back her fears and looking intently at her adversary, she blurted out.

'I slept with Jacob.'

Appearing to digest her admission, her adversary fell silent. Then, shooting forwards the woman slapped her hard across the face. She swayed but remained on her feet. Dissatisfied with the end result, the woman went berserk and pummelled her wildly. She parried the blows as best she could.

'Did I not warn you not to sleep with him?'

'Yes, Mistress Bradshaw, you did.'

'I can have you burned to death or skinned alive.'

'Yes, Mistress Bradshaw, you can.'

The woman eyed a heavy pewter candlestick, which she suddenly hurled. It struck Florence on the forehead with a glancing blow and clattered onto the floor.

'Did I not warn you against sleeping with him?'

Reeling backwards clutching her head, she felt something sticky trickling down her fingers, dripping onto her pinafore dress and spotting the bare boards. The sight of her own blood stirred her wrath. She stepped forward. Faith backed away.

'What do you hope for, white woman?' she snarled. 'What more do you want? You took everything I had. But that's not enough. So you take my man as well. You have white skin. I am black like him. I sleep with my own kind. You should sleep with yours.'

A knife materialised in the Faith's hand. Florence stiffened.

'You dare to answer me back, you insolent slave. I shall cut out your tongue. I . . . '

There was a knock at the door.

'Who is it?'

'Cook, Mistress Faith. I come to wake Florence, Mistress Faith.'

'Be about your work, cook. I shall send Florence down when I am finished with her.'

Without another word, the cook dropped back down the stairs. Her swollen-eyed tormenter sheathed her knife. Florence heaved a sigh.

'I am not finished with you. I shall ponder on your fate. In the meantime, if it comes to my ears that as much as your apron string has been sighted anywhere near Jacob or his house, I shall have you hanged by that apron string in front of him.'

No longer able to contain herself, Florence unleashed her fury.

'Nothing will come of your feelings for him,' she said. 'Like mine, your feelings for him are forbidden. And your people will never allow your union to bear fruit. You will lose both of us. If your father ever finds out that we have been sleeping with the same man, he will either kill Jacob and me or sell us.'

Stopping inches away from her tormenter, who fell back, she continued.

'What will you do when you weary of him?' she asked. 'Sell him or work him to death? Me and him are of the same blood. We struggle just to stay alive. And we fight for freedom from your kind. You fight only to find a man to sleep with. We are slaves because of your greed. You, bitch, are a slave to lust.'

So much of what Florence says is true, thought Faith, sinking slowly onto the cot. She was suddenly afraid. Rising unsteadily to her feet, she took a few faltering steps to the door.

'Stay away from Jacob,' she snapped, 'while I think on the fate of you both.'

I must warn Jacob, thought Florence, or get a message to Ol' Bones. In the meantime she would go downstairs and act as if everything was as it should be.

The sun leapt above the horizon. Jacob set off for the outhouse. A light shower produced a welcome reprieve from the rising heat. By the time he arrived, steam was rising off the ground around the outhouse. Energised by his night with Florence, he hammered the planks onto the floor joists with a robust vigour. Sniggering from behind made him stop working. He caught the carpenter wiggling his skinny hips inside his baggy breeches.

'You have pum-pum with she, Jacob? She put fire in them balls?'

He laughed.

'She gives me the strength of a lion, Sunshine.'

The carpenter snorted.

'Hold up, Jacob. We take a week or two to build this outhouse. Ferrers will make us build another in half the time if we finish this one too quick. This day we finish the floor.'

Downing his tools, Jacob stopped to mop his brow.

'And I will say build it yourself, Ferrers. And since your fat white backside won't take me back to Ake, I will row back. Another night with Florence and I will even swim back.'

Throughout the morning he toiled in higher spirits than usual. At midday, a girl brought a piggin of corn soup. She was a shy scrawny thing, in a bright vermillion dress with the letters DC burned on her right arm.

'What they call you?' Jacob asked.

She dropped her eyes and began fidgeting with her dress.

'Ruby,' she replied, weakly.

'Have you seen Florence?' the carpenter asked.

Her eyes jumped from one man to the other.

'She's frit,' said the carpenter.

To win her confidence, Jacob exposed the DC brand on his arm.

'Be not afraid, Ruby,' he said. 'Florence? Where is Florence?

Jumping back with fright, the girl took to her heels.

Was she scared because of something that had taken place in the Great House?

Twilight brought the sonorous wail of the conch. Having finished the floor of the outhouse, Jacob headed for the Slop House where he ate his last meal of the day in tense silence. Leaving the Slop House, he found Ol' Bones waiting for him outside.

'You was quiet, Jacob? What is wrong? Has that bitch found out about Florence?'

'Not sure.'

'I heard 'bout no trouble in the Great House,' said Ol' Bones reassuringly.

Inside his chattel house, his fears came flooding back. His head pounded with anxious thoughts. Was Florence alive and healthy? Could he trust Faith Bradshaw?

Soon after eleven o'clock he heard her footsteps. She looked flustered and she seemed on edge. Little by little she mellowed. If she had maimed or sold Florence, she showed not a trace. Her voice was soft.

'Let us meet in the summer-house this night, Jacob. My father has gone to Jamestown and will not return for two days.'

Had her father taken Florence to be auctioned? He must act non-chalant.

'Jamestown?'

'Be not so anxious, Jacob. His visit to Jamestown will not affect you. He has merely gone to buy more slaves. Ferrers is going to order you to build a shelter for them. Make haste to the summer-house, I shall go first. Follow me shortly.'

His thoughts were in turmoil when he started out for the summer-house. She had agreed to help him. If she had found out about Florence would she change her mind? He resolved to be very attentive to her that night.

It was early morning. Plainly deep in thought, she stood naked with her back to him by the open shutters.

'I am troubled, Jacob.'

An edge in her voice bothered him.

'Have you changed your mind?'

'Who will share your bed in the mountains, Jacob?'

He sat up wide awake.

She knows something, he thought.

'Will you be taking Florence?'

His head exploded with alarm. Sweat seeped from his armpits. The words he had most feared hearing had finally been voiced. She knows all about us, he thought, gritting his teeth, I shall hide nothing.

'Yes I know Florence very well. We come from the same village on the coast of Guinea. I owe her my life many times over. Before we were taken by Captain Blunt, we had started walking out together. Never did we have the chance to find out how fruitful the years might be. Or what those years might have done with our lives. Your people destroyed that hope. If I escape, how long do you think it will be before your father finds out about my friendship with Florence? He will surely kill her.'

Spinning around, her eyes flashed. He knew his words had pained her for she was close to tears. He persisted.

'I ask for my freedom. You ask me who will share my bed? Do you think I bumped into Captain Blunt strolling along the shore? That I fall to my knees and say, Massa please Massa, make me a slave? Put chains on my arms and legs, them too free. You think that I was joyful to see white people storming onto our shores? You say that if I stay here, Ferrers will kill me. You know I must escape or I will die. Florence will die if she does not go with me. I cannot leave this plantation without her. If I did, what kind of friend would that make me?'

Her throat dried. She had squandered the past days eaten up with jealousy and rage. Although his outburst had distressed her, she could not deny that what he had said was true. His words exposed her self-interest. She had thought only of herself, not of the two lives that hung in the balance. His pointed reference to Captain Blunt had focused her thoughts. A cloud of shame descended on her. She was his owner and with spurious authority wielded unlimited power over him. It was a power she could not now use on him. Throughout her refined life in the Great House, she had seen and stomached an ocean of cruelty. Her conscience was in turmoil. She was awash with remorse. Tears rolled freely down her cheeks. She turned to him.

'I shall help you, Jacob,' she said. 'You can both put your trust in me.'

Later that afternoon a courier arrived with a message from Nathan Greensleeves: come to the summer-house poste haste. A deep frown creased her brow. She tidied away her papers and set out from the Great House. Walking quickly down the path by the lake, she was panting by the time she arrived. He was sitting, tricorne in hand, on the topmost step.

'What troubles thee, Nathan?'

'Sit thee down here me lass.'

Frowning at his tone of voice, she scrutinised him closely. The urgency in his message was disturbing enough, she thought, but witnessing his anxiety was more unsettling. Opening his container of Blackamore's Head for a pinch of snuff, he sighed. Excusing herself, she strode into the house. Returning with two tankards and a jug of sarsaparilla, she sat facing him.

'What troubles you so, Nathan?'

'During the last three months, Ferrers has driven the cane gangs unremittingly. I fear he is stirring up unrest on your plantation.'

'Might you not be exaggerating his role, Nathan? You well know that I find that oaf beneath contempt. But even he would not be so foolish as to fan the flames of unrest.'

She noted the look of forbearance she received throughout her reply. He cleared his throat.

'He's been forcing your slaves to work harder,' he said. 'But they're still not cutting enough to satisfy him. So there is always a deficit. He is branding those shortfalls sabotage.'

Her mouth fell open. Sabotage is an automatic death sentence, she thought. How long before Ferrers settled on Jacob?

'What say you, Nathan?'

'He seeks to flog your slaves into greater exertion and the plantation's accounts into larger profit.'

'How does Ferrers plan to boost revenues, Nathan?'

'By dispensing the whip for the slightest indiscretion – six lashes for jostling, six for being slow to work after a break and twelve for quarrelling. Believe me when I say his activities are having a deleterious effect. So much so, the unrest produced by his actions in the canefield is spreading. Nay, it fast becomes an epidemic. And presently it is as if a hidden hand directs the acts of defiance. Can you not see lass? The hapless bastards can cut no more cane than they are already doing. The bugger is working them to death. They are certain to rebel sooner or later.'

'And you say Ferrers has instigated all this by himself?'

'Yes, and more. Reports from several plantations have prompted Randolph Fleming to convene a conference between the Governor and the plantation owners.'

'Mother of God!' she cried.

'At that meeting, which I attended as an interested party and observer,' he said, 'it was decided by a majority to introduce more persuasive measures. Ever since then the slave gangs have suffered terribly. Slaves were deemed expendable and mutilation was the favoured deterrent. Given that decision, slaves by the dozen have lost a leg, a hand or an arm and the mutilated are still worked intensely. Did you know that the death penalty is now imposed for sabotage and running away?'

'Yes I did know that,' she mumbled dryly.

'I wager you did not know that the death penalty is now the sentence for merely answering a white man back?'

'Holy Mary Mother of God! I did not know that. A nightmare has indeed arrived in Pertigua.'

'This island was spawned in a nightmare, me lass. At China Lights, in a fit of temper, an overseer boiled a slave alive in liquid sugar and had another skinned alive. Yet, acts of sabotage have persisted. What does Ferrers expect?'

His hands slid reassuringly over hers.

'In these treacherous times, me lass, I feel apprehensive for Jacob.'

She put a hand to her heart, for she feared for him as well.

The following night, Jacob was dropping off to sleep when he heard footsteps on his verandah. Bursting through the door, Florence stood trembling, flushed and breathless, her dress saturated with sweat. Not once had he ever seen her so afraid, but now, even her lips were quivering. Putting his arms around her, he felt the tremors of her fear shuddering against him.

'Why is so much water washing your face?' he asked, gently stroking her back

'I'm with child, Jacob.'

'How do you know?'

'I know I am. Mama Jezebel say so.'

While the full impact of her disclosure took time to sink in, words eluded him. Above everything he was excited. He smiled at her.

'Are you sure?'

A scowl wrinkled her brow. She snapped at him.

'I know I am with child! Mama Jezebel is never wrong!'

Drawing her closer, he advanced the escape date. I am to be a father, he thought. Somehow the prospect of a child gave him hope. On this godforsaken island, to have a child with a woman of one's choice was the province of white men. If they stayed at Tamarind Trees they would never see their child grow up.

'We must flee sooner,' he said. 'I want to be able to kiss this child and feel him in arms. And I want him to be born free.'

Her lips parted into a broad smile.

'What if he is a she?'

He chuckled.

'Then she shall be born free and be adored by her Baba.'

Laying his head on her shoulder, he envisioned savannahs and skies of freedom. In an attempt to surround her in the flimsy refuge of his devotion, he tightened his embrace.

Monday of the first week of November proved to be a warm day. He rested on the steps of his chattel house after his day's work. Clearly distressed, Moses hobbled up and slumped down beside him.

'You heard 'bout China Lights, Jacob?'

'What happened?'

'Overseers flogged three men so bad them die in that canefield.'

'That Fleming's plantation?'

The old man nodded.

'Why were they flogged?'

'Bad work when them patch up his fences. At first his overseers call it laziness and then them call it sabotage.'

'The owners are using murder instead of flogging, Moses,' said Jacob. 'They aim to frighten us into obedience. I tell you my friend the sabotage on the plantations is slashing their profits.'

Shaken awake in the early hours, Jacob was dispatched with the carpenter to repair a stretch of fencing along Farthest Field. On site they set to ripping out the rotten fence posts on a section close to the First Gang. Exhausted canecutters were sprawled down Liberty Lane at midday break. Surly-faced and close at hand, on guard and on horseback beneath that hated floppy hat, sat his archenemy, Ferrers. Shouts and screeching gulls turned Jacob's head. Smoke was rising out of a canefield a few fields away.

That does not bode well, he thought.

Assisted by a southerly gust, the smoke was rapidly fanned into a blaze. The biting stench of blazing cane drifted across Farthest Field. Grinning at the carpenter, he prayed it was sabotage. Getting down from his whinnying mount, a purple-faced Ferrers stomped across to the smirking cane cutters. The overseer hauled a skeletal slave to his feet. The smirks turned apprehensive.

I know that man, thought Jacob. Ferrers sleeps with his woman two times a week.

'You set fire to that canefield, nigger,' Ferrers snarled.

'I been cutting cane, Massa. I know nothing about them flames, Massa. Ask all slaves, Massa, I have never left this here canefield.'

Winking at Ferrers, a hatchet-faced overseer jabbed his musket at the slave.

'I sees you do it nigger. You know the punishment for sabotage?'

The slave shook. Stepping forward en masse, the overseers yelled vulgarities at him. Jacob's hackles rose. Clasping his hands in supplication, the slave dropped to his knees.

'Mercy, Massa, mercy,' he cried. 'I done nothing, Massa, mercy.'

Seven hard-faced overseers unfurled their whips and surrounded their quarry. An edgy silence gripped the witnesses in the canefield. The field rite began with a kick from Ferrers. Next, the boots of the overseer's peppered their prey. Then, they laid into him with their whips. Betwixt the screams and waning cries for mercy, time crawled chillingly by until at last, the overseers stepped away.

'O God!' the canecutters gasped.

A crumpled blood-soaked figure lay motionless in the dirt. Without pausing for breath, Ferrers picked up a machete and hacked the corpse into pieces small enough to fit into a wooden crate. Clenching his fists, Jacob's nails cut into his palms. He looked at the carpenter, whose cheeks were wet. What he had just witnessed further hardened his resolve. Sweating and drenched with blood at the end of his butchery, Ferrers crashed against a tree out of breath.

Narrowing his eyes along the men of the First Gang, Jacob thought he glimpsed signs of revolt. On all sides every man and woman stood gaping, their eyes fixed intently on the crate inside which was the remains of one who, until a moment ago, had been a living breathing being. What is in their heads and hearts is also on their faces, he thought. From where he stood by the fencing, he could feel the hate spewing across Farthest Field. Dusk was drawing near when the overseers readied the First Gang for the trek back to the Slop House.

'Machetes accounted for,' shouted an overseer.

A blood-spattered Ferrers mounted his horse.

'Count the niggers,' he yelled.

Predictably as in field practice, an overseer ambled down the line kicking the slaves into a single file. He then wandered back counting aloud.

'We got 'em all,' he shouted.

'Chain 'em,' said Ferrers.

Signalling the off, the hatchet-faced overseer cocked his musket, pointed it skywards and pulled the trigger. A blinding flash and the weapon exploded, blowing away a section of his skull and his right arm. Blood and brain tissue sprayed about. Crashing to his knees, the dead man keeled over. Ferrers' mount reared, though its rider managed to remain in his saddle. Jacob clutched the carpenter's arm.

'Now *that* is sabotage,' he said.

The carpenter grinned. And the glee that gripped the First Gang was palpable. In the waning light, six jumpy overseers hastily examined their muskets. Cracking his whip, Ferrers screamed.

'Get cracking you shiftless niggers.'

With grunts, groans and laboured sighs, the First Gang set off on the three-mile slog back to the Slop House.

During the second week of a sultry November, six slaves collapsed and died. Four more were found dead in their chattel houses. Right before Jacob's eyes, two more succumbed at morning line-up. They just lay there and expired. Ol' Bones groaned.

'Hope passed them by in this life, Jacob.'

'It was as if they were set on dying in the sight of witnesses,' he replied.

As if assembling evidence for a report, Jacob began keeping a tally of all acts of sabotage. The subversive tactics came in a multiplicity of guises. Farm gates were left open, allowing the milk and beef cattle to wander off, stables were set alight, tools continually disappeared and the sugar mill machinery was caused to break down frequently.

At dawn, on the third Sunday of November, Faith Bradshaw was in her bedchamber weeping beneath the mosquito net. Having missed her monthly cycle, she felt queasy, her breasts were swollen and her nipples were tender. Certain she was with child, she was just as confident that the father was Jacob.

I will call on Mama Jezebel. No no, she thought, I have never shown any consideration towards her. Mama Jezebel might denounce her condition, which would certainly get back to her parents. Common sense told her that she should find a way to terminate the life inside her. But she could not bring herself to even consider such an act, even if she knew how. This child was fated to be born and would need all her love.

Rising from her bed, she dressed quickly. I will seek the counsel of my friend, Rose Greenwood, she thought. As the bells summoned the faithful to Mass, she cantered out of the stable-yard heading north-wards for Sun Valley.

At the Greenwood plantation, she was admitted into the Great House and shown to the withdrawing room. Waving a bouquet of flowers, Rose swept cheerfully into the room.

'My dear Faith, it is a joy to see you. And in such blooming health, you . . . '

'I need your help, Rose.'

'You have it.'

'I'm with child!'

Rose turned ashen.

'Jacob's?'

She nodded.

'We had better keep our voices down, Faith. My mother is here on a visit from England. What do you intend to do?'

Turning to look out of the oval window, she threw her reply over her shoulder.

'No one had better try to take my child from me.'

'Keep your voice down. Don't be so ridiculous.'

'My child shall live with me in the Great House.'

'You are quite out of your mind.'

'We are Catholics, Rose. In our faith, it is the greatest sin to even *think* of giving away a child.'

'Your father will never allow the child to live in the Great House. Can you not see that you will endanger Jacob when your father finds out about this? One of his slaves is bound to tell him. Nothing happens on a plantation which the slaves don't know about.'

Rose was right. My father might even drown this grandchild, she thought. He would most certainly put Jacob to death. She trembled at the notion.

'I have to get Jacob away from here as soon as possible.'

'You do know that we are dining with you this night?'

'Of course.'

'Let nothing slip, Faith. You well know that my mother is exceedingly prying, if not downright meddlesome.'

Rising to her feet, Faith strode to the door.

'I should return home,' she said, 'to make certain that Jacob quits the plantation tonight.'

The following hours were spent cot-bound. At midday, she left her bedchamber only to receive a messenger bearing a sealed letter addressed to her. Disturbingly, the courier waited for a reply.

The Greenwood Estate

My dearest Faith – Soon after you left, mother began to plague me about your romantic inclinations. She angers me so with her snooping and prying, though she masks it with a specious interest in the comings and goings of Pertigua. She pressed me closely on your marital interests. My dear friend, I must confess that I inadvertently let slip that although you are not interested in any man in particular, you are well satisfied without a husband. My mother is now very keen to ascertain to whom you may be granting your favours. She suspects it is a slave. I hope and pray she does not find out about mine. Henry would be mortified. That is the entire extent of it. The secret of your condition is safe. However, since we are dining with you this night, I thought to warn you. For our mothers, acting as judge and jury, are bound to conduct an inquisition. Your father will no doubt interrogate his slaves, from one of whom he is bound to learn Jacob's identity, even this very night.

Your devoted confidante

Rose.

Uttering a cry of despair she tore up the letter. Composing herself, she gave her answer to the messenger.

'Inform your Mistress that I shall take care of this matter,' she said.

Retreating to her bedchamber she burned the fragments of the letter in the grate. Pacing back and forth, she racked her brains for a way to forestall the inevitable cross-examination at dinner. Disconcerted by screams from the carriage-drive, she rushed to the window. Shackled to a flatbed cart on the driveway were four children, howling hysterically.

These must be the infants who have been sold to Jamaica, she thought. Is this an omen?

Close by, four overseers were restraining the struggling enraged parents. Putting a hand to her temple, she closed her eyes. Tears rolled hotly down her cheeks. Wiping her eyes, she looked out the window once more. By the doorway and patently indifferent to the proceedings stood her own parents, keeping a close watch on the conclusion of the contract. When the cart began to roll, she saw the housekeeper dabbing her eyes.

Breaking free from the guards, the dispossessed mother dashed towards her mother slashing her wrists. Throwing her arms around her mother's waist, she saturated her fashionable gown with blood. Her mother passed out and was gently carried inside the house. Kicking the dying woman aside, her father left the woman bleeding to death.

Weighed down with guilt, she reeled back from the window in despair. Her spirits were crushed by what she had witnessed.

It is essential I meet with Nathan Greensleeves without delay, she thought.

In the afternoon, having resolved to make no mention of being with child, she set out for the home of the propagator.

At the foot of Orange Mountain, Nathan Greensleeves swung up a wooded track and dismounted when he arrived on a grassy plateau. Securing his horse, he ambled through a gate onto the hectare of fenced land of his home. Bordered by herbal shrubbery and with tropical blooms obscuring its foundations, it was a sturdy two-storey weatherboard property, steeped in old world shadows and a raised verandah running around. The house was his fragment of security set in a sultry nightmare. He was content with his standing as principal propagator to the island's plantation owners. They came flocking to his gardens to praise his genius. Smiling to himself at the thought, he recalled the approbation of the fruit aficionados after he had crossed the large shaddock orange with the sour orange, to introduce the grapefruit to Pertigua. Accordingly, the grape-fruit, in the company of the mango and paw-paw, advanced in rows bordering the paths.

He was a man of science – botanical science. But he was more than happy to be the talk of the island on account of his 'unparalleled' kitchen gardens and his famed experimental beds where he grew the species he had introduced to the island: the soursop – *annona muricata* – whose fibrous white flesh combined the flavours of mango and pineapple, and could be strained to make a fortifying tea; the cerasee – *momordica charantia* – a wild cucumber, widely used across the archipelago as a remedy against earlier fever epidemics, and the fingle-go – *zanthoxylon spinifex* – a restorative, which he cultivated as an aphrodisiac for the neglected Katherine Bradshaw. Nonetheless, he believed that his most exquisite contribution to the island's horticulture was the Nathanense fern, a rare variety of maidenhair fern with fragile, disordered fronds.

Concluding his ponderings on his botanical collection, he strolled to the verandah, flopped down onto the planter's chair and began sprucing his beard. Beside him on a wooden box sat a bottle of rum and his favourite snuff, a flat container of Blackamore's Head. Lifting his legs onto the wings of the chair, he sat gazing thoughtfully at the distant harbour of Jamestown. Then he heard a familiar voice.

'Nathan.'

Dropping his legs to the deck, he sat up.

'Come on up, me lass.'

Beaming dotingly, he watched her pass the mango tree and up the path. Having had a close relationship with her since her birth, a wealth of experiences lay between them. From the time of her delivery, her father was typically absent whereas he had been characteristically close at hand to the Great House. It was her delightful arrival that caused him to grow the aromatic herbs he used to help her overcome all her childhood illnesses. In opposition to her priggish Northumbrian governess who loathed men, it was only he who sided with her. And it was also he, the ever open privileged ear, who counselled her a propos her intimate dilemmas and thwarted relationships. He knew her better than anyone. The moment she stepped onto the verandah, he knew that something was amiss. As she made herself comfortable on the adjacent chair, he noted the tension in her smile.

'What a charming surprise, me lass.'

'Your gardens are abundant, Nathan,' she said unconvincingly.

'Forgo pleasantries, my child; I can see you are sorely troubled. What ails thee?'

'I am in turmoil, Nathan. I have never loved another as I do this man, yet I am forced to let him go. I fear the time has come for Jacob to flee.'

He poured rum into two ruby glass goblets and passed one to her. He tossed the cane spirit down his throat and almost immediately poured himself another measure before responding.

'I have wondered how long before this might come about.'

'The parents of my friend Rose are dining with us this night. Even she dreads her mother's ill-timed visits. As you probably know her mother lives in England for most of the year, preferring the climate.'

'May you survive the martinet's visit.

'An intoxicated trollop with a mouth alike a harbour.'

'How so?'

'Everything she hears passes effortlessly out of it.'

Chuckling momentarily, he then turned serious.

'What concerns thee most?'

'My friend has inadvertently let slip my affection for a slave. And her mother is prowling about.'

'And you fear that the old vixen will serve up your secret with the pudding or the Madeira.'

'Precisely.'

'What have you in mind?'

She lowered her voice.

'What I'm about to say to you, Nathan, I say in the utmost confidentiality. I can trust these words with no other.'

'Have no fear lass. Your words are safe with me.'

'For several months, Jacob has been planning to escape.'

'Alone?'

'Nay with three others. As of now they are ready to go. As I see it, whatever happens between his companions, Jacob must be gone this night. If Father hears that he has been lying on my cot, he will kill him this night. So while we are at supper in the Great House, I want you to see him safely to Bamboo Bay.'

'Aye, that I will. I have no liking for the brutality these old eyes have witnessed on this island over these many years. They have seen too much, lass. When I reach the hereafter, I pray that Saint Peter asks them not what they saw before they left this earth. And I have no liking to going home to the old country. The cold and damp will lock up me bones and see me off. Anyway lass, if there be a chance that we can best your father and Ferrers, we should do it. And if what you say is true, Jacob must indeed be gone this night. Come inside lass, we have some scheming of our own to do.'

Arriving back at Tamarind Trees, she dispatched a house slave with a summons for Jacob to meet her at the summer-house. She left herself enough time to reflect on what she would say to him. Bereft by the surrender of the only man she had loved, she was also wracked with the image of him being entwined with Florence. Since she had decided not to tell him that she was carrying his child, she would concentrate instead on his escape and not dwell on the predicament her condition posed for her.

By the time Jacob arrived at the summer-house, stars were peppering the heavens. A light southerly wind came from the canefields. She was silhouetted with an outstretched hand in the doorway. His hand in hers, she led him into the candle-lit bedchamber. Turning to face him she stood trembling. She was filled with love and uncertainty. Certain his escape was near, he dropped his eyes. He did not want to acknowledge what he saw in hers.

'You must be gone this night, Jacob,' she whispered tearfully. 'We have so little time. Now heed carefully the words I give thee. My friend's mother suspects that I hold affections for someone on this plantation. Her family is expected at our supper table. I am certain her mother will make public that she believes that I have befriended a slave. The witch will do her utmost to expose who you are. She will then be set to discomfit me into severing my contact with you. You had best be gone before we rise from the table. If providence is with us, they will be too drunk to begin a hunt for you straight away. But they will certainly do so on the morrow. May good fortune go with thee my beloved.'

'We work not on the Sabbath, Faith. I am rested this day more than any other. I will leave this night while I am fresh.'

A shadow stole across her face. Then her eyes were streaming.

'I will come for you at ten o'clock,' she said, in a barely audible voice. 'God give me strength.'

Gathering up her skirts and bustling from the bedchamber, her sobs echoed through the summer-house. His spirits aflame at the prospect of freedom, he set off for his chattel-house, stopping only at the house of Ol' Bones.

'Be at the barracoon before ten o'clock this night,' Jacob panted. 'I will warn Florence. You get word to the Hungan.'

'Faith Bradshaw?' asked Ol' Bones.

'She gave me her word,' he said emphatically. 'I know she will keep it.'

Ol' Bones grinned and whispered.

'Soon Florence be in your arms in them mountains, boy.'

He grinned.

It was nearly ten o'clock. The barracoon was resonating with the Lord's praises. Two men stole away from the gathering and shadowed him back to his chattel house.

Inside the Great House, the housekeeper had dismissed Florence. On the way up to her bedchamber, nausea welled up inside her. She paused on the stairs to steady herself. Bile entered her throat and she felt faint. Fighting queasiness all the way back to her room, she dropped to her knees and threw up into the chamber pot. For the first time she noticed the inscription within the lip of the vessel:

'Fast and pray and pity the poor, amend thy life and sin no more'.

Scowling at the trite words, her hands shook as she wiped her mouth. Stripping off her pinafore dress, she examined her body in the looking glass. She slipped into a sleeveless jerkin and pair of breeches. In order to forestall untimely discovery of her absence, she placed a bolster lengthwise beneath the bedclothes. Donning a floppy-brimmed hat and quenching the candle, she tiptoed down the stairs into the hall. Laughter pealed out of the dining room. With a hushed sigh of relief, she turned to leave. The voice of a drunken woman stopped her in her tracks. She slid into the shadows of the stairs.

'My dear Faith, pray tell me to whom are you presently granting your favours?'

'To no one in particular,' Faith Bradshaw replied.

'Oh come, come,' insisted the drunken woman. 'Is it not rumoured that you're bedding a nigger?'

'And sheep might knit,' retorted a man acidly.

Laughter rocked the dining room. With a credible degree of irritation in her voice, Faith Bradshaw responded.

'Unless any person hereabouts is the executor of the truth,' she pouted virtuously, 'I cannot for the life of me think who might be spreading such wicked gossip.'

Florence smiled, especially when she recognised the voice of Rose Greenwood.

'Gossip, mother, gossip,' she said. 'Indeed 'tis not merely idle gossip, 'tis a most malicious slander.'

'Dearest Charlotte,' said a man with a deep voice, 'we sailed from England to tarry a while on Pertigua for our wellbeing. We are not here to indulge in the spicy gossip hereabouts. You well know that an island like this teems with all manner of tittle-tattle.'

'And all manner of scandal,' Katherine Bradshaw added. 'But when it concerns my daughter, I should like to know the source of that tittle-tattle.'

The sepulchral voice of Frederick Bradshaw entered the conversation. Florence trembled.

'I should also like to know,' he demanded.

Before the subsequent investigation could begin, she fled out of the back door into the night.

A mannish stranger stepped inside the chattel-house. Everyone stiffened. Jacob's blood ran cold. An instinct made him step forward for a closer look.

'It's Florence!' he announced.

Smiles and hushed salutations greeted her arrival. Jacob watched the Hungan when she nodded at him. Half-heartedly returning her greeting, the priest smiled feebly when she stepped purposefully up to him.

'Going my way?' she asked.

The Hungan's smile broadened.

'We go as one,' he replied.

Relieved, Jacob turned away and removed his tiny bag of gold from its hide. He affixed it inside his breeches. Turning back, he gave each of his comrades a machete, a sack of food and a coil of rope.

A knock at the door sent his companions diving for cover. Gripping the handle, Jacob inched the door open. Visibly anxious with bloodshot eyes, Faith Bradshaw stepped warily inside. A rich fragrance followed her into the sweaty interior. A palpable relief swamped the chattel house. Conspicuous against her demure white gown and garnet cotton mantle was the flintlock musket in her hands. Her complexion was flushed and strands of hair had blown free from her coiffure. He smiled at her hesitantly. It was the first time the two women had been with him in the same room. She passed him the musket, a leather pouch filled with gunpowder and a piece of pyrite flint.

'I want you to take these with you, Jacob,' said Faith.

'I will use it if I have to,' he said.

Lately, she had asked him if he was prepared to shoot anyone during the course of his escape.

'Yes,' he had replied unequivocally.

With a certain apprehension, he watched Faith scrutinising them all. Identifying Florence beneath her hat, she blinked. For several awkward moments, the two women gazed at each other. Taking off her hat, Florence ran a finger slowly along the scar on her forehead. Faith backed away momentarily. Given Faith's deep and personal involvement, a truce was inevitable. Florence dissolved into a smile. It was as if heavy rain clouds burst over a desert and a downpour of harmony drenched the collaborators. Through watery eyes, Faith smiled at Florence and then at each man in turn.

'I wish you God speed to a safe haven,' she said. 'Nathan Greensleeves awaits you in the quarry at Orange Mountain. Are you acquainted with its whereabouts?'

'Yes, Mistress Bradshaw,' said Ol Bones, 'I knows it well.'

'Now listen carefully, my friends,' Faith said, lowering her voice. 'All is quiet at the Great House and the dogs are in kennels. Our guests will be at table for some hours yet. The night watch will be about their rounds at one o'clock. Be sure to be gone before then. If all goes well, your disappearance will not be discovered until about five or six in the morning. I shall try and delay them as best I can. With good fortune you should get a six-hour start. Make haste, men and woman of Guinea. And may God go with you.'

'God bless you, Mistress Bradshaw,' said Ol' Bones.

'God bless you, Mistress Bradshaw,' they chorused.

Following her onto the verandah, Jacob experienced a fleeting sadness. An instinct told him that they would not meet again. Turning to face him, she took his hands and placed them palms-down on her abdomen. Puzzled by her action, he looked into her eyes. Cupping his face in her hands, tears rolled down her cheeks.

'I shall think of you often my love,' she said, her voice breaking. 'I shall think of you as a free spirit and I shall be glad. As I gaze across this unhappy island, I shall remember the blackness of your face and the laughter in your eyes. You who came with so much pride from the dark coast of Guinea have brought laughter and love into my life. I shall never forget you, Jacob.'

'The water that washes your face,' he said quietly, 'bathes me with your courage. I know not when or how, or what will make it happen, but I hope we meet once more.'

He knew that her burning desire was made hopeless by his feelings for another woman. He drew her to him. For the first time since she initiated their precarious liaison, he kissed her with a genuine tenderness and gently wiped away her tears.

She had violated him at their first furtive encounter in the summer-house. Despite that violation and the iniquitous dominion of slavery, they had grown progressively closer. Consequently, he had over time, risen above his hate to forgive her abuse of him. He acknowledged the time she had then spent bridging the vast divide between her life of privilege and the barbaric reality of his existence. He had no doubt that she loved him to the extent that an affinity and equality had arisen in their curious relationship. Now while she was bidding farewell to her lover, he felt he was saying goodbye to a remarkable friend.

27 November 1751

It was a little past midnight. Tiptoeing past the Great House under a lustrous moon, Jacob and his companions headed down the carriage-drive towards the main gates. By the stable-block, Bradshaw's prized red rock chickens cackled, flapped alarmingly and fell silent. Such was the silence Jacob could hear every breath he took. His footsteps echoed horribly. Snarling kennelled rottweilers halted him in his tracks. Expecting a barking cacophony to ensue, he waved his companions down and dropped to the ground. A short while passed before he gave the signal to pass between the iron portals – beyond the point of no return. Outside the gates they were classified runaways and would be shot on sight.

Pulling out his map, Ol' Bones took the lead. By the light of the full moon they headed for the quarry. Behind Ol' Bones came the Hungan clutching his dark paraphernalia for voodoo gatherings. Florence came next. Jacob brought up the rear.

Several miles later they reached Orange Mountain. Inside the shadows of the rockface Jacob discerned a bearded figure. Recognising the silhouette, he stepped forward and whispered hoarsely.

'Mister Greensleeves?'

A chuckle came from the shadows. He trembled. The old man stepped into the moonlight.

'Is thee to be a mountain nigger then, Jacob?' he asked. 'Right glad I am for thee. There be about thirty hard miles ahead. We head northeast for Bamboo Bay. Then you be on your own. Stay clear of the Great Houses. Keep a look out for their malicious dogs. By dawn tomorrow the Mongoose Gang will be sniffing on your trail. They'll not be easy if they catch thee. Be up in the mountains by then. Got that?'

'We're ready, Mister Greensleeves.' he said impatiently. 'We're all set.'

Taking Florence's sack from her, Greensleeves threw it over his shoulder.

'We have not a moment to lose, Jacob,' he said. 'We'd best be away from here. The dust ain't about to settle.'

For a considerable length of time, they plodded silently behind the old man. Eventually they found themselves in a shallow valley. Swinging to the left, by the smallholdings bordering a sugar plantation, they caught sight of four drunken overseers hauling up their breeches. Two exhausted slave women in leg irons were sobbing on the edge of the canefield. A rescue is not possible, thought Jacob. Stifling his fury, he ducked with the others into a canefield. They would have to wait until the group had moved on. Fully dressed, the overseers hauled the women to their feet and prodded them out of sight.

'Let's be gone, Mister Greensleeves,' he said eagerly.

'Yes me lad, let us go,' replied Greensleeves.

At first light the terrain began sloping downwards. In the distance, he caught sight of an immaculate moon shimmering on a tranquil sea. The old man increased his pace with the length of his stride. Jacob gladly followed suit. Gone four in the morning they stepped onto the fine white sands of the desolate Bamboo Bay. Never before had Jacob experienced the serenity that met his ears and eyes. Fringing the crest of the shore was a long steep embankment of sand dunes, swathed in a forest of marram grass bending and twisting in the easterly gusts. Behind the dunes a range of mountains rose like a towering rocky barrier. Rolling gently up the sandy shore, wavelets greeted them with a foaming hush. Sitting down for a breather, Jacob's only thought was of putting distance between them and their pursuers. Looking around guardedly, the old man waved at the mountains.

'I take my leave of thee here, Jacob,' he said. 'White men have a queer habit of not reappearing from those parts. I'm glad it is thee making a break. 'Pon my word, Jacob, think not that all white men are like them thee has met. Someday others will give thee a finer opinion than thee has had as yet.'

Try as he might, he found himself incapable of responding positively to the good-hearted apology, for slavery had deafened him. Nonetheless, he embraced the old man and shook his hand sincerely. Bidding farewell, he felt more than a vestige of attachment to Nathan Greensleeves.

'I shall not forget the risk you have taken for us, Mister Greensleeves,' he said. 'When one day we come down from the mountains to liberate this island, we will not harm you and yours.'

'I shall camp in this bay from time to time,' said Greensleeves. 'When I do, I shall light a fire on this here sand. That will be my signal. Come down if it pleases thee. I know Mistress Bradshaw will be fretting to know how thee be fairing. Make haste, men of Guinea. Go now and God speed.'

Following his heartfelt farewell, the old man disappeared into the dark.

Jacob grinned uncertainly at his companions. Turning around, he looked along the shadowy coastline of coral limestone peppered by inlets with white sandy shores. Raising his eyes in the silvery moonlight, he saw a monumental crack in the face of the southern slope of the nearest mountain. It was the primary fracture that had forged the precipitous MacDonald's Bluff, with a sheer drop of two hundred and fifty feet to the rocks and dunes. Appearing from behind the clouds, the moon illuminated the awesome step-like rockface. He baulked momentarily before he took a long look at the topography of boulders, steep-sided valleys, sheer faces, chasms and crevasses. Finally he spotted a track hidden between two lofty dunes situated at the midpoint of the crescent of the Bay.

'We go that way,' he said.

'We're behind you,' Florence said.

From the shore, they clambered up the sandy marram-grassed embankment and around the back of Orange Hill. Traversing a long gully, they reached the seaward facing side of Mount James. Beckoning his companions, Jacob linked together their coils of rope in preparation for the ascent of the Striding Edge Ridge. Reaching the top, it was with some relief that they scrambled down the long slope on the other side into a deep grassy valley. Before them lay a range of mountain peaks with the severe northern face of Mount James on their right. Jacob pointed at a faint trail snaking down into the long valley.

'That way,' he said. 'First we eat. Then we walk all night.'

Sprinkling the contents of a pouch over their tracks, the Hungan chuckled:

'Devil pepper, Jacob. When them dogs nuzzle on this, them sneeze out their guts. Them fill with rage and sink them big teeth into Ferrers' backside.'

They all laughed. It was a frivolous moment in their frantic dash for freedom. Apart from the familiar sounds of the night, the silence that met Jacob's ears said that the chase had not yet begun.

I reckon we have several hours on the posse, but not much more, he thought. Come dawn, the First, Second and Third Gangs would be in the yard and the count would begin. The hunt for them would begin soon after. They needed to reach the other side of the mountains before the posse caught up with them.

Taking Florence's hand, he put his other hand to her belly.

'You two feel good?'

She grinned at him.

'We feel better than good. We're both free.'

He pulled her cheek playfully. She kissed him.

'We three are on our way,' he said.

Hand in hand they walked for some distance until the track narrowed. In single file, he led them deeper into the mountains.

28 November 1751

Several times during the night Jacob halted to listen for the hue and cry. Whenever he thought he heard baying hounds, he stopped for a short time.

'We must be on our way,' he urged quietly.

He quickened his steps after each break. With plantation slavery fast receding, his thoughts fell back to the voodoo mass. The celestial fore-warning by Samuel's apparition about Elijah had yet to materialise. The mass remained a bizarre experience and he reflected on the fantastical spectres of Baron Septem and Papa Goodwill. Conscious of Florence's condition, he prayed that they would quickly reach their destination so that she might rest from the exertions of the trek and not imperil herself and their unborn.

Dawn found Jacob leading the way along a wide ledge. With a sheer drop on one side, they had a commanding vista of a yawning valley. Towering above them was the austere north face of Mount James. As far as Jacob could see, the north face prohibited pursuers from launching an assault or springing an ambush from that direction. Beneath cloudless skies, brightly coloured toucans and long-tailed parakeets winged across the deep valley. Following an exchange with the Hungan, he told Florence that he hoped they would reach Lake Disappointment by midday. Only then would they be beyond the reach of the whites and their Mongoose Gang.

'Keep moving,' said Ol' Bones. 'The count of the gangs will have started.'

'Cook wakes me at first light,' said Florence. 'When she sees me gone, she will open her big mouth and raise that voice. And that foot-licking nosey bitch know plenty. She sells herself and her words to Bradshaw. Her brother is one of the Mongoose Gang. He loves nailing hands and feet of runaways to a cross. So she will run to tell Bradshaw and Ferrers.'

The valley proper was a vast deep ravine, stretching from the base of Mount James to the south, a range of hills to the north and a sheer cliff of tropical foliage to the east. The western end formed a narrow entrance through which they had entered. The valley was bounded on three sides by walls of impenetrable foliage. On the valley floor, a river meandered along an ox-bow and out of sight. It was close to noon and the heat was rising in the cauldron of the valley. Sweat was running freely down his body. Drums brought them to a standstill.

'Them knows we're here,' said the Hungan. 'Keep moving.'

Pointing at the rocks ahead, Ol' Bones pushed his way confidently to the front.

'Snake country, Jacob!' he announced. 'I'll lead from here. I know them snakes.'

The drums stopped abruptly. Peering from one side of the track to the other, Ol' Bones walked on. Jacob felt a hand on his shoulder.

'Somebody shadows us, Jacob,' the Hungan said. 'I feel eyes sinking into my backside.'

Jacob's heart was racing as he turned slowly around. A short distance down the path, four hostile characters stood their ground. Wearing ragged jerkins and breeches, they carried machetes and muskets. He shivered. I see why the Mongoose Gang avoids these mountains, he thought. Handing the musket to Ol' Bones and spreading his arms, to prove he was unarmed, he walked back slowly towards them. One of them yelled: 'Stay-where-you-is!'

Jacob halted.

'What you want?'

'To see Samuel.'

'What you want with Samuel?'

'He waits for me. We come from Tamarind Trees.'

'Who holds that plantation?'

'Mister Bradshaw.'

'Who his head overseer?'

'Ferrers,' he replied.

Stepping out onto the path, a stocky bald-headed man beckoned him forward.

'Come,' he said.

Reaching the four men, Jacob waited while the man examined the DC brand on his arm. Smiling lustfully at Florence, who scowled, the sweating bald-headed man addressed him.

'Them call me Truelove,' he said. 'I take you to Lake Disappointment and Samuel. Follow me.'

It was early afternoon when they stood on the edge of the legendary Lake Disappointment. Gazing around the dense mass of tropical vegetation,

Jacob's spirits rose. It was a lake of sorts, more a swamp, in a lively state of decomposition. Scarlet ibises and rose-coloured spoonbills waded through the shallows. Dotted with islands of marsh grass and impassable foliage, together with hefty thickets of mangrove trees sprouting vine-like roots, the vast expanse of water was in essence a huge watery quagmire. An outsider would have to be familiar with the channels and bogs to find a way through, he thought. The tangled vegetation will daunt any posse and the swamp dwellers know it.

Secreted up a creek and camouflaged by severed branches, Truelove uncovered a rickety canoe for the final stage of the escape. Weaving between the islands, the man paddled the canoe into a channel leading to a densely thicketed island – the runaway stronghold of Freetown. Thoroughly exhausted, Jacob stepped into the shallows and, disregarding everything in his new world, he waded through the reeds, onto the grassy shore and collapsed on the sunlit bank into a deep sleep.

Freetown

Fingers of sunlight prodded Jacob awake. He last remembered collapsing on the bank. Sitting up groggily, he yawned. He had a dim memory of being carried inside the shack. He looked around. Florence was fast asleep by the opposite wall. Rising achingly to his feet he stood for a while watching over her, thinking about what the past years had done to them. Free of barked orders, whips, shackles and chains, he was overjoyed that his pregnant lover was safe. Tiptoeing into the sunlight, he halted by the water's edge. With no sign of Ol' Bones and the Hungan, he began to explore the stronghold.

Freetown was a ramshackle set of huts roofed with banana leaves. Lengths of roughhewn planks and long grasses had been used to construct the makeshift dwellings. Twenty-two were arranged in the shape of a buckled horseshoe. Patches had been cleared for vegetables growing in untidy clusters of cultivation. An ideal setting, he thought, except for the deadly water snakes, mosquitoes, sand flies, bat ticks, bee lice and other nasty creatures.

Good fortune had blessed the location. Mangoes drooped from sagging branches. A freshwater spring bubbled up through the rocks near the heart of the island. Firewood was abundant in the russet-coloured clumps of dead mangrove roots. The sanctuary could only be accessed by boat and possessed a concealed entrance. It was for all practical purposes impregnable. Unless, he thought, someone was bent on a suicide mission. Across the swamp, he saw canoes disappearing beyond a line of trees.

Examining the abrasions left by chains on his ankles, he rejoiced at the thought of keeping company with the free – men, women and children. He would learn the runaway's ways of fishing and trapping around the stronghold. Free to do anything he liked, he wanted to shout with joy.

'Kayode. Kayode.'

The sweet sound of his right and proper name took him by surprise. It was the first time since being stolen from Ake that he had heard the name given him by his grandparents on free lips. Closing his eyes, his past life came flooding back in a torrent of sorrowful memories. Spinning around, he saw her flowing toward him like an oncoming wave. This instant heralded his rebirth. He was already beginning to see beyond plantation slavery. Throwing his arms around her, his lips yielded to the coolness of her cheeks. He pulled her down to the ground. Stretching out his hand, he twisted a yellow red mango off an overhanging branch.

'Daughter of Pategi,' he said solemnly, kneeling before her. 'Take this the mango from mother earth. And take back your name – Asabi.'

Sadness flitted across her face.

'Will we ever again set eyes on Ake, Kayode? I bleed for our people. Why did we have to live through such a long darkness? Slavery is a killer. The plantation is the wicked province of *Elegbara* – the Devil.'

'Tamarind Trees is far away,' he said. 'Here we are safe. We will never again see Ferrers, Bradshaw or Fleming. Never again will they whip us. And they will never take us alive. This I swear. From this day forth, Asabi, we own ourselves.'

He bent down and pressed his lips against her belly. Then he waved his arm in an arc.

'This hideaway, my dearest, is paradise.'

'Where is Ol' Bones and the Hungan?' she asked.

'Probably snoring.'

Flinging the mango aside, she lurched to the water's edge and vomited into the murky waters. Smiling to himself momentarily, he frowned.

'Baby does not like mango?'

Shaking her head, she smiled, stroked her belly and responded.

'Baby wants banana and fish.'

'Together?'

'Yes,' she laughed.

'I'll get them for you.'

'There are too many poisonous snakes here,' she said suddenly. 'This swamp is swarming with them. A flood ferrying such faithless things will be terrifying. We must find a place that is not infested. A place that is hard to find and where our children will be safe.'

'I know we should not stay here too long,' he said thoughtfully. 'I will try and convince Samuel to come with us.'

'And if he turns you down?' she asked.

'We'll go alone.'

Distracted by excited voices, he turned to see canoes coming into view.

'Ol' Bones and the Hungan have been hunting!' he exclaimed. 'They're back.'

Ol' Bones rose unsteadily from a canoe. Laughing aloud, he waggled a squealing piglet in the air, pointed into his mouth and rubbed his belly. Scuffing the rickety jetty, the canoes tied up. The fishermen and hunters landed their catch of fish and water hogs. Rising to his feet, Kayode felt his eyes straining in their sockets.

'It's the pockmarked Mogba who chased us from Oyo,' he hissed.

Springing to her feet, Asabi exclaimed.

'The serpent himself!'

The smiling object of their attention stepped out of the canoe with a string of fish. Catching sight of Kayode, his smile vanished and his catch tumbled onto the bank. Kayode was filled with hatred. The last sight he had had of this man was on the bloody shores of Badagri, in chains and waiting to board the *Pelican*.

'Perhaps Olorun wants the fight between us to end here,' he said. 'But how can I ever trust this man?'

'Never trust him, Kayode,' she replied.

Distracted by his loathing of the former Mogba, he failed to notice a slightly built man appear beside him. He had a toothy smile and wore a frayed tawny jerkin and shapeless breeches, sporting a large silver hoop through his earlobe. To his surprise, the man, who seemed curiously familiar, embraced him warmly.

'I knew you would come!' the man exclaimed joyfully. 'I've been waiting for you.'

Memories of his celestial rendezvous with the spirit at the voodoo mass came rushing back. He found it bewildering that he could recognise a man he had never seen before. Keeping a wary eye on the Mogba, he introduced himself.

'My name is Kayode,' he said. 'This is Asabi. My other friends are Ol' Bones and the Hungan. We escaped from Tamarind Trees.'

'Them call me Samuel. I ran away from China Lights plantation. And I . . . '

Following Kayode's gaze, Samuel stopped talking and asked:

'You know him before?'

'Another time, another place,' he sighed. 'It is all in the past. We all suffered.'

Though clearly intrigued, Samuel persisted with his tale.

'I break from China Lights plantation with others. Over long time we make this a safe hideout. Them call me Governor of Freetown. This here is Elijah. He was Mogba on the coast of Guinea. He's the Hungan for Freetown. Elijah break out of China Lights and been here 'bout four months.'

Raising his eyebrows at the name Elijah, Kayode winked at Asabi.

'We must leave behind what went before.' he said.

'Yes we should do that,' Elijah said, wiping his brow and walking hurriedly away.

'Come to my shack, Kayode,' said Samuel. 'There we can talk.'

Samuel's shack was situated at the heart of the settlement. Close to the entrance was the smouldering remains of a fire. It was a single room structure, sparsely furnished with crude planks laying across a box for a table. A straw-filled grubby pallet had been crammed in a corner. Pouring dark liquid into a coconut shell, Samuel handed it to him.

'Arrack,' said Samuel. 'We brew it from the sap of the sugar palm.'

Chatting throughout the hot afternoon, they were interrupted only by Samuel's woman and five-year-old son returning from working the family plot. After presenting his father with two ears of corn, the boy helped his mother cook food.

'There are small small settlements like Freetown not far from here,' said Samuel. 'We meet them from time to time. Not including them in the small camps, we think runaways run to around a thousand.'

Ending his description of Freetown, Samuel broached the subject of Piccaninny Farm where he was born twenty-five years before.

'Them rear slaves in that place,' he said.

Asabi raised a quizzical eyebrow at him. Slapping his thigh, Samuel laughed loudly.

'Did you not know them grow slaves like potatoes, Asabi?' he asked. 'Soon, them won't have to sail to Guinea to buy or snatch slaves, for them be all home-grown.'

Samuel exploded with laughter. Relishing the joke because he felt free to do so, Kayode grinned at Asabi. Another flagon of arrack appeared. The sounds of a brawl outside the shack forestalled their chat. Swapped punches could be heard. One of the combatants yelled, followed by a splash, boos from the crowd and a woman's screams. Jeers greeted the victor. Continuously shaking his head throughout the altercation, Samuel retained a blank look. When only weeping could be heard the fight was deemed to be over. Making no attempt to tender an explanation, Samuel simply mumbled.

'Every day them fight.'

From another shack came the cries of a woman reaching her peak, followed by gasps, fading into moans until she fell silent. Temptations of the flesh were suddenly and irresistibly omnipresent. Asabi ran the tip of her tongue playfully along her lips. Samuel grinned. Kayode smiled.

'Moses from Tamarind Trees talked of Piccaninny Farm,' he said. 'He said that he had fathered many babies on that farm.'

'Maybe Moses my father,' sighed Samuel. 'Never knew my father. Never knew my mother. I was born and given to a woman 'til I was 'bout five. Them sell me to Fleming of China Lights. That devil is cruel, very cruel. He never let mothers suckle baby. Them sold after cord cut and mothers never even hold newborn. One day I kill him.'

'I know that serpent,' said Asabi. 'Fleming came many times to the Great House to visit Bradshaw. Two hard men with hard ways. I will help you to kill him. I will show you how to peel his skin off.'

Kayode shuddered. Samuel grimaced and carried on with his tale.

'I been slaving on China Lights for gone fifteen years. 'Bout five years back, I escaped and found my way here. Them have been five hard years, but it safe here.'

'For how long?' he enquired.

'It been safe for five years, Kayode. Will be safe for five more. Why not?'

Following a lusty swig of arrack, Asabi blurted out.

'I'll tell you why not,' she said.

She began her list of objections. Kayode eyed her admiringly. With military precision, she proposed improving the stronghold's defences through an array of snares, trapfalls and lookout posts, from devices that hurled men high into the air, to traps that could hold them under water until they drowned. Proposing the kidnap of three white men left them aghast. She would force two to witness the roasting alive of the third, releasing the dead man's companions to spread panic in Jamestown. Samuel's frown deepened. Ending her account by urging a change of location for Freetown, she thanked them for listening. Mindful of her proven tactical expertise, her conviction in her own equality with men continued to intrigue him.

Shrieks and laughter of children brought the stronghold alive in the late afternoon. Swimmers were in the water. Cooking aromas wafted on the breeze. Heavy-bodied bullfrogs croaked. The mongrel pie dogs were on heat. Gazing across the swamp from the doorway, Kayode looked beyond the activities and boundaries of Freetown. Knowing the place had not measured up to Samuel's expectations, he reflected on the sour reality that five years of liberty had brought to the lives of those who lived there. Sitting back down, he carried on listening to Samuel's tale of escape.

Samuel had chanced upon the refuge in the tropical foliage of Lake Disappointment. Over the years, runaways stumbled across or were guided to the swamp by hunting parties. Never a day passed without dread of discovery. That was when he appreciated the stronghold had changed little since its foundation. Having been worn down by constant vigilance, it was obvious that Samuel was incapable of looking for another location and was thus content to stay put.

In contrast, Kayode was not only eager to relocate the stronghold, but was equally determined to strike back at the slave owners. Unlike most runaways who ultimately settled for merely being free, he hungered for a return to the coast of Guinea. If they had to remain on the island because of a lack of navigational comprehension, he intended to establish an assembly house and a militia. He envisioned the children learning to read and write. As a free people, they could do as they pleased. In the quietude of Freetown, he believed his dream was a shade closer to being realised.

'I agree with Asabi,' he said. 'I will lead a search party with Asabi, Ol' Bones and one you trust. We will explore along the coast until we find a safer place.'

'I like what you say, Kayode,' said Samuel, lowering his voice. 'It will take time and planning.'

Jabbing a finger up at the sky, Samuel leaned towards him.

'I warn you 'bout Elijah up there, Kayode. When I see look you gives him 'fore you even heard his name, I knows you know him. I tell you straight, I don't trust him.'

'You're wise not to trust him,' Asabi said.

'You know Elijah very well,' Samuel observed. 'I know his ways too. And I know he'll squeal on us quick to save his own skin. I heard when he was slaving at China Lights, he start out as Fleming's toady and back-scratcher.'

'He was a Mogba who lived by treachery in Ake,' Kayode replied. 'Tried to cheat my father out of his land.'

Apart from the occasional interruption from Asabi, he gave Samuel the account of Sango's visitation and the role played by Elijah in the catastrophe that befell the village of Ake.

'That sounds like Elijah,' said Samuel, shaking his head. 'Them say he had a fleshy time with Fleming's wife and made her really happy. 'Cos of her, he was given easy tasks and quickly become Fleming's eyes and ears. Unluckily for him, Fleming's wife fell for another slave. Elijah lost his exciting job and was sent back to the canefields.'

Following a fit of laughter, Samuel continued.

'Cutting cane nearly killed Elijah's grovelling backside, so he give it legs and turn up here starving,' he said. 'When we run into ambush a while back, I catch him sloping off into the forest. I sent a man to tail him. He met someone from the Mongoose Gang, who he said was a fellow he knew back on the coast of Guinea and would not reveal our where-abouts. I know the devil was lying. The fellow walks in the valley of shadows. We help his poor backside and he sweats like pig to hurt we. Keep our plans out of Elijah's sight. I put an eye on his back to shadow him.'

'So the struggle with this Mogba goes on,' Kayode said to Asabi. 'I will watch him like the viper watches his prey. My father said to keep my enemies closer than my friends.'

Chuckling, Samuel got to his feet.

'To welcome you among we, Freetown has cooked for you and your friends, Kayode. Come eat and drink the cup of freedom.'

Throughout the following weeks he continued regaining strength. Night by night he slept like a dead man. During the day he ate huge quantities. Together with the spur of Asabi's heady passions, he recovered a level of fitness that would enable him to begin a comprehensive exploration. At the Voodoo mass, it was a rejuvenated man who informed Samuel that he was ready to begin the search for a new stronghold. The Hungan gave him a protective fetish and Papa Goodwill's blessing. Later in the after-noon he met with Samuel alone.

'Asabi is with child,' he said.

Samuel chuckled.

'Overseers let you have rumpy pumpy in canefields?' he asked.

Kayode grinned.

The runaways gathered in the evening. Bellowing for silence, Samuel announced that he was sending out a search party. Kayode would lead it. Rising confidently to his feet, Kayode stamped his authority upon the assembled. The search would begin around Ocean Bay, on the seaward facing side of the mountains straddling the wild Atlantic coast. After that, he would turn his attention to the unexplored subtropical forests, well away from the whites. Truelove volunteered to be Samuel's man in his search party.

At a secret meeting with Samuel, the Hungan agreed to remain in Freetown to keep Elijah under close scrutiny. Asabi's condition also meant that she would have to remain behind.

Week after weary week his three man patrol combed the north-western peninsula. In that region the forest canopy was at times so dense that light itself never entered. Sometimes for days on end, tropical storms flooded the way and delayed a return to Freetown. For the duration of these storms they sought shelter in caves on the rocky seashore and lived on flying fish. Occasionally he thought he had found an ideal location, only to discover it was infested with snakes, flooded readily, or afforded little protection. Although he did discover much that had been unknown to the runaways before. During one such foray, Ol' Bones demonstrated his unique method for dispatching snakes. On another foray, beside an ancient well he stumbled upon a hideous configuration of mutilated torsos in the final stages of decomposition. The arrangement bore the signature of the Mongoose Gang. Set in a macabre circle, the skulls were assembled as if in conversation. To honour the men who had suffered an untimely demise, Kayode called the place Seething Wells.

The weeks of reconnaissance drifted into months. Returning to Free-town on one occasion, he met with the Hungan who spoke of his burgeoning friendship with Samuel. A spiritual impasse had been reached between the Hungan and his voodoo practices, on the one hand, and Elijah's *juju*, on the other. The stalemate apparently began when the Hungan urged Samuel to propose him as the High Priest of the stronghold's voodoo mass.

Kayode considered the Hungan's arguments persuasive. *Juju* was a long way from its roots. Elijah's practices with *juju* were conducted in Yoruba. Only a few of the runaways spoke that language. *Juju* belonged to the coast of Guinea. That land was now too far away. *Juju* did not work well in Pertigua. Though the power of *juju* was undeniable, it was not born in Pertigua.

'This island is steeped in voodoo,' the Hungan growled at Samuel. 'Voodoo spring from this very soil. Come a time when all we been born here. *Juju* and the coast of Guinea will then be a distant memory.'

'What you say, Kayode?' asked Samuel.

'This Hungan is convincing,' he replied. 'We are forgetting our language. Take those that are born here and sold before their parents could teach them Yoruba. They will grow up with a faith rooted in this island's tongue and religion. *Juju* requires too much Yoruba. I've noticed that this Hungan, who too is Yoruba, doesn't even speak the common words like '*e'kabo*' or '*e'kasan*' or '*adupe*'. The Slave Codes forbade us to use the tongues of our homelands. Thus this priest's memory of Yoruba, like mine and all others, founders little by little on the jagged rocks of time.'

Samuel readily agreed that the Hungan should be the High Priest of Freetown's voodoo mass. Additionally, the mass would henceforth be conducted in the patois of Pertigua. Kayode saw at once that, in his new role as High Priest of Freetown, the sparkle in the Hungan's eye said he understood well the nature of his task and he set about it eagerly.

In the Name of the Son

Christmas, 1751

In the aftermath of Jacob's escape, Faith found herself, together with stacks of plantation books, confined to the Great House. As she had intended, the finger of blame was laid on Ferrers, who was at first threatened with a flogging. To her chagrin, he was merely disciplined, with the value of the four runaways deducted from his salary. From behind account books, she heard her father initiate an era of fresh terrors in the barracoon – cancelling Sunday as a rest day, ordering lengthy periods in solitary confinement and severe beatings for the slightest misdemeanour. Heavy-hearted, she witnessed the cane-cutting regime reach new levels of barbarism. An acrimonious silence descended between herself and her father.

A month flew by. Growing industrious with crochet and needlework, a few days before Christmas Day she also began feeling unusually buoyant. In spite of the cruelties taking place on the plantation, she could not suppress her sense of optimism. Though physically she blossomed and her skin glowed, she experienced sporadic bouts of queasiness. At first her mother reasoned she might have contracted the earliest symptoms of a yellow fever genus known to be prevalent in the region. One fateful morning she caught her in her bedchamber retching into a chamber pot. Her mother's hand was instantly under her chin, lifting her head, to look hard into her eyes. Dropping her hand, striding to the door and turning, her mother fixed her with a withering stare.

'You are with child!' she spat. 'Your father shall be informed.'

Within the half-hour, a sharp knock on the door was followed by the housekeeper's strident voice.

'Mistress Faith!' she called through the door. 'Your father requests your presence in the drawing room.'

Smoothing the creases in her dress, she set off down the stairs with icy resolve. Briefly bracing herself at the bottom, she strolled into the pale yellow room. On a sofa by the French windows her mother clutched her habitual large glass of gin. At the writing table was her father, wading briskly through slave auction notices and shipping bulletins.

'You requested my presence, father?'

He looked at her. She could see the loathing in his cold grey eyes.

'I am told you are with child. Is that true?'

'I am with child, father. What of it?'

'Your name has not been matched with anyone in Jamestown, or in any of the Great Houses,' he said, rising to his feet. 'Which spineless rogue is responsible for the brat?'

Her mother garbled.

'Yessh, who issh the fellow?'

Steadying her nerves with a deep intake of breath, she spoke with barely concealed rage.

'Not only is the identity of the father mine and mine alone,' she said. 'But I am set on having and keeping this child. And my newborn and I shall live on the funds bequeathed to me by my grandfather, which neither of you can touch.'

'Harlot! Have you taken leave of your senses?' demanded her mother.

Her father rounded angrily on her.

'Is it that nigger you bedded?' he asked.

'It is, and I shall keep my child.'

'We shall see about that,' her father snapped, striding to the door. 'We'll have no disgrace with lazy niggers in this house. You shall go to your bedchamber and you'll see and speak only to Widdecombe. Until that nigger brat is born, you shall remain confined in this house. Then, Mistress Faith, you shall see what kind of man I am!'

He stormed out of the room and his fading steps echoed the threat that hung in the drawing room. Rising unsteadily to her feet, her mother staggered across to her and put an arm around her shoulders.

'You cannot keep it, Faith,' she said. 'It will be shunned; in fact we shall all be spurned by good society. Good god woman, have you lost your wits? A white woman with a nigger brat? What will you be thinking of next?'

'I am thinking that I am twenty-eight years of age, mother,' she said. 'I am capable of bearing and mothering a child. I care not about the colour of the child's skin, for it shall still be of my body and a Bradshaw by blood.'

With her mother draining the contents of her glass, Faith strode to the door.

'I shall keep my child. And I shall go this instant to begin preparing a nursery.'

Throughout the next six months, relations with her parents degenerated. Now that her tryst with Jacob was known about, the antipathy that had been growing between herself and her father became overt. He kept his distance from her and made certain the household knew it. In the second week of June, 1752, she began her labour. A midwife, sworn to secrecy, arrived late in the night from Jamestown and delivered her son. Following a taxing but uncomplicated birth, she succumbed to a deep sleep.

Awaking in the darkened house in the early hours, she lay momentarily in maternal euphoria, listening to birdsong. Dreamily, she gently swung her feet to the floor. Donning her Indian gown, she trod softly to the nursery and peered into the cradle. Horror gripped her. The cradle was bare. A cold clammy sweat ran down her face and neck.

'Mother of God!' she cried. 'He's been stolen!'

Staggering backward, she careered into the wall, let forth a heart-rending cry and crumpled onto the floor. Wracked with dismay, she frantically looked around. It was then she grasped that, except for the cradle, the chamber had been cleared of its entire contents. She lay trembling.

'Not once did I press him to my breast,' she whimpered. 'Not once did I hear him call me mother. Not once did I see him smile or feel his touch. Father is behind it all. What kind of devil is he?'

Nightmarish images tormented her. Picking herself up, she stumbled down the passage into the adjacent bedchamber. She found her mother weeping with her face buried in her hands, being comforted by the housekeeper.

''Tis Mistress Faith,' the housekeeper announced awkwardly.

Without raising her head, her mother mumbled.

'Your father has taken the child to the Auction House.'

The words exploded in her head. Her grip on reason slipped. Bursting out with rage, she picked up her mother's treasured tea-making set, flung it hard against the wall, and collapsed in tears.

In the late afternoon her parents entered her bedchamber.

Sitting upright, she snapped at her father.

'Where is my child?'

'Where the half-breed belongs.'

'My son is my breed and he belongs with me. I am his mother.'

'A nigger brat doesn't fit in this Great House.'

'You cannot see, can you?' she countered angrily. 'You who has been so blinded by such unimaginable hatred that you cannot see what you have done.'

'You shall not speak to your father in that tone,' her mother snapped.

'He is worthy of no other.'

'I have done what any respectable Englishman would do. I have done my duty.'

'Respectable? You? Your duty?' she sneered. 'Then ask yourself, you narrow-minded Catholic bigot, how many English men would sell their own grandchild? And for profit at that.'

Tight-lipped, seething and ill at ease, he shifted uncomfortably from one foot to the other.

'You who are so blinded by hate that you see my child as contamination of your ancestry,' she spat acidly. 'Such is your repugnance of black skin, you cannot see nor understand that the child you sold in the Auction House is actually related to you by blood.'

Flinging back the coverlet, she leapt to her feet. Pushing them out of her way, she walked unsteadily to the Queen Anne chest of drawers. Picking up her crucifix, she kissed it. Turning to face them, she thrust the hallowed icon at her father and passed judgment.

'Until my dying day, as God is my witness,' she cried. 'I shall never speak to you again.'

A sudden startling stillness filled the room. Silently fuming with a twitch in his cheek, he made no reply. He glowered at her and then, turning on his heels, he stomped from her bedchamber with her mother stumbling closely on his heels.

New Freetown

One balmy late December morning in the year 1751, Kayode stood with his back to the sea examining the cliff face. About thirty feet above the shore, he spotted what appeared to be the entrance to a cave. As he began climbing the rock face, nesting birds shrieked in alarm. Gulls and terns skirred, swooped and cried at him, while marauding birds of prey wheeled ominously above. During rest breaks in Farthest Field, he had often watched the falcon-like birds harrying the gulls to make them drop their prey, snatching it before it fell into the sea. The avian skirmishes had served to relieve the gruelling grind of the canefields. From the mouth of the cave, he yelled.

'Ol' Bones! Truelove! Get your backsides up here! We've found it!'

Of such huge proportions was the dry cavern that he reckoned the runaways of Freetown could easily fit inside. The lofty ceiling was coated by teems of bats and the undulant floor encrusted with their droppings. From the tidemarks, he ascertained that the high water stopped ten feet below the lip of the cavern, while at low water a crescent-shaped sandy shore materialised. Close by, a short promontory jutted out, thus concealing the presence of the grotto from passing vessels. Acting as a windbreak, the outcrop also deflected the full force of any headwind, so the cavern was continuously swept by a gentle breeze.

'This cave is out of reach of the whites,' he announced, gleefully. 'And it can only be found by chance.'

Gazing up at the roof, Ol' Bones chuckled.

'Them bats can hang about in another cave,' he said. 'I'll smoke them out.'

Shadowed by his companions and machete in hand, Kayode trod warily and deeper into the cave. Fifty yards inside he swung to the right. Sloping gradually downwards, the ceiling descended to the height of a man. At this the lowest point daylight poured through a large crevice in the ceiling above the boulders littering the floor. Stepping onto a boulder, he hauled himself up through the gap to emerge in strong sunlight above the cave. The plateau upon which he found himself was bounded by dense forest. In the distance to the south was Mount James, and to the north were the rolling Atlantic breakers scouring the giant outcrops of the Three Apostles huddling in a choppy sea. Gazing intently at Mount James, he declared:

'We bide this side of the mountain, the whites on the other. This is a fine place to build a settlement. Right here my friends, we build a new Freetown.'

And so it was. Lake Disappointment was systematically abandoned. At the end of June 1752, he heard the first cries of his son inside the sanctuary of the cavern. They named their son Abisogun, meaning 'born in war'. To his familial delight, his son had inherited the large nail on the index finger of his right hand, a feature unique to the males of the Sodeke family. The sight of Asabi breastfeeding the babe filled him with joy. Their prospects sparkled.

Turtle Island

Angrily lashing out with his riding crop at the ribbonback chairs in the passageway, Randolph Fleming stomped into the library of Beaumaris and called out.

'Bess! Bess!'

Flinging his tricorne onto a high-backed chair, he wondered aloud.

'Where is the woman?'

Throwing impatient looks around the book-lined chamber, he frowned and raised his voice.

'Elizabeth. I am in possession of the most disturbing Intelligence.'

His wife sallied through the French windows, one hand clutching the hem of her skirts and the other a fan.

'This sultry climate troubles me so, Randolph. The servants have not watered my roses properly. I have been in the gardens. I am here now. What is this dire report you have received.'

'The slaves at Harmony Hall have rebelled. Robert Ellis has been decapitated. His head overseer is dangling from the scaffold. The Great House itself is in flames.'

Gasping, she slumped into an armchair.

'Holy Mary, Mother of God! From whom did you obtain this dreadful report?'

'From none other than Governor Ashleigh himself. I have been summoned to a meeting of the Secretariat this instant.'

The Huygens long-pendulum clock tolled seven o'clock.

'Set off this instant, Randolph, and hasten back with your report. Does the Governor say what has become of Robert's wife, Hannah?'

'Nay, though I am confident he would have made certain she was safe.'

'And the Ellis children?'

He shook his head dolefully.

'I pray they escaped to Jamestown,' she mused aloud. 'I should be at

your side, Randolph. T'would be remiss of me not to be there. Hannah
will need a woman's hand.'

'As you think fit Elizabeth. As you think fit.'

Striding to the door with tears gathering in her eyes, she shouted.

'Abraham! Serenity! Come here this instant!'

An elderly white-haired house slave shuffled into the library, followed
by a young female slave.

'Yes, Mistress Fleming?' they chorused.

'Serenity, the Master and I are leaving for Jamestown within the hour.
Fetch me my bonnet, pack a portmanteau and . . . '

Raising his hand, he stopped her in full flow.

'Abraham,' he said, 'run and tell Mister Baxandale to make ready the
cutter with well-armed men. Well-armed I say, is that clear?'

Repeating the directive, Abraham stood aside.

'Serenity, I shall wear my Gainsborough,' said his wife, continuing her
instructions.

The two house slaves bowed out of the library. Fleming put an arm
around his wife's shoulders.

It was seven forty-five in the morning when Fleming stepped into the
cutter. With the head overseer, Baxandale, at the tiller, six groggy dishevelled men sat waiting at their oars. Scrutinising with satisfaction the two
neat stacks of swords and muskets lying across the thwarts, he looked up.

'I trust you have heard about Harmony Hall, Mister Baxandale?' he
asked.

Touching his forelock, the sandy-haired overseer answered.

'I 'eard 'bout the bloodbath, Squire. Right livid I am at the outrage.'

Assisting his wife onto the stern thwart, he was unequivocal.

'Let's be away to Jamestown to put matters right, Mister Baxandale,'
he said. 'Shoot any nigger who comes near. Cut him down first and ask
his name after that.'

Stroking the musket across his knees as if fondling a woman, the
overseer gave him a twisted gap-toothed smile.

'Aye, Squire,' he replied. 'I've long wanted to give them niggers a right
good pasting. Me and my men will give them what they need. We'll be
away then, Squire?

'Aye, Mister Baxandale.'

'Oars!'

The laden craft nosed across Raleigh's Passage for Little Pertigua. Smiling weakly at his wife perched proudly under her favoured white-plumed bonnet, he looked beyond her at his mansion house, Beaumaris. Built in 1630, the house had since given refuge to every generation of his family. It was the tropical replica of Augustfields, his family seat in Yorkshire, depicting the unique feature of a central Dutch gable.

Fleming mused upon the audacious deeds of his ancestors. In January 1616, his ancestor Squire William Fleming, had sailed from England's shores to land on the island of Pertigua, annexing the archipelago for the English Crown in exchange for being allowed to return to his birthplace. Ending his exile to return to England in March 1619, his Yorkshire estate was restored with a knighthood. In addition, he was gifted Turtle Island in perpetuity and appointed the first Governor of Pertigua by King James. Additionally, William Fleming purchased from the Crown three thousand acres of prime land on the western tip of Pertigua, which he christened China Lights. In time, he acquired another five hundred acres south of Crab Mountain on Little Pertigua.

On Little Pertigua, they transferred to another cutter, crossed Drake Sound and landed at Fort Patrick on the north-eastern tip of Pertigua. Boarding a black lacquered carriage, they completed the last leg of their journey to Jamestown. On the outskirts of the capital he was alarmed by the mayhem on the streets. He kept his feelings to himself.

'The intelligence of the rebellion,' he said calmly, 'has evidently reached our capital.'

'Indeed it has,' she said, anxiously looking out of the window.

A burst of musket fire drove the citizens into panic and the resulting chaotic activity in the street shook his carriage.

'Order must be returned to our capital, Randolph,' said his wife forthrightly.

Noting the anxiety in her voice, he knew in his heart that 'returning order' would not be such a simple task. Around his carriage the air grew thick with orders. Anarchy seemed to reign in a town squaring away for action. Soldiers dashed about reinforcing established lines of defence. Carriages were hurtling by at full pelt. He was glad to see cannons being trundled into position and muskets loaded. Arriving at Fort James barracks in the heat of the day, he saw a log barricade being erected across the main road into the capital. Soon, they were trotting through the iron gates of Drake House – the island's palatial seat of government – an edifice characterised by eight Doric columns.

'It fills one with a certain confidence,' sighed his wife, 'to see such a splendid icon at a time like this.'

At the guardhouse, he dispatched a messenger to China Lights with orders for his head overseer to report to him at Drake House, post haste. They were met by the Governor's wife in the vestibule. A vacant look dulled her blue eyes and exhaustion strained her refined features. Yet Jamestown's fashion-setter had evidently decided that the occasion warranted a cool blue and white gown.

'Anthony awaits you in the Cabinet Room, Randolph.' she said.

'I shall go there at once,' he replied, striding away towards a door.

Elizabeth Fleming turned to the Governor's wife.

'I too have been shaken by these calamitous events, Matilda. Together with the perilous expedition to reach here, I find myself quite fatigued.'

'Come, Elizabeth. We shall take Madeira in the Yellow Room. I fear our work has barely started. You will have some refreshment no doubt?'

Trailing the Governor's wife down the passage, she entered a large lemon yellow room that was bathed in sunlight. Taking a seat at the Hepplewhite table, she had a commanding view of the English Gardens. A manservant promptly appeared to serve dark Madeira. Sensing the underlying panic in the Governor's wife, she removed her hat and took charge.

'Shall we begin by comparing a list of the white residents at Harmony Hall against the list of known survivors you have in your hand.'

With some concern, she watched the eyes of the Governor's disorientated wife drift slowly down to the document in her hand. Giving her a sympathetic smile, they began to cross-reference the names. The quiet order inside the Yellow Room contrasted with the bedlam on the streets. Elizabeth sought to distract her hostess.

'We came the instant we received Anthony's Intelligence,' she said. 'Along the highway there appeared to be no signs of insurrection until we entered Jamestown. If Anthony and Randolph act speedily, I trust it will not spread far.'

'Pray God, Robert Ellis died instantly and did not suffer,' said the Governor's wife. 'We still do not know what those ghastly slaves have done with Hannah. Anthony has dispatched Redcoats to fetch her and any others who have survived, with orders to bring them back here. Major Cedric Thorndike commands. Divine he was, Elizabeth. He looked utterly dashing in his red coat at the head of his men.'

'I remember him,' she cooed. 'He is most fetching.'

'Of course Sarah Adams was the most noticeable in her regard, my dear,' she prattled on, 'when she dropped her glove by the hooves of his stallion. The forethought behind her action was beyond belief. When the gallant officer dismounted to retrieve the silken glove, hotly perfumed no doubt, a musket was accidentally discharged. At the deafening report, his mount reared and the hooves struck her carriage, which was stationed perilously close, causing her horses to rear up and bolt. Her mares dragged her carriage out of sight, spilling its frilly trimmings onto the highway. Half the ladies of Jamestown witnessed the whole affair. Her subsequent discomfiture should be an object lesson to her. Did you know that her husband is the distinguished furniture designer? And that his creations are very much sought after by London society?'

She gave the Governor's wife an understanding smile.

'You lead such an exciting life here at Drake House, Matilda. We are out-of-the-way at Beaumaris. Nevertheless, 'tis time to teach these slaves a lesson. After threatening us in our cots, they abscond to subsist on heaven knows what. The extent of their numbers in the mountains is not known.'

'You are secure on Turtle Island, are you not?' asked the Governor's wife. 'Why, a goodly number of your workers are well armed and white. Runaways could not possibly muster enough firepower to overwhelm your island estate. The same cannot be said of the estates on Pertigua, as well as your China Lights plantation. And I do so remember . . . '

Giving a long sigh, the Governor's wife continued her reminiscence.

' . . . when last we were out at China Lights,' she said, 'the sun set so romantically on Hurricane Point. China Lights enjoys a heavenly Great House, but not nearly as exquisite as your Beaumaris on Turtle Island.'

Rising and making for the door, the Governor's wife picked up her wide leghorn hat trimmed with flowers.

'Speaking of survivors, come, Elizabeth. Let us brace ourselves to receive the unfortunate.'

At the conference table in the smoky Cabinet Room, Randolph Fleming sat patiently listening to the grim deliberations. Chairing the meeting was the Governor, Sir Anthony Ashleigh.

'I have invited Parson Merriweather for a spiritual contribution,' he announced.

The convened Secretariat comprised Squires Wheatcroft, Brigstocke, Ogden and Bradshaw. Heated exchanges were taking place when the Parson effected a somewhat flustered entrance. Throwing a frown at the clumsy cleric, Fleming turned back to the dreary report being delivered by Colonel Thomas Applegate, the commander of Pertigua's Redcoat regiment.

Applegate droned on for what felt an age. Fleming pondered. Is this thickset officer the right man for the task? Certainly the man had been a leading light in the military force that had seized the island of Trinidad from Spanish and French settlers in 1737. Additionally, in 1739, Applegate had survived the War of Jenkins' Ear fought against the Spanish. Despite such laudable credentials, Fleming was unimpressed by Applegate's tactics. He thought they were invariably costly, both fiscally and in men.

Applegate paused to set light to a dark shuruttu. Banging his fist on the table, he thrust forth his advice.

'Teach the niggers a lesson!' he cried. ''Tis not enough to drive them back to the canefields. I say while we are about it, dispatch a substantial detachment to drive them from the mountains as well.'

Taking a goose bone pipe from his valise and cramming it with hemp, Brigstocke set it alight and proffered his opinion.

'Easier said than done, Colonel Applegate,' he said sourly. 'And with what do you propose we remunerate the musketeers of the garrison? Especially in the likely event your expedition lasts not weeks, but months or even years? I have a notion that it would be better if, from this instant, we increase the penalties on anyone caught doing anything we don't like. A few blindings and maimings should set them right.'

Taking note of those who concurred with Brigstocke's proposition, Fleming raised his eyebrows disdainfully when the Parson coughed for attention. Fleming remembered the account of the cleric's recent experience on the coast of Guinea, he'd heard it had been troubling the clergyman's conscience. And certainly, the priest had been seen in the taverns of Jamestown, drinking heavily, gazing into his ale while keeping his own morose counsel. He was however not prepared for the preacher's contribution.

'If you blind them, they may not be able to see the ways of Our Lord,' said the Parson. 'If you maim them, Squire, they will not be able to do

His work, such as cutting cane. Leave them with their eyes and legs, and Mother Church will take them under her wing and show them the light. Once their eyeballs have supped on that, they will have an improved appreciation of their position in the scheme of things.'

As the cleric was speaking, Fleming was watching Bradshaw's darkening visage.

'What do you suppose that will achieve, Parson?' asked Bradshaw, 'apart from bamboozling them with pious mumbo-jumbo that will find no abode in their heads. I'm with Applegate in this matter. 'Tis well known that I have a problem with accommodation as a policy. Robert Ellis, God rest his soul, was my neighbour. A right fine neighbour he was too. Had we set about your niggers with purpose after the matter was last discussed, we would not be holding a post mortem over how his head came to be separated from his body. What we have here is a mere debating guild.'

Persisting with his silence, Fleming noted the subsequent protestations. Alfred Wheatcroft raised a hand for attention. Brusquely ignoring his hand, Bradshaw persisted.

'I suppose you will be waiting on Fleming's judgment, will you not, Wheatcroft?' he asked. 'Gentry always stick together. But all of you had better take note . . . '

Looking pointedly at him, Bradshaw completed his sentence.

'There are more niggers on this island than whites, Squire Fleming,' he said. 'Consider that in your noble estimates.'

Bradshaw's censure heightened the awkward silence that descended. Fleming could see that. The blighter has put his finger on that most sensitive of subjects, he thought, the racial imbalance of the island's population. Looking around the table, he could see them all eagerly awaiting his contribution.

'I see merit in what you both advise, but consider this,' Wheatcroft said equably. 'What if Applegate's recommended course of action were to become an enduring military action? Can we afford the revenues it will then require to succeed? And we cannot count on the support of the Exchequer. I fear as well that His Majesty, King George, knows not what is occurring in or out of his kingdom. It is said he is more interested in the comings and goings of the House of Hanover. In this age, the real world is, for the King and his courtiers, rather irksome. By the 'real world' gentlemen, I mean those matters that concern the well-being of England's common people.'

'This black flock is not consequential enough,' said the Parson, 'to inspire the interest of Archbishop Herring and The Lords Spiritual. They are far too embroiled in the divisions and politics of the reformed Church. Nay, sir, you can count on no support from that quarter, I can assure you.'

'The business they should be minding is England's trade and interests,' said Bradshaw. 'Dotted about the distant lands of His Majesty's possessions are men like us who feed and clothe England. We are the buttresses of the new age of invention and discovery for the betterment of all. We lead the world in sugar production. England demands cane. We are also the cane that feeds England by whipping idle niggers into activity. If we fail, gentlemen, England fails.'

The circuitous arguments exasperated Fleming, the fifty-three year-old patriarch of the island. He was known for few words but decisive action. It was in his family mould. Moreover, he was well aware that regardless of what was discussed at this meeting, it mattered little if he disagreed. Most certainly, he was not about to put white lives or his assets in jeopardy by giving support to a gratuitous military expedition.

'What say you, Squire Fleming?' the Governor asked.

Rising slowly to his feet, Fleming ambled to the window to survey the Savannah. On these green acres, he thought, I have frittered agreeable hours watching races on this racetrack. I shall have them again. But first we must put a stop to this revolt.

'Crush this uprising!' he snapped. 'Execute the ringleaders! Institute such intimidating instruments to divert any nigger from running off into the hills.'

Turning around with intent, he faced the gathering.

'Station soldiers in the foothills to apprehend the runaways. Cut off the flow, gentlemen, before they multiply into a force to be reckoned with. Otherwise, effortless escapes, merely an idea at present in the slave's mentality, will not only turn into reality but speedily into legend. Then, even if we moved heaven and earth, gentlemen, we could not kill a myth. If the thought of free slaves, sniggering and swaggering in the mountains, were to leave this island, it would spread and sweep us from all our islands into the sea. Nay, we must put a stop to all escapes. That, gentlemen, will not necessitate an armed expedition into the mountains, the expense of which would be far too onerous.'

His evaluation at an end, Fleming resumed his seat.

'Capital, Randolph, capital,' said the Governor. 'Doubtless we are all agreed on the prudent course proposed by Squire Fleming?'

There were a few mutterings of dissent. His strategy was more or less unanimously accepted. Rising to his feet and expecting all to do likewise, Fleming made for the door.

'We leave for Harmony Hall at once,' he said. 'Will you ride with us, Parson?'

The priest writhed visibly in his seat. He is vacillating, Fleming thought. It is apparent he wishes to play no part in the forthcoming proceedings.

'I shall remain here, Squire Fleming,' said the Parson. 'I have no doubt that the dying and injured who have been carted into Jamestown will necessitate the attention of my ministry.'

'As you wish, Parson,' replied Fleming. 'But I trust that if they are injured runaways, you will let them die without ceremony?'

'Nay Squire, I cannot do as you ask,' the Parson said, shaking his head.

'For the tenets of the Church oblige that the last rites be equally applied to all.'

I am moved by the heartfelt manner with which this cleric utters his philosophy, Fleming thought. Despite his bedraggled appearance and alcoholic tremblings, the man speaks with conviction.

'As you fancy, Parson,' he replied thoughtfully. 'As you fancy.'

Escorted by a troop of Redcoats beneath a shimmering moon, Fleming set out on horseback for the Harmony Hall Estate with members of the Secretariat. Sporadic musket fire and shouts from the darkest shadows of the canefields dried his throat. By the Bay of Thanksgiving, he saw flames soaring into the night sky half way to the horizon. I wager that's Harmony Hall, he thought. Proceeding in silence down the rugged winding dark road, they eventually arrived at the portals of the plantation.

The Governor groaned.

'Good God, Randolph,' he said, 'it is worse than I envisaged.'

Even from the gates Fleming could feel the heat from the blazing Great House. Striding towards them like a cockerel, bloodstained blade in one hand and the reins of his mount in the other was a panting, helmet-less Major Thorndike. His stony face and dishevelled appearance conveyed its own story. Purple-faced, Colonel Applegate dismounted and snapped an order in a tone designed to produce a swift response.

'Your report, Thorndike!'

'Over there are the remains of the overseers, Colonel,' said the Major, waving his hand towards the stables. 'The rest are slaves. Mistress Ellis and all the white residents were butchered in the stables. It's carnage in there, sir. The site is awash with blood. I had their bodies removed, covered and laid out on the carriage-drive. Squire Ellis has been arranged with them. I found his head in the yard with his eyes gouged out. I would say they were massacred soon after the niggers broke out. But we have taken control, sir.'

Inflating his chest and clicking his heels, the Major wound up his report in a stentorian voice.

'At present we are securing the area, Colonel,' he said. 'We have twenty dead niggers and six alive. My men and the Mongoose Gang are hot on the heels of the runaways. I expect to have more prisoners in the morning.'

'You have done well, Major Thorndike,' the Colonel said.

Fleming sighed heavily. His worst fear of a full-scale rebellion had been averted. While his distress had been ostensibly of a political nature, it was also a personal one. Robert Ellis, the best man at his wedding, was dead. The enduring bond between their families made the pain all the greater. Ellis's mother would be devastated – he would write to his father instead. Also, he would compose a letter to the dead man's sister. He had had a lengthy tryst with her, long before she married a village parson back in England. Like the other four white women at Harmony Hall, Ellis's wife, Hannah, had been forcibly taken. Spread-eagled onto cots in separate rooms, they had been subjected to acts of such depravity, he was thankful that Thorndike omitted the grisly details. The thought of black hands fondling soft white flesh sickened him. The Governor's mutterings through gritted teeth interrupted his thoughts.

'These niggers shall pay for this outrage,' he said, 'they shall pay.'

'They shall indeed,' Fleming avowed.

'My compliments on the promptness of your action, Major Thorndike,' said the Governor. 'Make arrangements for our dead to receive a Christian burial in the morning. I shall mention your action in my dispatches to London, Major. Leave behind sufficient men to safeguard the plantation. Return to Jamestown. Have your report ready by the morning.'

Clicking his heels, the Major snapped to attention.

'As you wish, Sir Anthony,' he replied. 'I shall see that your orders are carried out precisely.'

'By the way, Randolph,' said the Governor. 'I believe your proposition was the correct one. I shall support any measures that you might have to put a stop to niggers escaping. And when we apprehend runaways, as a deterrent example they shall suffer an exacting ordeal before death. After that, the rest will readily accept that slaving in the canefields is akin to taking healing waters.'

'I have no doubt that the Secretariat will support my counsel, Anthony,' said Fleming. 'Bradshaw can suck on that. China Lights lies close. Come, there is moon enough to reach there. Tarry this night on my estate and we shall ride to Jamestown in the morning.'

'Gladly, Randolph, gladly,' said the Governor. 'A game of Quadrille should ease the exertions of this mutinous day.'

'I shall partner you,' said Fleming, 'and over cards we shall devise an abysmal demise for the recaptured niggers.'

Turning to Bradshaw, he asked:

'Will you join us, Squire?'

Shaking his head tetchily, Bradshaw delivered his counter argument.

'What we have here at Harmony Hall, Squire Fleming,' he seethed, 'is the primary manifestation of a much deeper malaise. I foretell that your stated solution of harsh treatment and torture as a technique to forestall revolt will in fact provoke further rebellion. Clear them out of the mountains and put a stop to it. It is March 1753, Squire Fleming, and the plantations are bleeding.'

Mounting his horse with manifest irritation, Bradshaw cantered away and was soon lost in the darkness. Shrugging his shoulders at his difference with the man, Fleming climbed on his grey and set off with the Governor for China Lights.

The wind scoured his face as they galloped. He peered into the dark distance for signs of China Lights.

It was unimaginable to him that anything could possibly change the existing state of affairs. Three thousand acres of tall waving cane were his property by right. Consecutive disasters had caused a series of ruinous harvests. Five years previously, the rains came too early and stayed too long. The resulting floods washed away the seedlings. A hurricane devastated half the island, destroying the next year's plantings. Fire destroyed another. By means of his inherited fortune, he had cushioned the disastrous financial effects and retained his white workers. The last two years had been infinitely better, the income from which had bolstered his estates and his exceptional and somewhat exotic lifestyle in Pertigua. It gave him some satisfaction that the profits of China Lights provided a sound financial base for the improvement and enlargement of his estate in Yorkshire.

In company with the old guard of the island, he hunted water hog, ruffed grouse, geese, duck and woodcock in his leisure time. Four house slaves satisfied his carnal desires at night. His wife, who had long since performed her duty by giving him an heir, was presently pledged to Our Blessed Virgin Mary as a fervent leading light and prominent member of the island's Catholics. During his many absences, she entertained herself with officers from the regiment in distractions organised by the ladies of Jamestown. And, until he had sent Elijah on a secret mission into the mountains, he knew she could be found in the arms of her favourite slave.

China Lights

Nearing China Lights, Fleming's apprehension grew. Had the uprising spread this far? Glancing to his right, the slant of the Governor's chin showed determination. Turning abruptly off the road, Fleming pressed his grey into the ripened canefield.

'Whatever the cost, Anthony,' he said, 'we will trounce these niggers.'

'Aye, that we will, Randolph,' the Governor replied, turning into his wake, 'that we will.'

Cantering down the long cane alley, Fleming was reassured by the thundering hooves of the Governor's mount. Through the tall spindly cane, he caught sight of the flambeaus topping the gateposts of his plantation. A lone figure was standing close by. His heart beat hard until, drawing near, he made out the taut features of his head overseer.

'Is that you there, Squire Fleming?' asked a familiar voice.

'It is, Mister Hardwick. By the looks of you, I daresay you have heard about the uprising?'

'Aye Squire. A bad business it is too.'

'Are my slaves displaying any signs of agitation?'

'I came up to the gate to watch out for any signs of trouble on the road, Squire. Lest the runaways venture this way, I have men concealed hereabouts in the trees and the woods. We're more than equipped to give 'em a mouthful of shot. Not anything as yet. And not anything has bestirred your slaves, Squire. They be well quiet and under lock and key this night.'

Relieved by his overseer's attitude, Fleming heaved a sigh – the insurrection had not yet infected his property.

'What have you heard about the runaways, Mister Hardwick?'

'I did hear that the niggers are led by a slave who escaped from Tamarind Trees, Squire. Went by the name Jacob. They call him Captain Sodeke.'

'What fresh felonies has the villain perpetrated?'

'Fired the Eden plantation, Squire, a few miles from here. 'Tis owned by old man Winchester who is away visiting his Hampshire estate in

England. They killed the head overseer. And cook who had just kindly dished out slops to them.'

'When we apprehend them, they'll never eat again,' the Governor fumed.

'I'll lop off his Sodeke's balls when I get my hands on him,' said Fleming.

'They sacked the storehouse and swiped six muskets,' Hardwick continued. 'These runaways seem well organised. They got order. I suspect they got a strategy as well.'

'Warn your men to be particularly vigilant around the slaves this night,' said Fleming. 'I'll tolerate nothing less. They're to take scrupulous interest in that big one called Jack. Did you know that he sold his own people?'

'Sold his own people?' Hardwick exclaimed. 'Now I knows why I've never liked that blackguard. I've had my eyes on him these past days. I have a feeling our Jack is mixed up in this uprising in one way or another.'

'Is he indeed?' said Fleming. 'Then I say 'tis time to dispense some pain about his person.'

The next few days of Jack's life were excruciating but no amount of pain could ever surpass the lasting torment he suffered for the part he had played as a cabiceer. In his previous life, he was Captain Tomba. Purchased by Randolph Fleming and sent to China Lights, he was renamed Jack. On the Guinea coast he had conducted similar trans-actions to Fleming. He had sold men, women and children, who were either prisoners of war or those condemned by the Mogbas. Initially, he had sold his slaves to chiefs and kings along the coast – until the white men had arrived. They had given cabiceers a far more profitable return for their merchandise. Men like him had been central to the trade in slaves, until the white men had shoved them aside and started kid-napping their own. Had it not been for men like himself, some of his people who were now suffering enslavement would have never even seen or heard of Pertigua. Etched into the features of every slave was an anguished, unending reminder of his complicity. Plagued by night-mares, he knew his past would remain with him to the end of his days. His own captivity had made him understand precisely the pivotal role of the cabiceer.

He had been a slave for nearly two and a half years. And unless he escaped, he knew he would never again see his wives and children. In his hometown of Badagri, he had acted as he pleased. Owner of one of the largest houses, he had also retained an armed force. To his townspeople he had been a man of substance, whereas to Pertigua's whites he was merely a slave.

The overseer's fresh campaign against him compelled him to strike back. Fixed on the pursuit of anything that caused distress to or endangered the lives of the overseers, he pulled the pins from cartwheels, introduced wet sand into the barrels of unguarded muskets and contaminated the molten sugar with broken glass.

Beatings, hangings and maimings had increased significantly during his time at China Lights. He was certain that the Harmony Hall revolt was due to the brutality of the overseers. Now China Lights was also in the grip of latent rebellion. He was confident that Fleming dared not leave his plantation for too long. Even with the cat, the whip and the musket, his overseers could not curb the escapes. Every time Jack heard of a runaway raid on another plantation, he became even more determined to break out of China Lights.

One sultry afternoon Jack was ordered into a long wheel base cart with four other slaves. Due to the presence of a musketed six-man guard, all were left unfettered.

My guts tell me my time has come, he thought.

'Where we going?' asked one.

'Overseer tell his mate we go to port on the north coast,' he whispered, 'to empty a ship.'

'What's on the ship?' asked another.

Shrugging his shoulders at the question, Jack turned away and groaned. His principal tormentors, the head overseer and his assistant, were in charge of the guard. Climbing onto the driving seat, the pair set the cart off down the track. Even before the cart had taken the first bend, the pair were swigging rum from a hip flask. Desperately scouring the unfamiliar scenery, Jack gripped the edge of the cart hoping for a break. Vibrantly coloured hummingbirds, nicknamed kiss-flowers by the slaves, hovered either side of the mud-baked track. The tiny birds sought the nectar of the scarlet poinciana and the yellow poui. A cool south-easterly blew from the sea. Jolting past the swaying canefields, Jack committed the lay

of the land to memory. The track ran along the cultivated boundary of the
China Lights plantation, and then entered a forest where the branches of
the trees conjoined to form a virtually impenetrable canopy. It grew dark
and eerie. A hoarse jittery whisper burst from the head overseer to his
assistant.

'Runaways been seen in these parts lately,' he said. 'I don't like this
here silence.'

A shot rang out. Dropping down, Jack lay flattened against the boards.
Another shot exploded. The horses whinnied and reared. Toppling from
the driving seat, the assistant hit the dirt with a distinct thud. Inching
forwards to peek over the edge, Jack grinned at the wound in the
assistant's temple. Blood trickled from the entry hole. The man was
stone dead. From the corner of his eye, Jack saw the head overseer drop
from the cart into the dense undergrowth. Four slaves followed the
overseer onto the ground. Tumbling down, Jack rolled in the opposite
direction. He came to a halt some distance away. There he remained
hidden.

'Can you see them, Ezekiel?' shouted the head overseer.

'Nay, looks like the cowardly killers have fled.'

From beneath the tops of the fern-fronds, Jack saw the head overseer
rise warily to his feet.

'We've lost the big one!' he cried. 'I tally only four!'

Jack lay stock-still, knowing that the overseers would not initiate a
search without the aid of dogs.

'We'll be back, nigger!' shouted the head overseer. 'So if you be
listening, we're away to fetch the dogs. They'll rip you apart!'

Restraining his joy, Jack watched the assistant's remains being carried
to the flatbed. Hastily turning the cart around, the overseers headed it
back towards China Lights. As it trundled by, Jack stifled a jubilant
laugh. The outing to the north coast had undoubtedly been called off.

Waiting until the cart had rumbled out of sight, Jack made his way
slowly to the coast. There, he hid himself in a crevice in the cliff face for
the remainder of daylight. At last darkness fell and he set out for the
mountains.

London

28 December 1753

As snowflakes swirled on the streets of Whitehall on a gloomy December day, Randolph Fleming cast his eyes over the group of solemn-faced men, all Honourable Members of the West Indies Cabinet Committee, who had convened in the vestibule of the Banqueting House. Fleming recalled his father's schoolroom lecture to him regarding the Kingdom, and their visit to Somerset House to see the masterpiece of the Royal Palace of Whitehall by the portraitist and painter Hans Holbein the Younger. He remembered it well, for they had journeyed there in a yellow-lacquered hackney carriage with high stepping horses. His father had told him too that the great fire of 1698 had virtually destroyed the Palace of Whitehall.

The Banqueting House, which was all that remained of the palace after the inferno, now stood as an architectural curiosity, with freshly painted white Corinthian and ionic columns.

The high-level meeting was to be held in the splendour of the dining room. Fleming was aware of how much he needed the support of his eminent but irritable guest, to salvage the precarious circumstances of the white population on the island of Pertigua.

His attention was drawn to the window by the arrival of two curtained carriages. Onto the snowy pavement stepped the Prime Minister and his entourage. In stark contrast to the beggars shivering on the streets, a blazing log fire welcomed the Honourable Members into the walnut-panelled dining room. Scratch-wigged footmen served watercress soup, roast goose and chestnuts on silver platters, with a pudding of strawberry trifle. A dry white Chateau Sernin from Bordeaux accompanied the meal.

At the head of the table was Henry Pelham, the Whig Prime Minister, his face pallid with almond paste under a white full-bottomed wig. To the Premier's right sat Lord Ramsey, the Cabinet Secretary. On his left sat Lord Cliffont, the Secretary for Colonial Affairs, and just beyond, the Lord-Admiral, Lord Howell. The gathering included the Duke of Chandois, Principal Shareholder of the Royal African Company, and Lord Blair, Principal Shareholder of the West Indies Company. In attendance, as representatives of the Honourable Company of Guinea Venturers, were Squires Christian Brigstocke and Alfred Wheatcroft.

As the emissary of the Governor of Pertigua, Fleming rose to address the Committee.

'Prime Minister,' he began. 'We, the Honourable Members of the West Indies Cabinet Committee, seek your assistance to counter the grave state of affairs that has arisen in the crown colony of Pertigua. Six months ago, a nigger who calls himself Captain Sodeke, sacked a plantation. I have an account of the very incident I speak of in the latest edition of The Gentlemen's Magazine. Let me read it to you.'

'Twenty-five negro slaves, refusing to put up with the inequality of treatment have violently captured and continue to hold as hostage, two gentle ladies from the estate of Mr. Pilsbury, who owns a plantation near Jamestown, in the crown colony of Pertigua. These slaves are no more willing to perform the laborious offices of servitude than our own people. They are generally sullen, spiteful, treacherous and revengeful.'

'Squires Wheatcroft and Brigstocke will doubtless support my report,' he said. 'For nigh on a year, this nigger has been attacking the plantations. His killers descend like a black plague, ravaging the women in their cots and butchering the men. Squire Ellis, owner of the Harmony Hall Estate, and I might add a confidante of His Majesty's Governor, Sir Anthony Ashleigh, was decapitated and his eyes gouged out. His wife Hannah was violated and strangled along with three other white women. We bear witness to such goings on. Do we not, Wheatcroft?'

'Aye, that we do,' agreed Alfred Wheatcroft.

'I hear no mention, Squire Fleming,' asked Brigstocke, 'of the brazen Captain Sodeke in your article?'

'It would almost certainly be unwise to identify his infamy with a name,' the Prime Minister said tersely.

'With regards to these reports, Prime Minister,' Fleming asked. 'How are we to protect our womenfolk from the ravages of such bestiality?'

'Revise your methods, Squire Fleming,' said the Lord-Admiral. 'Niggers own no moral standards. They have witnessed their women being forcibly taken by white men and they want revenge. It seems to me that it would be wiser to ravish slave women out of sight of their menfolk.'

'A sound notion,' said the Prime Minister. 'But these murdering niggers need to be punished. You say this Captain Sodeke has established a stronghold in the mountains? A sizeable settlement, you say. And you say you were taken by surprise. And that the impudent rascal calls his stronghold Freetown? Why then has this nigger been allowed to progress thus far? Surely you have underestimated him, Squire, have you not?'

Not wishing to answer the Premier's query directly, Fleming turned diplomatic.

'Prime Minister, with your attention drawn to the politics of the many strands of His Majesty's business in his colonies, you may not be familiar with the inhospitable terrain in parts of Pertigua. The stronghold of Freetown possesses only one known narrow entrance, is bounded on all sides by mountains that cannot be scaled and gives sanctuary to runaways. Over time their numbers have risen considerably. Indeed, we would lose an army trying to take the stronghold. The colony of Pertigua, my noble Lords, is in crisis. We must act now, lest it spreads. Prime Minister, your judgment is compelling. The niggers must be punished, and to achieve that we must have the army. Before my colleagues and I departed from Pertigua, Sodeke and his gang of criminals had already begun to lay siege to Jamestown. As I speak, the niggers may have already taken it.'

The dismay registered by his audience gave him some cause for satisfaction. Thoughtfully resuming his seat, he was encouraged by the set of the Premier's jaw. Lord Cliffont, the Secretary for Colonial Affairs was candid.

'Make examples of the ringleaders, Prime Minister,' he said. 'We must devise an exclusive demise for this Captain Sodeke. I'll wager if we castrate his lieutenants in front of the rest of his kind, they won't be so willing to use their tools on our women. In future the niggers will stick to their own kind. We must make it clear, gentlemen, that even to think of laying a finger on a white woman is akin to sacrilege.'

'Enough, sir, on the condition of the womenfolk,' said Lord Blair, the Principal Shareholder of the West Indies Company. 'I believe their very presence is an incitement in itself. They get nigger's blood fired up. Noble Lords, we are at war. Are women not the spoils of war? What is of greater significance, Prime Minister, are profits. What of our profits? How fare they with these niggers on the loose?'

That should send alarm bells ringing, thought Fleming, for the profits

Lord Blair refers to affect us all. He smiled wryly to himself when he recalled that after the War of the Austrian Succession, Pelham had ruthlessly carried out a major reduction of government expenditure and the military establishment. Surrounded by such important representatives of colonial trade, this colourless head of government would have no choice but to reverse his infamous cutbacks.

The Prime Minister turned to his Cabinet Secretary.

'What regiments have we?'

'Send the 46th Foot Regiment, Prime Minister,' replied the Cabinet Secretary. 'They gave a sterling account of themselves repelling a French attack against our Virginia colony and in doing so, decimated the Regiment du Roy and sustained less than fifty dead. They are presently in barracks at Woolwich.'

'See to it,' said the Prime Minister. 'Put them on notice that they will shortly be deployed.'

Turning to the Lord Admiral, the Prime Minister snapped.

'What's at hand to transport our forces?' he asked.

'The *Resolution, Sutherland, Leopard, Lion* and *Weymouth* are at present berthed at Greenwich dockyard, Prime Minister,' the Lord-Admiral replied. 'It would be prudent to dispatch the five warships and ten troop transports. Give command of the flotilla to Commodore Sykes of the *Resolution*, Prime Minister. He was the officer who wrung the neck of the pirate Israel Rogers in action off the coast of Guinea. With your agreement, Prime Minister, he is your man.'

Content that his prayers for assistance had been answered, Fleming sat back in his seat. Thoughtfully dabbing his lips with his napkin, the Prime Minister gave his orders.

'Send them on their way with Sykes in command to sort out the insurgents. And inform the Commodore that we expect him to make it decisive. We cannot have niggers in control of an English colony.'

The Prime Minister snapped at his Cabinet Secretary.

'Summon the editors and newspaper proprietors, Ramsey,' he said. 'Issue the usual threats. Play down the revolt. Focus their eyes on the massacre at the Harmony Hall plantation. Feed them the account of the decapitation of Ellis and the violations his wife was forced to endure. That should guarantee sympathetic headlines and raise the passions of the populace to ensure their support. Make no mention of the fugitive, Sodeke, his slave army or the siege of Jamestown. It may spread panic in the coffeehouses. Not a word about the Expeditionary Force, at least not of the transports. Draw attention to the dangers faced by our defenceless women and children. Tell them that the government is confident the ringleaders will be apprehended and punished. Inform those publicists of the fourth estate that we will of course send warships, but only as a precaution.'

With so much at risk, Fleming closely watched the Cabinet Secretary to make certain he entered the Premier's orders in his Cabinet Orders Book.

'As you wish, Prime Minister,' replied the Cabinet Secretary. 'Will you be making a statement in the House?'

Following a sip of wine, the Prime Minister shook his head, then smiled and answered.

'I shall inform the correspondents of the whispering gallery,' he said, 'long after the Expeditionary Force has left.'

The Premier's remark provoked laughter and a toast. Amid the mirth, the Duke of Chandois made an announcement.

'In this expedition to Pertigua,' he said, 'the Royal African Company will stand four square with the Navy and the Army.'

'As will the West Indies Company,' said Lord Blair.

Fleming winked at Brigstocke.

'We thank you, Prime Minister,' said Fleming. 'Your judgment is visionary. I propose a toast to the success of the Expeditionary Force.'

'Aye, we'll roast the niggers,' said Lord Blair. 'That should make for a just peace.'

The snow continued to fall throughout the afternoon. Having agreed to share a carriage with Wheatcroft and Brigstocke, Fleming stepped out into the white streets. They were bound for the Drury Lane Theatre to see The Lying Valet, a farce with a highly acclaimed performance by the actor David Garrick. Taking into account the tribulations of the past year and the crucial conference with the Prime Minister, Fleming found Garrick's farce a cheerful distraction. Returning from Drury Lane he sank back contentedly into the comfort of a carriage to Buttons Gentlemen's Club in the Strand, where he would remain until he sailed with the Expeditionary Force for Pertigua.

Pertigua

Gulls screamed furiously about her masthead as the *Resolution* led the task force inside Darwin's Reef, the coral outcrop that, even at high water, jutted above the surface of the Bay of Thanksgiving. In the bright morning, black-headed terns plunged into the waters around the *Sutherland, Leopard, Lion* and *Weymouth*. The warships were on picket duty, a few cables astern of ten transports, each conveying two hundred infantrymen to enforce England's will.

From the deck of the *Resolution*, Randolph Fleming caught sight of an unfamiliar flag fluttering above Drake House. His mouth dried, he closed his eyes, crossed himself and spoke quietly to Wheatcroft.

'I fear we are too late, Alfred,' he said. 'Jamestown has fallen. I cannot see the Union Flag.'

'We have a fight on our hands, Randolph,' said Wheatcroft.

Raising his telescope, Fleming confirmed his fears. Scrawled in crude white lettering on the banner flapping cheekily above Drake House, he made out the word 'Freetown'. The Expeditionary Force had indeed arrived too late. Half a league from the shore, the *Resolution* dropped anchor close on the Bay of Thanksgiving.

'They have renamed Jamestown,' he exclaimed. 'They are calling it Freetown.'

'A choice description, Randolph,' said Wheatcroft dryly, 'particularly since it is our town with which they are making free.'

'We will search along the coast, Squire Fleming,' said Commodore Sykes, 'to determine the whereabouts of the Governor and his troops. It is apparent to me that Sodeke has taken Jamestown.'

Looking closely at Sykes, Fleming thought the rank of Commodore reinforced his conceit and added stature to his portly frame. Conversely, the weeping pustule on his cheek marred his otherwise distinguished appearance. Turning to the commander of the warship's Marine detachment, the Commodore was succinct.

'I see little activity outside the town, Major Stirling,' he said. 'I fancy that the niggers are concentrated inside Jamestown and its environs. If we fail to determine the whereabouts of the Governor, we shall sail into the Bay of Thanksgiving. There we shall assess the nigger's strength and possibly even disembark our troops.'

Raising his voice, the Commodore gave orders.

'Captain Fletcher,' he said. 'Post lookouts, and tell them to keep their eyes peeled for any signal, particularly from the Governor.'

'Aye aye, sir,' said Captain Patrick Fletcher, the *Resolution's* former First Lieutenant.

An hour went by. Fleming gazed intently at the island. Every now and then, the dispiriting crash of the gallows's trapdoor echoed from the shore, followed by shrieks of delight.

'I'll wager that white necks are being stretched,' Captain Fletcher murmured.

The flippancy of the remark struck a jarring note in Fleming. A shout fell from the crow's nest.

'Cutter on the starboard quarter, sir.'

Appearing from around the headland of the Bay of Thanksgiving, he saw the Union Flag fluttering at the masthead of a cutter bearing a handful of men. Raising the telescope to his eye, he exclaimed:

''Tis Ashleigh and Applegate!'

Looking worriedly at the Commodore, he said:

'The Governor is on his way, and with him is the commander of the garrison.'

Fleming kept his eyes on the clinker-built cutter making it's way towards the *Resolution*. At last, the vessel scraped alongside the warship. A grim-faced Colonel Applegate clambered up the Jacob's ladder. Bloodstained and bedraggled, with a strip of cloth around his head, the Governor came next with an outstretched hand.

'Thank God you have returned, Randolph,' he said, grasping his hand.

'We come to rid Jamestown of the niggers, Anthony,' he replied.

'You have arrived not a moment too soon,' said the Commodore. 'I had almost given you up for lost.'

The Commodore directed the Governor towards his quarters. Fleming followed. He sensed the tension the instant he stepped into the Great Cabin. Here they were to sit in counsel over a hitherto inconceivable scenario – slaves had expelled an English military force from over half an island colony. Their objective was clear – the slaves had to be engaged and routed.

'Compliments from the Prime Minister, Sir Anthony,' said the Commodore. 'He will be delighted to hear that I have found you in good health. I myself am relieved to see that your command has not entirely dissolved. However, I need to ascertain the whereabouts of the niggers, their strength and weaponry.'

Reaching for a bottle, the Commodore was unequivocal.

'A glass of Madeira, Sir Anthony?' he asked, thrusting forth a goblet. 'How sir, has your command fallen into the hands of niggers?'

Downing a mouthful of Madeira, the Governor began his account with a noticeable quake in his voice.

'We were outnumbered six to one, gentlemen,' he began. 'The nigger with Jamestown in his grip has been identified as Captain Sodeke. You will recall, Randolph, that when you sailed for London he had already taken Jamestown's outlying plantations?'

'That he had,' he agreed.

'Since your departure,' said the Governor. 'All the plantations close to Jamestown have been sacked . . . '

Raising his hand, Fleming stopped the Governor in mid-sentence.

'And China Lights?' he asked.

'I believe not, Randolph,' the Governor replied. 'In fact, I believe that none of the western estates have as yet been breached. Many of the eastern estates have fallen, from which I might add, the niggers obtained more muskets, ammunition and cannon. An angry delegation of residents stormed up to Drake House demanding that I take action. On my orders, the Colonel dispatched patrols into the foothills. Not one man returned.'

Brigstocke whistled. An uneasy silence befell the Great Cabin. Looking around at the astonished expressions, Fleming pondered on the significance of this information. Visibly taken aback, the Commodore gasped.

'Good God man! How many have you lost?'

Ignoring the question, the Governor continued with his report.

'When events began to get a little ugly,' he said. 'I dispatched a company of fifty Redcoats under Major Thorndike, with orders to reach Fort Patrick on the north eastern tip of Pertigua. He was to commandeer another fifty and make a southerly sweep down to Englishman's Bay. From there, he was to march back to Jamestown and shoot on sight every nigger in possession of a musket. The company started out on a Thursday morning . . . '

Interrupting the Governor, the scarlet-faced Commodore snapped.

'Something tells me, sir,' he said, 'that you have lost a significant portion of your command?'

Clearly thrown by the Commodore's outburst, the Governor persisted with his account.

'No more was heard from Major Thorndike,' he said, 'until a soldier with his forearm torn off, staggered into the barracks at Fort James on the Saturday afternoon. He gave a ghastly account . . . '

'I daresay he did,' the Commodore retorted.

'It transpires that they were ambushed by runaways on the road to Fort Patrick,' said the Governor. 'In the skirmish on that road, the niggers went berserk with muskets, swords, pikes, staves, machetes and cudgels – in fact, anything they could lay their hands on. Thorndike and his men were forced into a quarry, where in front of his men the niggers hacked off his head . . . '

'Are you saying, Governor,' asked the Commodore, 'that mere slaves bested your trained soldiers?'

'It would seem so, Commodore,' said Brigstocke. 'Otherwise your services would not have been so ordered.'

'They shall not escape us,' said the Commodore. 'We shall kill the agitators in a protracted manner.'

'I doubt that the slowness of their demise, Commodore,' said Brigstocke, 'will make any difference.'

'Although the soldier was bleeding profusely,' the Governor continued, 'he rolled into a gully and secreted himself underneath branches. From his concealed position, he heard the niggers order his comrades to dig a long trench. Then the niggers shot them, dumped their bodies into the trench and covered them with dirt. The instant it was dark, the soldier made his way back to Jamestown.'

'We shall exhume them,' said Wheatcroft angrily, 'to give them a Christian burial.'

'Do you honestly trust, Squire Wheatcroft,' asked Brigstocke, 'that they would feel better in a Christian grave?'

The Governor persevered with his account.

'The soldier's condition and his lurid tale caused much consternation on his return. Frederick Bradshaw called a meeting, at which it was decided to bring the white citizenry into the security of Jamestown where it was considered that the militia would afford them better protection. In less than a week, Sodeke had control of the roads leading into Jamestown, effectively cutting the capital off from the rest of the island. It was reported to me that the niggers intended to leave Turtle Island alone for the time being.'

Raising his eyebrows, Fleming interrupted the Governor.

'And why is that?'

'Because there are too many white men protecting your island estate, Randolph,' replied the Governor. 'Moreover, Sodeke knows your men are well armed and considers it too well defended. I am certain that Elizabeth is safe at Beaumaris.'

'Safe until Sodeke subdues the island of Pertigua itself,' Fleming replied. 'No doubt after that he will turn his eyes on Little Pertigua and Turtle Island.'

He lowered his voice.

'I have an informer inside Sodeke's camp,' he said. 'His name is Elijah. Has he been in touch with you?'

'He has, Randolph,' the Governor replied. 'Your man kept me well informed. It was with Elijah's help that our escape from Jamestown was effected. You all know niggers have no stomach for strong liquor. I contributed, through Elijah, two hundred barrels of my best rum for their victory celebrations. I was hoping that they would drink themselves senseless and sink into fornicating. Luck was with us. That night they got to carousing and the rum did the rest. Applegate and I escaped with the women and children and a contingent of soldiers. We were making for the harbour and . . . '

The Commodore butted in.

'Just how many white men did you leave in Jamestown?' he asked.

'I cannot be exact,' replied the Governor. 'I think about fifteen hundred would be a fair tally.'

'Do you mean to say,' Wheatcroft asked, 'that you left fifteen hundred white men to the mercy of niggers?'

'We could not take them all,' the Governor snapped. 'They were located at different sites in Jamestown. As it was, we suffered a long and frightening night, which was exacerbated by hearing the executions of white men on the scaffold. We made it to the docks and boarded the *Pelican*. Captain Blunt transported us to the Bay of Thanksgiving. I set up my headquarters in the settlement nearby. There we have remained for the past six weeks.'

Following the Governor's account, disbelief hung in the air. The Commodore broke the silence.

'What are the niggers up to now?' he asked, quietly.

'Entrenched in Jamestown,' the Governor replied. 'Sodeke has established his headquarters at Drake House. I send out patrols every day to determine the whereabouts of his runaway units. Commodore, I daresay they are alert to your appearance.'

'They would be blind if they were not!' Brigstocke snapped.

Fleming turned to the Governor.

'What more do we know of this Sodeke fellow?' he asked.

'The killer was owned by Bradshaw,' said the Governor. 'I am told that he was snatched from a village on the Guinea coast by a raiding party off the *Pelican* and, I believe, your *Resolution*. He had been slaving on Tamarind Trees for over a year when he got it into his head to make a break with three others. They fled into the mountains from where he began to organise the runaways.'

'What brought him down from the mountains?' asked Wheatcroft.

'Muskets,' the Governor replied. 'According to our estimates, he has about two thousand men and women to supply with weapons. We believe that after stealing a sufficient number of muskets, he launched raids on the poorly defended plantations. He followed that with hostilities against Jamestown itself until his incessant assaults became a siege. Jamestown fell a few days later. Randolph, we should have listened to Bradshaw's counsel. Had we pursued his suggested action against the runaways in the mountains, we would not now be in this position.'

Fleming sighed irritably. Maybe Bradshaw was right, he thought.

Coughing to focus attentions, the Commodore was resolute.

'Shall we put our minds to the task in hand, gentlemen?' he asked. 'I would remind you that we have a crisis on our hands. One of His Majesty's possessions has been lost to a pack of savages. Thus, we must take Jamestown by force before we become the laughing stock of the world. It is indeed fortunate that the niggers have not attended military academy nor faced a well-drilled force before. I cannot see that our troops shall have much trouble. Gentlemen, here is how I see it . . . '

'A moment, Commodore,' said Brigstocke. 'It would indeed be a grave mistake to underestimate Sodeke. Having aroused his followers with fanciful tales of freedom, he has them convinced that he is their deliverer. It is said that he leads a pack of villains who uphold order by dispensing punishments to all transgressors of his Rules. *This* nigger is shrewd and it would be folly to take him too lightly. Take his life and the uprising will collapse. However, killing him will be easier said than done. You can be certain of one factor, Commodore, though he may not have attended military academy, this nigger most definitely understands our tactics.'

Without responding to Brigstocke's categorical opinion, the Commodore unfurled the map of Jamestown.

'I shall test out his fortifications,' he said, 'by sending a contingent of, say, fifty men to land at night, here at the harbour entrance in Sho'town and on the opposite side of the entrance at Deadpan. From these locations they shall engage the niggers, draw their fire and pin them down. A mere manoeuvre, gentlemen, for under cover of that musket fire I intend to disembark the transports in the Bay of Thanksgiving . . . '

The Way of Sorrow

The sun rose over the colonnaded grandeur of Drake House. Slumped in the principal chair in the Cabinet Room with his boots sprawled on ex-Governor Ashleigh's desk was a battle-worn character. In white breeches and a sleeveless silk jerkin, Captain Kayode Sodeke was open for business as Governor of Jamestown.

The Cabinet Room was cool, august and tidy, very much as the previous occupant had left it. Two sets of tall French windows over-looked the harbour, while against the opposite wall stood a baroque cabinet inlaid with pietra dura – a plaque said Domenico Cucci made it for Louis XIV. Neatly spaced across the yellow pine floor were carpets from the Aubusson factory in France. Occupying the centre of the room was a rectangular cherry-wood Cabinet table surrounded by twenty matching high-backed chairs. The walls adjacent to the table were lined with bookcases filled with books on constitutional, legal and political matters.

The rite of passage from slave to soldier had not been easy. Kayode began his transformation the day he discovered New Freetown. From the outset he had taken responsibility for all scouting and hunting patrols, a vital function in the organisation of the unruly settlement. In reality, Samuel had already yielded to his plans on a number of issues. Thus, he spent the following months reinforcing his position. Convinced that a stable supply of food was an effective way of winning recalcitrant hearts and minds, he made certain his patrols returned with a steady supply of meat and fish. Through his knowledge of the mountain trails, from time to time, un-observed, he tracked down and picked off members of the Mongoose Gang. It was commonly accepted that since he took over the organising of the stronghold, fewer runaways had been killed or recaptured by the Mongoose Gang. He was happy with his growing influence.

Following every hunt he would seek out Asabi. Since escaping, his unhindered access to her had fortified him and he had vowed to do everything to keep her safe.

Motivated by imminent fatherhood and the desire for order, he had sought out Samuel. He needed to make him understand that unity was the key to survival. That if they intended to escape from the island or overthrow the whites, they must begin by reining in the stronghold's hotheads.

'We'll go on brawling among ourselves, Samuel,' he said, 'with even more terrible injuries than we suffered before. Dog eat dog is our way of life. We quarrel over water, fight over food and throw punches over women. Constant worry about being taken by surprise causes many to lose sleep and sink into despair. And we have a lot of skin problems because of lice. We lose three men every month. If this goes on, we will soon be easy pickings for the whites.'

Duly alarmed, Samuel agreed to a shake-up of the stronghold. Kayode introduced The Rules. They were a set of laws that regulated the lives of the runaways directly, from penalties for stealing and interfering with another man's woman, to murder and treachery. The Rules could not cover all eventualities and it was decided that in instances where The Rules fell short, he, Samuel and Tomba would sit together to arbitrate. His calls for order required a sharp adjustment in the lives of several of the stronghold's inhabitants. As a result, the pig-headed became his enemies, but support for his way of doing things was also growing. When half a dozen members of the Mongoose Gang ambushed one of his patrols and killed a well-liked runaway, his moment came. Thoroughly incensed, he alone tracked the gang for three difficult days until they camped in a dead end gully. Once darkness fell and during the course of the night, he dispatched three of them in a long drawn-out shadowy action. Witnessing the proof of his action in the three corpses, confidence in his tactics mushroomed. Creating a defence force would be more exacting, but he wholeheartedly believed that such a militia was the only option.

At the end of a sweaty day, just before twilight, Kayode was sprawled in front of his shack when Samuel arrived. A moment later and in high spirits, Asabi brought three coconut shells and a jug of arrack. Intrigued by the joint appearance, he sat up and smiled. Kayode sensed something looming as dusk fell over the settlement. At last Samuel broke the silence.

'Let me tell you why we're here, Kayode.'

'I'm listening.'

'Since you joined us we have grown strong. Your scouts make us feel safe. We no longer walk so dangerously. Some of us have been meeting for the past days and have come to a decision. We want you to be Governor of Freetown.'

Pursing his lips, he looked at Samuel. The time has come to put my plans into action, he thought. He could put an end to the squabbles and brawls and be free to strike at the plantations and free slaves. And then there is Elijah. In the sanctuary of this stronghold, this Mogba still posed a problem. He was certain the 'we' in 'we want you to lead Freetown' could not possibly include the likes of Elijah. Being Governor would give him the power to take care of Elijah.

'Take it, Kayode,' Asabi breathed, 'it belongs to you.'

Crickets bruised the sudden hush as a light southerly breezed through the trees. Under the darkening sky, he smiled at Asabi. Turning to Samuel, he nodded.

To begin his Governorship Kayode formed a Council. It comprised Asabi, Samuel, Truelove, Ol' Bones, and the Hungan. Soon after Tomba arrived in the mountain stronghold, Kayode invited him to join the Council. Tomba's knowledge of munitions was a vital resource for the runaway militia.

Following the success of the siege of Jamestown and taking control of Drake House, he delegated areas of responsibility. Given that he knew well the capabilities of some Council members, his options were clear-cut. Asabi would lead around two hundred fighters for pillaging the Great Houses. Alongside Asabi's forays, Samuel and Ol' Bones, familiar with the merchandise and armaments held by the island's Great Houses, were responsible for filching swords, muskets and food. Tomba was chosen to teach the workings of the culverins and cannons because of his knowledge of heavy weapons acquired on the coast of Guinea. Truelove was given the sentries and scouts. The Hungan he appointed to sanctify all endeavours with his voodoo rituals. Kayode himself would lead an armed force of about a thousand.

Kayode outlined the tactical objectives to his Council. Their task was to commandeer ships to carry them back to the coast of Guinea. Failing that, they would form an administration in Pertigua. The problem of 'how to get to the coast of Guinea' otherwise known as 'navigation' he would deal with, when and if they succeeded in seizing a ship. Jamestown's defences were next to be given his attention. His plan was ambitious. He was not certain that they would all pull together. Moreover, his militia had almost nothing in common with trained infantry. Additionally, when fighting in close formation, the Redcoats were famed for the devastating effect of their directed firepower. He was convinced that he must avoid a head-on confrontation, whatever the cost. At the end of the meeting he met with Tomba alone.

'I want you to take a thousand men and women,' he said quietly. 'Divide them into groups of fifty. Choose twenty to be the leaders. Send them five miles from Jamestown on all the main highways. They are to surround the capital. Tell them to steal food and weapons from the Great Houses. Lie low in the hills and forests. From their hiding places, they must carry out hit and run tactics. Ambush the Redcoats the instant they set foot on shore, and then vanish into the hills.'

Hardening his tone, he said:

'Attack the moment the Redcoats set foot on land. And Tomba, don't forget, we need the Governor and Fleming alive.'

'I would never have believed,' said Tomba, shaking his head, 'that that skinny green youth who stepped foot on the ship at Badagri had the guts you have shown. You have become a great man, Kayode.'

Putting two small dark brown beans, grooved along one side, upon the desk, Tomba was almost inaudible.

'The Hungan sent you these,' he said.

'What are they?' he asked.

'*Esere* beans from Calabar on the coast of Guinea,' replied Tomba. 'The Hungan said eat them if you are taken prisoner. They will take your life, Kayode. It is better for slaves if you give up this life by your own hand, than the lingering death the whites will give you. They will make a big event of killing you slowly before all. The Hungan says you will feel nothing and will reach the next world quick.'

'You agree with him?'

'I do,' replied Tomba, without emotion.

He shuddered. At first glance, the two pulses looked innocent. Given his faith in the Hungan's expertise with poisons, he knew the beans were certain to be a reliable way off the island. Suddenly feeling very cold, he picked up the beans and looked grimly at Tomba.

All morning, as usual, he had been receiving contradictory reports about the activity around the Expeditionary Force. Messengers were dashing in and out of the Cabinet Room. From the steps of Drake House, he saw cutters weaving between the warships and transports. He was convinced that the assault from the Expeditionary Force was imminent. Given the location of the flotilla, he ordered the long-range culverins be moved down to the docks. There, they were sited both sides of the harbour entrance and tended by Tomba's hastily trained gun crews. Given that the Redcoats might try to sneak ashore at night, Asabi secreted men in the region of the culverins.

What to do with Elijah gave him restless nights. One sunny evening in the stables of Drake House, Tomba had overheard Elijah divulging the weaknesses in Jamestown's defences to a member of the Mongoose Gang. In that instant, Tomba had strangled the contact with his bare hands, while Elijah was detained for questioning.

At a convened meeting of his Council, Kayode tapped his temple.

'Elijah is a slave in here,' he said. 'I thought slavery would make him leave behind his hate for my family as an ancient story. But not him. He brings with him the cunning ways of the Mogba. Behind every quarrel in Jamestown, I see his face. His shadow haunts me all the way from Ake. It will end here.'

Slamming his fist onto the table, he snapped:

'It will end this day!'

In an instant, Asabi's blade was out.

'Why wait for day to end?' she asked. 'I will take his head off now and . . . '

Raising his hand with a twisted grin, the Hungan was firm.

'We can profit from this, Kayode,' he said. 'For that we need him alive. We have an opportunity to find out what he knows. Let *us* break him down.'

Nodding to the Hungan, Kayode turned to the window. The door closed behind the interrogators, leaving him alone. Since they had moved to New Freetown, his suspicions about Elijah had increased, particularly when he went hunting. As a free man, Elijah could come and go as he pleased. It allowed him to be gone for days at a time. It was true that he always came back with something, such as a hog, a buck or a doe. But where else had he been on his hunt? And with whom had he met? There was the time when Elijah was sighted by Nathan Greensleeves in Bamboo Bay. The old propagator had sent word, via a scout, that he should be on his guard where Elijah was concerned. Despite the tip-off, Elijah managed to talk his way out of trouble. Kayode had him placed under close watch, which was how the traitor was finally trapped. His thoughts were interrupted by the return of the interrogators. Ol' Bones was terse.

'Elijah is dead! Tomba gave his neck one chop. Not before the turncoat squealed to Asabi. Them whites plan to attack Sho'town and Deadpan this night. We're going to give them one big surprise.'

Elijah had also confessed about his escape from China Lights. It seems that Randolph Fleming had freed him for the purpose of joining the runaways and reporting back through a member of the Mongoose Gang. A black man collaborating with plantation owners saddened Kayode. The door burst open. A messenger dashed into the room.

'They're bringing whites from the Great Houses, Kayode,' he cried. 'Frederick Bradshaw is with them.'

Kayode froze. Fleetingly incapable of action or words, he looked at Asabi. Her eyes acquired a sudden menace. He picked up his whip.

We come full circle, he thought. The tide has finally turned.

'Fetch Bradshaw,' he said quietly.

'I want to see him too,' Asabi said. 'That devil forced himself into me many many times. I will never forgive him for the agonies I suffered. This very day I will bury a hatchet in his head. Before his cruel eyes, I will slice off his wicked tool and toss it on the fire.'

The dimensions of the blade she pulled out drew gasps.

'Our escape was made possible by his daughter, Asabi,' said Kayode, softly. 'Without her aid we would never have given life to a son who will never know slavery.'

'What if she is with him and pleads for her father's life?' she demanded hotly. 'What then?'

'I will give it to her,' he replied.

'Maybe we must show mercy to the daughter,' she argued, 'for she has risked much. I cannot stay here with you, Kayode. If I so much as lay eyes on that wicked father of hers, I will kill him.'

Without another word, she stormed out.

Hands lashed behind him, the plantation owner was led into the room. His daughter limped after him with her hands also tethered. Kayode shook his head. Her cheeks were tear-streaked. Her hair had fallen over her face and shoulders. Her stained yellow gown hung in shreds. The pair came to a standstill before his desk. Avoiding her eyes, he leaned back to scrutinise his battered and bedraggled former owner, whose clothes were in tatters. He appeared a chastened man.

Rising deliberately to his feet, Kayode picked up a dagger off the desk, approached the planter and halted a step away. He leant across and severed the bonds securing Faith's wrists. I will give him some spice of his own making, he thought. He brushed his hand lightly against the front of her father's breeches. Recollection showed in the planter's face. His eyes were virtually agog with terror. Faith gasped and turned away. Seizing the planter's arm, he jerked him closer until he was staring into his cold grey eyes.

'My name is Captain Kayode Sodeke,' he said sourly. 'They call me the Governor of Freetown. Who am I?'

The planter's eyes bulged. He mustered a strangled word. 'Captain . . . '

'I can't hear you, Bradshaw.'

Clearing his throat raucously, the planter spoke more clearly.

'Captain Kayode Sodeke, Governor of Freetown.'

The gallows's trapdoor crashed open. The planter shook. Releasing his grip, Kayode ordered the guards to take the planter out of the room. Turning around, he smiled sympathetically at Faith and took her teary face in his hands.

'It brings me no joy to see you this way, Faith. That man and his people left us with no choice. To die as free men and women or to live as slaves is no choice. We have only moments. Come sit with me.'

For what seemed like time without end they sat gazing at each other. He was relieved that the woman who had saved his life had survived the conflict thus far. But he was certain that despite the affection she had for him and he for her, skin colour would remain the gulf between them. He dropped his eyes. She noticed.

'You keep something from me, Kayode.'

'I'm struggling with words.'

'What is it, Kayode?'

'I seek words that soften pain.'

'What are you keeping from me?'

'I cried for liberty. I craved for something that was mine by rights. What I say now is yours. Nathan Greensleeves is not just your friend. He is your blood-father.'

'What you say is foolish, Kayode. You have just sent my father from this very chamber.'

'That is not true. I sent away a man who believes he is your father. He does not know you are not his blood-daughter. Your mother and Greensleeves kept your making a secret. On the plantations the slaves know the secrets of the Great House. I heard from Mama Jezebel who was under oath to the slave wet-nurse who breastfed you. Soon after your father married your mother, he quickly lost his interest in her. Instead, he spent his nights with fancy women in Jamestown. Your mother got very lonely. She turned to young Greensleeves. He gave her time and love. They spent many many nights together. Greensleeves is truly your blood-father.'

Mists of conflicting emotions flickered in her eyes. He watched her begin to resolve the knotted ambivalence of her feelings for her purported father.

'So that is why as a child,' she said, almost to herself, 'the man I believed to be my father never once held me in loving embrace.'

Wiping her cheeks and helping her to her feet, he embraced her. Cradling her head on his shoulder, she spoke softly.

'I want you to spare my mother and her husband.'

The gallows crashed. Flinching and drawing back, she continued without waiting for his answer.

'I know you have reason to hate him. I know you feel he deserves to die. He has wronged you deeply. But he has afforded my mother and I protection for all these years. For her sake, I am duty-bound to ask for his life. My mother stands with others in the courtyard. They are due to hang. Give me her life and the life of Frederick Bradshaw – or take mine as well.'

'I knew you would ask this of me. You gave me back my life. How can I give you less? I'll give you men for your protection. Take your mother and Frederick Bradshaw. Stay in Jamestown. It is dangerous out on the roads.'

'You have long been in my thoughts, Kayode,' she said quietly. 'I was comforted by what I heard about your life in the wilderness. On many a sunny evening, Nathan would sit with me, to acquaint me with your exploits. Whenever a runaway was recaptured, I feared it might be you. I do so remember our nights in the summer-house, Jacob, I mean Kayode. When you came down from the mountains I thought I might see you. I have lived in the hope that we might meet again. You see, Kayode, my love for you remains as strong as it was on the day you escaped.'

Her words affected him. For some moments he gazed out of the window. He turned back to face her.

'The path I take is not for you, Faith. The road I take is the way of sorrow. When one day your kind sees my kind as equals to themselves, this struggle will also be part of yours. We have little time. I want you to listen carefully to what I have to say. I want you to give me your word. I can trust this with no other.'

'What do you ask of me?'

'I have a son with Asabi, who you knew as Florence. If she agrees, I want your word that you will take them to live with you in the freedom of the Great House, or find her a safe haven – if I die in this fight.'

Watching his petition scythe into her consciousness, he knew that the mere thought of such an arrangement would cause outrage within the island's white society. Already he could hear the indignation caused by a former slave and her infant living freely in the Great House. He had deliberately told her that he might die. Following his escape from Tamarind Trees, his own death had never really crossed his mind. But with the armed force ranged against him, they both knew that the odds were stacked against him.

'I promise to care for them both, Kayode,' she replied sincerely. 'What's his name?'

'Abisogun. It means born in war. I pray he grows up in peace.'

Blinking back tears, she embraced him and repeated her pledge.

'I promise to take them both to live with me in the Great House, if Asabi will accept it. Do not fret. I shall not let you down.'

'Your word is enough,' he said.

Striding to the door, he called for the guard to bring back her parents. A short while went by before the door opened. The planter and his wife tottered abjectly into the room. Kayode approached them.

'You have your daughter to thank, Bradshaw,' he said. 'Take your family home. And thank whoever you pray to for sparing your miserable life.'

The planter heaved a long audible sigh. Grateful for the reprieve, he mopped the torrent of sweat from his face and neck.

'What do you expect from me in return, Captain Sodeke?'

'Nothing from you, Bradshaw. Tell the former Governor and that skunk Fleming that we will fight them to the end. Your daughter will tell you what I want – if the time comes.'

The gallows crashed. Kayode paused, certain the chilling reverberation of the scaffold would further unnerve the planter.

'We can have peace between our peoples, Bradshaw,' he said, 'if your people are prepared to cut their own cane. It is too hot in the canefields. We want to go back to the coast of Guinea. I will give the former

Governor and Fleming only a little time. They must come and talk terms for our exodus before more blood is spilt.'

'I thank you for sparing my family, Captain Sodeke,' said Bradshaw. 'I shall not forget the compassion you have shown. Whatever my daughter has promised you, I promise also. I give you my word and my hand. I shall, as well, give your forewarning to Governor Ashleigh and Squire Fleming. I have no doubt that you will be hearing from them. But pray sir, let me speak my mind if I may.'

He nodded at the planter.

'I have to say I pity you, for you cannot win,' said Bradshaw. 'King George will send ships filled with Redcoats armed with muskets and cannon. You cannot win. You cannot win.'

'Farewell, Bradshaw. If we are defeated, we will take many of you into the next world with us.'

Her parents stumbled out of the Cabinet Room. Reaching the door, Faith turned around slowly. His eyes met hers. Tears rolled freely down her cheeks. He smiled. She smiled tearfully back at him. He knew that it was the very last time he would ever lay eyes on her.

Faith stood trembling beside her mother in the antechamber of Drake House. In the depths of her reason, she knew that what Kayode had told her was true. Frederick Bradshaw has always felt a blood-stranger, she thought. As a child, she had often thought that he was merely disconnected from his own feelings. But to her chagrin, she had to progressively accept that he had no fatherly feelings for her. It was a wicked stranger who had sold her son. She rounded on Bradshaw.

'If I had divulged to Kayode that he was the father of the child that you have sold, he would have dispatched you on the spot. You should be dead for what you have done.'

Her mother snapped.

'That is no way to speak to your father.'

'And you, my sanctimonious mother, with all your airs and graces are diseased with hypocrisy. You well know that this philanderer is not my father. Indeed, you have always known and you kept it from me and from him.'

Utterly bewildered, Bradshaw's mouth fell open. He gazed from her to her mother.

'What's this you say?' he demanded.

Crimson-faced, her mother stood with her mouth opening and closing, her eyes screaming at the husband who stared angrily back at her. Giving him little chance to recover, Faith shook when she faced him.

'I have always sensed that a spineless degenerate like you was not ever my blood-father. Nathan Greensleeves is my real father and the grand-father of my son. You, Mister Bradshaw, who spent your nights forcing yourself on the slave, Florence, castigated me on the propriety of bedding a slave and a man I loved at that. You stole my baby in the dead of night and sold him to the highest bidder. What kind of humanity infests your being? The blissful truth is that you are without issue. Do you not see, Mister high and mighty Bradshaw, you are childless?'

Breathing heavily, she turned to her speechless mother.

'You withheld the truth of my making from your husband. You allowed him to sell your own grandson. What breed of mother are you? You spent days reeling from one decanter to the next, colluding with the subjugation of human beings and supervising the monstrous atrocities taking place on your plantation. You are in no position to lecture me on the difference between right and wrong. Both of you are guilty of cruelty and murder. Because your victims are black, the white man's law turns a blind eye to your actions. Have you ever considered how many generations it will be before the descendants of these slaves forgive and forget what you have done to them?'

Plainly discomfited, her mother lowered her eyes to the ground. Looking like a man barely holding to his reason, Bradshaw stood quivering. Was that a tear she saw in his eye? Hundreds of lives have already been lost, Faith thought, I am not about to relent.

'If this uprising does not succeed, he has asked me to take his woman and their child to live with us in the Great House. There is no guarantee that she will consent. She hates you both. I for one think she has every reason to do so. You, Mister Bradshaw, have just told him that whatever pledge I made, you would uphold. You had better not even think of going back on your promise.'

'So that's it,' he seethed. 'You want me to take a nigger woman to live with us?

'If you want to go on living, yes.'

Staring blankly at her, he kept his mouth shut. She persisted.

'Through me you have given him your word. Both of you had better keep that word. Otherwise, shall I go back in there to inform him that you refuse to give his woman refuge?'

Fear flickered across is face. Seeing his apprehension, she pressed on.

'Do nothing to obstruct this agreement. You will indeed rue the day that you try. I tell you now, if his woman chooses not to ask for my help, I shall be returning home to England. There, I intend to combine with the League Against the Importation of Negroes from the Coast of Guinea. Together, we shall defeat your breed to end this contemptible traffic in human beings. I cannot think why I did not wake up from this nightmare long ago. No just God can possibly sanction the possession of one human by another. There is no man or woman alive who can provide any justification for it. What your kind has perpetrated on this island is the reason why we stand here in this predicament. Lives have been squandered. We stand at the portals of a conflict that will terminate many more. The price paid by both black and white has been too high. I am ashamed to know you.'

Kayode stepped out of Drake House. Asabi had already left for Deadpan jetty. Picking up a quarterstaff, he mounted up in the stables. Thoughtfully, he trotted down to the waterfront to check that Tomba's cannons had been loaded, tilted and readied. In a depression below the muzzles of the cannons, he found Asabi with her musketeers. By eight o'clock the ambuscade was ready. Flopping down beside her, he began the wait.

A crescent moon cast an insipid glow over the harbour and a light breeze capered about. Campfires had been damped down. Few lights showed. Soon, all activity on the streets of the capital had subsided. Owls and laughing gulls lent an eerie tenor to the occasion. Now and then she rose to test the readiness of her detail. He caught anxious faces in the watery light. The clock at Drake House struck ten. I must encourage them, he thought.

'You don't look so happy tonight,' he said. 'Maybe you would prefer to cut cane? I will go get your Massas and tell them that you pine for them.'

Soft laughter rippled through the dark.

'I had a rum with Woodham Ferrers on his verandah last night,' he said. 'He told me that he was choked with grief now that we have all gone. He said if you return you can all live with him. He says he really misses his niggers.'

Nervous laughter tittered through the shadows. Hardening his voice, he continued:

'We won't die in shackles, my friends. If we're to leave this life behind, we'll do so as free men and women. I tell you if we cannot laugh in the face of this battle, our struggle will have been for nothing.'

Beckoning Asabi to follow him, they slipped behind the warehouses.

'I love you, Asabi,' he whispered, embracing her tenderly. 'We still have a lifetime to live together. Keep a very close watch. And take no risks.'

She laughed.

'Fret not, Kayode,' she said earnestly. 'I will be safe.'

'We knew this battle would come,' he said. 'Defeat the whites and we'll have peace. I love you Asabi.'

Embracing her yet again, Kayode whispered.

'I must return to Drake House.'

'I love you,' caressed his ears as he rode away.

The plaintive cry of gulls besieged the darkness. Waves swashed against the harbour wall. Beneath the barrels of Tomba's cannons Asabi sustained her vigil. A little past midnight she thought she heard a thud. Was that oars she heard? She was certain she heard voices on the incoming breeze. She whispered: 'They come!'

Her fighters tensed at their posts.

'Wait for my signal.'

Then she made out the shadowy outline of a boat.

'Oars,' said a hoarse English voice.

The sound of paddles rising out of the water reached her ears. Elevating her bow into the night sky, she let fly a succession of arrow-flares. Silhouettes of two invading brigs could be seen in the feeble glow of the orange-yellow light.

Tomba yelled.

'Fire.'

Four cannons roared. Searing balls hurtled above their heads. Three plumes of water spewed upwards, violently rocking the boat invading Deadpan. The fourth cannonball sped across the harbour entrance and struck the boat attacking Sho'town. Luck, she thought.

She shouted.

'Fire your muskets.'

Musket fire raked the remaining boat. Anguished cries filled the harbour. No Redcoat set foot on that hostile shore. Not one Redcoat made it back to the Expeditionary Force. She was jubilant.

Darwin's Reef

It was hazy at first light. From the spruce silent decks of the *Resolution*, the disaster was all too visible. Clenching his teeth, Randolph Fleming scrutinised the carnage from the forepeak. Ashen-faced and aghast, the Governor and Commodore stood rooted either side of him. Sighting the alien flag fluttering above Drake House, Fleming bit his lip with vexation. The sea teemed with seagulls around the Expeditionary Force. Bobbing on the swell, they sat plucking eyeballs out of the drifting corpses. Grimly shaking his head, Brigstocke kept his distance and his thoughts to himself. The man had warned the Commodore not to underestimate Sodeke.

Stunned by the sight of dead comrades drifting by on the tide, soldiers and sailors lined the rails of the warships and transports, muttering oaths and threats. The commanding officer of the *Resolution's* marine detachment had been shot to death. All that remained of the boats employed in the attack were thwarts floating on the surface, symbols of failure.

Questions are bound to be asked, Fleming thought. How could mere slaves who had never even heard of the Royal Military Academy at Woolwich trounce a well-drilled force? How could it happen? This Governor had forfeited the principal element of an English possession, in as much as he had lost control of it. Jamestown was in the hands of slaves. This Commodore had gambled away the lives of fifty English soldiers. Sodeke remained in firm control of Drake House. A fine state of affairs.

In resolute mood by the larboard forepeak rails, the Commodore said:

'Sodeke will be expecting another attack, Squire Fleming. We'll not disappoint him.'

'What have you in mind?'

'To mount a diversion, Squire,' said the Commodore. 'I shall despatch two warships and four transports around the westernmost tip of the island at Hurricane Point, to land a force on the northern coast. Sodeke will have us behind him. Under cover of darkness, I shall land my main force in the Bay of Thanksgiving. He shall then be sandwiched between us. You say that Harmony Hall and Tamarind Trees have fallen to the niggers, Sir Anthony? I'll wager that they'll not expect an attack from that quarter. We shall force him to fight a rearguard action into the Bay of Thanksgiving. There, we shall spring our trap. He will have us before him and his back to our militia as well as the sea. We shall take him there, gentlemen.'

The captain of the *Resolution* arrived on the forepeak. A shout fell from the crow's nest.

'Movement in the harbour, sir.'

Fleming scanned the waterfront through his telescope. In breeches, headbands and neckerchiefs, four men were strolling along the harbour entrance towards the jetty at Deadpan. Dropping his scope, he scowled at the quartet.

'Impudent rascals,' he muttered. 'Chantwells, Commodore. So called because they sing songs which are moral tales.'

Three Chantwells plonked themselves down at the end of the jetty. Soon the cadence of the bottle, spoon and conga floated across the bay. Standing behind his mates, the fourth man began strumming the four-string quarto, cheekily serenading the English flotilla.

> White men sail from London Town.
> To get a piece of the sun.
> It proved too hot.
> In the flaming pot
> And they find themselves on the run.
> Massa Ashleigh and Fleming and hototo.
> Stick their nose where it don't belong.
> So we send back their sons.
> Without their guns.
> And the Captain he laugh and say.
> Don't come my way.
> In Freetown me going to stay.
> Next time whitey find him leave his head behind.

Fleming scowled. The Commodore had turned purple with anger.

'The impertinent nigger goads us, Squire Fleming,' he said. 'We'll see about that.'

'We shall indeed,' said the Governor, striding aft. 'Two can play his game.'

Moments later, he saw the Governor muttering at Colonel Applegate. Soon after, the strains of Rule Britannia burst forth from the sailors on the poop deck.

> Rule Britannia.
> Britannia rules the waves.
> Britons, never never, ever.
> Shall be slaves.

'Methinks we won't recapture this island by singing each other to death,' said Fleming.

The Commodore's set jaw implied he was of similar mind.

Turning to leeward, Fleming saw an ugly black sky fringed by ragged clouds. Line squalls on the horizon showed thunderstorms scudding in their direction. The Commodore's voice broke into his thoughts.

'A storm is brewing, Squire,' he said. 'That should dampen Sodeke's ardour. Batten down the hatches, Captain Fletcher. Anchor outside Darwin's Reef, lest we be driven onto a lee shore. Signal the fleet. We shall return when this storm has passed.'

'Aye aye, sir,' said the warship's Captain. 'On second thoughts, Commodore, perhaps this storm is to our advantage. Sodeke, who knows nothing of the dangers for vessels on a lee shore, might think that we are sailing away to regroup and rethink our strategy. Better still, some of them will even think that we have been demoralised by the failure of our attack.'

'I think not, Captain Fletcher,' said Fleming. 'We have lost Major Stirling and over fifty men. I think it is about time we acknowledged that we have misjudged this man.'

'I don't agree, Squire,' replied the Commodore. 'Sodeke has had the luck of the devil. That's all. Otherwise he is tutored in nothing. The white man taught him everything he knows. Consequently, we know what he knows and much much more besides.'

'I deeply disagree, Commodore,' countered Fleming quietly.

'You seem to think they comprehend more than we've taught them, Squire?' the Commodore asked. 'I'm not convinced.'

'Neither am I, Randolph,' said the Governor.

Eyeing them thoughtfully and drawing a deep breath, Fleming leaned against the bulwarks.

'Pray, hear me out, gentlemen,' he said quietly. 'While slaving on the plantations and Great Houses, the slave is all-eyes. He lives his life watching every move we make. Because of that condition, he understands our language, our likes and dislikes, the way we think and our habits. By virtue of his enslaved state, he understands our motivations entirely.'

Tossing his head petulantly, the Governor said:

'He comprehends not my motivation, Randolph.'

'Oh but he does, Anthony,' he insisted. 'In truth, he understands yours most of all. By observation alone, the slave has grasped that as His Britannic Majesty's Governor, you are duty-bound to uphold his enslaved state. Furthermore, he knows that it is also your function to see that the sweetener we call sugar is continually shipped to England as a result of his labours.'

'I daresay that is very observant of him,' said the Governor sarcastically. 'How then does he think we view him, Randolph?'

'When you look at a slave, Anthony?' he asked. 'What do you see?'

'An abject sub-human rascal, Randolph,' said the Governor, 'one step removed from the ape.'

'That proves my point precisely,' he responded superciliously. 'You understand not the language of this so-called ape nor how he thinks. You comprehend even less his customs and traditions. And you certainly could not survive in his natural environment. Sodeke is a perfect example. While cutting cane, this close relation of the ape, as you put it, has learned to read, write, clean, load and fire the musket and cannon – all to instigate an uprising, as we have witnessed. Did Brigstocke not say that it would be an error to underestimate him? Last night confirmed it. It is virtually impossible to deny that Sodeke has indeed grasped our thinking. Was he not waiting for us at Sho'town and Deadpan, taking us completely by surprise? Putting it bluntly, Anthony, it is your ape who sits in the safety, comfort and sanctuary of Drake House. Whereas we suffer the grief of the seas in tempestuous conditions with our mission stalled. Gentlemen take note. We fight an enemy who understands the white man from inside his own camp. Pray don't get the wrong impression. I believe that we shall prevail. And indeed accomplish our objective to take back this island. Nevertheless, it might prove to be at great cost. Which is why I now believe that slaves who think like Sodeke are the morrow. This uprising supports my contention. He foreshadows the end for our trade. The continual uprisings of the last few years on some of our island possessions, such as Jamaica, though not as serious as this revolt, have proved that. We must, I fear gentlemen, begin to think of a world without the slave state.'

'What then do you suppose is the nigger's primary motivation, Squire Fleming?' the Commodore asked.

'Have we not taken his women by force and attacked his land?' he asked. 'We sell him, his wives and his children for profit. We destroy his family unit by policy. Needless to say, this furnishes him with ample motivation to regain his freedom and a feverish thirst for revenge. By that, I mean we have furnished him with the self-same weapon that sustains his appetite for escape and revenge.'

By the look in the eye of the Governor, Fleming knew that the man's curiosity had been clearly aroused.

'When we have put down this uprising, Randolph,' said the Governor. 'I would be interested to hear more of your thoughts.'

'I for one am now more inclined to agree with Squire Fleming,' the Commodore said. 'Right now, gentlemen, we have a fight on our hands. Sodeke must surely know that we cannot return to England empty-handed.'

Therewith, the captain of the *Resolution* hoisted a signal instructing the flotilla to disperse and return when the storm had passed. With the imminent storm the wind intensified. A brooding Governor lurched his way below decks. The Chantwells scampered for shelter. Fleming scanned the waves. A cavalry of white horses pranced on the curling wave tops. Rain thundered onto the decks and streamed into the wash-ports and scuppers. Huge drops from the tropical downpour pounded the cleared decks of the *Resolution*. Weighing anchor, the Expeditionary Force ran with the wind on the starboard quarter. A near gale was howling by the time the flotilla passed the southeast margins of Darwin's Reef.

With a deepening frown, Fleming turned to look at the other five warships and ten transports scurrying before the wind, away from the tidal protection of the coral outcrop. Lashed by driving rain, they were wallowing in choppy seas a league astern on the starboard quarter. At times he could see only stalk-like topgallant masts. Limping along the coastline five leagues out from the influence of the land, the convoy cut into the sway of the mayaca, a near gale force wind. Steadying himself against the binnacle, Fleming held his oiled weather cloak as a shield against the howling wind.

'Helmsman,' the Commodore shouted, 'steer southeast by south.'

'Southeast by south, sir,' the helmsman repeated.

'Make signal to the convoy, Captain Fletcher,' the Commodore shouted. 'They are to run to the lee of the land. Heave-to if the weather worsens.'

'Aye aye, sir,' said the warship's Captain.

Drake House was ringing with preparations for battle. Pondering over the next stage of the uprising in the Cabinet Room, Kayode sat alone eating red snapper and sweet potato off the Governor's finest china. The movement of the English ships had not gone unnoticed. Asabi entered the Cabinet Room wreathed in smiles.

'The English ships are sailing away, Kayode.'

'The English do not give up so easily,' he replied. 'This is a strong wind. They are too close to land. They'll come back when the storm blows itself out.'

'I can make them go,' she said, with a mischievous tone of voice. 'They will not want to hurry back.'

He narrowed his eyes. I've seen that headstrong look before, he thought. Asabi clearly had a plan. Without her snares and strategies, Kayode and his brother would have perished in the rainforest. Kayode trusted her skills.

'How can you make them go?'

'Terrorise them, Kayode,' she said, without emotion. 'Set fire to one of the ships while they sleep. It will frighten them. Hang seven overseers in sight of that big warship – one for each day of the week.'

A twinkle entered her eye.

'Hang Woodham Ferrers.'

He grinned at her. Thus they spent the afternoon thrashing out how this fresh attack against the whites could be delivered.

The storm halted all further action for the next three days. From the poop deck of the *Resolution*, Fleming scanned the scattered Expeditionary Force floundering in the trough of stormy seas. The vessels were riding out the gale in disarray. Seasickness in the flotilla was certain to be dire. Astern, an albatross sat above them like a desolate omen. Together with the Commodore and the Governor, Fleming went below to the Great Cabin to study the plans for the invasion of the island. Four days after the storm had begun, it blew itself to a standstill.

A bright blue sky proclaimed the new day. By the time the

Expeditionary Force anchored inside Darwin's Reef, he had succeeded in persuading the Commodore to let him make a final attempt to end the uprising by negotiation.

The sun had reached its zenith. Through the French windows of the Cabinet Room, Kayode saw a small boat depart from the *Resolution* flying a white flag. He kept his eyes on the craft as it crawled slowly towards the harbour entrance. Ol' Bones stood patiently beside him.

'A white flag,' said Kayode. 'See no harm comes to them. We'll meet them in the Careenage. That way they won't walk up here examining our defences along the way. Come.'

From the steps of Drake House, he counted three men in the boat. Two rowed against the tide. The third man stood arrogantly with his foot on the gunwale of the boat nosing into the Careenage. Making his way down to the harbour with Ol' Bones, he joined his Council at a makeshift table.

Dressed in black frock coat and white breeches, a white man alighted from the boat and started up the ramp. Randolph Fleming came to a halt before the table. When the planter sighted Tomba, Kayode heard him groan. The proximity of his former master proved too much for the big man and he seized Fleming by the lapels of his frock coat and snarled into his face.

'I will chop off your arms and legs. Let me chop off his head, Kayode.'

Throwing themselves into the fray, Ol' Bones and Truelove pulled the big man away from the planter.

'Let him alone, Tomba,' said Kayode.

Visibly shaken and keeping his eyes fixed on his assailant, Fleming picked up his tricorne, straightened out his rumpled frock coat and wiped his brow.

'Sit down, Fleming,' Kayode ordered coldly.

The planter remained stubbornly on his feet. Kayode fanned his face.

'It's hot. Give him water.'

'I don't sit or drink with your kind.'

Drawing his sword in a manner designed to intimidate, Kayode laid it upon the table.

'Then you'll never drink or sit again, white man!'

Springing to her feet and whipping out her dagger, Asabi plunged it hard into the table. Fleming dropped instantly onto a chair. Pouring a

tankard of water, Tomba thumped it down on the table. Instantly raising
the mug, he gulped down half its contents before uttering his next word.

'Captain Sodeke,' he spluttered. 'I come with a message from the
Governor, Sir Anthony Ashleigh.'

'I will hear what you have to say. But no tricks!'

'The Governor wishes you to consider an offer of . . . '

'He is not the Governor here. He is not in a position to make any
offer.'

'Sir Anthony proposes a truce and a treaty, Captain Sodeke.'

'What does the devil want?'

'Sir Anthony knows you desire to return to the coast of Guinea.
Through lack of fortune, he does not know from where you all come
along that coast. It would be nigh on an impossible task and . . . '

'When you needed slaves, Mister Fleming, did your vessels not find
the way to the coast of Guinea?'

'We did.'

'The answer is simple is it not? You send your ships back to the coast
of Guinea. We will be on those ships. When we land on that coast, we
will find our own way back to our homes.'

'Governor Sodeke,' responded Fleming obsequiously. 'I am authorised
to offer you King George's Pardon, a stipend for cutting cane, better
living conditions and an end to slavery on this island.'

'Words, Fleming, nothing but empty words. We don't need King
George's Pardon. It is him and his men who have committed the crime of
slavery and murder? King George should be asking for our Pardon. We
don't want to work or live on your cruel island. So we need no wages. We
want to go back to our homes, our families, our people and our land.
White man, why does Mister King George need so many soldiers to end
slavery? Why make a promise he won't keep? What are you hiding, white
man? You come here not to end slavery. You come to buy time by making
an offer you know we will not accept. What are you hiding, white man?
Make no mistake Mister Fleming, we will fight you to the bitter end.'

'I shall inform Sir Anthony of your decision,' he replied, diplomatically
backing away.

Taking due precautions, Fleming turned for the Careenage. Tomba's
foot struck him full in the buttocks to help him on his way. Following the
planter's humiliating withdrawal, Kayode spent the remainder of the day
with Asabi. After a careful scrutiny of the Expeditionary Force transports,
they settled on the target for her assault later that night.

The sun was tiring. From Deadpan dockhead Asabi gazed intently at her objective. It was a grubby-looking transport at the tail end of the flotilla. In the meantime, her crew of three men were priming a gig for the attack. Cramming wads of oil-soaked rags, marlinespikes, flints and four loaded muskets into the bilges, they lashed a six-pounder onto the forward thwart. Around eleven o'clock, cloudbanks obscured a gloomy moon. With poor visibility, the conditions were favourable for the action.

From the sheds at Deadpan, the gig slipped out of Jamestown harbour. Outward bound on an ebbing southerly tide, Truelove was at the helm. Given his experience of handling small boats, he had assured Asabi that rudder alone would take them out to the transport. They would return under oars. Making way out of the influence of the spit, he set the gig on a south-easterly course. Turning around, Asabi gazed at the rugged silhouette of the brooding island under the pallid moonlight. Gulls and terns masked the plunk of oars sliding into rowlocks for the return passage. Drifting on the tide towards the targeted transport, she thought back over the past day.

During the early part of the afternoon following Fleming's departure, she had spent tender moments with Kayode and their son. Such was the sense of fulfilment and love between them that they had even broached the subject of life beyond the conflict with the whites. Recalling the birth of their son, she smiled at the thought of her family. For now, Truelove held the rudder. Trusting that her pilot and the set of the current would carry them out to the flotilla, she was content to sit back.

Reaching the transport a little after one o'clock in the morning, the gig was secured to the transport's sternpost. The posting of a solitary guard reinforced her belief that the English were not expecting mere runaways to take the fight out to such a large force. A brisk southerly and a light swell made the creaky vessel roll. The lone sentry was deep in slumber as were the men below.

Closely followed by three men, she tiptoed along the deck and pulled out a blade. Dropping below the bulwarks, she waited until she was satisfied that the sentry had not stirred, giving her time enough to work out the layout of the deck. Staying in the shadows, she crawled along the starboard side. A snore identified the sentry, sitting upright, fast asleep against a coiled hawser on the forepeak. Sneaking up behind him, she cut his throat. Gagging him with her hand and with Truelove holding onto his feet, they held securely, while he shuddered from a furious discharge of blood until he lay still.

To prevent the soldiers from breaking out, Truelove barred the door of the companionway leading up to the main deck. Setting light to oil-soaked rags, two men tossed them into the sail stowage locker in the foc'slehead and through the portholes of the sleeping quarters. Almost instantly acrid fumes filled the nostrils of the slumbering militia. Panic followed. Stricken men frantically pounded on the barred doorway.

Sprinting to the poop deck amid the growing confusion, they shinned down the rope to the waiting gig and pulled away. By the time they reached the sheds at Deadpan, the masts and spars of the transport were toppling under the fierce blaze. Soon, the incapacitated vessel was lying on its starboard side. Boats from the flotilla were picking the injured out of the water. Woeful cries and towering flames marked the transport's position in the darkness. She grinned at Truelove.

Shaken from sleep, Fleming was given the tidings by a grim-faced Lieutenant. Hastening to the poop deck, he found the Commodore and the Governor composing a response.

'A doubled guard and a round-the-clock watch on all vessels, Captain Fletcher!' the Commodore snarled. 'I want gigs acting as pickets and as water patrols around the fleet. Not forgetting the casualty list if you please.'

'Should we not strike back, sir?' asked the Captain of the warship.

'I will risk no more men in this light,' said the Commodore. 'Casualty list, Captain, if you please. And fetch the Surgeon!'

'Aye aye, sir,' replied the Captain of the warship.

'The Governor and I are in agreement, Squire Fleming,' said the Commodore. 'Before we lose any more men, we'll mount our invasion of the enemy stronghold. Niggers caught us napping. Sodeke must be splitting his sides at our failings.'

Thumping the bulwark with his fist, the Governor said:

'We'll apprehend the rascal, Randolph, and make of him such an example the niggers shall never forget it.'

'They have left us with little choice,' Fleming replied.

A Sub-Lieutenant passed a slip of paper to Captain Fletcher. Close by stood the severe figure of Benjamin Gooch, Surgeon of the *Resolution*.

'I have the casualty list, Commodore,' said the Captain of the warship. 'One hundred and thirty-five dead, sixty-five wounded and ten are badly burned, sir.'

The casualty figures are inexcusable, Fleming thought.

'You heard that, Mister Gooch?' the Commodore asked. 'We have many burns.'

'Aye, Commodore,' said the Surgeon.

'I trust you have your *Chirurgus Marinus* at hand?' asked the Commodore. 'It will be sorely needed this day.'

'Aye, sir, I have it with me,' said the Surgeon, displaying his copy of the Sea Surgeon.

Fleming liked the look of the man. In his late thirties, the Surgeon was a large, fine-looking haughty character, with an outsized brow. His unblinking silver-grey eyes were direct, sincere and probing.

'May I see that, Mister Gooch,' he asked.

'Aye, you may, Squire,' replied the Surgeon, handing over his volume.

Flicking through the pages, Fleming was struck by the detail of the information. Compiled by John Moyle in 1693, the surgeon's bible advised treatments for a variety of conditions occasioned aboard a man-o-war during 'times of fight'. It was well considered, for instance, that rum and opium were the best analgesics. That a patient could bite on a leather wad during the fierce pain of an amputation.

'What action is recommended for burns, Mister Gooch?' he asked.

Taking the tome and leafing through, the surgeon put his finger on a paragraph.

Now whatever part of the body happens to be burned; the moisture of that part is dried up and causeth an eschar, but if superficial, then blisters and fiery heat insues. You have first here a Twofold Scope; that is to Mitigate the Pain and fetch out the Burning.

To achieve this, Moyle recommended the use of refrigerants such as, 'egg white, rose oil, white camphor and poplar bark'.

'A specialist work indeed,' he said, 'but is his cure effective?'

'It is, Squire Fleming, but not well enough,' replied the Surgeon. 'Since its introduction, the *Chirurgus Marinus* has remained the Royal Navy's standard medical textbook. It has not as yet been superseded, whereas treatments have progressed significantly since those early times. Thus I have penned my own Chirurgical Works which I trust will succeed Moyle's publication. I advance the use of a cerat of oil, wax and powder made into a soft plaster. My remedy has already been proven to fetch out the burning with superior results. 'Tis well-meant for those from the fired transport, on whose burns I shall apply my medication.'

'Good man,' said Fleming, 'I can see you are well set to moderate our losses.'

'You'd best be about your business, Mister Gooch,' said the Commodore. 'Prepare your treatments.'

'Aye aye, sir,' replied the Surgeon.

Since anchoring off Jamestown, Fleming thought, we have fired not a shot, either in defence or by way of attack. Yet Englishmen were losing their lives, for which the Commodore and the Governor were entirely responsible. Moreover, they had regained not an inch of territory. He knew the extent of their losses had raised the stakes.

Next morning, Fleming paced the main deck in the company of the Governor. The Commodore stayed by the larboard rails with his telescope fixed on the dockhead. Spars, masts, sails, rigging, barrels, rope and objects rendered unrecognisable by the conflagration, littered the waters around the *Resolution*. The stench from charred corpses made up his mind.

'I think you'd best launch your invasion, Commodore,' he advised, 'before morale falls any further.'

'For the love of sweet Jesus, Randolph,' the Commodore cried out, dropping his scope. 'They intend to hang white men!'

Fleming slewed his telescope. Strung in a row along the dockhead at Deadpan, seven white men were facing the sea. Men were hammering at a something on the ground behind them. Then taking a step back, they pulled ropes. One by one, seven evenly spaced scaffolds jolted upright. He was aghast. Hands lashed behind them, the seven men were shoved towards the nooses.

''Tis Woodham Ferrers!' he gasped. 'You know, the head overseer of Tamarind Trees, Bradshaw's plantation.'

The bright morning light cast sombre shadows on the grisly proceedings. Fleming grimaced when he caught sight of Captain Sodeke in the Governor's uniform. There's no mistaking that arrogant gait, he thought. His breathing deepened and his heartbeat quickened. He looked at Governor Ashleigh, whose face had turned puce.

The sun climbed into a turquoise sky as a light wind drifted in off the sea. A crowd of runaways had gathered around the scaffolds. With the arrangements for the execution completed, Kayode walked slowly down the line of condemned men with Asabi, Ol' Bones and Tomba. He looked over the seven sleep-starved overseers, with injuries sustained during their captivity in hostile hands. With absolute determination in righting one wrong, on what he regarded as an island of forsaken hope, he was not about to falter. The blood-spattered memory of pared men fortified his conviction. In his bones, he knew that as far as the runaways were concerned, the seven men needed no trial. They were all demonstrably guilty of managing a regime of slavery and murder. On reaching the end of the row, he approached Woodham Ferrers, put his mouth to the ear of the overseer and whispered.

'*He* will be there to greet you one day.'

Sweat exploded from the face of the overseer and his voice trembled.

'Who who wh–what do you mean? H–h–how can you hang an innocent man?'

'I have witnessed your thirst for killing slaves,' he said. 'We fled from Tamarind Trees and many you butchered were our friends. *He* will be there to greet you one day.'

He paused to let his words sink into the head of his erstwhile tormentor. Pointing at Asabi, he went on.

'She was called Florence and you are looking at Jacob. Now does that not stir your memory?'

He felt the overseer's eyes searching his face, and then Asabi's, until recognition dawned.

'Your escape caused me grief,' said Ferrers.

'You slaughtered so many,' he countered. 'You killed people who you knew were innocent. *He* will be there to greet you one day.'

Visibly shaking, the overseer's bladder suddenly opened.

'Wh-wh-who will be there?' asked Ferrers. 'How can you hang a man without a trial?'

Flinging his arm at the *Resolution*, Kayode retorted.

'Your friends out there will give you a trial. They will listen to what you have to say. But they are not here, Ferrers. On this side of the water I will put you through the same ordeal you gave the slaves of Tamarind Trees. You're here to receive a slave's justice. I have seen your appetite for crippling slaves. You chopped off the foot of my friend Moses. What breed of serpent are you? You visited on Moses the lingering pain of Satan. It is Moses who will be there to greet you one day. Fleming and the Governor can watch helplessly while you go through your agonies.

They will witness slaves send you and your guilty friends into the next world.'

Ferrers screamed angrily at the skies.

'If I burn in the fires of Hell, Moses, I will see your ugly mug roasting beside me.'

The overseer rounded on him.

'You cannot win, nigger. And you . . . '

Raising his hand, Kayode cut him short.

'Where you're going white man, you won't be taking tea with Moses. And you won't be around to see who wins or who loses. Look upon the sky for the very last time.'

Raising his eyes to the skies, the overseer began to weep. Kayode clenched his jaw.

'Set?' he asked.

Nodding their readiness, the executioners slipped nooses over the heads of the seven men. Knots were pushed to the right under the chin and tightened. At sword point, they were forced onto stools. As if sensing something terrible was in the offing, terns and gulls flapped and twittered with a sudden frenzy. Drawing his sword, he turned and waved it at the *Resolution.* Spinning around he thrust the blade into the ground. Stools were kicked away. Seven bodies jerked and twitched in the light breeze – and Woodham Ferrers was gone. Cheering engulfed the dockhead.

Fleming observed the reaction on the *Resolution.* To a man, they removed their hats and bowed their heads.

'We attack this night, Squire Fleming,' growled the Commodore.

'And not before time, sir,' Fleming replied.

''Tis the season to give them a taste of our mettle,' said the Governor.

Noting the change in attitude the execution had wrought, Fleming was more than content with the Commodore's orders.

'Captain Fletcher you are ordered to take the *Leopard,* the *Lion* and four transports to the west around Hurricane Point. Effect a landing on the northern side of the island, which should place you behind Sodeke's lines at Harmony Hall. I believe it is deserted. From there, you will strike out for Tamarind Trees and cut down any resistance. In that department I give you carte blanche. Force the nigger to fight a rearguard action into the Bay of Thanksgiving. My main force will be waiting behind him on the water's edge.'

I feel certain I have heard that plan before, Fleming thought. I hope this time he performs his duty.

'Furthermore, I want a gig dispatched with orders for Captain Portillo on the *Sutherland*,' said the Commodore. 'This night he is to effect a diversionary invasion of Englishman's Bay, that large crescent-shaped bay on the south-eastern coast. He must take it and commence his attack on Jamestown from there. Failing that, he must hold the bay until he is relieved. Pray God he is victorious.'

'Aye aye, sir,' said the Captain.

Captain Fletcher boarded a gig to take command of the *Leopard*. The crew of the *Resolution* squared away for action. Fleming stood by on the poop. Bearing sealed orders, a gig was dispatched to Captain Portillo on the *Sutherland*. Escorted by the *Leopard*, the invasion force sailed for Hurricane Point in the late afternoon.

Discerning a change in the strategy of the Expeditionary Force, Kayode put a watch on the *Resolution*. Furthermore, he dispatched scouts on horseback to follow the westerly sailing fleet along the coast. Setting out by moonlight with Asabi and Tomba on Governor Ashleigh's Arabian stallions, he kept the easterly sailing *Sutherland* under surveillance. Trailing the vessel for some considerable distance, they eventually trotted into Englishman's Bay. Wide at its south facing entrance, the bay was also sheltered from the prevalent easterly. A smaller bay lay tucked into the eastern peninsula of Englishman's Bay.

The *Sutherland* sailed on. He sent scouts to keep the warship under observation while he addressed the two hundred men and women stationed at Englishman's Bay. Some time later the scouts trailing the *Sutherland* reported back. After the warship had passed the small bay to the south-east of Englishman's Bay, they had seen her come into the wind with her mainsail flapping wildly, turn into a wide sweep and sail back. She was last seen anchored in the roads outside the small bay, lowering her boats in the long shadows of the cliffs. He chuckled.

'So the fox thinks we're sleeping,' he said. 'Let him come – we will give him a surprise.'

With Asabi, he set off for the mangroves of the small bay. They both agreed it was where the warship was clearly intending to land her men. There she positioned around seventy men and women armed with muskets. Camouflaged in the labyrinth of mangroves along the fringe of the sand and shingle shore, he lay quietly beside her at the base of the small bay's towering cliffs. Geared up behind them sat seventeen levelled cannons poking silently through the mangroves, barrels asymmetrically trained at the warship.

Signalling the dawn commencement of hostilities, a broadside from the warship landed short of the mangroves. The cannonballs scattered the gulls and threw up plumes of water. Streaks of daylight appeared, casting a shadowy light on the engagement. A golden orb sat on the eastern horizon. Kayode peered through his telescope.

'They are finding range,' he murmured. 'Won't be long before they find us.'

The warship's next salvo landed in the mangroves, killing three runaways. Pinned down where he lay, he closed his eyes and gritted his teeth while heeding their deathly agonies.

'We knew we would lose some,' he breathed. 'They will also suffer.'

Raising his head, he yelled at the gun crews.

'Shoot at the boats.'

His cannons discharged grapeshot at the inward bound gigs. The bay echoed with the cries and screams of the warship's injured and dying. Two gigs were sunk by the second salvo. About thirty men could be seen flailing about in the water. Shark fins were suddenly slicing through the water, rapidly followed by shrieks cut short when the victim was dragged under. The sea foamed red. Soldiers in the four remaining gigs continued paddling for the shore. Others fired a fusillade of covering musket shot at the mangroves. Several runaways died where they lay.

Daylight unveiled a grisly panorama. On the surface of a choppy sea, human remains drifted with the currents in an expanding band of bloody water. In frenzied sorties, gulls swooped to peck out the eyes. High above, delicate white strands of cloud stretched across the lightening sky.

'Shoot your muskets at the boats,' Kayode ordered.

Unskilled musketeers fired at the approaching gigs. Nearly all missed their target, but just enough balls holed the heavily laden gigs below the waterline. Frantically turning the leaking gigs away from the mangroves, the soldiers paddled for the *Sutherland*.

From Saint Xavier's Church in Englishman's Bay, the culverins opened up on the warship itself. Inside the mangroves of the small bay, Kayode watched the end result. Cannonballs tore through the *Sutherland's* rigging. By pure chance, one dislodged her main topgallant mast. The others landed over her larboard side into the sea. Many rounds were discharged by the culverins. And then, with another stroke of luck, a cannonball tore into the *Sutherland's* foredeck. Fire broke out. The diversionary invasion had turned into a fiasco. Devoid of her main topgallant mast, the smouldering warship was soon under way. Moments later, her mainsail unfurled. Making way to the west, she was abandoning the remains of about thirty soldiers floating in her wake. He grinned at Asabi.

'Come,' he said, 'let's go and make plans with Tomba.'

From the high vantage point of Saint Xavier's Church, Kayode sat watch with Tomba on the south-west bank of Englishman's Bay. Late in the afternoon, he caught sight of a lone figure cantering along the shore. Recognising the scout who he had sent to track the movement of the fleet bound for Hurricane Point, he murmured to Tomba.

'Find Asabi.'

Slipping inside the Church with the scout, he heard the bad tidings – six ships had anchored on the northern coast near the runaway stronghold of New Freetown and troops were disembarking. Needing to warn Samuel of their imminent return to the capital, Kayode sent the scout on to Jamestown. Tomba was waiting for him outside the Church.

'Asabi?' he asked.

'Alone on the headland.'

'Be ready, Tomba, I need to be with her,' he said. 'We may be some time. Tomorrow we return to Jamestown and then we go on to support our people at Tamarind Trees.'

Tomba grinned.

'Go to Asabi, my friend,' he said warmly. 'We will be ready.'

The sun was hovering above the horizon. He wandered pensively along the rocky path at the end of a bloody day. Freshened by the breeze off the sea, he was stirred by the thunderous roar of waves. His brother's words came flooding back to him.

'You worship at the high table of arrogance, Kayode,' his brother had told him back home in Ake. 'That is your weakness. Come a day when arrogance will bring you to your knees and to your senses. Only then will you be master of yourself.'

But the dead had curbed his headstrong ways and he felt daunted by the mission ahead. It needed arrogance to fight the whites. I am a free man, he thought, but I am also the humbled leader of an uprising.

Following the hostilities in the small bay, he took pleasure in the lush woodland, the absence of conflict and the breathtaking dimensions of the basalt boulders. A frigate bird landed on the rugged face of the peninsula. Laughing gulls swooped about his head. Heaving a long thoughtful sigh, he caught sight of Asabi perched proudly on a large flat rock overhang close to the end of the promontory. She was lost in watching the waves smashing into the cliff face and spouting through a fissure, high into the air. Sneaking up behind her, he whispered.

'My *kadara.*'

She chuckled.

'You're my destiny too,' she said. 'It is *kadara* we met and had a child.'

Sitting down beside her, he kissed her on both cheeks.

'He can say your name now,' she said.

He smiled.

'I love you and our family, Kayode.'

'All the love I have is for you and our son,' he said. 'Right now he plays with other children in Drake House, but one day he will learn, no, all our children will learn, to read, write and count.'

She gazed into his eyes and deep into his soul. It is strange, she thought, despite all the suffering he has endured on this island, I have never seen him shed a tear.

'Why does the water in your eyes,' she asked softly, 'never wash your face?'

He stiffened.

'Not on this island,' he said tersely.

The ache in his voice was unmistakable.

'Twenty-three dead and sixteen wounded,' he said, 'and most of the injured will die.'

'People die when they fight for freedom,' she countered. 'That has always been true. Talk to our people, Kayode. Ask them why they fight. They will tell you they fight to end slavery. Not to be slaughtered like cattle while cutting cane for feeding white faces.'

'Many more of us will die, Asabi.'

'You always knew that many would die, Kayode. When we took up weapons and followed you, we did so knowing that we put our lives in great danger. We have always known that an uprising is the only way off this island. You showed that whites could also be made to suffer like us. After so many deaths, we know that it is by musket alone that we can change our destiny. Our people believe in you, Kayode. I believe in you. We live as free people. Or we die.'

'Redcoats have landed on the northern coast,' he said.

'How many?'

'Hundreds.'

She shivered.

'It begins,' she murmured.

She heard the quiver in her own voice.

'Why north?'

'They'll camp at Harmony Hall, and then strike out at Tamarind Trees from there.'

'When will they attack?'

'In the next few days.'

The light was fading. Shrill screams shot from orange-throated parakeets. Sighing, she fell back, drawing him gently on top of her.

'I love you so much I can almost not breathe,' she whispered. 'When the slavers seized me, I felt dead inside not knowing what my *kadara* would be. You and your brother freed me, shared what you had and made me want to live again. The walk to the Bariba and back to Ake was difficult and dangerous. When I boarded the *Pelican* I was sure that I would never see you again. My heart bled when I was sold. Only to rejoice when I saw that the man who bought me also bought you. Ake is a long time ago, Kayode, my village even longer. Ake would be proud of what we have done.'

Tenderly, she caressed his neck.

'I love you, Kayode.'

Wearily, the sun dropped below the lighthouse at Hurricane Point. He kissed her. Cupping his head in her hands to look into his eyes, she pressed against him. His hand brushed against her breast.

'I love you, Asabi.'

His hand was on her belly. Slipping his fingers deliciously down the crease of her inner thigh, he touched her moist veiled sanctum. Tears crept into her eyes. Arching her back against the basalt neck of land, she pushed against him again and again. An age elapsed before they rose to stroll to the edge of the promontory. Holding fast in the moonlight, they gazed into the shadowy restless ocean. Lulled by his strong heartbeat, she drifted into thought.

Close to the cliff face below them, a flight of birds winged eastwards to the rocky islet two leagues away. She had met this man in tragic circumstances and ever since, violence had dominated her life. On the island of Pertigua, she had been moulded and shaped by brutality – the currency of the slave owners. In these turbulent times, moments for love and friendship were precious. With her man, at the dawn of battle, she stood against those who sought to whip them back to the canefields.

Night fell gently on the lovers.

Early next morning, with Asabi, Tomba and the Hungan, Kayode set out for Jamestown riding northwest through a banana plantation. To avoid an unnecessary encounter, they kept well away from its Great House, a residence that was still holding out against runaways.

'They have Redcoats in the house,' said Tomba.

Leaving his companions at the foot of Mount James, Kayode ascended, on horseback, the thickly wooded green mountain to take a good look along the coastline. He returned with a pithy report.

'I count nine ships near the Reef,' he said. The scout was right. It means six ships have taken soldiers to the north to camp out at Harmony Hall. Come, we ride to Jamestown. Then we go on to Tamarind Trees.'

Asabi grinned.

'Man of action,' she said.

Tomba was matter-of-fact.

'Mister Cut an' Dry,' he said.

Kayode smiled.

Arriving in Jamestown in the early afternoon, he found it in total confusion. From the outskirts of the capital, the streets were littered with upturned carts and carriages. White soldiers dangled from scaffolds used for slaves. In the town proper, the burned out shells of houses were still smouldering. Doors hung awry. Fires flickered in the ruins of the hotel and the general store. The gable-roofed church of Saint Francis of Assisi had been razed to the ground. Apart from a small number of runaway fighters who appeared to maintain ranks, drunkenness and disorder was the rule of the day.

Men sagged senselessly against buildings and lay comatose in the street. Intoxicated sentries had collapsed in front of padlocked buildings filled with the white populace yelling for food and water. Two guards were violating a screaming white woman on the steps of the prison. Three naked white men were sprawled head-first in a horse trough. Heads, arms and legs of whites unable to outrun the mob lay strewn across the highway. An overpowering stench of rum, hemp, opium and death struck his nostrils. The uprising had degenerated into drunken lawlessness. Bearing countless empty bottles, a long table had been erected at the intersection facing Fort James. Amid the debris on the thoroughfare, two naked white women sat in the dirt, weeping and traumatised from the effects of multiple assaults. The offenders dispersed on Kayode's approach. He had left a defence force in Jamestown and returned to a rabble.

He pulled up his mount. A lump entered his throat. Sprawled ignominiously on his back in the dirt was the body of Nathan Greensleeves. Fury seized his senses. He heard Asabi gasp. After dismounting, he stood over the lifeless remains of the man who helped them escape. He looked up at her.

'Her blood-father is dead,' he murmured. 'Faith will be heartbroken. I revealed his identity to her, but I will not be able to tell her that he is no more, for we will not meet again.'

Kneeling down and swatting away the flies gorging on the wound where a musket ball had entered the left eye, grief clouded his senses. The propagator's skin was a deathly pallor and his bushy grey beard was matted with blood. Nearby lay his black tricorne. Asabi and the Hungan joined him beside the body.

'I'm filled with sorrow, my dear friend,' he said to the dead man. 'I regret that my freedom cost you your life. I have never met a white man like you. When I was in need you gave me your friendship. You guided us to Bamboo Bay. You always kept your word. I will never ever forget you. My children also will cherish your memory.'

'We will bury this great man at Drake House,' said Asabi.'

As he lifted the body, he caught the still mounted Tomba frowning at Asabi and the Hungan.

'What is this?' Tomba mouthed.

The Hungan smiled at Tomba. Purposefully ignoring the big man, Kayode draped the propagator's body over his saddle. Greensleeves is gone, he thought, and he was killed by a runaway. Anger and grief welled up inside him. He rounded on his companions.

'Do they think we rebelled for this?' he said, spitting into the dirt and waving at the destruction wrought by the runaways. 'The drunken fools. Redcoats with blazing muskets will soon wake them up.'

Drake House galloped into view. On the steps of the mansion house, his son was waving. He grinned. His family were reunited inside the house. Momentarily the uprising slipped from his thoughts. A ceremony was hastily arranged for the burial of the propagator in the arboretum. In the shade of a magnificent brown rosewood tree, Nathan Greensleeves was laid to rest. By the mid-afternoon Kayode stood at the foot of the grave. He reflected on a man who was prepared to thwart his own kind by helping the slave who was the lover of his daughter. As he laid the tricorne on the propagator's grave, his throat grew taut. Greensleeves believed that slavery was an offence in the eyes of any God. But in the eyes of his own people, Greensleeves would be deemed a traitor. In truth, he thought the grizzly old man was a stubborn white rebel. Being familiar with the dead man's Catholic faith, Samuel mumbled something unintelligible over the grave.

Late that afternoon, Kayode convened a meeting in the Cabinet Room with Ol' Bones, Truelove and Samuel. Since they were about to enter into battle, he wasted no time in ascertaining how Jamestown had deteriorated into disarray. Instead, he outlined the measures he wanted them to put into effect to return the capital to some sort of order.

'If they're so keen to kill,' he shouted, 'they can try their luck on the Redcoats. Tell them that if this uprising fails, we will all be flogged back to the canefields.'

Kayode left the three men in no doubt that it was vital the Jamestown brigade was readied to respond, if he called for reinforcements. With Asabi and Tomba, he was bound for Tamarind Trees. Ol' Bones was to join them later. Before setting out, Samuel presented him with a gift found among the chattels of the mansion's ex-residents. It was the former Governor's favoured weapon, a Kentucky flintlock rifle wrapped in oiled fabric.

'It's true up to a distance of two hundred yards!' said Tomba

Once again, Kayode found himself kissing his son farewell.

Sighting the gates of the plantation, his heart beat hard. It was the first time he had laid eyes on Tamarind Trees since his escape. Tomba rode away to inspect the plantation's defences. Taking a deep breath, Kayode crossed the threshold of the plantation. A scene of shambolic activity met his eyes. Aghast, he dismounted with Asabi. At first appearance, the near to six hundred encamped runaways seemed resolute. And by the way they carried their muskets they appeared readied for action. Closer scrutiny showed that there was a complete lack of discipline and order. Many were drunk and others had failed to load their muskets. For the most part, the few cannons faced the wrong way. He was exhausted and incensed.

The Great House had been turned into the quarters of the runaway militia. Ruby, the slave of Widdecombe the former housekeeper, was living comfortably there. She related the events at Tamarind Trees since his escape and since the uprising had begun. Ferrers had forced himself on Rebecca over and over again and then starved her to death. Since the start of the uprising, Sunshine the carpenter had for months kept Widdecombe the housekeeper locked in the summer-house as his slave. He forced himself upon her night after night, until one day she disappeared. A year ago on a dewy April morning, Moses died in the Slop House.

'Kayode he done us proud,' he had said with his last words. 'I have had a long hard life. I sleep now.'

At the end of Ruby's account he rose thoughtfully and stepped away. Her words had affected him deeply. Asabi wiped her eyes. Hand in hand, they strolled to his old chattel house to grieve for his friend Moses. A stale odour hit his nostrils the instant he entered the empty dwelling. Gone were the few possessions he had left behind. In fact it felt as if it had never been occupied. Slumping down heavily, he leaned against the wall and stared out of the doorway. Asabi flopped down beside him. In the sanctuary of his former home, he exposed his fears.

'I say this only to you.'

She frowned at him.

'What is it that you must tell me?' she asked.

Lowering his voice, he said:

'We have only a small chance of defeating the Redcoats.'

'I know,' she said quietly. 'I realised that when I saw so many soldiers at Harmony Hall. We can go back to the mountains if we lose. We can go on fighting from there.'

'When we came down from the mountains,' he said, 'our strategy was to hit and run because we had surprise on our side. To defeat them in pitched battle will be hard, almost impossible. They have greater weapons and preparation. If we fail, Asabi, then we must be remembered by the way in which we suffered defeat. We will take a great number of them down with us. Then they will know that slavery comes at a high price.'

Gazing through the doorway with his back to her, silence held sway. His confidence wavered. Turning around, he looked at her keenly. Her face was dark, striking and solemn. Her eyes were bursting with questions. All the same, he needed to make her understand the possible consequences. Sitting down beside her, he said:

'If we fail, many will die.'

Taking his hand, she put it against her cheek and spoke softly.

'Knowing they will die if they are sent back to the canefields,' she said, 'will make them fight and fight bitterly.'

What she says is true, he thought. Slaves died or were butchered every day in the canefields. Runaways had every right to kill or be killed. He kissed her. Dropping his eyes and barely audible, he said:

'I might die.'

She stiffened. He felt her eyes searching his face.

'If they catch me,' he said quietly 'I will die by my own hand.'

Visibly shaken by his words, she cried out.

'No No No. We cannot end like that.'

Rising to his feet, he walked unsteadily onto the verandah. He scanned the defensive activities taking place at the barracoon. The cannons were being loaded, run into position and carelessly trained. Despairingly, he shook his head. She followed him out.

Facing him with tears in her eyes, her lips quivered when she spoke.

'You said you loved me. You said how we would make babies. And how they would learn to read and write. You said that we would clear this island of whites if they did not want to share it with us in peace. How one day we would go back to Ake. Now you are saying that if you are captured, you will take your own life. I ask you, how are we going to do all of this if you are dead? If you know you're going to die, it would be better if you had never said that you loved me at all.'

'I do love you. There is more than us to think about. This uprising is greater than you and me. I have spoken to Tomba and the others. They all agree. I will take my own life if I am captured. I have no choice.'

He had made up his mind. A lingering public death would crucify the spirits of the island's slave population forever. It would undo so much.

He would do his utmost to make sure that such an occasion would never arise.

It had been a long sweaty day. Campfires were sprouting around the barracoon. Inside the chattel house dark thoughts charged the atmosphere. The uprising had accomplished the impossible. It had turned the tables on their former masters and, openly, he had had a child with the woman of his choice. Yet, looking back, it seemed that he had succeeded only in bringing her to the possible face of defeat. There she stood in the tallow-light, her lips slightly parted and her chest gently heaving. Her face dissolved and down rolled tears of despair.

This was the first time he had seen her frightened. He found it almost unbearable. Sinking to her knees, she looked up at him through her tears. Dropping down beside her, he wiped her eyes and drew her close. He was heartened by her bodily response. From somewhere in the fog and confusion of his heartache he found his voice.

'All I have done, Asabi, I would do all over again.'

'I would too, my beloved,' she said.

On that warm moonlit night they stood gazing at the configuration of the stars. With the instincts of the Yoruba, steeped in superstition and astrology and honed by a belief of the next world, he judged the positions of the heavenly bodies significant. Was it an accident that his chattel house was aligned with that bright star? Or was it a fragment from *Oduduwa's* grand design? Greensleeves had said that the star was called Vega, the falling vulture. And it was the fourth brightest in the night sky. Squeezing his hand, she nestled into him. A warm wind gusted across the plantation. He kissed her with longing. A short distance away, men and women cheered themselves around a fire.

'Comes first the hush before a strong wind,' he whispered.

Early next morning through a telescope trained on Harmony Hall, he watched the 46th Foot Regiment standing by for action. Readied fighters lay behind the barricades, in the trees and in the ditches. They must only fire their muskets from behind cover. Mindful that it would not be long before the Redcoats closed in on Tamarind Trees, he called together Tomba, Ol' Bones and the Hungan.

'If we have to retreat from here,' he said, 'I want you to swear you'll see Asabi and my son safely back to the mountains.'

Solemnly linking arms with him, the three men endorsed the pact.

'We swear it.'

Agreeing to meet in the Great House when the fighting was over, he embraced them solemnly one after the other.

The day was sweltering. In the afternoon Kayode was scanning the field through the drawing room windows when: boom boom boom. That comes from Harmony Hall, he thought. Asabi dashed into the room. The stables burst into flames. Shards tore into the Great House with splintering crescendo. Jerking her down to the floor below the sill, he screened her with his body.

A series of explosions followed the cannonade. The room shook. Unearthly screams pierced his senses. Warily, he brought his eyes level with the foot of the window. Clumps of earth, rock and debris were slicing dangerously through the air. Flames and dense smoke obscured the stable-block and outhouses. A chattel house disintegrated before his eyes. Splinters of wood fatally lanced three men. Blood spurted out of the chest of another lying on the carriage-drive. Cannon fire stopped as abruptly as it had started. Making sure she was unhurt, he rose impetuously to his feet.

'Come, Asabi,' he said. 'We must find Ol' Bones.'

Ol' Bones was close by the summer-house. Following a whispered exchange the old man hurried away.

'You are the mother of our child, Asabi,' he said earnestly. 'It will be safer for you in Drake House. Ol' Bones has gone to fetch horses.'

'I'll stay here with you,' she declared firmly.

'One of us must stay close to our son in Drake House,' he said.

At the mention of their offspring, she yielded. With little time to lose, they exchanged faltering, stifled farewells. His throat grew tight and arid. Her lips trembled and her eyes filled with water. For an inordinate length of time he held her until tears soaked his shoulder. Watching her leave with Ol' Bones, his spirits departed with her. In a few painful moments she was gone. Lifting his moist eyes to the heavens, he prayed that *Oduduwa* would watch over her and that all they strived for would come to pass.

From the drawing room, he watched runaway fighters bobbing about in ditches, in the trees and behind barricades. Some were swigging rum as if the threat presented by the Redcoats was fantasy. Shaking his head irritably, he raised his telescope at the perimeter fence. Redcoats were advancing on the plantation. Stopping half way across a slashed canefield, they unleashed a fusillade. Musket balls felled several runaways by the perimeter fence. Closing his eyes, he blotted out the scene. Opening them on the canefield, he saw runaways scattered across the ground. Musket fire from the dead men's companions was for the most part ineffective, though he did see four Redcoats fall. Tomba materialised next to him.

'Not good,' he said.

'Chaos,' he agreed curtly.

'They are stupid to wear red, Kayode. It makes them easy targets. They are also lucky. Our fighters have had little practice in hitting targets.'

Ever since the big man had succeeded in uniting bickering prisoners in the dungeons of Cape Coast Castle, he had admired Tomba's restraint. And though the big man was a warrior without equal, he knew that they were both inexperienced in their understanding of the white man's tactics – even more so, his weapons. Throughout the hot afternoon the casualty rate of the runaway militia rose perceptibly.

Evening shadows were sifting through the Great House. A panting messenger limped into the drawing room. Jamestown was suffering a major assault. Kayode frowned intensely. Every day brings fresh rumours, he thought. He could not be certain if messengers carried trustworthy information or were merely the bearers of another rumour? If what this messenger said was true, then they could not depend on any support from Jamestown.

'Pull them back, Tomba. Tell them to take refuge in and around the Great House.'

'And if they force us from the Great House?' Tomba asked.

'Head for the mountains and New Freetown,' he answered, 'or fall back to the Bay of Thanksgiving. Swim to that empty island in the bay where you'll find a few boats. Sail or row round the coast to New Freetown. We'll mount our revenge from there. Get some help to pull them back.'

The sun was waning when he surveyed the field. Step by step the fighters were falling despondently back from the perimeter fence – four hundred and fifty men and women. Having abandoned the dead and wounded, they spilled into the grounds of the Great House. One hundred and fifty of the runaway militia were missing.

I pray that Asabi and my son are safe, he thought. Picking up his musket, he set off for his chattel house where he sprawled on the verandah. Tomba slumped beside him.

'Many are dead because I said we would win,' he confessed.

'You did not force them, Kayode,' Tomba countered. 'They chose to follow you.'

'Tell them every musket ball must have a white face on it,' he said coldly. 'And every machete must lop off a white head.'

During the next few days they were forced into a rearguard action. After being ejected from the Great House, they were pushed continuously back towards the sea. Eventually, the only protection left them was the densely thicketed marram-grassed dunes on the crest of the Bay of Thanksgiving. Some distance before and below them stood ranks of Redcoats straddling the coast road. Behind them lay the disembarking troops of the Expeditionary Force and beyond them, the sea. They were trapped.

On 28 March 1754, his runaway militia fought the Redcoats in the Bay of Thanksgiving. Towards the end of the afternoon, Kayode surveyed the battlefield from where he lay atop a grassy dune. He lost count of the dead littering the ground between the front lines. Many white bodies lay in evidence. He shook his head regretfully for the majority were black.

'Krreearr. Krreearr,' cried the gulls. 'Krreearr. Krreearr.'

Onto the corpses swooped the web-footed scavengers. The acrid stink of munitions drifted across the front lines. Stripped by gulls, the rotting bodies had lain for a day decomposing in the heat of the sun. His nostrils smarted from the stench. A lull descended on the battleground. Blinking back tears he closed his eyes. He opened them on two soldiers with a white flag. They started weaving their way towards the front of the English lines along the coast road. Grasping at once the negotiating significance of the flag, he leapt to his feet waving his arms.

'Stop shooting,' he shouted. 'Stop shooting.'

His order rippled out across the dunes. Dropping back down, his heart beat wildly. The musket fire stopped. He smiled uncertainly at Tomba. The big man squeezed his arm in a heartening gesture. For a timeless age, they watched the makeshift banner meandering through the scrubland between the road and the dunes. Twenty yards from the foot of the dune on which he lay, two infantrymen came to a halt. Bent on giving his enemy no time to compose themselves, he slid forwards on his belly, delivering his challenge in a voice chosen to unsettle.

'What you want?'

'Jamestown has fallen,' shouted a soldier. 'The Governor demands your unconditional surrender.'

'What Jamestown does is Jamestown's business,' he replied. 'We will never surrender. Give up if you want. Then you can all go back to your hovels in little England.'

Cheering engulfed the dunes.

'We will take your reply to the Governor,' a soldier shouted.

He turned to Tomba.

'If it is true that Jamestown has surrendered,' he said, 'I hope and pray that Asabi got away.'

'Never fear, Kayode, Ol' Bones will make sure she got away.'

The two soldiers started moving apprehensively back towards their lines. An ear splitting shot rang out. A fragment flew from one soldier's head. The white flag dropped from his hand as he crumpled soundlessly onto the sandy grass. Freezing in his tracks, the remaining soldier turned around slowly with his hands rising. From his position, he could virtually smell the man's fear. Another shot rang out. Screaming and flinging his arms in the air, the man crashed to the ground.

A fleeting silence overshadowed the battleground. It felt a dark moment. Glancing at the dune to his right, smoke was rising from the marram grass from the barrel of a nearby musket. Suddenly, angry jeering broke out from the English front line. Dismissing the cries with a wave of his hand, he got to his feet. Incensed that a runaway had killed an unarmed man carrying a white flag, he scowled at the culprit. His next thought stalled his impulse. What of the slaves who have been maimed and slaughtered on the plantations? They possessed no weapons. He dropped down to the ground.

'Those soldiers were taken off guard, Tomba,' he said. 'When we were taken on the coast of Guinea, were we not surprised? Those murdered by Bradshaw and Fleming were also surprised. It is good we use surprise. It is their way. They have taught us how. We escaped and surprised them by their failure to recapture us. And we surprised them again when we overwhelmed Jamestown. The English don't like surprises. So we should try and give them one more surprise.'

'You're right, Kayode,' Tomba sneered. 'We shocked them.'

Sporadic runaway fire from the dunes peppered the sand before the English lines. He felled a soldier with the Kentucky flintlock rifle. At this distance, he thought, our muskets are having little effect. That English front line stays firm with few losses.

'They are too far from us,' Tomba said quietly, 'as we are from them.'

Through his telescope, Kayode beheld three mounted men before the musketed Redcoats of the English front line. The triumvirate sat irritatingly in conversation as if time was of no great essence. Governor Ashleigh was the central rider. His companions were very conspicuous by the sparkle of the sun off their bemedaled chests. Infuriated by the spectacle, he passed the telescope to Tomba. After scanning the English front line, the big man jabbed a finger at the Kentucky flintlock rifle.

'Let me use that, Kayode,' said Tomba. 'It is a good time to deliver our surprise.'

Conceding Tomba's superior marksmanship, Kayode grinned and passed him the rifle. Putting the butt against his shoulder, Tomba levelled it.

' 'Bout hundred and fifty yards from here,' he said. 'Well in range of this nasty weapon.'

'Knock that big peacock off his horse,' said Kayode. 'It will wake his people up and give them plenty to think about.'

Steadying himself and taking aim at the Governor, the big man squeezed the trigger. There was a loud report. One of the bemedaled men toppled off his horse. Kayode ducked down. Raising his head to grass-top level, he peered through his telescope. The Governor had dismounted and was hurrying to the aid of the stricken officer with a coterie of officers. He scowled.

'Missed him,' said Tomba, 'but I hit his best man.'

'A good surprise, Tomba.'

The response from the Redcoats was immediate. Musket fire began their counter-attack. It was followed by a regimented roar of cannons that rent the Bay of Thanksgiving. Heads, arms, legs and torsos of runaways were soon scattered along the front line. The dunes were rendered bloody. Desultory fire was sent back at the Redcoats on the coast road. An impulse made him turn around.

From the water's edge, Redcoats off the *Resolution* were beginning their advance. Having been encircled by a greater number of soldiers, they were now pinned down in the dunes, by a force who owned superior weaponry and a history of training in the art of war. They had undeniably been outmanoeuvred. He bit his lip with vexation. Darkness fell. He lost count of the comrades falling around him. With around two hundred men and women, he retreated into a crater ringed by four dunes. After posting a lookout atop each tufted dune, he gathered his militia around a fire to settle on the way ahead. Tomba was terse.

'We must get off these dunes, Kayode.'

'Get off these dunes?' asked a woman. 'What we must do is not get taken alive. I will kill myself before they take me. If we cannot escape from here, Kayode, the Redcoats should find all of us dead.'

Her words reminded him of his suicide-pledge to Tomba. Instinctively, he groped for the *Esere* beans fastened inside his thigh. I carry a poison that will take my life painlessly, he thought. How would they take theirs? With muskets? It would be butchery. They must flee together and live to fight the Redcoats another time. He mopped his neck. He must get them out of this hell. He imagined himself leading a charge down the dune's steepest incline onto a long narrow, rocky overhang, down onto a smaller stunted plateau, along a dried up riverbed, down to the sea and away. All we have to do is get past the Redcoats . . .

'You talk of surrender yet we still carry muskets?' he asked scathingly.

'Hundreds are dead, Kayode!' a disfigured man exclaimed. 'We will squander more lives if we don't surrender.'

'If you surrender,' Tomba asked incredulously, 'do you think they send your backside back to the canefields?'

'Them need slaves in the canefields,' the disfigured man retorted. 'Them lose profit if them kill us all.'

'You think like a slave!' Kayode snapped. 'They don't need your poor black backside cutting cane. They can get more like you from the coast of Guinea. Brothers and sisters we have three choices. We die here. We die on the gallows. We escape or die trying to escape. Tomorrow we fight. This night we find a way off these dunes – without waking the Redcoats.'

Unanimous agreement followed his appraisal. Slipping away to be alone, he slumped down onto a clump of grass. Lying on his back contemplating the stars, he thought, and what of you my beloved Asabi? Where would she lay her head this night? He prayed that all was well with her and his son.

They were trapped in the dunes. For three perilous days they held out, repelling attacks. He sent fighters into the gaps left by the dead to shore up their flagging defences until the next attack. On the fourth day the Redcoats stormed the encampment. Before he even sighted a white face or red coat, he shouted.

'Follow me.'

Loping down to the foot of the steepest slope, he dashed along the waterless riverbed heading towards the sea. Outwitted and outgunned, they ran into an ambush. He was finally apprehended by the water's edge. With his arms pinioned by Redcoats, he witnessed the crushing surrender of one hundred and forty of his comrades. Chained together, they were whipped onto their knees.

Shackled and hauled through the dunes, he was dumped at the feet of the mounted Governor, Sir Anthony Ashleigh, who was handed the only weapon 'found in the possession of the prisoner' – the Kentucky flintlock rifle. Following a close inspection of the hot firearm, the Governor raised hostile eyes. It was the first time Kayode saw the measure of the Governor's loathing of him. Opening his eyes wider, he held the Governor's stare. The uprising had clearly caused His Majesty's envoy a great deal of trouble and personal embarrassment.

'You're a dead man, Jacob,' he said coldly. 'I have plans for the likes of you.'

Twisting in his saddle, the Governor addressed his officers.

'Drag him slowly past the other niggers,' he said, 'then throw him into the cell we have prepared for him in Fort James.'

In the sticky heat of the afternoon his hands were pinioned behind him. Bodily lifted onto an elderly nag, he was tightly lashed belly-down. Puffing and wheezing alarmingly, the mare began lumbering the twelve miles from the Bay of Thanksgiving to Fort James. Raising his head occasionally, he saw the devastation fashioned by the uprising. The agony on the faces of runaways being flogged by the wayside drove him into powerless fury. Sorrow wracked his spirits when slaves trudging down the roadside heeded the overseer's order.

'Stop!' he cried, 'and sink your eyes on a dead nigger.'

He was pierced by lifeless looks from vacant eyes. The spark produced by the uprising had been extinguished. He swallowed hard on the bitter taste of defeat.

Manhandled off the nag at Fort James, his wrist bonds were cut, leaving his legs shackled. Prodded across a courtyard and down a bleak passageway, he arrived at a doorway. Scrawled on a piece of wood nailed to the door was one word – JACOB. His wavering spirits plummeted. The door was wrenched open and he was kicked into the dark dank cell.

Dragging himself upright, he leaned against the wall. His tight iron anklets made the brutal sound of bondage. Devoid of freedom and sunlight, he shivered with cold sweat. The grille in the door crashed open. A commanding voice burst through the lattice.

'You stand trial in the morning, nigger. Then you go on to meet your maker. Whatever ungodly thing that might be.'

'Why waste time with a fake trial?' he asked.

In the wake of the man's fading laughter and footsteps, he sighed.

It was a hot and humid morning. Through a tiny barred window set high in the wall, the sky was indigo. Gulls wheeled below the lone cloud that obscured the sun.

To be home in Ake with my beloved Asabi and our son, he thought. I would give two life spans to be trampling the red soil of my motherland with them. It is all over for me now, but my family go on. Though I pay with my life, I would do it all again.

The wind fell to a flat calm. He heard the footfall of the guard. The moment for him to leave Fort James had arrived. Filled with righteous anger and foreboding, he rose shakily to his feet and felt for the *Esere* beans secreted in his breeches. Reassured of their presence, he turned to face the door. It burst open. The jail-watch stomped in, hoisted him clear off the ground and hurled him into the passage. Rising unsteadily and wiping away the blood trickling from a gash on the bridge of his nose, he smoothed down his dishevelled jerkin. He braced himself for his ordeal.

Hemmed in by guards with levelled muskets, he was prodded across the road to the Courthouse. Mounting the steps he felt little apprehension. He shuffled through the doorway of the crowded courtroom. All the old anger welled up in him. Gazing around the large mahogany-panelled courtroom, he knew that his was to be a trial of consequence. The pomp of the judicial drama strengthened his conviction. The uprising had effected the utmost chaos to the regimen of slavery on the island. And the planters had come to gloat.

Directly ahead on a raised platform was the Judge's chair. Seeing the

Union Flag on the panelled wall behind the chair, he scowled. Occupied by richly dressed planters and pallid wives, the stifling courtroom comprised four tiers of seats on three sides. Inside a chamber that owned an air of celebration, officials, overseers and planters sat with scorn and triumphant looks.

Taking a deep breath he stepped forward. Chattering ceased. Faces turned and then a torrent of abuse assaulted his ears. Hampered by leg irons, he continued shuffling towards the dock.

'You'll die horribly nigger,' a woman shouted.

'Not if he's already dead, he won't,' retorted a gravelly voice.

'How's that?' the woman asked.

'I'll dispatch him before your grubby mitts botches it up,' the gravelly voice replied.

The courtroom rang with laughter. Following a stumble into the dock, he gripped the rails and glared at the finely clad women along the front row. A saturnine black-cloaked Governor entered the court. Striding across the platform, he plonked down on the Judge's chair. The stage was prepared.

From the very beginning his trial was a mockery. Greensleeves had told him that the pronouncement of 'not guilty' had never been heard in the trial of a slave. Under the law, being the property of the said Frederick Bradshaw, he was deemed not fit, competent or able to plead.

'In this case, counsels for the prosecution and defence will not be necessary,' the Governor said. 'All that is required is the statement of charge, the plea and the sentence. Everything else will be at my discretion.'

Silence reigned momentarily. With an inflated flourish, the Clerk unfurled the lengthy statement of charge. The straitlaced official read the document with such rapidity, Kayode caught only the words 'on the night', before the charges of 'mutiny, rebellion, theft, murder and treason.'

The remainder of the statement was a blur. Asabi and his son streamed through his thoughts. He was awoken from his reverie by the Clerk's voice.

'Who will enter a plea for the prisoner?' he asked.

'Guilty,' the Governor said, without hesitation. 'Jacob pleads guilty.'

Turning affable, the Governor addressed his words to a seat in the front row.

'You are the title-holder of this prisoner, Mister Bradshaw,' he said, 'I daresay you will have much to say about him.'

Shaking his head from side to side while watching his erstwhile owner rising to his feet, the countless lives lost thanks to this man's gluttony and malice passed through Kayode's thoughts. Dressed in a black waistcoat and breeches, the planter was gaunt-faced and his once intimidating stare had been replaced by a tormented look. A shade of his former self, the planter kept his eyes averted from the dock.

'I have nothing to say about this prisoner, Your Lordship,' he said, almost apologetically. 'Since my wife and daughter also have nothing to say, they have chosen to remain in the Great House and absent themselves from these proceedings.'

With such few words, the planter resumed his seat. Awed and conspicuous was the hush that followed. Anticlimax hung in the air. The Governor was undoubtedly taken aback. His expression said as much. Kayode smiled to himself – for he knew how the planter's silence had come about and what guaranteed it. Nonetheless, there followed a hotchpotch of white witnesses who swore that he had planned and led the revolt. And yes, they had all seen him firing muskets at white men. Nothing was said in mitigation.

A manicured figure stepped into the arena. Kayode recognised Squire Christian Brigstocke at once. He had often seen him swaggering about on the *Pelican's* deck, keeping close company with a dark-haired man. Raising his eyes to the ceiling, he yawned perceptibly.

'In an effort to keep this impertinent villain awake,' said Brigstocke, 'I bring testimony that should rouse him from his apparent tedium.'

A ripple of laughter followed the Brigstocke's barbed aside.

'I have with me a house slave,' said Brigstocke haughtily, 'nay an eyewitness who can shed much light on this villain's deeds.'

A grouchy voice shot from the back of the courtroom.

'In accordance with the Slave Codes, a slave is not permitted to give evidence in an English court.'

Murmured concurrence rippled through the courthouse. The Governor brought down his gavel to silence the commotion.

'At my discretion I can waive that clause,' he cried. 'I therefore do so now, particularly since he is a house slave. Squire Brigstocke, you may produce your witness.'

'I am most grateful for your indulgence, Your Lordship,' said Squire Brigstocke, snapping his fingers.

Into the witness box stepped a handsome, shaven-headed young house slave. He had a hunted look and quietly said his name was John. Yes, he had been close enough to hear the prisoner planning the uprising. Yes yes, he had seen the prisoner kill several white men with a musket. No, he did not know why the prisoner 'did it'. And yes, he had given his evidence of his own free will.

Kayode grimaced. Free will rings hollow in this wicked place, he thought.

'And that my Lord,' the Clerk declared, 'concludes the case for the Government of Pertigua.'

'Prisoner at the bar,' said the Governor. 'You have heard the horrifying deeds attributed to you and your murdering thugs. What have you to say in your defence, Jacob?'

Gripping the handrail and clearing his throat, he addressed the court-house.

'I know no Jacob,' he replied tersely. 'My name is Kayode of the Sodeke family from the village of Ake on the coast of Guinea.'

'Bloody cheek,' cried a croaky voice.

Ignoring the interruption, he continued.

'For years I suffered terribly on Bradshaw's cruel plantation. I escaped. I am guilty of all charges. I am honoured to say that I led the uprising. I am also guilty of wanting to steal a ship for the purpose of returning to my homeland, from where I was kidnapped by white men. I am guilty of fighting those who chop off the arms and legs of my people, leaving them to bleed to death. I am guilty of wanting to kill the men who carried out that evil. Thirty-two guineas for my life. That is what Bradshaw paid for me. Am I not like you? You have two hands like me. Why can you not cut your own cane? If a man tried to kill you, would you not defend yourself? Can you not see that slavery is an assassin? It butchers the slave and prolongs the hate we have for plantation owners? In the uprising, I acted in self-defence and killed white men on the field of battle.

Yes, I am really guilty of loving my family so much I wanted to see them again. I am prepared to do anything for that to be so. I am very guilty of wanting that which all white people possess – the right to speak my mind. The right to go where I please. And the right to be free. You will find me guilty. You will sentence me to death. If I must die because of my awkward thirst for freedom, then I die for a good cause. When you take my life, Ashleigh, all you will do is put an end to my suffering. Beyond the gates of this life I will never again have to watch the wretched step of the slave and the arrogant strut of the white man. And for that, Governor Ashleigh, I thank you with all my heart.'

Tightening his hold on the rails, he looked along the ranks of animosity before uttering his final words. And this time his voice held a ruthless edge.

'Make no mistake, Ashleigh,' he said, 'we will rise again. Many more of you will perish in the flames next time.'

Relief cascaded down his body. Gripping the rails, he swayed. His audience shifted uneasily. The suffocating chamber was inundated with coughing, angry mutterings, papers being shuffled and the incessant rustling of fans. Silence once again descended.

Rising like a phantom from the front row, Randolph Fleming looked hard at him. He stared angrily back at the plantation owner, who then turned, strode up to the bench and began to whisper. Following a huddled consultation, the Governor threw a hostile look at him and cleared his throat.

'Prisoner at the bar,' he said. 'By the evidence and by your own words, I find you guilty of murder and rebellion, which is a treasonable offence. Furthermore, you are also guilty of attempting to deprive the island of Pertigua of a lawful government. The sentence of this court is that you be taken instantly in chains from here to the Auction House in Sho'town. From there, you will be paraded slowly through Jamestown as a conspicuous warning to those who attempt to follow your wicked example. You will then be incarcerated in the death cell at Fort James. On the dawn of the morrow, you will be taken from the chamber and put to death. May God have mercy on your soul, though in your case I doubt that he shall.'

Clapping and cheering assailed the courthouse. Staring ahead and impervious to the sour looks and hateful words flung in his direction, he noted that the Governor had avoided saying how he was to meet his end. His trial had lasted under two hours.

Outside the Auction House, he was secured to an upright post on a flatbed cart. He could not fail to see slaves being whipped for averting their eyes. To complete his humiliation, an iron mouth-gag was clamped around his jaw. Having seen this device used on a previous occasion, he knew he now presented a fearsome appearance. Governor Ashleigh, Randolph Fleming, Colonel Applegate and Squire Brigstocke trotted past on horseback. They were now positioned behind him preceding government officials who were on foot.

Fifty paces in advance of the column, a drummer from the 46th Foot Regiment stepped onto Promenade Road and set off with a slow, stirring beat. His cart jerked forward to begin the dawdling journey along the perimeter of Jamestown Bay, past slaves whom he knew would be lining the three-mile route. Stumbling behind the Governor's party, shackled and linked by an endless chain, were the one hundred and forty who had been captured with him. Every so often by the side of the road he saw white people clapping and cheering, alongside jubilant members of the Mongoose Gang, raising their flutes, goblets and wineglasses to his downfall.

At the bridge on Promenade Road, the cortege halted beside a tall wooden cross. He saw the island's clergy clustered around a makeshift lectern. Straggling wisps of grey hair identified Parson Merriweather. The Governor and Fleming rode up to the clergyman.

'A benediction for a contemptible nigger who is about to die, Parson,' the Governor said. 'And your prayers can begin the ceremony which shall culminate on the morrow.'

The pained expression of the cleric spelt reluctance.

'Ask this not of me, Sir Anthony,' he pleaded. 'From what has transpired before these eyes on the Guinea coast, at Cape Coast Castle, on the *Pelican* and the mortal conflagration I have latterly witnessed on these islands, I fear, sir, that I have not the stomach for what is about to occur. I implore you, sir, ask this not of me.'

Thoroughly incensed, Fleming rose up on his stirrups.

'White men have lost their lives and white women raped, sir,' he said. 'Yet you can stand there to tell me that you have no stomach for the execution of the nigger who is directly responsible? Are you saying candidly, Parson, that the catastrophe that has befallen your own people matters not to you?'

Fleming's polemic produced the desired effect. Clutching the lectern with one hand, the gaunt clergyman raised his other hand to dispense his blessing.

'Here stands before you, Captain Sodeke,' he said, 'who is said to be a sinner. It is also said that he has perpetrated the foulest deeds against God and man. Yet even he must be granted the blessings of Our Lord.'

Making the sign of the cross, the clergyman intoned:

'Do me justice, O Lord. Fight the good fight against all faithless people. And from deceitful and impious man, rescue me. Amen.'

Fleming was dismayed by the priest's emotional display, by the ambiguity of his expression and by the fact that he had failed to make use of the name Jacob. Under the aegis of the Church, the priest's words were such that not a soul could raise objections. Scowling intently at the priest, Fleming wheeled away.

'What an incoherent benediction,' said the Governor. 'There stands a devil-dodging nuisance who possesses not the belly for justice.'

'This sermoniser is set to be an abolitionist,' said Fleming. 'I only pray that he does not muster with that mischievous League Against the Importation of Negroes.'

Rumbling onwards, the procession eventually rolled to a stop at Fort James. Freed from his fetters he was flung into the condemned cell. Fleming and Colonel Applegate were close on the heels of his armed escort. They stopped in the doorway.

'You begin to die at dawn, Jacob,' said Fleming. 'Believe me when I say I wanted none of this. You are the designer of your own downfall. You and your cutthroats are entirely responsible for the deaths of your masters. You think we will simply hang you? Well, there you are mistaken. The Governor and I have decided to have pieces hacked off you. It will take you two or three days to die. Your fellow slaves will be compelled to watch the entire process. Your screams will help them understand that *their* masters, given that *you* won't be about, will not abide rebellion.'

Pulling himself upright and leaning against the wall, Kayode eyed his enemy menacingly.

'When you take my life, Fleming,' he said, 'all you will take is the life of a slave. It may surprise you, but my death will not rid you of your troubles or end our struggle for freedom. My people will never let you forget, until they have reason to forgive.'

Taking a step forward, Colonel Applegate was candid.

'You deserve to be where you now find yourself, Jacob,' he said, 'for we will not sanction revolt. Nevertheless, you have earned my admiration, sir. Never before have I fought against a more resourceful enemy. Captain Sodeke, I salute you.'

Delivering a scornful smile, Fleming was cold.

'Slumber deeply, Jacob,' he said, 'for you have but a little time.'

'The war is not over, Fleming,' he said. 'Sleep deeply this night for at dawn you begin your passage into the heart of the darkest shadows. Night spirits await you. The fate of your children and your children's children will be decided by the actions of our children. They shall visit them with the wrath of time because of the sins *you* carried out on this island. From this terrible day, your people will be forever fearful of us.

Your people will never know what we will do. Or when we will do it. Time will be my judge. On the morrow, I die once. From thereon, *you* will die a little each day.'

Flinging a furious look at him, Fleming swept out of the cell and slammed the door.

Paying no attention to his injuries, he rose shakily to his feet to inspect his cell. About ten feet long and six feet wide, it had a solid oak door and a spy hole. It was a rock-solid prison with no escape route. The stolid step of the sentries said he would not be allowed to cheat his execution.

Slumping onto a mound of verminous straw, his thoughts returned to Asabi and their son. Holding up the large nail on his right index finger, which was twice as big as his left, a tearful smile crossed his lips, for his son carried the trait unique to the males of his bloodline. Through five fleet years, he had lived a lifetime with Asabi. In the cavern stronghold of Freetown where they had finally found sanctuary, they planned the uprising together. Their fight had ended in defeat. Not knowing whether she had escaped or had been recaptured preyed on his thoughts. Nonetheless, he clung to the belief that she would keep her promise to take their son back to the protection of the mountains. For she was just as set as he that their son would never endure the life of a slave. Closing his eyes, he muttered to himself.

'What did my family do when they could not find us? What torments have you suffered as you searched for us? Did you ever give up hope? How many of my people lie at the bottom of the Ocean Sea? I pray that my beloved Asabi is well hidden in the mountains with our son.'

For only the second time on the island of Pertigua, tears tumbled down his cheeks.

'I know now why *Olorun* draws close,' he muttered. 'He comes for me.'

He was to die in the morning. Thanks to the Hungan, he had been prepared for such an eventuality. Certain that a long drawn-out demise before the island's slaves would sap morale on the plantations, he would deny Fleming and the Governor a complete victory. Reaching inside his breeches, he extracted the *Esere* beans. He rolled them solemnly about in the palm of his hand.

'You will feel no pain,' he had been told. 'You will meet *Olorun* in a very short time.'

On the *Pelican*, he was slave number two hundred and twelve. At

Tamarind Trees, he was named Jacob. Captain Sodeke led the slave uprising. Now he was destined for the unknown.

Slipping the beans into his mouth, he began to chew. They were almost tasteless. In fact the flavour was akin to the haricot beans he had eaten with Faith Bradshaw in the summer-house. Swallowing the masticated beans, he lay down and closed his eyes. He envisaged Asabi skipping and playing with their son. For a while he felt nothing. Then, a creeping numbness progressively grew from his belly. It spread perceptibly into his chest. Strangely, he could no longer feel his hands and feet as he drifted into oblivion . . .

Daybreak crept into the morning room of Drake House. Two men sat in gloomy company at breakfast. In preparation for the impending execution, the Governor was fortifying himself with gin. Fleming sipped China tea while half-heartedly picking at his plate of devilled kidneys.

The door crashed open. Colonel Applegate stormed in.

'The blasted nigger has tricked us!' he cried.

Fleming turned ashen.

'What did you say?' he asked.

'Jacob is dead, Squire Fleming,' said the Colonel.

His thoughts churned. A prickly heat seized his temples.

'Who found him?' he asked, barely holding his temper.

'The turnkey on his rounds,' replied the Colonel.

'How came he to be dead?' he asked. 'Were his guards and the turnkey carousing?'

'Poison,' said the Colonel. 'The nigger must have taken it into the cell with him. By the state of his body he had been dead for some time. Guards never searched him. He evidently made no sound in his dying.'

He shook his head with frustration.

'The half-wits!' he snapped. 'How could they fail to notice something on a villain wearing only a sleeveless jerkin and breeches?'

Snatching a scribbling pad, the Governor began writing furiously.

'Your orders, Colonel,' the Governor said, handing a sheet of paper to his executive officer.

He frowned at the Governor.

'My dear Randolph,' said the Governor pompously. 'I have just signed an order consigning one hundred runaway rebels to a roasting.'

Sitting further back into his chair, Fleming smiled contentedly.

1 May 1754 at two o'clock in the afternoon of a hot and airless day, the sound of buzzing gadflies climbed to a higher pitch. Fleming stepped onto the raised platform that had been erected on the Savannah. Seated were the executive, judicial, mercantile and spiritual men of the island. They faced a squared-off arena where one hundred Y-shaped iron frames had been constructed. Each had a long iron shaft between them connected to a turning mechanism. These were the essential appliances for roasting one hundred men alive. A pile of wood lay beneath each shaft. The field of death covered one hundred square yards.

The name of each victim had been crudely scrawled on a piece of wood. It was nailed to a cross in front of each pyre, a grisly attempt to personalise the torment about to be endured. Three infantrymen stood uneasily in attendance beside each device awaiting the command to light the fires. On three sides of the field of death, massed slaves stood mute, giving the occasional cough. The fourth side comprised soldiers and white residents from Pertigua's society, on horseback, on foot and under umbrellas in open carriages.

Fleming breathed with satisfaction. Sodeke was dead. Power was back in white hands. Thank God. Onto the stage stepped the Governor. Sir Anthony Ashleigh looked resplendent in his crimson dress uniform, purple sash and military decorations, topped by a stiff white hat with a pointed crown and white plumes. The Governor nodded. Unfurling a scroll with a flourish, the hooded crier beside him began to read aloud in sombre tones.

'Hear ye. Hear ye,' he shouted. 'The wretched villains you see before you have been found guilty of the foulest acts of treason. Furthermore, they did wilfully and with malice aforethought rebel against their lawful Owners. By their actions they did seek to deprive the island of Pertigua of its lawful government. In the name of His Most Glorious Majesty, King George the Second, it is the decision of His Excellency, Governor Sir Anthony Ashleigh, that they shall suffer the prescribed penalty of death. And may God have mercy on their souls.'

Rolling up his writ, the crier stepped aside. The drum major fell into a slow beat. After being chained securely to an iron bar, the prisoners were lifted onto the Y-shaped iron frames. Fires were lit and fanned. The handles turned. The spit roasting began.

June 1754

From the stern rails of the *Gold Coast* of Dover, Faith Bradshaw gazed sadly at the hasty reconstruction of Jamestown's sun-drenched water-front. She was sailing on a vessel of the Royal African Company, bound for England with a cargo of sugar, timber, molasses and passengers. Turning to her left, she recognised a lugubrious Parson Merriweather standing close by against the rails. Moments later he was approached by a fair, blue-eyed, fresh-faced officer.

'Going home aye, Parson?'

The cleric turned to face the officer.

'Captain Thomas Wimborne,' the officer continued, removing his hat to greet him, 'previously First Officer of the *Pelican.*'

At his mention of the *Pelican,* the captain's name nudged her memory. 'Tis serendipity, she thought. By taking passage on the *Gold Coast,* she had chanced upon the erstwhile First Officer of the very vessel that had shipped the particular consignment of slaves who had revolted and shaken the island to its roots. During those long sultry nights in the summer-house, Kayode had spoken well of this man. He had portrayed him as a kind-hearted officer, who had tried to manage the *Pelican's* prisoners with some regard for their well being in defiance of the orders of Captain Blunt. When the two men exchanged a clearly heartfelt embrace, she saw the clergyman's face light up.

'Great Heavens, Mister Wimborne,' said the Parson, 'and how it gladdens my heart to see thee.'

'It is providential, Parson,' said the officer, 'that you survived the bloody uprising.'

'Happily do I take my leave of this ghastly province,' said the Parson, 'to go home to England's green pastures and sceptred shores.'

'Is that not Mistress Bradshaw of Tamarind Trees, Parson?' the officer asked.

'Aye, that be so, Captain.'

Hearing the officer mention her name, excuse himself and head in her direction, she removed her calash bonnet and began fanning her face.

'Thomas Wimborne, ma'am,' said a gentle voice. 'Master of the *Gold Coast,* at your service.'

Marshalling her frazzled nerves, she blinked back tears. Turning to face him, she extended her hand.

'It is an undeniable pleasure to shake *your* hand, Captain Wimborne.'

'Welcome aboard the *Gold Coast*,' he said, smiling, and then, impulsively, he asked.

'Did you ever lay eyes on Captain Sodeke?'

For a telling moment, she gazed wistfully into the distance before water clouded her eyesight. Smiling tearfully she looked unwaveringly up at him.

'Yes, I met him,' she said quietly. 'He was a very fine man. On this dark island, he was awash with light.'

'Aye, that he was,' agreed Wimborne. 'I also had cause to make his acquaintance.'

Heartened to be beside a man whom she felt comprehended her heartache, she took his proffered arm. He drew her to him briefly.

''Tis over now, Mistress Bradshaw. Let us leave this ungodly colony behind us. Though you and I shall never forget Captain Sodeke or what occurred here on this island.'

Captain Wimborne spoke quietly to his First Officer.

'Get her under way, Mister.' he said.

'Aye aye, sir.'

The *Gold Coast's* breastropes and springs were hauled in. Soon she was making way. Outside the harbour entrance her sails billowed, and she crossed the bar.